CLEAR MOON TRIBE

CLEAR MOON TRIBE

A NOVEL

JAIYA JOHN

Soul Water Rising

Camarillo, California

Clear Moon Tribe

Printed in the United States of America

Soul Water Rising
Camarillo, California
http://www.soulwater.org

Library of Congress Control Number: 2015909387
ISBN 978-0-9916401-2-6

First Soul Water Rising Edition, Softcover: 2015
Second printing

Fiction

Editors:
Jacqueline V. Richmond
Kent W. Mortensen

Book design and cover design by Jaiya John
Cover photo: Stock photo from GraphicBlock.com

Or say the soul is a moon,
that every thirty nights
has two so empty,
in union,
that it disappears.

Rumi

THE TRIBE

Lake	Born for the Diné (Navajo) and Pueblo people.
Shonto	Born for the Diné (Navajo) people.
Ivory	African American.
Ashia	Ghanaian.
Maricela	Mexican and Panamanian.
Balanta	Sierra Leonian. Older brother of Mende.
Mende	Sierra Leonian. Younger brother of Balanta.
Pikea	Maorian, from New Zealand.
Cielo	Aztecan, Indigenous Guaraní, and Spanish.
Promise	African American.
Eloni	Samoan, from Hawai'i.
Binda	Aboriginal, from Australia.

PROLOGUE

Ivory showed out. The 18-year-old stepped to the lonesome podium like a prideful ninja. Despite his outward bravado, he was caught inside a time bubble of fear that would not budge. Not a darned iota. He heard muffled voices. Imagined they were making fun of his outfit: Best he could do on short notice. Shorter on cash. Light blue button-down with 70's era wing-flap lapels. Fat brown leather belt with a large silver buckle depicting a cowboy riding a bronco mid-buck. Gray flannel slacks with faint plaid print. Scuffed caramel-colored dress shoes with large pilgrim buckles, rubbed down with vegetable oil. All of this straight off the thrift store rack. His 'fro, tilted and emancipated, a shock of black wild grass reaching for the sky. He smelled pharmaceutical. Two swipes of bar soap across his underarms stood in for deodorant. Mouth gargled with orange soda. Lips topped off with bacon grease. Sleep gunk still in his eyes.

Sweat was holding a party in all his intimate places. And this venue: a ballroom. Too deep and wide. Fluorescent lights burning like Hades. Psychedelic patterns in the carpet. Stains. Coffee aroma lacing the air with notes of rote repetitive activity. Another conference. Another parading of the at-risk youth attractions. Whole lotta grown folks with glazed eyes. Slouched faces. Zombies with nametags dripping condescension and too much sympathy. *Too quiet up in here.* A thousand eyes staring straight at him. A thousand eyes set in 500 professional skulls. Professional clothes. Professional notepads, pens, briefcases. Professional legs crossed, professionally. A sea of tightness and here he was, trying to get loose. *Get loose. Tiger in a zoo exhibit. Watching me move. Acceptable as long as I'm in this here cage. Speaking zoo language. Domesticated stuff. Nah. I'm not down for that.*

Ivory broke loose.

"Before we get into the stuff I'm going to tell you," he said, "can we please agree that you won't freak out? No pity parties. Or worse, no scoldings, calling us ungrateful. Those are both ways folks try to avoid swallowing the truth. You ever seen a baby in a high chair being fed food it doesn't want to eat? Man, there isn't anything like a baby throwing a fit like that, face all balled up like the rear end of a tomato. Eyes squinting, looking like spiders with those crow's feet. Fists squirting food everywhere. Spraying and spitting stuff out its mouth like a leaf blower. Hollering and crazy with anger. Pounding and kicking. Man, when that baby decides it's not going to eat that food, game over.

"Grown folks are like that with the truth. Once they decide they don't want it, they'll do anything possible not to swallow. Don't be like that, okay? Don't go tomato face on me. Cause I'm fixin' to tell you some stuff you won't believe."

Concerned murmurs in the professional audience. *Did anyone prep this kid?*

1

Is he on his meds?

I hope this isn't going to be another one of those rambling, directionless rants.

Ivory was undeterred by the subdued response and strained facial expressions. He was determined to stay true to the cause. *Revolutionary, that's what these folks need.* He stretched his neck side-to-side. Pulled on his collar. Lakes of sweat were blooming on his powder-blue shirt. "Can I get a mic check? Can y'all hear me all right? Can I get some more water, please? Thank you. Any of you hot? Maybe we can get some A/C pumping.

"Now, where was I? Oh yeah. If I told you a secret, would you keep it? Of course you wouldn't. But then, that's why we tell a secret, isn't it? So it can get spread. First off, we should clear something up. I'm not who you think I am," Ivory pronounced, teeth gleaming like a toothpaste commercial. "Y'all have been drinking the juice way too long. Read too many posters and pamphlets about people like me. We aren't *resilient*. Man, we're straight up suffering. We aren't criminals. Crime's happening *to us*. We're none of that juvenile mumbo jumbo your training manuals and slideshows spew out. You can throw out that stuff right quick."

Fidgety movement by the nervous facilitator fake-smiling by the edge of the stage.

"See, I seen the light. Y'all got your slots for us. You live by those slots: 'Put this one here. That one there.' Slots give you comfort at night. Let you believe you're doing something: 'Well, we got that one into that slot today. This one's getting prepped for that other slot.' Then you take your Nyquil or your Valium or whatnot and you black out. Then you get back up in the morning and come to work and think about how you can get some more money to put more of us in some more slots. A sense of order. That's what this is all about. Without it, society gets too nervous. Gotta have a place for all these tragedies, right?" Ivory impulsively sipped warm water from one of the plastic cups that he always thought were strangely stunted. Like they were made for leprechauns. Like they wanted you to have the illusion that you were curing your thirst. Three sip capacity. *I'm a grown man. Can I get a full size cup?*

"Now, don't you go thinking that this here's a negative message," he continued. "I just came to tell the truth. Remember? We young people appreciate all you do... since you always need us to lead off with gratitude and shucking and jiving." Ivory was smiling, trying to convey jocularity. "It's just that we're on an island, man. And nobody's actually coming onto the island, feel me? Everyone's just throwing us bones across the water from the safety of their shore. Man, I'm saying, brave those barrier reefs." A paltry scatter of applause rose around the room. This only encouraged Ivory's flow.

"Way I see it, it's island time up in here. No more slots. As far as us young people, our agenda? Our agenda is to blow up these slots and just live. Feel me? Skip the labels. Nobody's giving us nothing. So today, I'm Moses up in here, and I'm saying, not asking, Let. My. People. Go." He gave the words as much dramatic authority as his seal pup-pitched voice could generate. By now, the professionals had reverted to their true human nature. Gossiping. Filing verbal grievances with each other, and with nobody at all. Shuffling papers in protest. Uncrossing professional legs. Some were laughing. Some needed to pee. The session facilitator was nervously twirling her hair. Hades burned hotter by the second.

Ivory was untouched and ignited. This was the moment of his life. His time to shine. His face glistened and his eyes sparked. "These days everything is such and such-free. Sugar free. Gluten free. Antibiotic free. I figure, why not slot free?" Ivory broke into song: *"We... shall... overcome... one day...*

"Yeah. Time to extinct all slots. No more people looking at us and seeing cartoon figures, all because they lost touch with their own childhood. Nope...

We rampage.
We take the stage.
We free our rage.
New page, my people.
New page.

"Now... before I get started with my main message, not the one they scripted for me, can a brother get a slice of pizza up in here?"

DAY ONE

It was rush hour on the seabird highway. Scores of grebes, egrets, and gulls drafted the winds, calling, climbing, carousing. Pelicans, sanctioned for Kamikaze dives, plunged into the swells with wings pulled back tightly, shaping their bodies into sleek missiles as they targeted their prey.

A continental wind howled its private language, ushering the jumbo sized pontoon boat slowly forward. The deep voiced gust spoke in verse, with ominous pauses and moody rhythms.

Gray, blue, humpback, minke, sperm, and pilot whales all migrated through these ocean channels, along with orcas, porpoises, and dolphins. Fins and tails arced out of and back into the water, leaving flute prints on the surface, condensation spraying up through blowholes, hulking bodies breaching, seemingly scratching their backs against the water's surface, like bears against the bark of pine trunks.

Whales were mating and calving. They were lunge feeding, creating hordes of bubbles, raking their baleen through massive amounts of sea water, devouring krill and other micro plankton by the tons. Sea water sprayed, an epidemic of salt against air, against boat, against all form, coating human lips, stinging eyes, berating and purifying at once.

The dark form of an unknown sea creature sliced forward just beneath the water's clear surface. It was enough to set off alarms in one suspecting soul.

"Girl, you betnot put that hand in the water like that," warned the dark skinned young boy with teeth like fresh snowfall. "Don't you know there's sharks in these waters?"

"Ivory, you're so extra," replied Ashia, her long, slender fingers skirting just beneath the water's deep blue surface as the boat moved along steadily.

"All I'm saying is, don't let the beauty fool you. The sea will hypnotize you with its waves, and you'll be all, this is sooo nice... then the next moment, wham! You got Jaws all up in your grill, and his grill is bigger." Ivory was painted like a desert night. Deep onyx skin jeweled with bright eyes and large blatantly white teeth. When he smiled, sun bleached gypsum pillars shone out in a broad dazzling.

"Ivory, you're a mess," Maricela chimed in. She came from a family of three brothers and rolled along with adolescent boy vibe with the ease of April dealing with springtime. "Why don't you let down your hair and enjoy the ride?" she said, laughing, her own long black hair a lush kite in the wind. "Can you believe this? I never thought I'd be in a boat headed to an island. Not to mention with some knuckleheads like you all."

The soft early summer water was an affectionate swell lapping at their faces—12 teenagers, most of whom right now were questioning their own sanity in choosing to get into what lay ahead. The sea sprayed its attention with each surge of the boat against a wave, wetting their faces, leaving strong salt on their lips.

A seagull whelped above, and a squadron of pelicans flew in tight formation just upwind, outpacing the boat and moving off into the distance. *Maybe they're racing us to the island*, Maricela wondered to herself. *I hope they can set up camp for us, cause I'm definitely going to be in minimum effort mode once we get there.*

Ashia dipped her hand deeper into the water. She had never felt the sea like this, so soft and natural against her skin, like a coating of moisture that came from her own pores. Not since Ghana. Not since the bubble that was a long ago season of her life, now drifting further away by the day on a breeze of poignant circumstance.

The sea was friendly. Until it was not. The liquid-casual, pensive boy named Cielo, with a penchant for unsolicited philosophical blathering, stood up to stretch his back, a little too close to the boat's railing. Just then, a gust slammed into his lithe form, lifting him from his feet as though he had slipped on a banana. "Oh!" he yelled out, alarmed and yet somehow still appearing to be spaced out. His body went horizontal in the air, blew out over the boat's edge, and for a moment, looked like a cartoon figure suspended out over a canyon, just before plummeting comically.

"Man overboard!" yelled out Ivory, none of his usual clowning in his voice. "I told y'all! You don't play with the sea! The sea plays you!" The boat's crew looked at each other, shaking their heads, not bothering to act. They were in no hurry.

Nobody paid Ivory any attention, as at this point, all eyes and thoughts were frantically on Cielo, now bobbing, a serene cork in the water, his eyes remarkably glazed over, and peaceful.

"Cielo! Reach for the rope!" the tall, broad shouldered boy commanded. His voice was assured, no quiver of panic or fear. Later, Ashia would recall Balanta's voice in this moment, and his leadership aura.

"Reach for the rope, Cielo!" Mende repeated after his older brother. Mende was 10 months younger than Balanta, less privileged with height, yet nearly as large in energetic presence.

"No teman, Amigos!" Cielo responded. "Don't fear. The ocean is holding me gently today." His grinning face, mossed over by his dark brown locks of hair, bobbed joyfully in the enthusiastic swells. "This is much like a Love ballad," he said, cryptically.

Most of the group looked at each other, perplexed. "I'm not playing, Cielo! You need to grab the rope," Balanta persisted. "This isn't safe. We need to get over to the island and get camp set up."

Cielo, a proud descendant of Aztecs, Guaraní Indians, and Conquistadors, smiled sweetly. Silently, he gave up his cradling in the sea and grabbed the rope offering. Balanta, Mende, and Maricela worked hand over hand to pull him to the boat. The two brothers lifted him from his sudden bath.

5

"Man… that was crazy, Cielo!" Ivory exclaimed, his sapling legs trembling with a cocktail of fear and excitement.

"Thanks, guys, Cielo said. I appreciate the lift. The water isn't so cold once you realize that your body temperature is adaptive." This gem was met with a collective groan.

"Cielo, you so deep," nudged Maricela, playfully.

"Let's get going, y'all," said Ashia, as the island loomed in the distance, a hulking host waving its invitation through sheer stillness. Her words had barely been released when she heard a loud splash. Ivory, caught in another gust and by his inattention, had now himself gone over the pontoon's railing. For a moment, only his afro was visible on the water's surface. It looked like a black sea urchin bobbing in the tide. Then Ivory shot up from below, a ballistic missile. "Help! I'm going under!" His high pitched quailing busted up Eloni, who folded at the waist in laughter.

Maricela was more concerned. "Someone get him! Can he even swim?"

"He told me just before we got on the boat that he was all-state in swimming," said Mende.

"What state?" Eloni asked through laugh spasms. "The state of panic?"

"I heard that, Eloni!" Ivory protested. "I'm not a saltwater swimmer!" he said between gulps of air. "Get me in freshwater and I'm like a torpedo."

"See…" Promise chided. "Everything was cool until someone had to start getting cocky on the boat." Just then, a seagull with a gifted sense of timing flew over and dropped a healthy payload, which landed supremely on Promise's forehead. "Eeeee!" she shrieked, her hands flailing as the hot yellow-white cargo dripped down her face like a runny egg.

"Eeewww!"

"Naaasty!"

"That's so wrong!"

The whole group pantomimed retching, some more than others coming close to the truth of it.

"Somebody get me something quick!" Promise screamed. She was bent over, attempting to avoid the unthinkable getting into her eyes and mouth. No one moved. Too much laughter, shock, and confusion. Plus, Ivory was still in the water.

"Little help here!" he shouted, his head barely above the surface.

Promise leaned over the edge of the pontoon to grab handfuls of water for her face. Half blind, she lost her balance and joined Ivory in the drink. Now, everyone was rolling on the deck except Balanta, who was just staring at the scene with a look of mock disappointment, like the team captain of a losing squad. He shook his head silently and moved to haul in the overboard crew.

Eloni, brawny, with a kind face, composed himself enough to grab one of Ivory's hands. Balanta grabbed the other, and they hauled the soaking stick figure up onto the deck. Coughing, gasping, playing the moment for all its value, the slender boy regained his words. "Thanks y'all. Coulda been shark supper. I think they can smell fear hormones."

"I'm sure they smelled something, man," said Eloni. "Maybe you better get back in and clean off."

Promise was still in the water, frantically splashing it through her hair, obsessed with the thought of bird splatter still caught up in her kinking strands. "Promise, you better come on out of there," said Maricela. We'll wash your hair up good once we get to camp."

The whole time, Binda and Lake, the smallest and quietest of the bunch, sat observing the chaos, their eyes attentive and without judgment. Binda, her sandy brown hair the texture of cotton candy, dropped her gaze periodically, writing something in her journal. Something that made her smile with a secret thought. Beside Binda and Lake, a young man slept completely undisturbed with a grin on his face, his plump belly sashaying with the rocking of the boat, his bare feet curling with pleasure in the sunlight.

A secretive benefactor had personally chosen this group. Not through the usual personal essays and recommendations. Instead, she had required the candidates to submit video and photo projects that highlighted their relationship with three things: Nature. Rebellion. And Truth. She also admitted to a fair dose of stalking as her final method of choosing her recruits.

Owner of a private island about an hour's boat ride from the mainland, she had grown up on the streets, moving in and out of a dizzying succession of shelters, foster homes, group homes, and detention centers before hitting rock bottom in the cold, absolute belly of a heroin binge. Twice, she was declared expired. Twice, she revived, to the shock of the attending medical team.

A medical social worker began to linger in her hospital room during the two weeks she was in critical care. The worker, herself a recovering addict, brought the woman hot soup and cool washcloths for her forehead.

Later, people asked the benefactor why she believed she had lived, defying expectations and statistics even during her time in critical care. The woman answered, "It was Myriam Obrigada, the young lady who cared for me. I kept wanting to die. I tried, but could only manage to fall asleep. I would wake, open my eyes, and there would be Myriam, her sweet face staring at me like she couldn't be happier to see me. In those moments, so cold inside my soul, I would think to myself, *I am a very sick butterfly who hopes to die. I flutter to break the bonds of earth, but a gentle heart brings me back. This woman, she keeps me warm. Maybe I can learn to warm myself.*

"Following Myriam's example of how to provide Love to another soul, provide Love as though you are sharing all that you care about in each single act, I did learn how to warm myself. Naturally, it occurred to me that maybe I can do this for others. Help them learn to warm themselves."

And so, Antonia Mercado rebuilt her life. Healed herself. And became a useful garden in which other wilted flowers could resurrect themselves.

Antonia came into her island through nothing but Grace. A dying woman, wealthy from her family's generational coffee business, bequeathed the island to Antonia's foundation, *Keep Warm*. It took three years for Antonia to emerge out of her shock and realize that she had an island on her hands. She turned the island over to Greater Hands, praying for inspiration. Looking to be guided toward the purpose of her island.

It came to her in the shower, after a particularly difficult day. Since that shower, Antonia had brought a group of young people to the island each year, on their own, to have whatever experience they were meant to have at that particular time in their lives. Her only stipulation: No technology. All of that would have to be left behind. She wanted the youth to push themselves through their walls of fear. Fear of nature, solitude, quiet, and freedom. Hopefully, they would break the scar tissue left by addiction to noise and stimulus. She prayed that they would shed their false beings, and find their actual selves. She prayed that they would learn to keep themselves warm.

Antonia showed up on this day at another of the many public humanitarian talks she scheduled wearing a flowing white cotton summer gown with all the moxie that a freedom fighter like her innately possessed. Her long hair was wrapped in a chartreuse and banana yellow scarf. After being introduced, she took her place at the podium under dramatic lights. She was freely eating a bag of nacho chips, her fingers, lips, and tongue a bright radiation orange. Antonia was not the least bit self-conscious. Rather, she couldn't be more tickled at her violation of formality and protocol, which she likened to the absurdity of finishing schools, cult codes, and frightened herds of buffalo pretending to be liberated swans.

"All of my clothing is handmade by a collective of entrepreneurial women in *naturally developed* countries," she announced, completely unsolicited. Media flashbulbs flared. Coffee-soaked vocal chords murmured.

"Why do you call yourself a refugee, Ms. Mercado?" someone in the audience asked.

"Whomever among us has been visited by violence against the soul and has survived to another land, we must regard that person as a refugee, mustn't we? Whether that new land is a nation, neighborhood, relationship, or attitude, we have sought refuge in its embrace, hopeful ever, even if in desperation, that something beautiful there may grow."

Antonia loudly crumpled her empty bag of chips and continued. "Leave something for the world. It doesn't have to be great works of art. But leave *something*. Kindness. An embarrassing habit of hugging strangers. An upgrade to your gene pool. People touched by your Love. If you don't leave something, then why on earth were you alive in the first place? If you do leave something, don't do it expecting rewards. Do it out of sheer stubborn consideration. Care enough to peel off a piece of you and offer it to the whole. Is that too much to ask? Give the people your bread.

"A person owes humanity many things. The least that humanity can do is offer a crumb of dignity to a person. I have a deep belief that enough crumbs, over a lifetime, can soothe the inflammation that comes with being human. I suppose that's what it means to honor someone: care enough to share some of your crumbs."

Antonia met with Ivory, Ashia, and the rest of this year's crop of youth at a horse stable. She required that they go on a ride with her as a final qualification for the island. She was dressed in a Mexican serape, a large woolen shawl, hand-died in red, indigo, and white. A small sombrero hung against her upper back, suspended from a thin black chinstrap. The sombrero looked like a kitchen utensil for pulping oranges, a coned teepee of a headpiece circled by a narrow moat that ended in a curled brim. Antonia had on knee-high cowboy boots, dark leather chaps over sangria red jeans, and a dramatically billowing white blouse just to add a splash.

They rode a long trail that grew slender as it traversed a steep hillside, and finished by the ocean. After dismounting, and feeding and watering the horses, they sat as a circle in warm sand. Antonia kicked off her boots and sank her bare feet, both ornate in toe rings, into the sand. Brushing her long black hair back over her shoulders, she let out a big exhale of satisfaction and smiled at her young protégés, who looked at her with a mix of anticipation and uncertainty.

"I hope you enjoyed the ride," Antonia said. "I'm impressed we made it here without losing any of you," she joked. "Nobody fell too hard, and nobody got stomped. That's a good start.

"I didn't expect you to be experts on the horse, Familia. Half of you fell off at least once, which was less than I anticipated. Then there's Ivory. Ivory, mi'jo. A horse is not a dog. It will not roll over because you scratch its neck. It responds to the reins and to flank kicks. Not *choo choo* sounds. It is not a train. But have no shame, mi'jo. You hung in there like a champion.

"Horses are good people detectors. They would have told me if any of you weren't fit for the island. So, the ride wasn't really a test of your abilities with horses. I know most of you never rode a horse before. I just wanted to run you through my trusted four-legged people detectors, so they could tell me what I already knew. I picked a good group."

Antonia scanned their faces. This part always thrilled her. Seeing them *before* the island. Before being touched by the impossible. Before having their sand sifted and swirled and blown away, hopefully to reveal themselves. Here, before her, were 12 artifacts of neglect and abuse, so shimmering and vibrating with potential. The brothers, Balanta and Mende. And the other young men. Shonto and Eloni. Cielo and Ivory. The young ladies. Ashia, Maricela, Binda, Lake, Pikea, and Promise. Antonia looked into their eyes and saw their vibrancy. *Your lightning inside is why I chose you*, she said to herself.

9

They talked for a long while, passing around dried fruit and slugging canteens of water with lemon slices. Antonia told many stories, got lost on many tangents. She laughed very easily, "...the sign of a saint," she joked. Her eager charges asked her many questions. Eventually, Antonia got to the pragmatic details. And the mystic ones.

Antonia spoke softly, yet with authority. "This is a big island you'll be experiencing. You'll find that out quickly. You have the lagoon on the western side, the dunes on the eastern side, and mountains and valleys all over the place. Camp is pretty much in square in the center of the southern shore, but close by the coast."

The island had no cell phone signal. That fact alone had narrowed down the interested candidates. Three satellite phones would be provided, to be kept fully charged in a fireproof lockbox stored in a small cabin at the campsite. Only in an emergency were they allowed to use the phones. They would be given a flare gun and a box of flares, and were to shoot one off in any true emergency. Someone would be spotting for them from a boat about a mile offshore, scanning the shore and sky for any distress signal. Antonia had also arranged for the lookout boat to be stocked with medical supplies, food, and water. Other than that, they were on their own. No chaperones. No staff. No parents or guardians. No judges, lawyers, teachers, principals, playground monitors, sports coaches, life coaches, mentors, therapists, counselors, advisors, preachers, shopkeepers, police, or any other form of authority. This also meant that no such presence would be available to get them out of trouble, to put things in order, to calm conflict, or offer a reasonable head. They would depend on their young heads. No old heads for an entire, hardly believable week.

Antonia continued her orientation. "As I mentioned from the beginning, I have only these conditions: No smoking of any kind. I don't care if you incinerate your own lungs. You're not burning down my island. No alcohol. Women open all the wrong doors when they're on that stuff. Men are more frantic than ever to step through those doors. And no phones or cameras. If I am so kind as to invite you to my island, you're not going to be there as some ghost, affecting the place with your presence, even while you're not really there all the way, letting the place get into you. You can masturbate to your technology on your own time.

"You're not going to need to bring food or water. I know that seems crazy, but you'll find all the food you need already growing there. You'll eat like royalty, I promise," Antonia said, glancing at Eloni. And the water is pristine. Cleaner than any water you've tasted. You can drink it right from the lagoon. And there are springs bubbling up everywhere. You have so many climates on the island. Desert. Subtropics. Woodland forest. Mountain."

Antonia told the group, "I'm trusting you in a big way here. I'm not having you sign waivers and all that. You're grown. You're either going to take advantage of me, or you're going to honor this opportunity. I'm going old school here. Como los Viejos. *Like the Old Ones*. I'm trusting that you're going to do right by me and not sue my Latin behind. It's not that I'd mourn the money. But I would mourn the ability to offer this island experience to other young people after you. So, let's spit on it or something. If anything gets broke between us, we gotta make it good with each other. The right way. Me sientes? *Feel me?*"

Antonia despised the legal system, and the litigious frothing of piranhas that was society. She believed that both dynamics existed for one sole purpose: to allow the wealthy to keep their loot, and to keep the rest from getting their hands on that loot. "Frankly," she told many a friend, "I wish I could be a techno revolutionary, with the skills to bring down all these systems. I'm still waiting for the young people to rise up and blow apart all these cannibalistic money pots like so many piñatas. Just let the money scatter to the wind. Reset civilization. I don't care about what chaos and suffering comes after that. It won't be as hollow and soulless as the chaos and suffering that already exists."

"Listen," Antonia said to the 12 youth, finishing her orientation, "I want you to know... the island... is not like other places. Things will happen to you there that don't seem to be possible. When that comes, don't run from it. Embrace it. It's like surfing. If you just let yourself crest that wave, you will discover something incredible. Something that science cannot measure and society cannot comprehend."

The boat's hull met with the loamy shore. The group spilled over with chatter, anxious as much as excited. Ashia, Promise, and Pikea stepped gingerly onto solid ground, their legs wobbly. "Now, what were you saying about rabid animals?" Promise asked, scanning the scene. Shadows were long and retracting as heat began to make its pitch for the day.

"I was just playing, girl," said Ashia. "Antonia (she insisted the youth call her Antonia) said there was nothing here larger than deer, foxes, and goats."

"Fox is too large already, if you ask me," Promise huffed. "I'll be sure to have my pepper spray on hand 24/7."

Balanta, Mende, Eloni and the rest were out of the boat, surveying the scene. "Are you serious!" yelled Mende. "Is this place for real?" They were staring at a slope of sparkling white coastline, crested with white foamy tide heaved up by waves of startling, clear water. The beach was a rolling stretch of impossibly white sand, its gypsum glistening in the sun like miniature flares. Up from the shore, they could spot their encampment. A cluster of cabins framed inside a convention of proud, diverse trees. Palms stood distinct, swooped in the trunk like arrow bows of the gods.

A striking mountain rose in the background, a towering, sweeping obelisk. There it stood, dynastic and tenured, without a single insecurity. *Jade Mountain.* A granite monument, green and sentinel. Jade Mountain earned its name honestly. A thick groundcover of avocado-hued shrubs and bushes blanketed much of its surface. Where emerald tribes of oaks and maples opened up into clearings more frequent with gaining altitude, rocky patches gleaming with quartz enjoyed sun's touch and offered back fertile clusters of wildflowers: Indian paintbrushes. Poppies. Lilac. Scorpionweed.

The mountain in its growth had settled on a variety of geological shapes. Relatively flat stretches advanced up to the bases of sheer cliffs. Folds of the mountain wove their way up its entire height, stretching into curvaceous passes, puckering into sharp ridges, plaining back out into modest valleys and errant canyons. Aspens and cypresses gathered in many of these low lying areas, along with orchid trees and red flowering gum trees, all suckling from the clear marrow of streams that ran through the low notches of narrows. The aspens wore bright maize and auburn puffs of leaves, accenting the greens of the higher pines and the reflective ramblings of granite and scree, which were in fact stained in jade. Nearer to its peak, the mountain presented many long scree slopes lorded over by large boulders. Dwarf goats with reverent beards and saxophone-looped horns ran here, leaping sideways against the mountain face from one impossible rocky pinnacle to another, braying away at any imperial imposition of gravity.

The peak of Jade Mountain was its own microclimate. Somehow, water pooled in flat stones. Large black beetles and miniaturized ferrets drank from those watering holes. Wind was a strong sonnet at the peak, howling and gushing erratically, washing everything flat. Rocks. Grasses. Air. Oxygen, thin and ambivalent, gave what it could, but this was not a place for breathing. It was beyond such comforts. The view spanned the island 360 degrees, making the ocean appear to be wrapped around land like remnant bathwater around a drain.

They gathered their provisions from the pontoon boat, whose crew of three, once they helped carry everything up to camp, wasted no time loitering through a goodbye. After rechecking the list of supplies for a third time, the crew unanchored and resumed their duties. Soon, the pontoon was back out on the open water, motoring back to the larger boat that had brought them all from the mainland.

Silence roamed the group as they gazed around their home for the next seven days. Their movements dreamy and unsure. A surreal sense of being left alone, by adults, *on purpose*, breached the silence. Wanting to be free of adult presence was one thing. Being completely alone for the first time was something else. Then... childlike instincts: "I got that cabin over there!" yelled Eloni, racing for the closest shelter, claiming a cot before Balanta and Mende could get through the entrance.

"It's three to a cabin!" Ashia called out, as the mad dash was already nearly over. Ivory bounded into another cabin, trailed by Shonto. Cielo made his way over on his own time. He was still savoring the fresh onion on which he was snacking. Lake, Promise, and Pikea took one cabin. Maricela, Ashia, and Binda filed into another. The four small cabins were seven feet high, single rooms, wooden floored, and walled with weathered pine logs shaved of their bark. A fifth cabin was for supplies. The smell of blooming star jasmine in the woods suffused the air. That and the scent of teen sweat and apprehension. Crickets in the grass were sending out word to their people: *New ones have come.*

The group began to reemerge into the open area, pulled by curiosity. A large fire pit in the center of the campground held shards of wood burned down to ash. The pit was ringed by blackened stones. Farther out from the pit, a circle of sitting rocks and logs.

Ringing the camp area were groves of cottonwood, willow, and oak. Also, angel trumpet trees and tipu trees with their bright yellow blossoms. Ferns competed with sagebrush just above the height of wild grass that gave the camp area its perimeter. Everything smelled of untamed, vivid life.

Ocean water lapped, just over 100 yards away, a pendulum against the coriander-colored clay shore, depositing its artifacts of shells and seaweed and bright silt. Seabirds in the distance parted the sky with their wings. So many new sounds. Unfamiliar rhythms. *Just another placement*, thought Pikea. And then, strangely, *I want my mother. Such an inappropriate thought. It doesn't even fit. I don't want my mother. I want the feeling that mothers are supposed to bring.*

"Hey, y'all, come over here!" Pikea yelled. "There's a *waka*!"

"What's a waka?" Ivory asked as they hustled over to the clearing behind the cabins where Pikea was on her knees in the sandy soil, running her hands along the edge of a long, faded white canoe.

"*This* is a waka," Pikea said. "It's our Maori word for it. I wonder if it works. It would be cool to get it out on the water."

Ivory jumped into the hull and lay down on the canoe's bottom. "This thing is deep," he said. "And long. I bet we could fit about eight, 10 of us in here." They milled about the canoe, some fantasizing deep sea adventure, others scanning the surroundings, trying to process the cultural displacement of being alone in the midst of so many living nonhuman things.

Maricela saw the garden first. Not far from the canoe, it was a large uncultivated space behind the cabins, piquant and aromatic. So abundant with fruits of the earth that it tumbled and spilled all over itself. They came over to it, their mouths watering as they saw what awaited. Eloni dropped, sinking his knees into the dark fudge soil. Maricela thought she saw wetness in his eyes. The garden ebbed with life. Yucca and Jicama. Squash, potatoes, radishes. Cucumbers and zucchini. Carrots and spinach. Garlic and bell peppers. Ghost peppers. Jalapeños. Habaneros. Tomatoes. Sweet potatoes. Peppermint and basil. Cabbage and melons. Fat clusters of blackberries, strawberries, and raspberries were scattered throughout. The berries were tight with juice. All of this splendor was oversized and swelled with vitality.

Eloni dug his fingers down into the black soil. He pulled up several egg-shaped tubers. "Look," he said. "Taro. And malanga root. The taro is West

African. Grows in the lo'ai in Hawai'i, too. Man, earth people eat this stuff all over the world. Fiji, Samoa, India, Nepal, Brazil."

Eloni lifted the brown malanga root, closed his eyes, and inhaled deeply. "This is packed with nutrients. You can prepare it any way you like. Sliced and fried. Stewed. Grilled."

"I Love malanga," Cielo said. "That's a Latin staple!"

Along one side of the garden was a thick stand of cornstalks, head high to Balanta. Sugarcane walled another side. "Who in the world is taking care of all of this?" Eloni asked. "I thought no one ever came out here."

"And why aren't the animals getting to this?" Promise asked. She kneeled and tasted a blackberry. Her eyes rolled back and she moaned. "This can't be real. I have never tasted a blackberry like that. Take me away before I gorge and die." They all gorged and died, berries staining their lips and clothes in splotches of decadence.

"I guess we should start by making a fire?" asked Ivory.

"A fire? It's already a good 75 degrees." Ashia responded.

"Yeah, but isn't that what you're supposed to do first when you go camping? Start a fire?"

"Well, maybe not a forest fire, but yeah, maybe if we get something started we'll be ready to cook some lunch when we're ready."

"Hey y'all, know what I'm thinking?" asked Eloni. "Remember what Antonia said? There's a lagoon not five minutes from here. A *lagoon*!"

That was all that needed to be said. So much for starting a fire. Everyone broke for their cabins, put on their swimming clothes, and raced for the lagoon. Eloni, as solid and hefty as he was, was light on his feet, and could run faster than most half his size. His arms were thick gourds strung together: shoulders, biceps, triceps, forearms. This arrangement was capped off by strong hands as puffy as winter gloves. Down below a wide torso were Samoan legs as sturdy and thick as a mountain might need for tap dancing. Quickly, he was in the lead, eyes blazing, the grin of a hyena taking over his face.

The island flora exploded visually around them. Passion fruit and trumpet vines cloyed their way through the underbrush, decorating the groundcover in ornate blossoms and stark hues of purple, violet, blood orange, and cold yellow. Thick vines of morning glory spilled over decaying logs, rich waterfalls jeweled in pastels. Squirrels, pompous and rowdy, leapt from the branches of jacaranda trees down onto lower lying branches and then to the ground where they darted their tails excitedly and scattered in search of harvest. Eucalyptus leaves rattled high in their crowns as swallows trampolined on the branches and wind ruffled the dark green arrangement.

The brush was thick along the dirt path. Arms swiped and were swiped at by a jungle of overgrowth. Vines. Branches. Weeds. And as they closed in, reeds.

"Last one to the lagoon is a loser!" Eloni shouted.

"Obviously!" Mende mocked as he raced by Eloni without the slightest straining.

"What are you, a track star?" gasped Eloni, who then noticed Balanta pull up alongside him, his breath still intact, as though he was chilling on a porch swing.

Balanta said calmly, "We've had to do a lot of running."

Twelve newcomers in t-shirts and shorts. Dashing through unspoiled woods. Hearts pounding with exertion. And with excitement. Something new and promising just ahead. Something that should feel more than good. And then, there it was.

The lagoon was a liquid turquoise impossibility. Too beautiful. It made you doubt you weren't dreaming. Its surface had a language. A very real one. If you were quiet, you could hear it: 1,000 monks chanting at a whisper. The water was large. Bigger than many lakes, and much deeper. The shore around the banks was dark soil and soft lush grass before it surrendered to a thick stand of willows and cottonwoods that ringed the area.

Mende jumped without pause as soon as he reached the waterline. His slender body slid under the water's surface. He felt his skin melt as the water seemed to reach his bones. Surfacing, he spouted unregulated ecstasy: "I have never been in wild water this warm! Not in a lake, river, or ocean!"

Balanta was next. He dove, his broad shoulders cutting the water as he plunged. Breaking the surface again, he showed off his first real smile all day. "You all need to jump in! This is insane! It feels so good!"

Pikea, Eloni, and Cielo followed Maricela into the water. Eyes bulging at the moment of contact. Shonto, Lake, Binda, Ivory, Promise, and Ashia were last into the water. Some, meekly. Others with delicate steps as they first toed the blue wetness and slid in on hands and bottoms. Ivory, once in, clung to the shoreline roots, eyeing the deeper water suspiciously. "Are there leeches in this water?" Ivory asked, not one bit discouraged at the collective hollering this brought.

"Man, will you just get in and enjoy it?" urged Mende.

"Okay, but if I come up with bloodsuckers in my shorts, whose going to remove them?"

"Ivory... just, ewww..." Promise responded.

Promise and Maricela giggled as they treaded water, splashing each other gleefully. "Oooh! I'm not coming out!" Maricela proclaimed. "The water feels like a feather. Even softer!"

Soon, most of them were drawn to the phenomenon happening before them, at the base of the lagoon against the cliff side. A singular, spectacular waterfall, 40 feet high. A waterfall that looked like God crying. Too pure. Crystalline. Mist so fine it barely held its tension between vapor and air. Emergent from the dense forest above, a river catapulting over the granite lip of a cliff, piercing the mist, blasting out in a bosom over the cliff lip, arcing in a translucent grace downward into a lush drapery. A freefall of enormous water particles, their skin a glimmering glass, plunging water singing divine hymns, gaining momentum, letting gravity shape their droplets, shape their union, still so far to go. Finally, landing in a steel drum whisper against black rocks, against a lagoon face caving in rhythmically to the force of falling water. It sounded like a giant cup of tea being poured. Mystical sounds of water arriving as a river, of water gushing out over cliff into space, water playing on air as it dropped, plunging water landing on lagoon water, entering it forcefully, joining. Always joining.

And this lagoon, like the waterfall, 40 feet deep, spread vast and palpable, spread like a liquid diamond across a meteoric crater. Its face, wavering, ever rippled by the waterfall's abundance. Lagoon, fertile and surreal. Its color. Spectral blush of greens and blues, yellows and reds. Reflecting sky and hibiscus blossoms nested in trees. Lagoon diaphanous and decadent. Deep and lapping. Sweet scents of mountain tears, mint and jasmine from the higher meadows, honeysuckle petals blown into its waterfall, stewed like tea leaves in its belly.

Sand, soft and sable, covered the floor of the lagoon, and was easily visible through the pristine water. The shore clung to the water with thick vining of jasmine and morning glory for fingers, holding, holding. Much of the lagoon was shaded by tall willows and cottonwoods, palms and silk trees. They stood over the river above, shading the falls, accepting stark golden sunlight shafts as décor upon the tumbling waters. The trees were mutants, drawing from the lagoon for size that made no sense to human eyes. Trunks twice the norm in diameter, canopy twice the usual height. The trees on the lagoon level reached to the height of the waterfall and much higher, bearding the cusp and overflow with dense, tussling clusters of green afros, dark, bright, streaked in yellow.

Birds rented every single branch of this canopy circling the lagoon, paying in song and rustling accent of feathers. They dived and drank and bathed in the opulence. Squirrels used high branches for springboards, in turn chasing and being chased by annoyed birds nesting and mating.

Fruit. A jewelry around lagoon's neck. Ripened and opining in fragrance. Orange and yellow and rust-purple fruit interrupting the green fabric of leaves. Papaya. Mango. Star fruit. Plums. Guava, lemon, peach. Fruit drawing bees that hovered everywhere like miniature helicopters jaundiced and striped black against the sun. Dragonflies flew just over the water. Water bugs danced on the surface tension. Nightingales took this as a dinner invitation and dived accordingly.

Eloni swam out to the lagoon center. A warm rush of water came up from beneath him and hit him in the stomach. "Whoa! What was that? Hey, y'all, check this out!" The hot spring came up from the lagoon floor as a translucent rope of current the circumference of a large tree trunk. It gyrated upward, displacing sand from around its mouth, gushing to the surface where it ended in a faint bubbling, sending out circular ripples that faded quickly.

Eloni, feeling very Samoan and in his element, dove down and swam through the spring's liquid rope. He felt its strong current boost him upward swiftly, a nearly invisible hydraulic lift. The spring current against his body was propulsive. Jacuzzi jets pumping water against his skin and muscles. He was inside of a tubular massage, and it felt unbelievable. Again and again, he dove down to the lagoon floor, pushed inside of the spring current, and rode its elevator up to the surface. The water inside the plume was hot, though not uncomfortably so. And there was no sulfurous smell. Rather, the spring's mineral content brought a sweetly detergent bouquet to the lagoon's surface that dissipated all the way to shore.

It was getting hotter. Thirst was awake and roaming. Skin was browning quickly in the sunlight magnified by the lagoon broad face. "Do you think we can drink this water?" asked Ivory. Don't want to be getting parasites and whatnot. Thought we were supposed to boil it first."

"I've been drinking it since we got here," said Cielo, treading near the lagoon center. He gulped some water and sprayed it up into the air. "This stuff is mountain pure. Don't think we have to worry about it. Tastes delicious, not like municipal water. That stuff tastes like rusted pipes. Storm drains."

"So, you've tasted pipes and drains?" Maricela asked, chiding.

"Sure. At least, the sediment of it."

"Okay," said Ivory, unsure. "If I take to retching later on today, it's on you."

"No sir," Cielo replied. "You're not going to get any of that on me. You'll get my compassion and a pat on the back. Nada mas, 'migo."

Binda was admiring Maricela's face. High cheek bones. Deep dimples. Large, dark eyes. And Maricela had a proud nose. That's what her abuela, her grandma, called it. That, and *presentable*. A smooth, pleasant ridge. *Presentable*. Her abuela had always referred to Maricela in these terms: Presentable for a true gentleman. Presentable for society. Presentable for a respectable job. When she was younger, Maricela wondered if her abuela saw her as no more than a fine porcelain doll on a cabinet shelf, needing frequent dusting. Later, she realized that her abuela had herself been raised entirely for social presentation. That's when Maricela began persuading her abuela into secret mud fights in the nearby arroyo. They screamed their delight as they slung and slipped and ended unrecognizable. Maricela remembered how she and her abuela showered off with buckets of water from the outside tap. She was determined to shatter the fine porcelain doll that was her abuela's identity, and to prevent her own flesh from hardening into porcelain. When she was young, Maricela had considered her project to be a grand success.

17

Ashia and Promise made for the foot of the waterfall, where it was shallower and they could stand mostly out of the lagoon, and directly under the falls. Ashia possessed full, ripe lips that had always been the object of either scorn or desire. Her auntie always told her she had been "blessed with blackberry lips and valentine heart hips."

People had a hard time knowing which way to fall with Ashia, so strong was her energy. By the time a few moments had passed in her presence, few had any memory of ever not being attracted to her. Her hair was a bountiful black fountain of tight, vibrant coils that she Loved to evolve from afro to braids, cornrows, locs, and back again. Now, it was loc'ed and glistening with Loving care. Moisturized and groomed, a single cowrie shell hung from a loc near to her temple, an ivory emblem of her African, Ghanaian roots. Every rare moon or so, she thrilled to cutting the whole thing down close to her scalp and feeling the lightness of being that only comes with having your head so naked and free beneath sky and sun. Her hair grew preternaturally quickly. So much so that she could go from a shaved scalp to shoulder length locs in six months. Some back in her village considered this to be a sign of destined greatness. Ashia just took it to the shower and Loved it up deliciously.

Ashia drenched her hair in the waterfall cascade as it showered over her. She leaned her head back into the strength of the plummeting current and opened her mouth, letting the sweet flow caress her throat. Her athletic body was engulfed. Taken. Promise joined her, letting the falls rush through her proud afro. A kinship of flowing.

Promise was long. Long limbs, hands, and feet. Even her lashes. Her enthusiastic, thick crop of black hair was so soft to the touch that it had invited far too many unsolicited hands throughout her life. She walked like a little girl who had just discovered a trove of magic treasures—with a spritely bounce barely restraining itself from being a leap or a skip. And she smiled. Smiled like she was giving away smiles for food at a homeless shelter—with undiluted gratitude at being the bearer of such gifts, and knowing the rampant soul hunger she was feeding. She smiled like her smiles were hot biscuits and rich gravy. Like they were fat stacks of waffles and syrup just pulled from the maple tree. And she would not give up her smile. Not to anyone's fear, anger, spite, blue mood, or coldness. Her smile was her homestead, and she wasn't leaving.

"Cielo. Um, no. What are you doing?" Ashia said, not really asking.

Cielo halted what he was doing, which was pulling down his shorts so that he could backstroke al fresco. "What else is a boy to do with all this paradise and freedom?" Cielo asked, his voice already anticipating a scolding. "No? Not good? Sorry. It was just a natural impulse for me. We were born naked, 'miga. Just trying to get back to the root."

"We don't need any of those kinds of roots, Cielo," Ashia said, smiling. "You just keep on enjoying the water, and let us keep on enjoying our innocence. Bet?"

"Bet."

"Why do they call it Lake of God?" Ashia asked, her voice softening as she changed the topic.

"What?" Cielo asked.

"*Lake of God*. That's what Antonia said this lagoon is called."

"I'm not sure," said Cielo. "I read something about the Native people coming here for sacred ceremonies. Maybe it's the spring coming up from below into the lagoon, or the color of the water. Or… just look around. You got a waterfall, mountains, sky, ocean in the distance. Who else's place could this be?"

Ashia felt Balanta's gaze linger. *Good*. She stole her own glances, just more discreetly. Balanta's muscles moved like ocean waves across his back and shoulders. Ashia wanted to swim there. Here she was, on a supernatural island, and she was thinking about a boy. She couldn't help it. She marveled. Balanta's sleek torso was terraced like a rice paddy. All rolling hills and valleys, crisply outlined. Polished geometries of muscle. Broad plates of smooth sandstone pectorals. Rows of symmetrically perfect abdominals. Even his back, a long deep spinal canal banked in muscle, with more muscle fanning out to his sides. Shoulders stacked like sculptured realms of power, striated with movement and set on a broad upper frame that tapered to a narrow waist. Thick tributaries of vessels ranged over those shoulders, and down his long arms, ending at the deltas of his sweeping hands. Cords of muscle tussled in his forearms, and his triceps flared into horseshoes every time he straightened his arms. Ashia kept gazing, indulgent and fluttering privately.

Eloni, Mende, and Balanta climbed up the black cliff face and took turns diving from the top of the waterfall. Eloni, not so much diving as jumping, landing with powerful cannonballs that sprayed anyone within 30 feet. Cielo chose to stay below, backstroking across the lake, pure joy on his face. Mende shouted down to Ivory, who was in the water but still hanging by the shore, "Ivory, you coming up here? You gotta try this jump, man!"

"If God had wanted me to jump from up there, he would have made me a flying squirrel!" Ivory replied.

Maricela, Lake, and Binda, their loose, knee-length shorts and t-shirts soaked, made their way up the cliff and slid repeatedly down the washed smooth obsidian riverbed preceding the falls, and thrust out into the air, before plunging into the lagoon, squealing and flailing in delight.

Romanced into this paradise of beauty, they all stayed for hours, daring to wash down with the waterfall, swimming out to the lagoon's center, diving down to the sandy bottom. The hours stayed with them. Locked in a moment. Happiness. Free and washed in water. Loosened like never before. Dreaming.

Only hunger pulls them from the lagoon. On the way back to camp, one of them wanders away from the dripping wet flock. The terrain changes from dense forest, to open beach. Her name is Lake. Born for the Diné, *the People*. Born also for the Pueblo people. Warm brown eyes perched on artistic cheekbones. Oval face framed in a falling loom of thick jet black hair. Scent of piñon. She has a penchant for following butterflies, following so entranced that she often ends up lost. Like now. Sitting on a brown chair of rock by water's shore, she silently says goodbye to the small cream butterfly lifting into the blue as her attention returns to earth.

She drifts next through an arboreal art gallery lain out over shallow rolling hills. A robust banquet of fruit trees. Pomegranate, oranges, and lemons. Avocado, almond, and apple. Limes and olives. Lake samples the delicacies, her mouth swooning with juices. She lifts her smiling face to the sky and spins, letting her spirit ascend into the fragrant openness. As she turns, water seeps up from the earth in several places near her bare feet. Just enough to pool with itself and run toward her toes. The wetness brings her back.

"Now where am I?" She is used to dislocation. Her question is not of urgency, only amusement. She notices sun is climbing down its daily hill. "They're probably starting the fire and preparing dinner. I better get back." She says this even as she remains fixed. Since she could crawl, her life was like this. Pulled by natural worlds, tugged by duty back to human order and routine. A water bug skating between two shores.

Giant jacaranda trees grew in fertile numbers on the inland side of the lagoon, dropping distinctive brown seed pods the size of silver dollars. The pods reminded Ivory of giant clams with their rippled lips. Larger than silver dollars, with rock hard shells, they were scattered everywhere. He gathered pocketsful of the seeds from the ground on the walk back to camp. "What are you doing?" Pikea asked in her chalky voice, a filmy remembrance of peace.

"I think these will make cool necklaces. I can hear them clacking together in the wind, like wooden chimes."

"Cool, I'd like to see what you come up with."

"Thanks. I'll make you one." Ivory enjoyed the friendship of females. It was his comfort zone. He had the longest eyelashes in the free world, female or male. It was impossible not to stare. The lashes extended out over his eyes, feathery awnings, creating an impression of dewiness, almost drowsiness, to his gaze. These features caused girls and women to fawn over him, which he did not protest. "It's like having a puppy dog permanently by your side," he joked with friends, "except you don't have to take care of it." At the same time, as he approached the end of his teens, he was developing a complex about the whole thing. Everyone wanted to pet him and coo at him. But no one seemed to want him. Really want him. He was beginning to feel impotent in the ways of Love.

Pikea slung a pile of palm fronds she had gathered over her shoulder and headed back to camp. She was looking forward to wrapping fish in these palms, then burying and baking them in the earth for dinner. She could already smell the scent of the feast in her head.

They came to a field of oats. Eloni ran through, Pikea and Mende after him. They brushed the stalks with their hands as they raced, tickling their palms, yelling nonsense sounds. Sunlight gathered in the tips of the stalks, which hummed with energy, appearing on the verge of catching fire.

Back at camp, Balanta and Mende gathered firewood from the stacks alongside the cabins, and some stray kindling from deeper in the woods. Balanta cut a leonine figure as he stalked through the undergrowth, focused, shirtless, and glistening. He draped his left arm over his brother's shoulder as they wandered, reminiscing and sharing private jokes. "You remember how we used to do this back home?" asked Mende, looking up at Balanta. Balanta's dark chocolate skin tone contrasted with his younger brother's mocha hue.

"Now, *that* was work. Mom had us doing that all day. In the sun. Cutting, carrying. The whole thing." Balanta, although just 10 months older than Mende, was three inches taller. Next to each other, they looked like varsity and junior varsity. Balanta stood erect, his shoulders broad and high, his posture resembling a conduit between sky and earth. Mende slouched and tucked, increasing the brothers' perceived difference in height. Lake wanted to run her hand over their smooth shaved heads, but decided she would wait until they knew each other better.

Several people left for the beach to fish for dinner, while Lake and Binda chased squirrels in circles around the cabins, luring them with almonds, squealing with them as they grabbed and fled. Lake enjoyed this moment with Binda, who seemed to Lake to be a kindred spirit of quietness. Lake noted Binda's smooth sable skin that caught sunlight uniquely. Skin that was a field of fertile earth, very few stones or weeds to be found. Lake thought: *Some Skin-God is clearly pouring fresh cream and brown sugar into Binda's complexion each morning.* Binda's eyes said, *Don't notice me.* Her lips betrayed this command, often seeming to just barely hold in a smile that said, *It feels good to be noticed.* The slope of Binda's broad, shallow nose reminded Lake of the ruins of an ancient pyramid, flattened yet still majestic. It was the centerpiece of a face shaped from river clay, tracing down to lips like swollen rivers.

Binda's skin tone *was* clay: smooth, rich; like from the mixing of old earth and new water. Her Aboriginal features seemed to do original things with the play of sunlight. Her color changed as the light moved. Dark umber. Autumn amber. Nutmeg. Sable.

And shadows enjoyed reshaping her features. She had multiple faces, depending on the angle at which you were looking, and the momentary expression she wore. Her smiling face sometimes appeared... tremulous. Her frowning face verged on comical.

Binda's soft clouds of hair managed to be grayish black in an elderly way, even though upon close inspection, she had no gray strands of which to speak. Depending on the humidity and the hour, her hair performed upright and bouffant, half-hearted and listing, or weeping sweetly around her cheeks.

Her clothes were casual. The way she wore them though, bespoke regality. Her movements were like those of desert rocks or water: You had to pay close attention or you would miss them. One moment she was here. The next she was elsewhere. Not stealthy. Just inconspicuous, efficient. And she walked gently, touching the earth with apologies in every step, her generous grove of hair waving enough to let Lake know it enjoyed being stroked by breeze.

As the shadows lengthened, the heat of the day backed off gradually. Lake saw most of the group returning from their fishing trip. "Where's everyone else?" she asked.

Ashia waved her hand dismissively. "Balanta, Mende, Eloni, and Promise got infected with caveman fever. It was Balanta's grand idea to go hunting. I guess they think they're going to take down a boar, or a Mastodon or something."

Maricela laughed. "More likely to take down a hamstring, or an ankle. People, let me know when it's time to make dinner. Too much adrenaline for me today. I'm going to catch a quick nap."

"Me, too," said Ashia.

"Great idea," said Ivory. "I need my second wind. Then it's grubbing time."

As they slept, the sun dipped, and the day's heat climbed into the trees. The falling sun cast a spell of colors over the world. Ocean became violet. Sky and its cloud children, a kaleidoscope of reds, oranges, and yellows. On land, tree leaves took on richer, somber notes, like old jazz musicians in a blues joint. Even the earth grew more dramatic, its soil darker and pensive.

Upon waking, appetites made themselves clear.

"Should we start making dinner?" Cielo asked, clearly self-motivated. "I feel the temperature dropping."

"Balanta and them aren't back from their great hunt and adventure yet," Maricela offered with a smirk. "But they should be soon. Maybe the smell from the food will bring them."

"They need to end the great hunt and start the great cooking," said Pikea, with her usual fragrance of attitude. "That's what they need to do. Look at Ivory, he's pacing by the fire like a panther on a hunger strike. Somebody give that boy a cracker."

Moments later, the hunting pack emerged from the forest and into camp.

"I don't see any meat swinging from any poles," said Maricela. "Unless you've got mice in your pockets, or something. In which case, I say, *gracias, no.*"

"Balanta almost speared a rabbit," said Mende.

"And my brother almost speared a leaf," Balanta said in his dry delivery.

"Man," said Mende, "for all the animal sounds this place makes, there's really nothing out there."

"Did it occur to you, brother that the animals might be motivated to hide from a noisy pack of hunters?" Cielo said.

"Okay, joke's over," announced Eloni, revealing the ice chest he had been holding behind Promise. We didn't get any land dwellers, but there's an amazing estuary just a little ways past the lagoon. Has more fish in it than water. Look see." He sat the cooler down and took off the lid. The container was fat with freshwater and saltwater fare: red snapper, sea bass, grouper, catfish, shell croakers, and trout.

Ivory jumped high, his hands pressing down on Balanta's shoulders. "We 'bout to feast tonight! Well done, my people! Who's cooking dinner first? I'm hungry."

"Promise said she would," answered Lake. "Hey, did anyone catch any fish earlier?"

"Ivory caught his toe," laughed Ashia, "and Promise caught Mende looking at her."

"Ha, ha," said Mende. "I wasn't looking at anybody. I was momentarily blinded by the sun."

"Blinded by something alright," said his brother, grinning heartily.

"If Promise doesn't mind," asked Eloni, "I would Love the honor of cooking the first dinner."

"Look at you, boy," said Ashia. "I'm sure Promise doesn't mind at all, right, Promise?"

Promise was still blushing at the comment about Mende. "Sure. Do your thing, Eloni. I'm not opposed to sitting back and resting my toes."

The fire pit spanned 10 feet. Rimmed with large fire bleached stones, it was circled by a series of large driftwood logs for seating. Charcoal lay in the pit's ashes, letters written in thick black font, telling of the numerous infernos that came before.

"Before we start the first fire, we should make an offering," said Shonto. He ran to his cabin and came back with a small pouch. "This is cedar," he said, pulling out a clump with his fingers. He spoke to the sky, tossing the cedar shavings to the four directions. He gave thanks to the Great Spirit for the gift of fire, and for the blessing of this island, offered to them for a purpose they hoped to discover. "Okay," he said, gesturing to Eloni. "We can start now."

Eloni kneeled and started the fire, working first with dried kindling, which he cupped in his palms and blew on gently. Soon, the kindling smoldered, then birthed a small flame. Eloni set down the flaming tinder in the center of the fire pit. Patiently, he placed small dried branches around the kindling in a teepee formation. As the fire matured, he added larger branches, then slender logs.

"Nice..." Maricela said, holding out her hands closer to the fire. The warmth moved through her, unraveling muscles. "First fire."

Outside of the fire pit, Eloni, Pikea, and Mende had dug a hole into which they placed rocks heated from the fire. Over the rocks, they put down a layer of sand, then a heavy layer of sea water soaked banana leaves.

Eloni rubbed corn cobs with butter, then dashed sea salt, black pepper, cayenne, and garlic over the cobs before lightly tossing on shreds of green chilé peppers and placing the cobs in the earth oven. In seconds, the camp smelled of the roasting peppers, tearing up more than a few eyes.

Eloni filleted sea bass, mackerel and halibut, then laid out a line of guava- and garlic-stuffed mushrooms down the center of each fillet. He closed the fillets around the mushrooms, securing the bundles with wet brown string. After wrapping the fillets in banana leaves, he placed them in the earth pit, its sandy bottom already releasing ribbons of smoke from the hot rocks and ashes buried beneath. Sand was placed on top of the fish, potatoes, and corn cobs.

The fish sizzling underground sent smoky tendrils into the cabins, aroma laced with black pepper and garlic. Shonto sniffed the air like a Labrador. "Ahhh... That's going in my Diné belly tonight," he said, with the most blissful expression on his face. The group ran down to the ocean to refresh in the bay while the food cooked. When they returned, the aroma coming up from the earth in steam was irresistible. The scent of guava, garlic, mushrooms, and fresh fish, all baked into a juicy tenderness in the earth, made the boys do joy-dances like two-year-olds and the girls simply issue a chorus of "Ummm, ummm, ummm..."

"I think those potatoes are done," said Ivory, practically panting. "You going to dig them out?" Before wrapping the potatoes in banana leaves, Eloni had sliced them down the center, parted them open, and filled them with butter, salt, pepper, garlic powder, and a dash of cayenne. Now they were baking in the glowing earth. The old way that Eloni was taught about a million times by his mom. *It is always best to let the earth cook and prepare what she herself has grown for you*, his mom would say. And it was true, Eloni believed. Nothing tasted better than food cooked in the earth.

They resurrected the food from its earth burial. It came out browned. Sizzling. Succulent. Night made its pitch to dusk, which wasn't yet ready to give up the floor.

"All living things have a soul, not just animals," Shonto said. "It is not so much what we eat, but the spirit in which we gather, care for, and take our nutrition that has sacred meaning. We need to give thanks for these plant and animal spirits that gave up their earth lives for us. We must honor the way they lived, and the purpose for which they shed their old skin and became our own form and heartbeat." Shonto followed with a blessing for the meal. Ivory's legs bounced impatiently throughout the blessing as though he needed to pee ferociously.

The cooling air brought the group closer to the fire, as Eloni circled around, serving the steaming fish, browned corn cobs, and smoldering potatoes. Eloni had made a soft drink with gobo root (burdock) and dandelion blossoms. He went around ladling it into everyone's mango wood cups. They sipped skeptically, then asked for more.

Twelve hungry bodies gathered around the fire, sitting on boulders and logs, stomachs growling. Wind whipped hair into faces, jackets billowed. The wooden serving bowls unleashed a ferociously good smell. This meal, however it might have normally tasted, was devoured over taste buds that regarded it as the best dinner ever prepared. Appetites were deeply earned this day.

Lake missed feast days, those magical days where whatever was good in the pueblo became manifest. She missed the long wooden tables piled with flat bread, grilled corn on the cob, the cobs with their beaded skin colored dark purples and blues and reds, now blackened and suffused with melted butter and snowfalls of salt and pepper. And frijoles seasoned with cayenne, and red punch, and limp salad, and fresh fruits and vegetables when possible, sliced and arranged like turtles on top of each other, and lamb stew and elk soup, and tortillas with jam, and roasted chilé peppers, chilé con carne, and carne adovada.

Lake missed the energy leading up to feast days, as children rebelled hopelessly against the nagging imposition of parents and grandparents, uncles and aunts, older siblings, stray dogs, all dragging, scolding, and motivating them to practice for the various dances they would be joining the grown ones in, children of two and three years of age, just learning alphabet in school, already linguistic and literary and licensed in tribal tradition and the sacredness of song and dance.

Lake missed watching the old ones, prideful, dress in their feathered and beaded regalia, regalia older than a human lifespan, worn and showing evidence of many dances. Cherished regalia. Not costumes. Not uniforms. This was no dress-up ball, no entertainment tradition that clung to the calendar over years through sheer lack of energy to stop doing what has been done for so long. No, this was something that could only be fully understood and honored from inside the circle. The circle of generations and families and community, once free as humans go, now, for so long situated and bounded in an arrangement never volunteered for, but imposed by those who had no hope of understanding these dances. This deep drumming. The food and nonperishables tossed by beautiful families of modest and far beneath modest income, standing on their own rooftops. Tossed down into the crowd, the estuary that was the entire community, the pueblo gathered around the house, swarming it like mystic bees around a precious hive. Tossing, sharing, providing food and drink and provision. Acting and reenacting the sacred tradition that *family is the community and community is the family*, and that what a true human does is *give*, not unto the self but to the people, so that the people may become rich in the ways of spirit and thus be well enough to give unto the family. Circle. Obvious. Should be, at least. But here, in the dust and territory of tumbleweeds and erosion, where water from the sky might monsoon in summer, but otherwise stays far away on some other rain errand, here where the people dwell, families give away all their hard earned, barely sufficient food to the community, and all *eat plenty*. Lake missed feast days.

Ivory grubbed so hard and fast, his stomach felt tumorous. He walked down to the beach to try and soothe his digestive distress. Night, still a couple of hours away, was closing in like an ominous storm. At least, that's how it felt to Ivory. "Walk through the valley..." he whispered. "Seems like it's about to be way too much darkness for a brother. How do I spot what's coming at me? And why is it so quiet out here? What's getting ready to jump off?" He began to shadow box, and shadow kick, bluffing at no one and nothing in particular: "Get up off me. I'm highly skilled. You haven't seen traits like this. Best get on your way, 'less you want a clubbing." By the time he was finished with his foolishness, Ivory was panting and still no less scared of the arriving night.

"I'm way past fat and happy," said Shonto, his voice sleepy, as he licked the stewed fish sauce from his plate. "That was the best food I've ever had."

"Eloni, you're hired," said Promise. "When I get my villa, you can be my chef."

"Thanks, y'all," said Eloni. His face was sheepish, his body language proud.

"Let's be real," Ashia said, "We're all extra happy to have Eloni on this trip because he's a master chef and all. It's not everyone who gets to go camping with a food wizard."

Eloni blushed silently at the compliment. He had dreamed of attending culinary school since he was 11. He figured, *I like to eat, so why not be good at preparing what I eat?* He could be logical like that. At least, that's what the psychological assessment ("We like to call it a personality profile," the overly syrupy woman in white had said) concluded.

Cielo came out of his cabin dressed in baggy white shorts checkered in pale blue lines, a white button-up not buttoned up, and a wide-brimmed straw hat. Cielo wore his wavy dark brown hair just long enough to flop over his ears. His mahogany eyes were draped in lazy lids and he bore a faint scar that ran for two brief inches from his left eyebrow down to the upper stirring of his nose. He was loose limbed like Pinocchio, and rose up on his toes with each step, splaying his feet outward like a charming duck.

"Right, right, Cielo," observed Eloni. "Looking splendid."

"This is pure campesino, bro!" Cielo bit. "They don't dress like this anymore."

"Clearly," Lake said under her breath, chucking Shonto in the ribs with her elbow.

Cielo's choices in daily fashion placed him squarely in the tradition of a colorblind peacock. Bright plaid slacks. Salmon and tangerine socks. Sandals and moccasins adorned with beads a little girl might wear in her braids. Banana boat hats and blatant white, embroidered, button-up short-sleeved shirts. And cowrie shell necklaces. Wide leather bracelets with yin-yang symbols and such burned into them. Lime green belts and suspenders. And Spanish-style scarves tied like a Boy Scout's around his neck. In short, and taken all together, Cielo was a completely manifested mess.

"Who's up for some ultimate frisbee?" Cielo cheerfully asked, as he pulled the bright yellow disk from his Sherpa bag. Most of the group joined him, spacing themselves out in the sand between the fire and the ocean tide. Cielo slung the disk with apparent ease across startling distances and with great accuracy.

"You play this a lot?" Ivory asked.

'Yeah. Me and some friends play in a league."

"There's actually a league for this?"

"All over the country. Other countries, too. We made it all the way to nationals for our age group last year."

They played until Ivory broke a nail, and, frankly, they were gassed from pounding sand as they chased down the disc from wind and water.

"Shonto, from the way you're built, my man, you're surprisingly light on your feet," observed Balanta, smiling. "You were moving around in that sand with a quickness."

"We played ball all day long on the rez," Shonto said, grinning. "Some of those Indian boys could dunk like crazy, contrary to popular belief. I saw this one guy named Eddie do a 360 in traffic, land, grab his power drink and, with a smile, just walk out of the gym. Game was still going on! I guess he figured he wasn't going to top that, so what's the point? One thing you could be sure of was a sky full of three pointers when we played on the rez. Diné like to make it rain. Must be the desert."

"Shonto, you're so *tuba*licious," Ivory teased. "Come here and let me drum your belly."

"You see?" Shonto deprecated, "Too much fry bread, I'm telling you. That, and I haven't seen exercise, other than basketball, since I was in sixth grade."

Shonto grew three inches his junior year, but still couldn't come close to dunking. At least he could see over more heads when he walked down the hallway at school. Made him feel less like he was drowning in bodies. He could breathe better, and began to dare to dream of life beyond the reservation.

Shonto was moon faced and dipped in seven flavors of sweetness. Girls had always hovered around him like honeybees, even back in preschool. And he had always been equally uncomfortable, shy, and overwhelmed. They were drawn to the puppy spirit that seemingly emanated from his skin.

Once, he tried being crispy with a girl who kept bringing him lunch in the third grade, just to see how she would react to his meanness. His performance was so unconvincing that the girl only laughed, and brushed his shoulder as she cooed out, "Oh, Shonto." She brought him lunch *and* brownies the next day.

Shonto's skin was a light brown highlighted with yellows. On sunny days, he had the skin tone of graham crackers. On cloudy days, his skin was cinnamon graham crackers. Either way, people were always trying to nibble on him. He often envied the bad boys and mean girls who seemed to have more say over whether and how people approached them.

He had a mop of black hair that hung in bangs all the way down to his eyebrows. He didn't mind this, as it offered him shelter and coverage against the harsh light of social attention. When he played ball, sweat brought his bangs down further, just enough that they got in his eyes. He was known for quickly brushing away his bangs just before he launched his three-point shots, a quirk that only infuriated his opponents.

"We need spears!" Eloni declared. He, Mende, and Ivory spent the next hour finding suitable branches, shaving off bark and stubs, and whittling spear heads. They made one for each person, custom made to length. Ivory promptly cut all four fingers and his thumb on his left hand. By the time they finished, Ivory's bandaged hand looked like a mummy's.

Mende made himself a new fishing spear, whittling the tip into a barbed head. He brushed his thumb over the tip to test its sharpness, which obliged, cutting through his skin. Blood filled the cleavage. Mende tasted it, satisfied with his creation.

"You got yourself, too?" Ivory said. "Hope cuts heal okay out here. You never know in the wilderness. Wish I could conjure up some antibiotics."

"I had this friend, Baijan," Mende said. His voice was nostalgic. "He was a magician or something. If he wanted something, it would appear. I mean, on the spot. I couldn't tell if he was prearranging it, or if it was an actual power."

"What did your instinct tell you?"

"I dismissed my instincts. Didn't want to know the truth."

"Why not?"

"Cause if that boy could summon whatever he wanted, it meant that laws exist beyond what anybody is even talking about. It would mean that all these adults that we lean on like they're gods, are just children like us, not even at the beginning of knowing the end."

"And what's the end?"

"That's what I'm afraid of the most."

Pikea followed the voices of bongos out to the granite boulder where Cielo sat, crossed-legged and bowed over his instruments. His fingers moved slowly, sculpting scalpels considering their clay before touching down.

A languid sound lifted from the bongos' faces into the night air and drifted up toward the cottonwood leaves.

"How are you doing, Cielo?"

"Hey, Pikea," Cielo answered, still gently tapping the drumheads. I'm good. How are you?

"Good, thanks. Just wanted to take a walk after dinner. I like the night air around here. It talks a lot in soft voices."

"Yeah?"

"Yeah. In the city, the noises are hard and harsh, mechanical. Everything's an emergency. Out here it's all wind, birds, croaking, chirping, and tree whispers."

"Don't forget the sound the silence makes," Cielo offered, still locked in his musical trance.

"You're right. That sound is the softest of all."

Balanta approached Binda and Lake, who were singing a made-up song about sand dune mattresses, giggling as they created more nonsensical verse. "How are you two doing so far?" Balanta asked. His measured demeanor during the day was softer now, more open.

Binda looked up. "That was sweet of you to ask. We're having the time of our lives, I think?" she said, looking to Lake for confirmation. Lake nodded her head, blushing.

"Maybe the two of you can have the fruit picking duties from the high tree branches," Balanta joked.

Binda was low to the ground. Brief of height. Vertically abbreviated. Still, she was taller than Lake, who was half Balanta's size. Lake was also twice the calm of Ivory. She existed on a wavelength somewhere between ethereal and Zen. Except when she was drawn to a creature of nature. Then she was a lost cloud, unmoored from prevailing weather systems and all the better for it.

"You have a thunder voice, Balanta," Binda said. "The kind that shakes mountains." Binda's own voice was a delicate flower. Lake's, a soft rain.

"Is that good?" Balanta asked.

"Good if you need a mountain shook," Binda said. "No, seriously. It's actually... calming."

"Okay, now you're making me blush," Balanta said, smiling. "I just wanted to see how you two are doing today. Lots of stimuli around here. And some louder types."

Lake spoke up. "You seem attentive. I bet you have a lot of people confide in you."

"I'm surprised you could tell that already."

Binda laughed. "Well, big brother. We see the way you are with Mende. He really looks up to you. You try to play all hard, but your big heart is sticking out all over the place."

"Thanks, Binda. Mende and I have been through it. That's for sure. We're getting to that time in life now, though."

"What time is that?" Binda asked.

"A boy has to become a man at some point. You can't stay so... dependent all your life."

"Are you talking about Mende?"

"I guess. Maybe I'm talking about both of us."

"Um, hmmm. You know, it's not like being an adult means you need to go your separate ways, like this culture seems to teach. You realize that, don't you?" Binda asked.

Balanta's laugh sounded like it came from earth's core. "Now who's counseling who?"

Balanta reflected on Binda's words, and the irony that it was Balanta who was struggling to let go. His journey with his younger brother had been a long, arduous intimacy. From *before* the beginning. When Mende went into fetal distress in the womb, his heartbeat fluttering like a panicked hummingbird due to the umbilicus constricting like a boa snake around his neck, and was surgically removed at seven weeks premature, it was ten-month-old Balanta who preternaturally watched over him for that first year, not leaving his newborn baby brother, so small and interrupted, not even to eat or sleep. By the time Mende stabilized and grew strong, Balanta had emaciated. Worn and drawn and foggy, he missed recognizing that his baby brother was going to be all right, and that he could put down his gut burning concern.

Promise was snacking on a cucumber. She playfully smacked Mende on the back of his neck. "It's so cute how you always follow along after your older brother, Mende."

"I don't do that."

"Yes, sir, you do. And don't be shamed. It's adorable."

"So, you saying I get points for that?"

"I guess so."

"Then I'm a tag along little brother."

Lake and Balanta approached, side by side. "Here comes the exclamation, and the point," Promise joked.

Lake paused for a moment in notice of Balanta's height. "Balanta, you go so far into the sky. Do you lose touch with the earth, or just see it better?"

"It depends on the weather," Balanta said. "The weather inside me."

It was the hour of the long shadows. Dusk thickened. No one was saying anything out loud, but the fear was there nonetheless. The first hint of darkness snatching light from the trees put a spook in the bones of most of them. This first night was a gigantic unknown about to pull itself over them like an unfamiliar tide. Imaginations began to crawl in tortuous directions.

"A place like this is paradise in daylight," Pikea noted. "Once night drops its weight, and you're not coddled inside of some five-star hotel but sitting duck against the buck naked blackness, paradise can become a haunted house."

Most of the group made their way down to the beach. They stood along the shore, quietly. The sun was dropping over the ocean, growing larger as it approached the waterline.

It was seabird happy hour. Bellies plump with greed, they waddled over the sand or labored in the air. Flocks of geese careened overhead, small juvenile trainees in tow. This lent the sky a familial sense, one that pricked Shonto's heart. A brief line of gulls skirted like levitated surfers an inch above a wall of wave just before it crested, scanning the water for their prey in the gloaming. Pelicans dropped, ballistic and aerodynamic, from the sky into the sea, plummeting beneath the waves. Some surfaced with fish in their beaks.

Shonto heard a low, repeating tuba sound in the distance. "It sounds like cows mooing out there in the ocean."

Pikea listened for it. "Whales."

"Whales? Whales moo?" Ivory asked.

Cielo laughed, kicking sand with his bare foot. "Why do you think they call the male and female ones bulls and cows?"

Ivory's face broke into revelation. "Are they migrating?"

"Probably mating," Pikea guessed.

The ocean's like a water pasture, Lake thought in wonder. *A very private one.*

As the distant circle of fire flattened and sank into the sea, Pikea walked away from the group, unnoticed. To her, sunset always felt like dying.

Binda Loved the sunset. It made her feel closer to her dreamtime, when she traveled so freely beyond the limitations of her circumstance. She wondered what this first night here on the island would be like in her dreams.

Cielo removed himself a few yards from the group and sat, folding his legs on the sand. He dropped his hands onto his thighs and rotated his shoulders backward in circles, relaxing his muscles. Promise called over to him, "What are you doing over there, Plato?"

"Getting my sunset meditation on. It's good to follow the example of the seabirds. They always face toward the sunset. I believe it is their way of paying homage. Any of you want to come sit with me, please, feel invited."

Promise came. "I'll sit with you, Socrates," she said, nudging him. They sat quietly for a moment.

Cielo broke the silence. "The ocean scrubs your brain clean. It has fingers. The wind. Reaches out and blows through your head. When I sit here staring out, my thoughts are clearer. It's like kenosis."

"What?"

"*Kenosis*. Emptying yourself to be filled with God's will."

"Maybe the salt wakes you up," Promise said. "Like ammonia."

"Sure," Cielo said, smiling. "Ocean is Enlightenment's candle."

Promise looked at him worriedly and shook her head.

The cape of night fell, and with it came the decibel of the nocturnals. Crickets. Owls. Frogs. And the night wind, solicitous in the trees.

Shonto scanned the black night and breathed attentively. "I feel the presence of Kokopelli around here," he said.

"Who's Kokopelli?" Promise asked.

"Kokopelli is a legend that came out of the ancient ones, the Anasazi, and was passed down through the Hopi, and the Pueblo peoples. He represents all kinds of stuff. Fertility. The spirit of music. Dance. Renewal or replenishment. Mischief. Rain. Ushering spring forth from the womb of winter."

"Is there anything he doesn't represent?"

"Ha... He has lots of names, too. Hohokam, for one. Hopi call him Kokopilau. Most of the Pueblo people call him Neopkwai'I, right, Lake? And he's known to have a female by his side: Kokopelli Mana."

Maricela yawned. "That's a pretty wild myth."

"No myth. Legend. Like biblical people are legends. They aren't treated as myths, right? Kokopelli, he's kind of a big deal to us. Kokopelli is kind of like the life of the party. A trickster. Always playing jokes, getting people to laugh and feel good about themselves. Laid back, like Cielo. Carefree, you know? And he is a magician. A mystic. Tells stories like no one's business, just oozing with charisma and aura. He can make a weed growing by the roadside into a story that'll keep you up all night."

"You talk about him like he's right here, in the present tense," Maricela said.

"Isn't he? People talk about us Native people as though we went extinct. We actually still exist. Our stories aren't past tense. They live in us today."

Lake joined in. "Kokopelli was da Vinci before da Vinci. Teacher. Healer. Inventor. Trader. Traveling harvest whisperer. Baby bringer. Joy spout. You'd want him along on your hunts, too. You'd be sure to bring home a nice fat buck, or at least a bunch of rabbits.

"Zuni see him as a rain priest," Shonto said. "Some of these droughts going on, people better start dancing for Kokopelli. He's the one who has his way with water."

"Him and Lake," Cielo added.

"My Masaani used to tell me some wild stories about Kokopelli," Lake recalled. "Said he was a spiritual priest who had some strong medicine. Healing powers. And in the old times, when the women had trouble with planting their child seeds, they would go to Kokopelli. He could restore their wombs to power. They would stay up all night dancing to his music, then wake up in the morning with a baby on the way. That's some strong stuff."

"That's right," Shonto said. "He carries a bag of seeds for every plant and flower on his back as he goes around, teaching people how to plant. Trades beads and shells and stuff like that. For turquoise. Loves that stuff. Thinks it's the ocean crawled up into a stone.

"Diné, we believe his hump is made of clouds filled with seeds and rainbows. Then, there's some who believe he's a song trader, carrying songs in his bag, trading them for new ones. He is the original hit maker. You get a song from Kokopelli and you're pretty much guaranteed a blessed life."

Cielo stretched his arms behind his back, then moved through a series of yoga poses, breathing audibly. "Sounds like he's a musician," Cielo offered.

Shonto smiled, nearly hopping up from his seat. "Kokopelli is the pure spirit of music, man. Happiness and joy bloom from the mouth of his flute. When he plays, nature comes alive and gets giddy. Sun shines brighter. Rivers clear up. Flowers blossom. Birds start singing. All that. His flute will even ignite your creativity and make your dreams come true. He's a bad boy."

"Look up at the moon," Lake said. "Even with it getting so skinny, I can see Kokopelli dancing and playing. You see that? Look close. You can usually see him in the moon if you just look up and get in touch with your heartbeat. That's our first human music."

Shonto went on. "Go look at just about any rock in the Southwest, or on a cave wall. You're likely to see Kokopelli drawn or carved or painted. He's been getting good PR for centuries now. Petroglyphs were the first social media. Did you know that?"

Ashia looked at Lake. "Can you draw it? Kokopelli? You're a wonderful artist."

Lake kneeled on the ground and with a small tree branch drew out a rough impression, little more than a stick figure. A hunched back form playing a flute. Legs positioned as though the figure were walking, or dance stepping. A crest of four long, slightly curved lines coming out of the head.

"Looks like a dreadloc'ed musician to me," said Balanta.

"Now I *know* he must be cool," Ashia said, a sleek smile on her face.

"Pushup contest!" Eloni announced out of nowhere. In the next moment, he was on his belly in the sand, huffing away next to Mende, Maricela, Ivory, Shonto, and Pikea. "Up, down! Up, down!" Eloni commanded. Quickly, he lost his breath and grew silent. Ivory dropped out first, claiming a congenital cramp. Then Maricela, Pikea, and finally, Shonto, leaving Eloni victorious and grinning with a quiet pride.

As night bloomed, they gravitated toward the fire. Ivory had thrown in some big logs. In a beat, the flames were a bonfire. Heat spread beyond the sitting logs all the way to the cabins. Mende sat his djembe drum between his knees as he shifted into position on a tree stump. His fingers wandered over the canvas drumhead, searching. His tips tapped, lightly. He massaged the drumhead with his palms, moving his knees up and down to a silent beat. Then he released the drum voice. A steady cadence rose with the flames. Calm beat. Meditative.

Cielo drummed his thighs, matching the drumbeat. Promise and Lake joined in. Ashia hummed. Ivory bebopped. Now, the circle was drumming. Thighs, chests, frisbee. Drum and fire. Ushering in the night.

Moon Time. The waning moon began its ascent, appearing first over the tree line to the east. A semi-circle, linen white and leaking indigo from its iris out into the blackness.

A sickly yapping broke out in the darkness. Chills ran through the group. "I see you moving closer to the fire, Cielo!" Mende pointed and called out.

33

Cielo smiled. "You're moving, too, Mende. Those foxes sound like guitar strings being broken five at a time."

"Sounds like suffering," said Binda.

"That and a warning to get up off their island!" Ivory joked.

The wind through the willows whistled in spurts. Bebop trumpets. Promise pulled her knees closer to her chest. She thought she could hear a whisper in the wind: *Turn to your name.*

With the drum and firelight as their chaperones, they fell into story. "Pikea, where'd you get your name?" asked Ashia.

"My grandfather named me Pikea. In Maori language it means *Tame Whale.* Don't laugh."

"Too late!" Ivory brayed.

"Anyway..." Pikea went on, "for my people, a whale is a sacred animal that tells the people about how well we are. If we don't see whales, that's not a good sign. When we see them, especially with calves, it means good fortune is coming to the people."

"Yeah, but why Tame Whale?"

"Whales are large and powerful, and can destroy humans if they wish when we are out on the water. But they don't. They are mostly very gentle with us when our boats encounter them.

"My grandfather said that when I was born, he saw how large and full of power my spirit was. He wanted me to always be mindful of how I used my power. He used to say to me, 'Pikea, my flower, learn to use your power for the people. Don't be a destroyer.'

"I asked him once what he meant by that: *Don't be a destroyer.* He said, 'each of us carries two fires inside. One fire is a destroyer. The other one is a creator.' Grandfather told me, 'Little flower, all you have to do is blow on either of those inner fires and they will grow.

Learn to blow on the creator fire, even when people make you feel like burning down the world. Because being a destroyer can be addictive, you get carried away with it. And if you burn down the whole world, where will you have to live? Where will you find Love?'

"It took me until I was about 12 before I realized that the word *tame* doesn't have to mean you're a punk or weak. It really means that you have learned to be at Peace inside, for your own sake. And for the world.

"I couldn't stand the meaning of my name for the longest. I guess when the hormones started running through me, they turned on some lights. I saw the gift that a name can be, if it has meaning. And we get the meaning."

"My name is Samoan. Means *Mountain,*" Eloni shared. "I think my dad wanted to make himself feel bigger through me. My mom though, she was the one who really found a deeper meaning for my name. For her, it was about how so many different climates and life zones can be found on a mountain. How much different life grows there."

"So, she was trying to be deep?" asked Promise.

"Don't mess with me, woman." Eloni was smiling, somehow proud of the thought of his mother being regarded as deep. "Mom is just into nature. She likes how everything has a place." *Everything has a place...* The thought lingered with Eloni like the fire's scent all through that night.

"My name means *Life*, or, *Hope*, in Arabic," Ashia said. "My parents are Ghanaian,"

"Aren't you, too, then?" Cielo asked.

"I mean, I don't feel like I know that much about the place. I left so young. Most of my memories now are of the last 10 years."

"But you're always talking about it," Cielo said. "I guess things get put into you while you're not paying attention."

Promise laughed. "And then they come out when you're not expecting, right?"

"Yeah," Ashia said. "I don't know. *Ghanaian*. Honestly, I wish I knew what that meant. At least then I could make my own decisions about being a part of it."

"Seems like you're already making your own decisions about it anyway," Mende said.

"Cielo means *Sky* in Spanish, if you didn't know," Cielo said.

"And Maricela is for Saint Marcella, a great woman of history," Maricela shared.

"My name is Aboriginal. It means *Deep Water*," Binda said.

"I can see that," Mende observed. "You're one of those deep ones. Thinking a lot, right?"

"Yeah, I guess. I like to think of deep water as the place where the things that live there feel safe. Far away from the turbulence of the surface."

"I've heard all kinds of Diné meanings for my name," Shonto said. "I think people just make things up as they go. I've heard *The light that reflects off water; spring on the sunny side; shadow on the water;* and, *do you remember the water?*"

"That's a lot of water," said Maricela.

"Yeah. You would think I would be like Lake, making water appear and all that. Nothing doing."

Lake was a water bringer. Where she walked, things tended to sprout water. People cried. Skies opened. Leaves budded with condensation. Drinking glasses misted. Even the desert surrendered its dryness when Lake was around. Its earth grew moist in strange places, then pools of water appeared. Sometimes even small ponds. Because of this, Lake was useful on the Diné reservation. People liked to ask her along on ceremonial walks in the desert, banking on her presence as an insurance policy in case of thirst.

Children gathered around her in summertime as though she were a spigot or a hydrant. In the heat ribbons of daytime, they hoped Lake would somehow become a fountain. Or lead them to one. Usually it was not so dramatic. She would touch their lips, affectionately, and drops of water would appear there. Or, she would place her palms against a tree and its bark would weep clean, cool water.

Such characteristics aren't always endearing. Many potential boyfriends stayed away, fearing that if they wronged her, she might drown them in their sleep. These fools, she was happy to keep at a distance. Some girls became a little too friendly, bargaining that Lake, with her water spirit, could give them an advantage in their quest for social power, by association or some such vague reasoning. But Lake was a shy whisper retreating from attention. A timid chipmunk peeking out from behind rocks of silence. Since the beginning.

When Lake's mother became pregnant with her, a stain of water appeared on the ceiling of the family's home. The stain began dripping. Soon, buckets couldn't hold the leak. Thing was, this happened during a moon when the sky did not rain even once. Soon, Lake's family had to move out of their home, as it became inundated with water. Water came from the walls, the floorboards, even the cement stairs out front. After eight weeks of pregnancy, Lake's family home stood in two feet of water, which now was beginning to consume the neighboring homes as well.

By the time Lake was born, a body of water the size of a football field had taken its residence. The water was so pure that it wasn't long before it was stocked with fish. Most of the reservation used it to catch their dinner, selling the remainder to tourists who were all too happy to pay top dollar for what they believed, of their own idealizing accord, to be special mystical Navajo fish.

Balanta, standing next to Lake by the fire, noticed her energy, studied her appearance. Her eyes were organic brown. Garden brown. Long lashes framed high, wide cheekbones. Her face was the moon. Her body shrub-like next to Balanta's tall form.

Ivory came over next to Lake, spitting sunflower seeds like he was in a major league dugout. Lake ducked away as inconspicuously as she could, went over by Ashia and sat. She leaned in close to Ashia's thick locs.

"Ashia, your scent reminds me of sweetgrass," Lake said in a soft voice the texture of summer dew. "My Masaani and I used to go gather it up north after the rains, when it smelled the best."

"Thank you, girl. That's sweet of you. No pun intended. At least, I think that was a compliment, yeah?" Ashia smiled.

"Oh yeah. My favorite baskets to weave are sweetgrass. I like the way it holds the light, softly. And it smells good when the basket is dry, too."

Balanta was waving his hand over a patch of tall feather grass that had learned to keep its distance from the fire. Its softness was soothing. He raised up on his feet and stretched. "The grass here is laid back. Not much anxiety. Same with the rocks."

"Balanta, you're always saying some far out stuff," Ivory noted as Mende smiled knowingly. "How do you know what rocks or grass feel?"

Balanta didn't just act like a river, he moved like one. His form shimmered through air as he walked, more fluid than solid. Loose limbed, muscles emptied of tension.

"Everything feels," Balanta said. "You just have to open up to it. I knew this old guy back in my neighborhood who was always walking the streets. One of his eyes was a glass marble. When he came up to a tree he liked, he would stop and caress it."

"That's where you get that from?" Ivory asked.

"Maybe. So, I was curious. He put his face up against the bark and seemed to be listening. I finally had to ask him about it. He wasn't used to having teenagers roll up on him. It startled him. Once he felt my vibe, he calmed down. I'll always remember his voice. Sounded like thunder moving over rocks. Balanta soon found himself deep inside the memory, seeing and hearing the conversation replay as though in a dream:

The man had said, "Son, I'm not doing anything any different than what you do when you put on your headphones and lose yourself in your music. I'm finding that sound that makes my soul stop fighting with itself. I get to feeling all those years running through the tree and it calms me. Puts life in perspective. A tree generally has seen a whole lot more than you and I ever will. Lived through a heap more, too."

Balanta had asked, "But do you really hear anything, or are you just imagining stuff?"

"I don't know. You tell me. When your sweetheart whispers in your ear, do you really hear anything, or are you just imagining stuff?"

"I'm hearing what she's whispering."

"Are you sure? Do you hear what she is speaking, or what you imagine?"

"Depends on if she's saying what I want to hear."

"Sure. Those trees are speaking something. We have probably mostly lost the ability to hear it. I try anyways. And if I'm just hearing what I want to hear, does that mean the trees aren't speaking, or that I might not one day hear something real?"

"You might have lost me there."

"No one laughs or questions when someone dangles their feet in a lake, or wades in an ocean, or makes a snow angel, or sticks their face out the car window to catch the breeze. We're trying to make contact with something we were once closely connected to. Now, we don't even realize we miss it. But that old urge is still there to commune with it. Check it out sometime: People are forever trying to make contact with the world. Whoever said we are above nature clearly wasn't raised to understand that we *are* nature. And we just want to be home.'"

Balanta emerged out of his daydream, and sat back down on a dark gray granite boulder, its quartz sparkling with firelight. He shared the story of the old man with the others. Afterward, he said, "What that man spoke got into me. The world seems... closer around me since then."

"Mende," Cielo said, "I'm glad you brought your djembe. I brought my bongos. Your drumming makes this fire feel even more warming to the soul."

"Thanks, man" Mende replied.

Shonto jumped in. "A drum circle is how we reconnect with each other and with all things. It's not entertainment. It's medicine. Sweet medicine. It heals what damage has been done during the day, or week, or year. Or even a lifetime.

"It helps to rebalance our spirit and mind, because life has a way of spinning us out of balance. Especially if we forget the old ways. The voice of the drum reduces stress, too. When we gather in drum circle, we are taking a tranquilizer that treats the roots of anxiety, not just the symptom."

"Deep stuff, Shonto," said Binda, smiling. "I thought I was supposed to be the deep one."

Shonto ran back to his cabin and returned with a hand drum slightly larger around than his palm and fingers extended. "This drum was made in a pueblo, in New Mexico. The design has a lot of meaning. The two snakes on it represent life waters. They're surrounded by lightning. The swirling creation dance of the serpents forms the land masses and reveals the *Sipapu*, the Place of Emergence. That's especially a Hopi concept."

"Okay," Shonto continued, "Now I'm going to give you a drum washing, Binda. Come over here."

"What's a drum washing?" Binda asked.

"It's like taking a shower, only with the drum vibration raining down on you. It gives you peace, and cleanses you. Come on, Mende, help out with your drum."

Binda stood by the fire, its light painting her face in flickering shadows. She smiled and closed her eyes. "Okay... go ahead."

"Make sure you're relaxed. Breathe out your tension. The drums are going to make the air move. It's a healing movement, an air dance. Let it sweep over you and through you." Shonto and Mende began with a slow, solemn beat, then slowly built up to a jogging cadence. The beat grew higher in pitch as it quickened. It sounded like the rhythm of the nearby surf. It felt that way inside of Binda. She could feel the air push into her, rhythmically, in waves. It entered her body, claiming her. She felt hands kneading her muscles, urging her tension away. Drumbeat all around her. Floating... in an ocean of vibration. Her boundaries erased.

"Okay," signaled Shonto. "You can open your eyes now. How did it feel?"

"Amazing," said Binda, grinning widely. "I feel all rubbery inside. Let me sit down. Wow. I'm going to sleep like crazy tonight."

"Who wants to go next?" They all did. The stark, eroding moon reached its apex as drumbeat washed so many knots away.

Lake spoke, her tone of voice surprising the others. "Us being around this fire is special to me."

"What do you mean, Lake?" asked Promise.

"When we are around this fire, we are in sacred circle. That's not just a name. It speaks to our way of conduct."

Ashia jumped in. "I agree with Lake. This feels different than during the daytime. I don't know. Fire is... there is something about it that is mysterious."

"Go on," Cielo coaxed.

Ashia paused, reflecting. "I just think that when we're here, the fire can help to chill us out, calm us down. Focus. Where I come from, a circle represents the way life is, the way everything flows. So, the circle is sacred for us. What happens here is ours, good or bad. We have to own it."

Ashia's eyes were teary. "Think about it, y'all. Maybe for the first time in our lives, we're alone together. No adults. No one with power over us. That's cool and all, but it also means we can't make excuses anymore. That people don't understand us. That we don't have any say."

"Ashia's right," said Cielo. "Do you really think we're going to have this experience again? This is like a miracle. Hopefully, we can use this somehow."

"How do you mean?" asked Eloni.

"I don't know. It just feels like something is supposed to change for us. Maybe I'm being dramatic. We'll see."

Just then, Ivory yawned extra loudly, blatantly reaching his left arm around Promise's back, to comic effect.

"Ha!" Promise taunted. "Bless your heart, Ivory. You're a sweet little squirrel scratching for acorns from an apple tree."

"But can I get an apple?" Ivory asked.

"Um... have you heard of the word *unrequited*? That's your word for the week, Ivory."

"Okay, you guys," Ashia said, "Not trying to be a chaperone here, but—"

"Awww!" a swarm of voices interrupted. "Here we go!"

"Come on, now," Ashia persisted, "I'm just saying, we agreed, limit the cabin creeping and all that while we're here. We only have seven days. We can go that long without the hot and heavy, can't we?"

"Sister, seriously," Promise responded, "have you been smoking the local herbs? The testosterone level on these here boys must be off the charts. And the ladies aren't far behind, myself excluded of course. Asking for 24 hours of ice-down is asking for a lot, not to mention seven days!"

Cielo ran his fingers through his curly bush of long hair. He thought of the abundance on this island. The garden. Fruit trees. The water everywhere. He added his thoughts to the fire, speaking professorially: "The people that came before our generation ate up everything on the planet. Air, water, trees, even the soil. Is our generation going to fight over the scraps, or grow a new garden?"

"We're the seventh generation, right?" Promise asked.

Mende considered the idea. "Seventh generation… I've heard of that. Isn't it about how we are responsible for how we leave the earth for our descendants seven generations after ourselves?"

Shonto slapped his thighs, engaged by the topic. "That's the popular way of thinking about it. It's not necessarily the Native way, the old way. Traditionally, seven generations referred to *us*, right here, right now. We are the seventh generation. We are the result of the lives and spirit and actions of our parents, grandparents, and great grandparents. So they represent the three generations before us.

"And then, our own lives, the way we exist and make choices today, becomes the reality of our children, grandchildren, and great grandchildren. So, they are the three generations after us. Three generations before, three after, and then us: the seventh generation. We are like the tip of an ancient pyramid, the part that shows above ground. The supposedly most able part.

"For my people, we see the seventh generation as a sacred assignment. We are responsible for carrying through on the assignments of the ones who came before us, including healing what they could not. And we are charged with supporting the assignments of those who come after us, by doing our part with what we are given to do."

"Who decides what the assignment is?" Ashia asked.

"Spirit decides," Shonto answered.

"Who?" Maricela asked.

"God, if you will. Or, the Great Spirit."

One corner of Maricela's mouth curled. "I always felt that *Great Spirit* term seemed strange."

Pikea jumped in. "That's because this culture has taken it over, like it does everything else, and made it into something corny and casual."

"For us," Shonto went on, "*Great Spirit* means the exact same thing as God. Isn't God a spirit?"

"Well, yeah," Maricela said.

"You're not going to tell me God is a bearded man, are you? Like a shepherd with a staff and robe, somehow magically hiding in the sky."

"No, no."

"And God is great, yes?"

"Yes. All the time."

"Okay. So if God is great, and God is a spirit, what's so hard to get about God being the Great Spirit?

Shonto wiped back his bangs, rubbed his arms, and continued. "To answer your question further, Ashia, God decides our assignment, of course. But, so do we. We each decide our assignment in the way that we interpret what our spirit speaks to us. No one else can do that for us.

"And no matter how we might misinterpret the assignment, because humans will misinterpret everything, it's still up to the next generation to do their best to interpret the assignment in their own time. In their own lives."

"That's some cool stuff," Ivory said.

Shonto glanced at Ivory. "No... Fads and fashions are cool. This is our Way. Our spirituality. Our existence."

"Man, that fish was good, Loni," said Cielo. "Can't get over it, bruh. Todo bien. *All good.* Reminds me in a strange way of something I saw one time." He rubbed his belly, and stretched his sandaled feet closer to the fire, elongating his body over the large rock on which he was sitting.

When Binda focused completely on Cielo's eyes, the warm, silent fire inside them pulled her in, like a friend bringing her inside a cave in a rainstorm. His energy hummed, strong, gentle. His presence touched her skin like wind passed through sunlight.

"Tell it," urged Mende. "Tell the story."

"Okay," Cielo obliged. "So, this Latino man was fishing from the ocean shore. Nobody around. Just him, and his wife who sat back on the hill, up from the tide. This old man comes along walking his dogs. Two big ones."

"What kind?"

"Big kind. I don't know. Anyway, one of the dogs goes and puts its head in one of the fisherman's fish buckets. I kept waiting for the old guy to call off his dog. I mean, this was probably the family's dinner in that bucket. Who knows how long it took to catch whatever was in there.

"Old man just kept strolling and watching his dog get at whatever was in the bucket. The fisherman was looking down at the dog, seemed to be kind of nervous. I mean, big dog. But the fisherman didn't say anything. Just kept looking at the old man, waiting for him to call off his dog.

"Finally, the dog lifted up its head from the bucket. Had a big ol' fish in his mouth. Pulled it over onto the sand and chowed down. Old man comes over to the fisherman and says, 'Howdy. Catch anything today?'

"I'm boiling inside, thinking, *Yeah, he caught what your dog just ate, you entitled, self-centered...*

"Fisherman never did really say anything. Just kept looking perplexed. He turned to his wife and shrugged. She shrugged back, like, 'What are you going to do?'

"Maybe the family already had plenty of fish. Maybe they had plenty of food and money back home. But maybe they didn't. What if that fish was how they were going to feed their children that night? What possesses people to move through the world like a bulldozer, not caring the least for how they are plowing over everyone and everything? Wasn't the dog's fault. But where's the sense of responsibility for another living thing that's in your care? I don't get it."

"I'm with you on that," said Ashia. "Some kind of people in this world don't have a soul. They aren't real humans. They look like humans, but on the inside, no soul. That's why they can't coexist with other people. They're basically allergic to the world. So they try to destroy it. It's their deepest impulse."

41

"Who else has a story?" asked Promise. "How about you, Balanta?"

"All right." Balanta stood up and moved closer to the fire, spear in his hand, moonlight a robe over his shoulders. He looked to Ashia like a Maasai warrior. She wondered what he would have been in another life. Before this time.

Lake looked at Balanta, his majestic lines, his proud length, and she wanted to sculpt him. Ashia just wanted to be inside the sculpting.

"There was this elder woman in the village," Balanta started, "named Osha. Her fingers were like roots of a mangrove tree. Mangled. Kind of flowing over and around each other. I remember her breath. You remember that?" Balanta asked, glancing at his brother. "When she spoke, the air changed. It became... older."

"That's cold," Promise said.

"No, I mean, it became like air from an older time. When the air was cleaner, purer. The scent reminded me of what the world must have smelled like before humans. More like the smell of dirt and trees and rain. Less like industry.

"Anyway, she had cataracts over both eyes. Clouds. One was a white cloud. One was blue. People were always pampering her. That's how I took it. Oiling her skin. Bathing her. Feeding her the best food. Singing her songs. Combing her hair, oiling it. I thought she had it made. I resented that woman. *Why does she get treated like that? Why not me*? That's what I was wondering. I was only six, so I didn't have a clue."

"I remember, she had this ox," added Mende. "Right? She was always rubbing its ears and whispering to it. That's mostly what I remember."

"Yeah, she had that ox and not much else. But everyone was so good to her. Then, one night, a woman was bringing a child into its generation."

"What do you mean?" asked Cielo.

"She was giving birth. It was a difficult one. I couldn't cover my ears tight enough. That sound. The pain. All night long. Made my bones huddle up. I got up just before dawn, when it was still black out. I don't know what got into me, but I crept up outside the window of the woman's home. I looked inside and I saw the old one, Osha, kneeling next to the woman. She was leaning close and whispering. Then the child came, which I didn't need to see. Osha, she took up the child right quick, even before the mother could, and started whispering to the child. All the other women in the room were silent. Still like poles.

"Then Osha gave the new child to the mother, who was smiling even though I think she was half delirious. I asked my mother later, 'What was all that whispering about?' My mother said, 'Son, some people keep the stories. For everyone. When a new child comes, first thing, someone needs to give them the stories, or they immediately start forgetting. Nothing worse than a human who forgets.'

"'But why does Osha whisper to her ox?' I asked.

"'She's not whispering to her ox,' my mother said. 'She's responding to what her ox is whispering to her. Osha gets her stories from all the people. The animal people. Tree and plant people. Water people. Even the sky people. Then she gives them back to us.'

"'How?'

"'By putting them inside the new children when they come.'

"'Why them?'

"'Because a new child is the best vessel to hold stories. They are water-tight then. Soon enough though, the world begins to whisper. So many lies and deceptions. So you must get the stories deep into a new child, so they can hold them all the way through their journey.'

"'And so they can pass them on?'

"'Yes, so they can pass them on.'

"'Is that why people treat Osha so nice, doing things for her?'

"'Son,' my mother said, if you had a vessel that held your most priceless possessions, wouldn't you take the best care of it, too?'"

"Mende, where'd you get that scar on your face?" Ashia asked, gingerly, waving away a moth attracted by the flames.

"Balanta," Mende answered, casually. "We were tussling one time. Big cat, small cat. You know how that goes."

Mende's mahogany face was landmarked by a long scar running vertically from his right temple down to just above his jawline. "Tribal marking. That's what I started telling everyone when I was nine. It was my power story. My sympathy story, especially as I got older and when I was around girls, was that it was a scar left by a powerful stream of tears after the Love of my life broke my heart."

"Mende, you're a clown," Ashia joshed. "Watch out, or a circus is going to come through and kidnap you and Ivory."

Mende laughed and took to his drum.

"Look at Mende getting it!" Mende's slender arms rippled as his hands beat the djembe's drumhead with a frantic pace. His hands moved at a blur, his torso glistening as a smile overtook his face, a spreading pool of teeth growing broader with each beat.

"We got cool beats and open mic in the firelight!" Ivory delighted.

"No mic though, Ivory," said Maricela, absent-mindedly twirling her hair, kicking her crossed leg.

"That's alright," said Ivory, "cause who needs a mic when you have firelight. Plus, we're only 12 deep, and you know my booming voice doesn't need any help to travel," he teased.

"Ivory, the only time your voice booms is when you're burping. Other than that, I often confuse you for a squirrel, to be honest." Maricela sported a satisfied grin.

"Oh yeah?" Ivory taunted:

43

"I'll wreck you with my left... straight to your cleft... leave all your kin bereft... so deft, I leave you out of breath... like cops chasing theft!"

"Watch out!" Promise shouted. "Ivory a fool!"
Maricela came back at Ivory:

"Don't come at me with your verbal toy, boy... bring me your grown up tongue... so I can put it back in your mouth with a rhyme to make your soul go south... Don't you winter up in here... My language is too cold... you'll end up frozen and supposin': how'd I end up with icicles hanging from my rear?"

"Oh dear!" Promise yelled.
"Maricela blasted you, boy!" Eloni blared.
"Yeah, yeah..." Ivory said, grinning as he sat his butt back down. Maricela snapped her jacket sides together around her, looking all kinds of satisfied.

Shonto told them the story of *the Stone Boy* who helped his people learn ceremony, prayer, and sacredness so they could become a true tribe. After that, he told them the story of *the Ghost Dance at Wounded Knee.*

Binda told some Aboriginal stories. *How the Native Bear Lost His Tail. How the Sun Was Made. The Giant Kangaroos. Why the Crow is Black.*

Cielo switched tracks, cracking everyone up with a mime impression that included him scaling a ladder to pick a peach and eat it before rubbing his belly in delight, chopping down a tree and carving it into a canoe before canoeing over a waterfall in horror, and going to great lengths and ingenuity to crack open a coconut only to pass out from sheer exhaustion right at the moment of triumph, allowing the milk to spill away on the ground.

Ashia followed that with an inspired performance in which she portrayed each member of her Ghanian family, with exaggerated effect. Her lazy sister, who wouldn't so much as cross the living room in order to get to the refrigerator. Her overachieving brother who studied so hard he darn near went blind. Her boastful and deeply insecure father, who littered every inch of the outside of the family car with bumper stickers proclaiming the greatness of his children, and therefore himself. Her decrepit and yet virile grandmother, who used her walker as a flirtation prop by blocking unsuspecting men with it in the produce aisle at the grocery store. And her bananas auntie, who sewed images of crocodiles riding elephants into her blouses, then wore them to church on Sunday, thinking they somehow bestowed her with a superior level of piety.

Shonto purred privately as the fire warmed his bones. He was getting hungry again. He looked up at the half moon and thought about ice cream sandwiches. "Hey, I've got a story," he said. "My great uncle was wiped out by alcohol all his life, but he told great stories. I heard that when my mom went through a bad depression and got suicidal, my great uncle literally storied her out of it. He spent months at her bedside, just telling stories. He told me this one that I keep thinking about now, with the moon the way it is.

"So, there was this giant with such a tender heart that everyone in the village came to him with their problems. The giant was gifted at calming and soothing people, and he had so much Love, that he couldn't help but to respond when people came for his help. People lined up by the hundreds, and for hours and hours each day, the giant listened, comforted, and reassured.

"Well, this took such a toll on the giant that he had to sleep whenever he could, just to recover and to have energy for the next day-full of people in need. Because of this, he could often be found lying on his side, at any moment, growing drowsy, with one of his eyes slowly closing. He always kept one closed, so he could rest. But he was so caring about how others were doing that he did his best to keep one eye open.

"One year brought a particularly harsh winter. People were even more depressed than usual. They lined up thousands deep to seek comfort and guidance from the giant. But something miraculous happened. The giant became so exhausted, and so filled with Love and compassion, that his body began to float up off the earth like a balloon. He ascended high into the sky where now he keeps one eye open at night, searching the universe for souls in need. Eventually though, he grows so tired and sleepy that even his one open eye begins to close. That's when we start to get what we call a *Clear Moon*.

"Other people call it a new moon. But we know that it isn't new. It hasn't disappeared and been replaced. It's just clear. Night's darkness passes through it. People can't see it. So they pay it no attention. Which is probably good for the giant, anyway. At least that way, he can finally get some rest."

"*Clear Moon...* I like that," Ashia said. "Hey, Mende and Cielo, can you give me a Latin beat on those drums?"

"Sure." Mende nestled the drum between his knees and started getting spicy with it. Cielo did the same with his bongos.

Ashia pulled Ivory up and brought his hands into position with hers, leading him into a salsa movement and rhythm. Ivory, lost as a skunk set loose inside a fragrance store, grinned and followed the best he could. He had never danced with someone this beautiful. Ashia's lips were full ripe rose petals decorating a strong chin and jawline. Her father's side endowed her with a broad forehead and cheekbones that nestled high and tight beneath wistful, searching eyes. And here Ivory was, dancing with her. It did not compute. Nor was Ivory functionally dancing. Mostly, he served as a prop for Ashia to do her thing, twirling, sashaying, flipping back her head, kicking back her lower legs, grooving. Flames highlighted their forms. The two were fire dancers, circling the bonfire. The others cheered them on, Eloni hooting the loudest at Ivory.

Ashia thanked Ivory and moved to Eloni, who was suddenly sitting recalcitrant as a stone with roots, pale in the face. Not to be denied, Ashia coaxed him into a listless cooperation, moving with him into a merengue, picking up speed and flavor as Eloni picked up blush and sweat. Still, he smiled.

Then it was Shonto's turn. Ashia led him through a swift, wild tango. Having not a clue what he was doing, he gave himself to Ashia's direction. Night's breeze moved over Shonto's face. He was dazzled. It was good to feel his body, to be in it all the way. *Feels good to be in the wind and remember peace.*

"Whew, that was great! Ashia said, breathlessly. Thanks, guys. That wasn't so bad, was it?"

"Woman, you are determined, aren't you?" Ivory said. "You were really moving though. Where'd you learn all that?"

"Thanks," Ashia, replied. "My dad used to play Tito Fuentes, Ruben Blades, all of them, at night when he got home. Didn't matter how tired he was. He'd come in the door, say, 'Where's my dance partner?' and put on the Latin music. Then he'd sweep me up and we'd dance until he was out of breath. We would laugh and just get lost in the music. I don't care how bad a day I was having, I would just think of dancing with my dad that evening and everything would be all right."

A few of them headed back down to the ocean, not wanting to face the unknown of dark cabins and a long night of stark stillness. Shonto, Lake, and Mende lost themselves in digging holes in the sand, and building sand castles. Mende laughed, and looked at the other two. "Eighteen years old and look at us, playing like preschoolers." They continued displacing sand. Letting water rush into the spaces left behind. Grading, evacuating, and reshaping the surface of things.

Pikea sat on the sand. Her leg kicked restlessly. "Why are you so twitchy?" Balanta asked.

"Those foxes are driving me crazy," she said. "They sound like cackling witches sucking helium. It's eerie. And is the air supposed to smell like this?"

"That's salt. That's the ocean out there. Remember?" Balanta put his arm around Pikea's shoulder. "It's kind of wild, us being out here, no one else around, right?"

"Yeah. And I appreciate your reassurance. The truth is, it's not just us being here. There's a fire in my head. It's hot enough that it usually keeps me from getting near to calm."

The six island sisters gathered in one of the cabins for a while before sleep. Quickly, the buzz started. "Okay, ladies," said Promise, girlishly, "What are these boys' colors?"

"What do you mean?" asked Lake.

"It's like with ice cream," said Promise, a sinister look to her eyes. "You have to have a flavor to describe their color, or a color to describe their flavor."

"Oh no," sighed Lake, blushing.

"No, no. We're all in on this. Innocent fun, right? So... Mende?"

"Toasted coconut," said Pikea.

"Ooh, girl! You said that a little too quickly!" shrieked Promise.

"And deliciously, I might add," said Maricela.

"Pluh-eese, Promise," said Ashia. "You know that boy is all up in your attic and down in your basement."

"Stop, girl. Hush," Promise replied, blushing. "Okay, Mende's brother, Balanta?"

A long collective pause. Then, "Deep dark chocolate!" simultaneously from Pikea and Ashia.

"With almonds," added Maricela.

"Yes!" from the group.

"Good, good. Cielo?"

"Caramel."

"No. Adobe."

"Keep it going. Shonto?"

"Honey."

"More like the whole honey pot."

"Now, now..."

"Okay... Ivory? Hold on," Promise interjected into herself, "I gotta take this one myself. Deep space!"

"That's not even a flavor!" Pikea protested.

"And it's cruel!" Binda pleaded.

"Only Love," said Promise. "And it doesn't have to be a flavor. It can be a color to describe the flavor."

"How about licorice?" Binda contributed.

"You go, girl!" exclaimed Promise. "Lookit Binda! I liiike it... Deep space licorice!"

"You're too much, Promise," teased Ashia.

"Last one. Eloni?"

"Hmmm. Ham?" Maricela said.

"What? That isn't even an accurate color."

"Well, how about browned ham? Or turkey?"

"Woman, you are harsh," said Promise, smiling.

"River clay," Binda said.

"Roasted piñon," Lake said.

"What about nutmeg?" asked Maricela, "Cause that boy can cook. He's spicy in the kitchen!"

"Ooh!" Ashia squealed. "And on that note, ladies, let's call it a night. It's getting too heated up in here!"

Ivory lingered in Mende's cabin, avoiding going back to his own. They sat on Mende's cot, talking about the various adventures they were going to pull off before they had to leave the island, each escapade more outlandish than the next. "I'm going to tame one of those mountain goats up on the peak and ride that thing," Ivory declared.

Mende clapped his hands, a pre-exclamation mark. "I'm going to swim with some dolphins. I'm going to ride one, maybe two at a time, doing the splits between them."

"Aright. Aright... I'm going to hang glide from the dunes all the way down into the ocean using banana leaves for wings. Then I'm going to drop into the water and dive like a pelican straight down on top of a nice, fat, delicious tuna. No, a sturgeon."

Mende laughed. "A sturgeon? Those things are wicked and have sandpaper skin and dagger spines and stuff."

A large black spider dropped from the cabin roof on a barely visible thread. "Aw, man! You know I hate spiders!" yelled Mende.

Alarmed, Ivory jumped to his feet and went into checklist mode. "Does it have a red hourglass on its belly?"

"Man, I'm not trying to get that close to see! What are you *talking* about!" Before Mende could finish speaking, Ivory had grabbed a shoe and flung it at the spider. His throw was on target.

"Case closed," Ivory said, huffing.

"Man, did you have to kill it?"

"I saw a threat and handled it. Memories are like a spider, you know," Ivory said, standing up to extemporize. "...hiding out in the corners of your mind, steady weaving webs. Eventually, you can see the webs, and you try to get rid of them, cause they creep you out. But the next morning, there they are again. Memories are constant weavers. Super spiders. And you can't kill them. I don't care how hard you try."

Mende reached for his drum to soothe himself. "Maybe that should tell you something about what memories are for. If you can't kill them, they must have some kind of powerful purpose. My culture teaches that all of life is about choosing *how* to remember."

Few slept soundly that first night, so acutely foreign, ominous, and untranslatable were the island's sounds. Back in his own cabin, night gripped Ivory, an incomprehensible horror. *How could the night possibly be so dark? This is another step beyond black. What's the word for that?*

Their cabins moved from nervous conversation to a delirious scattering of words simply to break up the silence. Then, their bodies washed all day in adrenaline, sleep took over. Their first day ended as a poem might. Abrupt. Spacious. Pregnant. Intangible.

DAY TWO

Light began to leak from the horizon up into the early morning sky, spreading cloudlike into a black ocean receding by the moment. Birds inspired by sunrise sirened, warbled, throttled, chattered, and clucked. Woodpeckers drummed on dying trunks losing bark in large swatches.

Coughing came from the cabins. Then, Ivory. Rubbing his eyes and adjusting his crotch, he stumbled toward the fire pit. "You move like Pinocchio," Ashia observed, emerging from her cabin.

"Pinocchio needs a cappuccino," Ivory slurred. Soon, most of the group was milling about the fire pit. Shonto stirred the ashes with a long stick. Mende stretched his back, feline and growling. Cielo was inside a patch of sunlight, progressing through yoga poses, his eyes closed, face serene. Maricela noticed Eloni looking at Cielo, frowning.

"What are we doing today?" Ivory asked.

"We're going to the dunes, right?" Promise answered. "That's what everyone was saying last night."

"As long as I get back to the lagoon today, I'm good," said Ashia. She was tying her locs up high on her head with a deep red scarf.

"I second that," said Maricela. "You boys can have your sand. I'm soaking in that water every chance I get."

"Ya'ah'teh, people!" Shonto said, greeting the group as he loped out of his cabin.

"Ya ya, what?" asked Maricela.

"*Ya'ah'teh*. It's the greeting of my people. Means more than hello though. Our language has more soul than that. It's like a ceremony in itself, a way of entering into another person's sacred space or moment."

"Like *Namasté*?" asked Cielo, rubbing his face and running his fingers through his hair, which looked like wild grass after a windstorm.

"Sure."

"What's *Namasté* mean?" asked Ivory.

"Many ways to translate it," Cielo instructed. "Basically, it means, the divine in me recognizes and bows down to the divine in you."

"That's a whole lot of words wrapped into one," Ivory surmised. "I like word economy. Matter of fact, I'm working on my own language. Forget 26 letters. I'm talking about 26 words!"

"Ivory, it's too early for your energy level," said Maricela. "Can you please turn down the dial? Maybe from a 12 to a 3?"

"Who wants breakfast?" asked Eloni. The question swung the group's focus squarely onto food and fire starting. As sunlight crawled over the trees and across the sand, the moment was doused with scents of fish frying in onion and garlic, and plantains searing.

They ate grouped in clusters around the camp. Binda, Lake, and Pikea had climbed up onto the roof of one of the cabins to eat in the sunlight. Lake, pausing from her meal, looked bashfully at Pikea. "Can I switch cabins with you?" she asked.

"You not feeling the Love in the other cabin?"

"It's not that. Me and Binda seem to be on the same wavelength. I just want to take advantage of that while we're here. We'll be leaving before we know it."

"I feel you," said Pikea. "I'll go get my stuff. It's no thing to me to switch up beds. Only done it dozens of times."

Intoxicating sweetness from the island's citrus blossoms filtered through the air, drenching the cabins in its charms as Promise bathed in morning sunlight just outside of the shadows of a big oak's crown. As she lay, a lightness unprecedented moved through her chest and spread its cloak inside her body.

She wondered about the staying power of peace. Is this what the great spiritual masters feel? How long can a person hold onto a feeling like this? What's the human limit on feeling this way? Promise wanted to be addicted to this, whatever it was. And if she could manage to achieve that addiction, she convicted herself in that moment that she would never let herself be rehabilitated.

The hike to the dunes started right after breakfast, when sunlight was still immature. They followed a faint trail left by animals into the shade of the woods, gradually veering onto a course parallel to Jade Mountain. Curling brooks emerged and dropped back down beneath ground. Soon, smells from the camp faded into a gaining aroma of foliage. Buttercups hung like earrings from the bones of bushes. They came to a clearing filled with sultry stalks of sunflowers, their dark faces pointing the way to the sun's morning position. The sunflowers were at least twice Balanta's height. Binda ran under one and looked up at its face, a small child looking up at a grownup.

A whelping came from the trees and persisted. "What is that? Promise asked. The sound was not clearly mammalian. Or bird. It rankled Promise's nerves. She moved closer to the center of the clearing, where she watched a small auburn fox scamper across, holding its kitten in its mouth by the nape. Its tail switched as it moved on silent paws. "First fox sighting," Cielo announced.

They moved through dense tapestries of trees and vines. The ground lifted into folds, became the rise and fall of hills. Their bodies were working now. They stopped to drink water from a brook, passing around fruit and fish jerky. As morning developed, their sense of adventure grew. Their pace increased, except for Lake and Binda, who lingered at the back, lost in wonderment as the forest palpitated around them.

A majestic blue heron stood frozen in the center of a shallow stream. "Do you really think I can't see you, buddy?" asked Eloni, laughing. The heron broke form, its spindle legs folding mechanically as it moved to the bank and into a fist of bush.

The group passed by several large flat stones, their faces cupped by time and filled with pools of rainwater. Eloni took note, the survivalist in him alerted. Agave and yucca grew in kindred patches, their leaf blades algae green and shaped like the heads of a spear reaching 10 feet into the sky.

Cielo placed his nose flush against the bark of a pine and inhaled enthusiastically. "Now we're smelling trees?" Promise joked with him.

"These smell like maple syrup. You should be able to smell it from where you are," Cielo replied. "Pay attention, 'miga. It's a virtual brunch all around you." Promise smelled the tree. After that, she was smelling every tree she encountered.

They came to a large family of cottonwood trees, morning's air still cool on their faces. The cottonwoods wore bark that was thick and deep with fissures, like a latticework of canyons running through mesas. Balanta trailed his palms over the bark, his nerves there soothing to the stimulation. Ant colonies paraded up and down the bark, dutiful in formation. Balanta studied their movement, fascinated at their social cohesion. Cielo leaned in, taking his own look. "Those things are to be commended," he said. Balanta assumed Cielo was being environmental. He was being culinary. Cielo licked his lips and said, "They taste great pan fried, flambéed, however you want them. The crunch is what makes them delectable. Add some sesame oil, and you're off to bliss."

The group moved in a loose line along a mostly undefined path through bright woods. Balanta, Mende, and Eloni kept to the front, the rest drifting freely. "Girl, that butt of yours sits so high, it's just about smacking you in the back of your head," Maricela joked, whacking Promise on the rear for good measure.

"Don't hate. Relate." Promise laughed. It felt good to her that Maricela was feeling comfortable enough with her to joke like that. Promise passed it on, whacking Ivory lightly on the back of his legs with a thin willow branch.

"Girl, you know I'm not your racehorse, right?" Ivory said, playing along. "I'mma walk this here hike at my own pleasure and pace." With that, he promptly slowed his roll; that is until he found himself at the back of the pack. After several nervous glances back into the woods, Ivory advanced himself back up into the center of the caravan.

Morning warmed and brightened. "I'm getting thirsty already," said Maricela.

"Here, have a piece," Ashia said to Maricela, handing her a giant peach, chomping one herself. "They'll hydrate us." The peaches were fat and white fleshed, crisp to the bite and sweet as a daydream. They came from a stand of trees between camp and the lagoon. Ashia finished hers and offered another to Promise, who had come up from the group lagging behind.

"Thanks, girl," said Promise, taking the fruit and sinking her teeth into its coolness. "Ummm... Now *that's* a party in the mouth."

They continued on, stepping over droppings left by small wild things that had, with their endless passages, earned the trail its surprising barrenness. They came upon a large patch of groundcover flaring with lavender-colored blossoms. The entire hillside droned with bees, a ghostly rotational howl of race cars against track; a deep, oscillating chant, as the bees labored away in a meditative state, landing on and lifting from blossoms. The bees swarmed the blooming groundcover, making the hill appear to ripple.

Eloni spotted the hive first. It was the size of an heirloom watermelon. Honey leaked from its pores and dripped onto a large piece of pine bark resting on the ground like the hull of a boat. Sunlight caught the amber honey as it dripped, brilliantly highlighting the bubbles in the thick drizzle. "No way!" Eloni exclaimed. He scooped the deep pool of honey from the bark and fingered it into one of the three small gourds he had tied around his waist. He licked each finger, his eyes rolling back, orgasmic. "Okay, we're about to feast this week like ya'll don't know!" he bellowed. "This is the manna!"

"Bees remind me of folks picking cotton," Promise observed. "Not cool history, I guess, but there's something beautiful about these bees working together as one, just humping it in the sunlight. Going through the fatigue collectively. The bees might feel otherwise, but it's... beautiful to me. Not their pain. The sharing of it."

Cielo rubbed his palms together, cherishing a philosophical moment. "I'm with you Promise. It's like fieldworkers. The migrant life. Everyone tethered on a string, a rhythm. Only way to get through the day and get your quota. These bees are invisible. Just like fieldworkers. Daily bringing the crops for the rest of the world, but invisible. No one thinks twice about them, except to complain about them as a nuisance. Bees do the dirty work. Pollinating. No crops without them. But folks call them a danger. A threat with stingers. But nobody gets stung like the invisible kind."

Cielo thought he had an audience, so he continued. "You know, funny thing about the term *beekeeper*. You don't actually *keep* bees. You make conditions attractive to them so they want to stay. They have their own nature, their own purpose, which does not change. You don't keep children either. Doesn't matter whether you're a parent, a guardian, or some kind of authority. It isn't your place to possess. Your task is to make your space with them something that appeals to their nature. Make it a greenhouse. So they can thrive. He turned as though to be affirmed by his audience. There was none. The group had moved on. He laughed and moved on, too.

"Okay, Cielo," Ashia shouted back, Lovingly. "You can keep pontificating over the bees. But we need to get to where we're going."

"Where are we going again?" Maricela asked, laughing. "Oh, yeah. The dunes."

Cielo caught up. He noticed Pikea chewing her lip. Her face seemed tight. "Como te sientes, 'miga?" he asked. "How are you feeling? You okay?"

"All this fresh air. No adults. No rules. No schedule. I feel..."

"Lost?"

"Naked. My skin feels raw against all this freedom. What do I hold onto? I'm floating."

"Life out there in the grownup world is gonna take getting used to. Don't matter the system we've been through. When you're on someone's list and living their program, lock up is lock up. Takes time to learn freedom."

"Thanks, Cielo. I appreciate the reminder."

The group came to a stretch of rolling hills. Silk trees lived in this neighborhood, their fernlike leaves wavering lightly as they ushered sunlight to the ground in brilliant slices. Beyond the silk trees was a neighborhood of plum trees. Plums seemed to leap from their branches at Promise as she walked beneath, so plentiful and perfected. They released from the branch with the slightest touch. Promise only had to cradle them gently in her fingers, and with a faint pop, they were hers. She gorged on five of them before she knew it, her fingers and chin sticky with the evidence.

They climbed as the earth rose. Now they were in the foothills of Jade Mountain. Still not far from the sea as they moved up the island. Gazing up at the towering face of granite puncturing the clouds, Shonto asked, 'Why do you think that's called Jade Mountain?"

"It doesn't look too green to me," said Promise. "More like... almost blue somehow, especially in the morning."

They came to a meager trail along a cliff side. Mende stayed in the cluster with Balanta and Eloni, with Promise and Ashia right behind. Ivory glued his body to the cliff face as he scooted sideways down the path. His eyes bulged. "You people are not getting me kilt over some sand dunes. Isn't there another way to our destination, cause this feels like some insanity to me." He couldn't help glancing out over the trail ledge and down into the canopy, which was alive. Cedar waxwings and mockingbirds told their stories from the podiums of elders and elms. The staccato knocking of a woodpecker echoed down on the valley floor and up, reaching the hikers.

The trail began descending. Soon they were just above sea level again, and back in the woods. The shade was welcoming. Sun was approaching its throne. They drank more water, ate more fruit and jerky. They passed by some fig trees and gorged, Cielo performing *Namasté* to the trees for the blessing.

The ground grew grainy, brighter. Trees departed the stage. The new breeze on Mende's face was refreshing. He broke into a trot. Now they were on the open beach and running. They could see the first distinctive shapes of their objective. The sea to their right side changed as they scanned to their left, transforming to waves of vanilla grain, a billowing apron of dunes flowing down the waist of Jade Mountain.

They left their shoes on the beach and raced up and down the sea of dunes, rolling, swimming, dancing. Lake flung her arms into the air and twirled in circles. Ivory did sand angels. Binda sat and buried her feet. She felt the sand grow moist around them. They all rolled. And rolled. Thrilling to the sensation of their bodies falling down slopes, displacing sand as though it were water.

Shonto and Mende came up with a pushing game. One person had to make it from a point on a dune ridge to another point, without letting the others knock her or him off the ridge. Eloni came closest to making it all the way.

Binda found ant lion funnels in the crux of a dune. She lay down, her face close to the funnels, and watched large black ants fall into the funnels. Monstrous pincers that looked prehistoric blasted up from beneath, sending grains flying. The ants went down, pulled under the sand, fates sealed and stamped.

The group's lips were chapped. They gathered to drink water and eat energy back into their bodies. Sun was now close to its prime. Balanta kneeled in the gypsum, digging his hands into its granary and lifting them up, letting the sand spill through his fingers in streams. Eloni was up ahead of the pack, still climbing. His eyes were on the dune peak, still far above.

Eloni was bull chested. Or rather, his chest made all his shirts look tight, no matter how much he stretched them out when wet. His older brother, Keola, warned him from a young age that his heart was in danger of exploding out of his body and that the only remedy was for, say, an older brother to mercilessly pound on Eloni's chest with both fists whenever possible, in the hopes that by flattening this freakish feature, Eloni's heart might remain in its box. More than once, child welfare and the police were called on Eloni's family, due to all the bruises adults noticed on the child's shirtless body at the park and playgrounds.

Eloni sprinted up another rise of dune, his calves and lungs burning by the time he arrived to its peak. Water blurred his vision, whipping across his face in the wind. Heaving and bent over with his hands on his knees, he decided to walk from this point upward.

A memory visited him just then. A memory more painful than what he had approved for his consciousness, though also comforting in a way. He had been on the big island of Hawai'i with a group of other boys from his juvenile detention center. They were mostly Pacific Islanders: Hawai'ians, Samoans, Tongans, Fijians. On a bus, going to a luau on the beach. The bus stopped at a grocery store to let a few of the boys take a bathroom break. As they strode through the store, with detention center staff moving closely with them, they passed by a group of fraternity boys going in the opposite direction. Eloni and another boy overheard the college boys dogging them under their breath: "I'm surprised they let them out without their chains."

"They need to put them in isolation, like they used to do with the lepers on Moloka'i."

"Somebody better secure the cash registers up in here. There's about to be some crime for sure."

The words were nonsensical and not worth a response. But it was Eloni who had overheard those words, words that landed directly on the raw scab barely containing his woundedness. Before Eloni realized his error, he had left his feet and was flying. Airborne Samoan. He slammed his already considerable heft into the chest of the closest frat guy, driving the shocked student off of his feet and into a devotedly stacked tower of canned beans and stacks of Hawai'ian sweet bread.

By the time the police left the scene and passersby had their fill and stopped window gawking, Eloni had been hauled away, his wrists bound in plastic straps behind his back, head dropped throughout his walk of shame to the police cruiser. The other boys were loaded back onto the bus, and continued on to the luau, where they got fat and happy on roasted pig and pineapple punch by the paper cups full. When Eloni returned to the detention center, the other boys were more than happy to let him know about the great party he missed out on, even as they slapped his back and raised his fist triumphantly for defending their kingdom of delinquency.

On the way back from the dunes, they ran. Hunger had assumed its priority. Until Promise shrieked. The group hustled to her, alarmed. Promise jumped up and down as though coals were under her feet. "Look! Right there!" she screamed. It was a snake. A large one.

"Is that thing eating something?" Ashia asked.

"Eeewww! That's nasty! It's eating a lizard!" Maricela shrieked.

"Poor lizard," Pikea empathized.

"Poor me," Eloni cracked. "I could have used not seeing that, especially right before lunch."

The garden hose-thick snake, oily obsidian in color, stared coldly at the humans, as if it was thinking, *This meal is mine. Don't even think about trying for it.* The shocked lizard was motionless. At least, the part of it, mostly legs, still visible from the corners of the snake's mouth.

"Is that a python?" asked Ivory, his voice quivering like a drunken arrow.

Ashia smiled. "Not exactly."

"You sure?"

"Yeah, about as sure as I am that you're not a wilderness guide," she laughed.

"Give it a name, Eloni!" Ivory shouted. "We gotta name everything we experience here."

"That... was weird," Eloni murmured. "A name? How about... Messed up?"

"Good enough," said Ivory. "Said what was said. Messed up, it is."

Eloni noticed that Ivory's hair seemed to have sprouted magically with moisture, like a chia pet. Shocks of hair went in different directions, as though reaching out like tentacles. It was pure Jimmy Hendricks. "Ivory, you've got an afro on steroids."

"An afro on steroids that's been run through with a malfunctioning weed trimmer," Promise said.

Ivory soaked up the attention. "Y'all are just fiending for my flavor. Admit what you can't git."

Ivory soon trailed behind the group, distracted by a squirrel that ran off with his last bite of jerky. Just when the others noticed his absence, Ivory rounded a bend, running at them. "I just saw a pterodactyl or something! I'm not playing!" he yelled.

"Calm down, Ivory," urged Ashia. "What are you talking about?"

"This huge bird! I was walking along, looking at the ground, when this shadow passed over me that took away the sun. And I heard a huge swooping sound, like the whole sky rushing over me. I looked up and this giant... thing flew over me. Its head was the ugliest, and colored like ketchup. The rest of it was black and its wings must have been 10 feet across!"

"Whoa! It's revenge of the dinosaurs!" joked Mende.

"I'm telling you all the truth!" Ivory implored.

Ashia was calm, with a smile on her face. "That... was a condor, Ivory."

"A condom? Real funny."

"No, a condor. You know, the big bird that almost went extinct? It's making a comeback."

"Well, it doesn't need to come back here. No exaggeration, that thing could have picked me up easily. I hit the dirt and closed my eyes. When I looked up, the treetops were still rattling.

"I wonder if that was what that goat bleating was all about the other day. What if that condor is picking off goats from up in the sky?"

"A condor is a scavenger, Ivory. You know... road kill?" Ashia explained.

"Either way, I'm thinking we need to institute an air raid drill or something," said Ivory.

"What do you know about air raids?" Promise asked.

"I read about them."

All at once, the group roared, "Of course! He read about them!"

"Ivory, maybe you won't stop talking because you're afraid of silence?" Ashia offered.

"I don't think so," Ivory replied. "I don't mind silence, as long as no one's forcing it on me. It's more like... you know, I lost track of my mother's voice after about three years. I couldn't *feel* what it sounded like anymore. Made me feel erased, partly.

"It's not like I think I'll ever have my voice taken away. But... hearing it run through me is soothing. I feel like, yeah, I'm still here. Plus, it's sexy you know, so how can you blame me?"

"Ivory—"

"I know... I'm a clown."

Heat followed them on their way back, clinging to their skin, wetting their clothes. Shonto found a passion fruit tree and picked a few. He parted the flesh of the passion fruit with his pocketknife. "Would you like some?" he asked Pikea. The fruit's juice glistened in the sunlight, dripping down along Shonto's fingers.

Pikea answered with her eyes and smile, taking a slice from Shonto's hand and closing her lips around the soft, sweet offering. "Thank you. That was good."

"It's good for when you're thirsty, too." Shonto's chest was pounding. He was faint, and tried to play it off by wiping sweat from his brow. *Man, it's hot.* Thank goodness he was sitting down, or else he would have been the first Diné who passed out on his face from offering a girl some fruit.

By the time they got back to camp, the sun was already on its slow downslope. "Man, it's way past lunchtime," Ivory growled.

"I'm starving," Mende added, as they all moved for the food stores.

Ivory pushed past Promise and Pikea. "Watch yourself, Ivory," Pikea said, elbowing Ivory in return.

"At this point, it's everyone for themselves," Ivory said. "No time for chivalry. Don't get between me and my chow."

"Okay then," Promise said, rolling her eyes. "I didn't realize you were on the verge of death, son."

Ivory piled gargantuan portions of the fish and fruits and vegetables onto his plate. He had always gotten nervous when it came to food. Food was for him a myth, much like a unicorn. No, a flying, singing unicorn. That unbelievable. He could see it, eat it, get sick on it, and still he would not believe in it. Ivory swore it was a phantom, a mirage in his desert of hunger. When it was presented, he felt those presenting it to be playing a cruel trick on him. So he played one, too. Swipe and run. After one too many times gripping random items from the shelves of grocery and retail stores, one security officer, large and heavy yet apparently still in condition enough to run down a teenager who folded into the breeze like dry leaf, had finally caught him. Busted. Long, surreal moments of shame and terror in the store's security office, followed by the violation of his soul and ancestry by the police with their eyes as they arrived and sized him, not up but down. Down, like a dog. Less than that. Down like something subterranean that had not been given permission to show its mole face above ground. Ivory was splintered down the fault line that held together his dignity, splintered long before the cold cuffs, back seat squad car resettlement trip, clanging of the bars, slamming of doors, mocking white paperwork, and all the while those wolf packs of eyes assaulting him, penetrating him, bending him over and forcing him to bleed for his sins.

"I can't believe how the day is blowing by," Pikea noted. "I always hear older people saying how time flies by for them. Like, summer flies by. Weeks fly by. Days fly by. I guess it's just me, but time barely moves, feels like."

"That's what happens when you're so hungry that you're in pain," Ashia said.

"Or when you're in so much pain that you're always hungry... for something to end the pain." Ivory added.

A pack of clouds huddled in the distant sky, feverish and undecided. Mende took his food and went over to a cluster of birds of paradise. A grove, really. The birds of paradise towered over him, beaks of vanilla, navy blue, persimmon, and turmeric-colored blossoms shooting out from high and low on the stalks. Mende sat beside the flowers and mindlessly chewed his almond buttered prawns and figs wrapped in kale. It was bothering him that Balanta seemed to be siding up to Eloni so much. Mende liked Eloni, too, but he was used to it pretty much being just him and Balanta. Since they had arrived, Balanta came off almost as angry at Mende. A new sensation. And it stung.

After lunch, thoughts turned toward the lagoon and cooling off from the afternoon heat. Shonto rubbed his belly like he would a basketball before taking a free throw. "I, for one, plan to be in the water the rest of the afternoon. Anyone has any chores for me, I'll catch them after dinner."

Cielo, wearing a technicolor vest and purple fedora, slugged down a conch shell full of carrot juice with gusto, smacking his lips after emptying the shell.

"Dang, Cielo," Maricela said. "You drank that like it was the best stuff on earth."

"Nearly was. Nothing like fresh pressed carrot juice. I could almost taste the soil in it."

"See, that's why people look at you sideways, Cielo. And by the way, I don't know if you were *trying* to look like a parrot, but bravo!"

"You know you Love my flavor," Cielo said, laughing as he pressed his vest and tipped his fedora proudly.

"Ivory, don't you have something to apologize for?" Maricela asked, shifting tracks. "You were kind of rude getting to the food."

Ivory's glance dropped. He was still finishing off a stick of carrot dipped in blackberry mush. "When I get hungry, I get territorial," said Ivory. "Sorry about that. Once I eat, my defensiveness evaporates. I lose that edge, and feel all touchy feely again. That's when you can cuddle up on me, in case any of you were wondering."

"You're a fool," said Maricela, "as matter of fact."

Everyone moved to get food put away and change their clothes for the lagoon. It was still mid-afternoon, with plenty of sunshine left for a few hours in the best waterpark of all time.

"Hey, Binda," Lake said, approaching Binda as Binda sat singing quietly to herself. "You want to go to the meadow with me before we go to the lagoon?"

Binda looked up. "Sure. Then we can go cool off after in the water."

"Yeah," said Lake. "I wanted to get to the meadow yesterday, but the day went by so fast. Antonia said the meadow is a magic place. I can't wait." The two of them told the others where they were headed, and took off, skipping.

The meadow was miraculous. Wondrously alive. Its body, an undulating wave of waist-high Mexican feather grass, bobbing bunny tail grass, and cheerful flowers pushing back at the forest. Pushing for more space to receive and bask in a sunlight that showered it so softly that the meadow was a thriving blossom on the earthly tip of sun's stamen and pistil. Its space extended in a nearly circular shape of breathless dimension. At least two football fields across. In illogical contrast to the island's white beach, the meadow's black volcanic soil, situated in this cup of caldera, an ancient volcano mouth having passed through eons of transformation from crater of fire. Its numerous tongues of magma darting upward as if from a giant monitor lizard. Geysers of earth's innermost forces spewing up to scald a blameless sky. From this boiling outburst, eventually to become a landing place for rain, a bowl suited to store water until that water became a lake, rich and thick with fowl and aquatic life beneficiary to the lake's volcanic bottom soil. A water heaven evaporating over millennia into this. This meadow in the maws of a dense island forest. A pause in the tallness of trees, giving way to a blanket of grass for breeze to play with as it circled and licked and eased itself before moving back out to sea.

Lilies of the valley, their pale purple blooms atop tall, thin stalks, clustered throughout the meadow, lending quirk to the display. Knee-high grasses blushed in golden tones, and dark purples, sage, and amber. Wind moved over their backs, an unseen hand smoothing down the plush carpet, changing directions at whim, fanning the carpet again. Sunflowers stood erect everywhere, their faces obedient to sun's arc. Sweet fragrances rose and danced about the meadow. Star jasmine. Lavender. Honeysuckle. These decorated the open meadow, happily soaking up sunlight. Hidden in the shadows of snow gum trees at the perimeter were hibiscus, giant fists of rare red and honey-yellow blossoms. Day lilies and birds of paradise dwelled there, too, each framing the meadow in stark patches of color.

Air in the meadow spoke an entirely different language than down by the beach or at the lagoon. Here, your breath came easier, left more lightly. The air here was entitled. It knew it was protected by the meadow's crater, the surrounding forest, and its distance from the ocean. And so it was less frantic, calmer. It was air for monks and souls that knew how to be still. Lake knew how to be still. Immediately, feeling the meadow's breath enter her, she entered the meadow, dropping to the ground like a dreamy ribbon, laying her head upon the warm, soft bed of grass. Laying her body over the small vibrations of this earth, so small as to be undetectable. Unless you were still enough inside your soul to register the micro tremors of movement in this wide open place, this pulsing prairie where dark orange dragonflies lifted and dived, and bees labored freely, and ladybugs strode grass stalks in their black dotted multitude of millions.

Light played on the meadow in a way that tipped its grass in sun sparks. Sparks everywhere. Touching off across the waving grains like fireflies jumping from stalk to stalk. Gentle fireworks of brightness, a drenching of sun pouring over every edge, diluting every angle into a softness that made Lake want to sleep. The songs of insects were gentle, their volume soft and librarian. Buzzing, chatting, popping. Birdcall optimistic and without worry. Tree crowns brushing each other sounded faintly like ocean brushing sand.

Lake lay on her stomach on a soft patch of tall emerald and golden grass and looked out across the meadow. Bridal parties of butterflies, bees, and hummingbirds frolicked in a sea of wildflowers, their forms and movement frosted in shafts of sunlight. She felt the warm ground against her face and sleepiness come over her invitingly. She wondered if it would be possible to merge into this meadow and become its magical heartbeat. Lake pulled all of this warmth over her, a blanket, and drifted, smiling, into a wonderful sleep.

When Lake awoke, Binda was chasing dragonflies and butterflies. "*Bunpa!*" she yelled joyfully. "Butterflies!" Clouds of glittering yellow, blood orange, and sail white butterflies danced in the air around Binda's head. She saw Lake sit up, and came over to her. "You ready for the *aroona*?" Binda asked, her face bright and satisfied.

"The what?"

"The water! The lagoon!"

"You go on ahead to the lagoon," Lake said. "I'm going to take a moment. I'll be soon behind you."

"Are you sure? Okay. I'll see you over there. Don't get lost."

In a moment, Lake was lost. She thought she heard the wind singing, then realized it was a bird. Pushing her way through thick tangles of vines, some larger around than her arms, she made her way in what she hoped was the direction of the birdsong. Insects in the undergrowth at her feet throttled and clicked. With each step, she imagined she was bringing destruction to whole families of small creatures. She mourned, even as she continued stepping, dry leaves crunching, soggy ground squealing.

A ray of sunlight brushed her shoulder. Somehow, its touch felt paternal. She sensed the canopy about to give away its blanket to the sky. Stepping over a large rotted log, she emerged into an opening in the trees filled with sun, like a secret storage place for a giant who hoarded light.

Squinting, she looked around for the source of birdsong that had been her guide. Her vision was still mostly flooded with brilliant shards and fragments. From this shimmering curtain, a small dark form appeared, moving in quirky spasms along the ground. As her eyes cleared, she recognized the bird as the same one that persisted outside of the campground the day before. *At least, I think that's you. What are you doing here?*

She felt something brush lightly against her cheek. She stepped back. A spider was manipulating its webbing in a moment of silence and sunlight. Knitting, unspooling, binding. Its web emerged theatrically, a perfect soliloquy of industry, a monologue reflecting light, quivering its verse and vowels, shimmering with predatory tension, with anticipation, as it hung suspended in the nook of air between two lemon tree branches joined at their base. Lake watched the spider craft its livelihood, her face just inches away. She Loved the story of web making, much more than the story of what such webs are made for.

Dreamcatchers. Medicine wheels. They were everywhere now, her sacred tokens rehashed into tourist ornaments. Absconded away with by a clueless culture that wanted all the sacredness of her people, but not so that it could dwell in sacredness. No, that would require making amends inside the soul. No, this culture just wanted trinkets to play with, to adorn their car windows, and necklaces, so as to appear sacred. Appearing sacred was good business these days. It was a big part of why children like Lake were valued by the millions of programs out there, over half of which, it felt like to her, she had been run through like a whole grain harvest on a conveyor belt. Appearing sacred was sufficient in a world where essence was never the point. But Lake wanted her essence back. They started taking it many generations ago, before she came, and now she was on a mission: repatriating the bones of her people's essence. Bringing them home. Even if home was so difficult to decipher for a people of genocide. Hard to know where you belong when you've been told for so long where you belong. And where you don't. She didn't care. She was going to bring all the bones back. Not the actual bones. The artifacts. The languages. The memories lost from shattered pots of clay, clay now serving, for appearance's sake, the glass cabinets of soulless ghosts who themselves were raised to believe only in the deceitful, ill-gotten appearance of things.

"Who's swimming out to the center with me?" Promise shouted excitedly. Ashia and Maricela had already stripped down to their shorts and t-shirts, and were running for the lagoon water. Their two grins revealed a joy that starts at birth and too often burrows upon adolescence, if not much sooner. The warm water was thick against their bodies, and buoyant. Promise's long arms rose and fell in turn like a waterwheel, churning water as she moved toward the deeper part of the lake. Maricela followed behind, in a combination of dog paddle and sidestroke. Sun was high, shadows short. Dragonflies flew reconnaissance missions by the lake reeds, scattering the few small white butterflies in their path.

Promise dove down, completely submerging herself in the heavenly element. Surface sounds muffled and echoed through the water. *This feels so peaceful. It's nice to be completely surrounded, every part of you touched so warmly.*

Mende, Eloni, Shonto, and Cielo repeatedly followed each other off the waterfall's ledge, kicking in the air, feeling the rush of free falling before hitting the water. "When Ivory gets here, we've got to get him to jump from up here," Mende said. "He doesn't know what he's missing."

"In his own time," Cielo said, sagely.

Mende looked at the shirtless Cielo and shook his head. "Cielo, are you sure you're not a man-ape splicing? You're hairier than any person I've seen, and you grow a five o'clock shadow by 10:00 a.m."

"My ancestors must have lived high up in the mountains, cerca de los nubes. Como los angeles. Near the clouds, like the angels. Up by Machu Picchu or something," Cielo responded, completely unruffled. "The fur is good insulation," he cracked.

Balanta stood under the waterfall, far enough under to avoid the plummeting divers. He closed his eyes and let the water's force drum on his face. The sensation loosened him from his thoughts. His body grew slack, unwound. His arms dropped, his long fingers appearing to join the water's shape as it fell. Ashia watched him, wondering what such a proud, pensive soul held onto in the privacy of his heart. She climbed up toward the ledge of the falls, wanting to take a few leaps. As she reached the jump off point, her head was down, focused on the terrain. She heard a low voice. "Here, let me help you up," Balanta said, extending a hand down to Ashia. He had somehow climbed up past her. She looked into his eyes. Balanta was looking down and away. She gave him his hand, and felt his strength bring her up onto the dark stony ledge.

Maricela's eyes were on Eloni's tattoo. Every time he emerged, bare chested, from the water to climb back up to the falls, Eloni's tribal markings seemed more alive to Maricela. The tattoo ran from just below Eloni's ribs down to beneath his calves. A matrix of blue-black lines and symbols. A turtle shell dominated the center of his back in dark olive plates. The legs extended to Eloni's sides. The tail was a dark triangle above his tailbone. The head of the turtle sat between Eloni's shoulder blades, looking up at the back of his head. Maricela wondered what age Eloni was when he had acquired these lines and the spirit that came with them.

At the lagoon's edge, Pikea lay on her back on a large flat rock, sunning herself like a turtle and smiling at the warmth penetrating her skin deeply. She was lost in the tranquility of the moment, eyes closed and water evaporating from her skin. *You can't buy this*, she thought to herself. This wasn't just water. This place was safety. Peace. The absence of judgment and labels. Scorn and fear. Here was a place they had each wanted, no, needed, for so long. It was very difficult for Pikea to process this place as a real thing. Still, she let her tension run from her body into the stone. When sun had warmed her to a sweat, she slipped back into the soft water and dropped loosely into its depths.

Eloni wasn't down with snorkeling, which the others were planning to do out in the bay. But he sure did like floating on his back here in the lagoon, grinning like a bobbing sea otter with fat clams on its belly. Floating made him feel somewhere between this world and another, lighter, more peaceful world. He wished he could float like this through the rest of his life. He looked over at Maricela and thought he caught her looking. Nah. She couldn't be attracted to him. The old ugly duckling feelings came up in his throat like acid reflux. He coped by laughing maniacally as he floated. This place was playing tricks on his mind.

Ivory was feeling badly about his behavior at lunch. He had held back from joining everyone else at the lagoon. "Gotta make amends, soldier." He said to himself. He went into his cabin and gathered up the jacaranda tree pods he had collected earlier. Finding a suitable rock on which to sit, he went about his business. His face grew focused. Sweat beaded on his forehead, and in his 'fro. After a day in the dunes, his skin was way past ash. He had already braided fiber from dried branches and bark to create cordage. The materials were everywhere around him: Milkweed, which made for the softest cord. Dogbane and cedar. Cattail from the lagoon and estuary, yucca and agave from the heights, and sugar maple, which grew liberally. His favorite twine was what he had rendered from willow, boiling the inner bark in water with ashes from the fire. Now, he had a complete set of rope and string with which to work.

Ivory selected the smallest jacaranda seed pods, setting a handful aside in a pile. Picking up a pod, he wrapped the hard, firmly attached stem of the pod in willow string, knotting the stem in place. He did the same with seven more pods until he had the anklet complete. He repeated the process until he had three anklets. Then, working from the largest pods, Ivory fashioned three waist chains. "These will do, champ," he assured himself. Dusting off his jeans, he thanked the sitting stone, and ran off for the lagoon.

Promise was having one of her moments. A tidal wave of pain terrifying in its sharpness breached her protective walls. And here, she had just had such a good moment at the lagoon. The water had felt so good. Then, someone had said the wrong thing. Or her clothes felt weird against her skin. Or the air wasn't right. She rarely knew what set it all off. But here it was. Sheer pain. And there, in her mind, the unavoidable face of her mother, *Shuraa*. Promise confirmed to herself that it was not Thursday. Then she found the most private place she could, and she cried. Awfully.

Then, spirit came over Promise, changing her from a person into an instrument. Her eyes went distant as she gazed up into the sky. Her body now swaying rhythmically, she opened her mouth. What came out was a voice so pure, so unearthly, even the forest paused. Beautiful notes emerged, winged and glorious, like monarchs in heat, and flitted for the trees, settling in the

63

leaves and raining down a mist of music so fine and original, the grass below cried tears of dew.

Camp was in a lazy moment, heat creeping through everything, welling up even in the shadows. Down by the surf, the boys tussled and jostled for no apparent reason. From this distance, it looked like the frenzy of rutting season.

"Why are they always pushing and wrestling with each other?" Binda asked.

"Practicing manhood." Ashia said.

"Why are Shonto and Ivory in each other's faces, flexing and grunting like two bodybuilders in a flex-off?" Pikea asked.

"It's like with whale song," Pikea said. "The males sing the same song to compete. Loudest male wins."

"Maybe it's mating season." Promise joked.

"Who are they trying to attract?" Pikea shook her head.

"Each other," Maricela said, smarmily. Pikea jogged over to break up the foolishness. It took her a minute to break up the ritualized head butting that was now being performed. Not to mention the poor Sumo techniques.

Pikea and Shonto grabbed snorkel masks and ran down to the water. Soon, they were swimming through glinting schools of silver fish. Bright pastel colored fish swam between their legs when they stopped and stood in the chest deep water to adjust their masks. The fishes' color was like bright, melted candy. From the surface looking down, the coral teemed with shadow creatures: octopi, squid, eels, sea cucumbers, anemones. A parade of starfish dusted up the sand beneath Shonto. Pikea pointed him up ahead, to his left. There, he spotted a large tomato-red octopus with a crab in its beak, skirting for a private place to dine. The warm water relaxed Pikea's muscles. And her mind. Down here, life felt and looked fluid, not abrupt and jarring as what she knew. Shonto listened to his breath circulate through the mask and tube, a deep, solemn thrush amplified in the water. The sound and rhythm hypnotized him, pleasantly. Sunlight poured down through the water around them, creating a forest of sun trees through which they navigated. The tide tossed them gently. It felt to Pikea like being held in the bosom of the world.

Lake and Balanta came down to the estuary late in the afternoon, drawn by boy laughter. The estuary teemed with congregations of gulls, cranes, storks, and cormorants, each bird an aspiring minister beseeching its flock to listen to its sermon. The result was an overwhelming vocal blizzard. Rimming the estuary was a necklace of tide pools formed in fields of sea-polished stones. Sea cucumbers, anemones, starfish, and kelp all doing what they could within shallow patches of water.

"What are you all doing?" Lake asked.

"Skipping stones!" Eloni shouted.

She noticed they were aiming at a group of turtles on a large branch out in the water. "Hey! Stop that!"

"Stop what?" Mende asked.

"Don't you know turtles are sacred? You can't be throwing stones at them. You need to be protecting them, because if even you don't know it, they are always protecting you."

"How's that?" Eloni asked.

"My people see turtles as messengers to the human race. They carry old traits, like patience and endurance that are being lost from the world. They are spirits that bring healing and peace to those who are open to them. People think turtles are fearful, because of the way they duck back into their shells. They are not afraid. They are at peace inside their shells, secure and independent. Their shells magnify the energy of the outside world, like good acoustics in church or a concert hall. Or a singing bowl. Their wisdom tells them to go inside their shells so that they can have a deeper experience with the world. They are monks, basically. And I for one like the way they get down."

Mende shrugged his shoulders. "Okay, Lake. You're the resident animal expert."

"I don't know about that. But turtles are my spirit animal, and the fact they are all over the place in this estuary tells me that this water has good energy. Wisdom has been drinking here."

Balanta's face was stern. "Our *Balanta* tribal people hold the tortoise and its shell to be sacred, too," he shared. "Mende, you should know better."

"Excuse me, captain," Mende said, sarcastically.

The boys dropped their heads. Ivory tried to lift the mood. "Look at you, Lake. At least we got you speaking loud and strong!"

"Okay, Ivory," Lake said. "Just be good to those turtles." She pointed with two fingers toward her eyes and then toward him. They all laughed, including the pelicans and gulls, who quickly turned the estuary into an amphitheater of the absurd.

"I'm going for a hike," Promise announced.

"You want company?" Ivory asked.

"That's okay, Barney," Promise said, smiling. "I want to take a moment to breathe."

"Barney?" Ivory inquired.

"As in *barnacle*," Promise said, busting herself up in laughter.

"Good one," Ivory acceded. "Don't worry, I'll get you back."

"Arm wrestling contest! Eloni called out. Everybody pair up. We'll do rounds."

"C'mon, Eloni," Maricela implored. "Can't we all just take a walk or something?"

"Walking's for people who can't run!" Eloni declared. "Now, who's ready to get their arm blowed out?" Before he could finish the sentence, everyone scattered, leaving Eloni to compete against himself. He found a suitable branch on a large tree with fragrant, pink flowers, and did pull-ups until his arms screamed. Then he grabbed his spear and ran to the bay to find something in the water to stab.

Promise's legs burned something fierce as she scaled a steep scree slope, the stone strewn earth giving way beneath her feet. The thinner air up here felt good entering her lungs, and she fantasized that she was climbing an ancient pyramid.

She stopped and turned to look out over the ocean, catching her breath in deep gasps. The wind was cool against her afro, bobbing it side to side gently, even as she stroked it. Promise Loved nothing more than to run her fingers through her hair, knowing that every wondrous sensation was coming from her own being. It was hers. The personality of her kink, ribboning and springing against her skin. The soft suppleness. She gardened her hair like this, with her fingers, to soothe herself. A form of massage or meditation. She Loved the evolution of her hair. The way she could shape it to her mood. It answered her faithfully. She could set it free, into a bold treetop crown billowing against the sky. Or braid it up into creative weavings she piled atop her head. Crocheted. Macraméd. Plaits. Coils. Pinwheels. Spools. Whipped cream swirls. Or shave it down to the scalp and let her face blossom. Folks had always praised the shape of her skull, saying, "More power to you. I couldn't get away with that." Promise thought it funny how people justified their need to hide themselves. For her, she figured hair and the absence of it were clay to play with, miraculous gifts she got to explore for a lifetime.

To Promise's right was an inset embankment, its façade a rock outcropping. Promise noticed branches, leaves, and spider webs at the center of the outcropping moving in and out, rhythmically. As though the mountain was breathing. She moved closer, her left leg slipping downhill over the scree and dirt with each step.

Darkness peered out from behind the breathing lattice of branches. It was an opening. Wondering how far back the opening went, Promise pulled away the cluster barricading the way. The top of the opening reached her chin, and the dark space was about as wide as her body length. Kneeling down, Promise tentatively poked her head inside the darkness. *A cave!* Daylight penetrated nearly 20 feet deep, and she saw the contours of jagged rock walls framing a black throat with no visible endpoint. Tentatively, Promise moved just inside the cave mouth. A phosphorous smell clung to its blackened walls, incense of ceremonial fires lit for centuries. She took deep breaths and felt the cave air moisten her skin. *Okay, lady, that's good enough*, she told herself. *Time for you to leave.*

She backed out into daylight, and glanced up above the cave, at the continuing rise of mountain. Cypress and pines blown against the mountain face pointed the way uphill. She ascended the slope for several steps, and sat on a large flat outcropping uphill from the cave mouth, letting breeze wash over her face. Promise sat and opened her journal. Her soul ran out across the page. She saw some of the group moving around on the beach between camp and the ocean. From this distance, they were no more than abbreviations in the sand.

"What are you doing?" Ivory asked Shonto. The two of them, plus Mende and Pikea, were wandering the woods, making use of the late afternoon coolness.

"Here, take this," Shonto said.

"What is it?" Ivory asked.

"It's sweetgrass. We burn this stuff on the rez. Purifies the spirit of things. I just Love the smell though. Takes me back to when Grandma was alive and I can remember feeling Peace."

"How does it work?"

"I don't know. I guess if you burn anything, it releases its Truth into the air. Sweetgrass just smells sweet.

"I heard an old man once say that sweetgrass started as regular grass in the old times. Then one day a young warrior who was deeply in Love had his heart spilled open on the battlefield. The grass his heart spilled on soaked up his Love, and that's why today sweetgrass smells like it does."

"You believe that?"

"Man, these sacred things aren't about what you believe. It's about what you remember."

"What do you mean?"

"You can believe in Santa Claus, but if you remember seeing your old man drunk and stumbling, putting a used basketball by the foot of your bed on Christmas morning, then what you remember is what lives in you. Not what you believe."

"But I believe in God."

"Do you remember God?"

"What are you talking about?"

"If you want your belief to come alive, then you better start remembering. My uncle told me, 'Whatever is true in Creation can be remembered by anyone. Anytime. It's all a matter of opening your spirit. Humankind's problem is that we are good at forgetting.'

"So if you want God to live in you and not just be an idea you *believe* in, then you better start remembering God."

"How do I do that?"

"By seeing. See God in that willow tree. See God in the sky, in the lake, in the mountain. In the breath of our words. If you see, you'll start recognizing God's true face and nature. Then you will remember."

"You're deep, man."

"Life is deep. I'm just trying to remember." The breeze around Shonto's shoulders like a cape felt soothing. His muscles relaxed, which opened a rusted lid over an old memory. He was nine, just before his 10th birthday when he hoped to gain eagle vision, a new, more mature way of seeing the world. He and his friends Amber John and Sammy Begay were playing kick-the-can in a deep arroyo. Suddenly the summer monsoon howled. It birthed a flash flood. A wall of water raged through the arroyo, catching the three of them off-guard. The water tried to take their lives, and nearly did. Since that day, none of them had managed to shake the trauma. It was the kind of memory, that when visited enough, stole from children their belief in a thing called safety.

Lake and Binda walked down to the beach, seeking reprieve from the noise that humans produce. Ocean, though tidal, was a certain silence of its own. A consistency of sound falling into a hypnotic grace. White noise. *Sometimes people dwell too much in meaning and words*, Lake thought. *We miss out on existence*. The ocean offered respite from distraction. Allowed Lake to come back into herself. Into just being.

Clumps of foam flew from the surf like spittle, and bounced up the sand, propelled by the gusts of high tide. They rolled like tumbleweeds along the beach, eventually losing steam and settling into the sand, giving themselves back to the earth.

Binda smelled the sweet musk rising from the ocean, that unmistakable scent of a universe of marine life living and dying. She drew in deep breaths of it. Wished she could preserve it, like fresh wild berries in a jar. Binda noticed the ocean's scent change slightly, to something more acrid. She wondered about death in the ocean, and just how much of it happened without anyone on land ever knowing. *Instant graveyard* were the words that came to her mind. It was not a morbid thought. It was, a thought of convenience.

As they came to the edge of the water, the ocean moved toward Lake. Binda noticed it. She couldn't tell if Lake did. Lake was looking out at the distant water. But Binda was sure of it. She saw and felt the entire ocean come up to Lake. Like a pet animal would. The water surged over the bare feet of both of them, and the tide was fairly high. But the ocean. The whole ocean. Came for Lake. Binda took a step back in awe and wondered about the power within that a person doesn't even begin to grasp.

Binda sank her bare feet deep into the bold white sand. Beneath the hot surface, coolness enveloped her skin, the grains massaging her as she shuffled forward. Sunlight traipsed the ocean water with its paintbrush. The wind cooled her face, made her spirit feel as though it were flying. Wind always did this to her. She wondered: *How many journeys does the mind make backward into its memories in a lifetime*? The open nature here made her long for a place she had really never known, except through her family. She wished she had grown up there, where her ancestors had. She wished she could be one of them in that way. Not some outsider stranded in a world that could not care less for the people she came from. Nor for their own memories which now carried on in her.

Ivory joined Eloni for a hike over to the estuary. Ivory liked the busyness of the estuary, its varicose highways of activity. From the fish and turtles under the water, to the ducks and geese cavorting on the surface. And the dragonflies and damsel flies. The warbling conflicts. Fevered mating calls. Delirious juvenile horseplay. It felt like the energy of a city. Complete dysfunction, somehow all moving forward collectively. Even the estuary's odors managed to mesh, at odds as they were. Ivory walked the water's edge, thrumming the cattails, ever on the lookout for stealthy predators lurking beneath the rippling surface.

Underwater, a giant salamander shimmied along over the silt, barely disturbing it. The salamander had vestigial limbs, barely developed. It was nearly a snake. Its skin was fire red blotches on a canvas of black. In a flash, it swirled its body in the shallow pool and was gone. A school of fish darted by, a silver spoon of light beneath the surface.

Birds were at work at this hour, splicing the water with their beaks for fish that were themselves feeding on insects in the changing light. "Look over there in those reeds. You see how they're moving?" Ivory asked.

"Yeah, I see a little rustling," Eloni responded.

"A little?" Ivory pushed down on the words. "They're practically dancing. I'm thinking it might be gators... or snapping turtles."

Eloni dropped his head and shook it side to side. "Mmm, mmm, mmm. I'll give you turtles, maybe. But gators? Ivory, you ever hear of *natural territory*? We're a whole lot of miles from gators. But that doesn't stop the conspiracy theories from running wild up in your head, does it?"

"Okay, then *you* go see what it is," Ivory urged.

"I have no reason to do that. Can't you be at peace without knowing what every little thing is?" Eloni asked.

"It's all in the details, brah. Gotta know or gotta go."

"Then let's go. I need to get to cooking."

Pikea and Shonto lay under a monkeypod tree not far from the meadow, listening to the concerto of the cardinals and blue jays. Shonto looked up at Jade Mountain in the background. As the air cooled into its late afternoon persona, the lowering sun lent a lusty red hue to the mountain's skin. It made Shonto silent. *What kind of place is this?*

The monkeypod tree had nurtured its own verdant circle of lush, soft grass around its trunk, grass advantaged to have cover from the sun on hot days, and therefore plentiful moisture in its earth bed. This was prime napping real estate, and more than a couple of friendly squabbles and races to the tree had already broken out.

Shonto grabbed at his leg. "I think I pulled a hamstring snorkeling."

"Maybe you should start stretching before getting out of bed, Old Man. Soon you'll be seizing up like the Tin Man."

"You could give me a massage."

"Ivory doesn't ever take off his shirt," Pikea said, ignoring Shonto's comment. "You notice that? Not when we go to the lagoon, or in the ocean, or when it's baking on the dunes. What is that about?"

"Huh. Hadn't noticed."

"Don't know... Hey, Shonto. Have I ever told you that your belly is drumable?"

"No. In the handful of days we have known each other, you have not told me that. Good to know." His mouth parted into a giant smile that broke the skin of his chapped lips.

Shonto pulled something out of his pocket. "I made you this," he said, placing a small carved wooden turtle in Pikea's hand.

"This is so kind of you. How long did it take you to make this?"

"Just a minute. This morning. Turtle is a symbol of Mother Earth, everlasting peace. When you wear the turtle close to your heart, you will feel the peace and harmony within her."

"Maybe you need one then, brother."

"Yeah. You funny. And here, have this, too." He gave her a single white feather. It was downy, with streaks of faint brown. "Found it on the path back from the dunes. Maybe quail. Or owl."

"I feel like it's my birthday. What inspires all this generosity?"

"You're good people. A little wild, but good."

Pikea pushed him in the ribs.

"Anyway, feathers are a symbol of cleansing the soul," Shonto said. "They carry prayers."

"I just want to curl up and sleep with my head on your belly. Is that okay?"

"Sure. Go ahead." They stayed there, silently, while the monkeypod showered them in blossoms. To Shonto, nothing else on this island could possibly matter.

Ashia joined Binda and Lake in weaving baskets from sweetgrass they had gathered on the way to the dunes. Ashia watched two hawks gain altitude in the sky, then drop steeply. She thought of her own rises and falls. The painful humbling she had been brought through so many times, apparently not learning the lesson sufficiently each time. "When you try too hard to be perfect," she said to no one person, "your insides get wound up like a coil. Eventually, you pop. End up being less perfect than the people you were trying to rise above."

Dinner's aroma taunted the camp. Eloni was offering crab legs dipped in olive oil as an appetizer while he prepared the other food.

"How in the world did you make olive oil?" Ashia asked, slurping down another crab leg, her lips glistening with oil.

"Oh, I extracted it," Eloni said, as though the answer should have been obvious to anyone. "I made some cuts in the skin of the olives, so the oil could get out. Then I put the olives in a glass that I placed inside a larger jar. I found a sand dollar on the beach. It already had holes in it. Perfect for a strainer. I placed the sand dollar on top of the glass, and filled the glass with spring water until it overflowed a little into the jar. Then I let the olives soak overnight, and all day, to let the oil separate from the water, rise to the top of the glass, and overflow down into the jar. When it was ready, I took the glass out of the jar, and voilà, olive oil in the bottom of the jar!"

"Wow," said Ivory. "That's a whole 'nother level."

Eloni boiled plum juice in a gourd that was settled into the water bowl of one of the large rocks at the edge of the fire. Stirring with a length of dried bamboo stalk, he watched for the juice to congeal to just the right thickness, lifting the stalk to see how the syrup dripped back down into the gourd. "Mmm... plum sauce. This stuff's unbelievable with fish, plantains, whatever."

"You're crazy, Loni." Mende said. "I don't even know how you come up with this stuff. Let me just stay out of the way. Sooner we can eat."

Cielo took a big slug of water from a conch shell, smacking his lips afterward and burping. "Amen, Mende. Hey, the water I've been drinking is making me feel more lucid," said Cielo. "More aware. All of us, I think."

"Not sedated, but calmer," added Binda.

"Have you noticed," Mende asked, "that things keep happening here that are impossible, but somehow you don't feel shocked or scared?"

"Like the glowing in the lagoon water?" asked Maricela.

"The raining trees," Shonto said.

"Yeah. Everything," said Mende. "It just happens and it folds into us and we accept it like it's the most normal thing. I feel like we're dream walking."

"That's a good way to put it," Ashia affirmed. "I feel all of this vividly. And it all feels... natural. Even though it's crazy."

"Did any of you notice what I did, with Antonia?" Ashia asked.

Lake looked up. "What do you mean?" she asked.

"I'm not sure. The outline of her body. She seemed to shimmer. Like she wasn't completely there. I have this weird feeling. As though she isn't even real. And I wonder, how did we even get here? Is all this a dream?"

"Do you think we can carry this dream with us, back in the world?" Binda asked.

"That would be the life," said Ivory.

Eloni served up a steaming hot mango wood pan heaping with paella. The paella was chock full of mussels, white beans, saffron and rosemary, olive oil, tomatoes, sweet paprika, and jalapeños. They ate like athletes in training, devouring massive quantities in no time at all.

Balanta came over to Ashia. His expression was softer than usual. His stride truncated. "I cooked this for you," he said, holding out a plate heaped high with a mound of food smelling of brown sugar.

"Is this plantain fritters?" Ashia asked, smiling as she took the plate.

"I did the best I could. Used some of Eloni's spices."

Ashia picked up a bite with her fingers and took it into her mouth. "Mmm... Mmm! This is good! What did you—"

"Family recipe," Balanta interrupted.

A thought sprung up in Ashia. She wanted to join the family. Balanta's family. *Girl, get yourself on track.*

They sat in the sand, eating plantains until their stomachs protested, licking the sweetness from their fingers and beholding an ocean of mysteries.

Ivory walked around camp after dinner, settling his stomach. He approached Promise, Pikea, and Ashia, who were positioned in a tight circle, oiling each other's hair, massaging scalps, awash in sandalwood and vanilla fragrance. "Wow, can I get some of that?" Ivory said, vaguely.

"Ivory, don't start your business," Promise said, her voice cooing from Pikea's fingers on her scalp.

"No, no. I come in peace this time," Ivory said. He reached into the mudcloth sack he was carrying and pulled out three jacaranda pod anklets. "I made these for you."

The ladies broke their trance and reached for Ivory's gifts, their faces brightening. "What are they?" asked Pikea.

"Ankle bracelets," said Ivory.

"You made these for us?" said Promise. "And just when I was about to fire you, boy. You done redeemed yourself." They fastened their anklets and stood, twirling and posing. The sods knocked against each other, birthing a chorus of wood chiming.

"Nice," said Ashia. "I Love the sound these make. I really appreciate this, Ivory."

"Yeah, Ivory," said Pikea. "Sometimes the sweet in you pops up from nowhere. Kind of like a gopher."

"Ha," Ivory pronounced.

"Ivory, will you make me one for my waist?" Ashia asked. "It would be so nice to dance with one around me like that."

"Already ahead of you, sister," Ivory replied. He pulled a waist chain from his bag and presented it to Ashia with a bowing of his head.

"Wow," Ashia said. "This is amazing, Ivory. Perfect. You've got some real skills there."

"I know," Ivory said, beaming. "Don't put out the word yet. I need to get a patent on this stuff. I'm making some for the rest of the girls."

"Women, Ivory," Ashia corrected. "Women."

"That's what I said. Women." Ivory grinned and walked away, redemption thick in his stride.

Shonto was down by the ocean, watching the water colors change as the sun descended. He saw Lake approach the water down shore. She was running her bare feet through the sand. He could barely hear her humming through the soft sounds of the tide. Shonto and Lake had known each other back on the reservation. Theirs was a massive reservation, sprawling over countless miles of desert and plateaus, so their connection was not a given. The system had brought them together. The Correctional System that Shonto felt should go ahead and be honest with itself and call itself the Punishment System. Not because he hadn't known plenty of staff who cared about him, and sacrificed on his behalf, but because the system's policies, he believed, were drenched in a spirit of spite and resentment. Even deep in the southwestern desert, he felt the cold touch of politicians in distant lands satisfying themselves with conceiving *no tolerance* laws for *juvenile delinquents* like him. And where was their *no tolerance* for all the adults who had failed him? Hurt him? Lied to, burned, and scalded him? It was this spirit of vengeance that he witnessed staff and administrators struggle against as they wrestled with their hearts and consciences in making decisions that so often landed on Shonto like acid rain.

Lake came over to Shonto, shuffling through the sand. "Maybe the ocean clears your mind because of the salt in the air," she said, her tone gentle, humble.

"Like a boxer with smelling salts?" Shonto replied.

"Yeah."

"Or, it could be just getting away from human noise," Shonto said.

"For me, it feels like bowing before God," said Lake. "You get to the ocean and you just... grow quiet and still inside. Awe takes over."

A seagull moved past overhead, squawking with tremendous volume, its chest ballooning in and out. "That gull sounded like it had a chicken in its throat," Lake said.

"Yeah, and like the chicken had a frog in its throat," said Shonto.

The seagull circled back and landed. Lake recognized the gull from earlier in the day. Its left leg was contorted upward at the ankle joint. The bird held its wounded appendage aloft, as though afraid to put its weight on the tenderness. It appeared to stare at Lake. She wondered what it might want. "Who are you, friend?" she asked. The gull cawed, pivoted on its good leg, and lifted away.

The ocean bay continued to kaleidoscope toward sundown. Shonto ran his fingers through his bangs, sweeping them to the side. As he did, he saw the spirit of the water rise up around Lake. Translucent and wavering, it nuzzled under her chin, poured over her ears, and washed down over her chest. The water spirit bent sunlight into crimson and opal streaks. It was a prism of iridescence, bejeweling Lake as it curled and danced. Shonto wondered if anyone else could see, back by camp, what he was seeing. Now, the water spirit entered Lake, flowing in through her *Sipapu*, her umbilical place of emergence. Shonto saw Lake's body arch, her eyes dilate. Then, the water spirit gushed out of Lake, out of her every pore. Her body grew gossamer. Clear and luminous. She was water spirit. Shonto kneeled in the moist loam and prayed.

When Shonto opened his eyes, Lake was gone. Assuming she had left him to be at peace, Shonto headed back to camp. But Lake had entered the ocean. She stayed there for a long while. Submerged. When Lake did step from the ocean, she was wearing nothing but a blouse of water and seaweed sandals. As she dressed and walked up to camp, her spirit and body found each other again.

Eloni had asked Maricela if she wanted to walk with him down the beach. They headed up out of the cove, over into another small one. The sand there glimmered with silica and fine grains of quartz. "Hold up," Maricela said. "You walk fast. You can't just enjoy the steps along the way?"

"Come on, Cela," Eloni urged. "You gotta power through if you want to hang with me."

"Oh yeah? What is this, some sort of test? If it is, I'm not applying for whatever position you have in mind."

"Don't act like you're not measuring me up, too." Eloni's voice quivered slightly, his face tensing even as he pushed out a smile.

"Don't put *you* on me, Loni" Maricela said. "That's your stuff, your way. Don't be assuming that's how I am."

Eloni's tone grew sharper. "And just how is it that you think I am?"

"You're hyper competitive, E—lo—ni. You can't help yourself. So, you assume the whole world must be competing with you."

Eloni was silent.

"Don't get a rash over it," Maricela said.

Eloni stared up the coastline, spotting a lone cypress tree outlying from the edge of the woods, though not exempt from the winds. Its trunk leaned severely, and its crown was blown back. "Race me to the tree?" Eloni asked, mustering up a sense of humor.

"Funny," Maricela said. "Why don't we sit and watch the sun go down? It's nearly there now." They sat on a piece of driftwood, its knots stained dark against the bleached trunk.

Eloni thought about his competitiveness. "Maybe once you've been stranded in the ocean, you hug the shore tighter than most for the rest of your life. Even if it squeezes the life out of the shore."

Maricela put her hand to her stomach. She had been feeling the familiar queasiness and off-kilter equilibrium that came to her monthly, but it seemed to have arrived a few days early. "I'm feeling seasick."

"Don't look at the water where it breaks against the shore. Look at it out there in the distance, where it looks like frosting on a cake."

They grew silent as the air changed. A breeze ran through, a subtle messenger. Slowly, with consistent pace, the ocean swallowed the sun. Soon, only an amber glow remained as evidence of what was the day's most radiant jewel.

Ivory had spent dinner stewing over what might be in the reeds. He hardly noticed his food growing cold, or Maricela nabbing his plantains with a grin. As soon as he had blessed the ladies with his jacaranda pod jewelry, Ivory ducked in his cabin, threw on a hoodie and headed for the estuary. In the evening gloaming, forms began to lose their outlines, starting to sink into the shadows. The reeds were beginning to look like dark whiskers along the bank. Ivory assumed his best predator pose and crouched forward toward a thick gathering of reeds. He focused his flashlight at the foot of the reeds, squinting for a glimpse of movement. A bright blue dragonfly or two, plus a hula-hooping moth were all that appeared. As the ground grew softer and muddy water sprang up around his footsteps, he paused to grab a long stick. He used it to separate the reeds, jabbing and twirling like a fencing champion. "Walk through the valley..." he repeated, steeling himself.

He cleared a patch enough to be able to see into the water. Just inside a stand of reeds beyond his reach, he saw movement. *Better get ready if it's a gator*, he thought, calculating his reflexes and speed. *Been a minute since I was in shape.*

With a flourish in the water that flustered the reeds more tellingly, he narrowed his vision and spotted his culprit. *I'll be. It's some minnows. How can something so small move reeds like that?*

His next vision was of 11 hyenas back at camp on the ground, rolling and laughing at his gator-turned-to-minnows. *I better come up with something good.* Pulling his feet up from the mud suction with each step, he retreated to the base of a willow tree and sat down to come up with a suitable fable.

They grew their fire for the night as darkness first began to dye the air. The dunes. The lagoon. Good eating. All of this began to exert its sediment, bringing a sweet fatigue. And with the fire, came stories. They all stared deeply into the burning, its dancing flames heating and hypnotizing them, taking them in spirit to a place far beyond their youthful age. When they did speak, breaking a long silence, it was in the voices of those many generations before their time, and many generations after.

Promise circled the fire, staring into the fierce alchemy of wood and ash. "I had this history teacher who pulled me aside after class," she said. "He told me, 'Promise, you're exceptional for an *at risk youth*.' Can you believe that?"

"What did you say to him?" Binda asked.

"Nothing. I was too off guard. First it tasted like peppermint. Then, by the time I swallowed, it tasted like paint remover."

Promise continued. "And did you ever have a teacher call you out in the middle of class about being in care?"

"This one teacher thought she would be all enlightened after she found out I was in placement. She had the class do a whole section on what it means to be family. So there I am, and we're all expected to talk about our families. What do I say? Do I lie? Do I dog my parents? I didn't know what she expected from me cause she never bothered to pull me aside about it, and I was afraid to get a bad grade, so I made up some stuff.

"I ended up feeling worse than ever about my situation. She just smiled at me the rest of the semester, like we were best friends and she had handed me a bone. Thanks, Teach. Not cool."

Pikea jumped in. "How about when you're walking down the street with your foster parents and you run into kids you know from school, or their parents. I froze up this one time. I didn't know how to explain who these people were who I was with. Felt like erasing myself, just closing my eyes and not existing anymore.

"Afterward, my foster parents said, 'Pikea, we're kind of hurt you didn't introduce us. Are you ashamed of us? You know we Love you like one of our own.'

"First of all, how about how *I* felt right then?" Pikea said to the group. "I was horrified. Ashamed of myself. Second of all, you think I had a script for how I was supposed to introduce you? Did we go over that before you decided that I should be proud walking around with you? And third—

"Of all?" joked Ivory.

"Skip you," Pikea huffed. "Third, what exactly does *like* one of our own mean? That's supposed to make me feel better, you saying I'm *almost*, but not quite one of your own?"

"People talk about housing like it's a given for them," Mende said. "They can't imagine not having shelter, or a place that is their privacy that no one can enter without permission. When I hear the word housing, I think *miracle*. I struggle with believing that I can have housing. I wake up in the middle of the night sweating, with my heart racing, because I'm panicking that someone's going to bust through the door and kick me out onto the street.

"I dream about being evicted more than I dream about anything else. And I can't get warm enough, no matter how hot the room is. I have this cold in my bones that haunts me. I got to stay in a hotel room once for the first time last year. I blasted the heat to the maximum. Something like 85 degrees. My roommate got dehydrated overnight and had to go to the hospital to get an IV. That's the thing about being homeless. It becomes what you believe in. You can't believe that you ever get to own something. Not just a home, but anything. You hoard because you just know whatever comes your way ain't going to be yours for long."

Binda's mind drifted back to that first night out on the street. Her family was woefully unprepared. Their clothes alone made them a target. And they were way too naked with the fear on their face. Recalling this, Binda thanked God that they were fortunate enough to make it through to the next morning alive.

Balanta leaned to Binda and whispered, "Loni's about to rant."

Eloni did not disappoint. "I'm not a freak in a cage for you to poke at with a stick, with your programs and *best practices* and conferences and white papers. I'm a 100-percent certified, grade A, Samoan Love monster, pound for pound the most delectable. You better recognize. Speaking of cages, my juvee was no joke. When I got there, soon as the staff turned their back for a second, the predictable knuckleheads rolled up on me, whispering about, *I better watch my back.* 'What, you think that impresses me?' I said. 'This is my seventh stretch, fool. Get on back to your boys. You don't want none of this.'"

Shonto had his own kindling for the talk fire. "Seems like a lot of juvee staff are trying to compensate for not being in the big leagues, in the adult system. Like they've got a Napoleon complex. They puff up more, talk harder, look harder, act harder. They get more OCD with the rules, too. Whatever they think it means to be a big time prison guard, they do that, times two. I wish they would just chill. Half of them..." Shonto's voice broke.

"I could use a big brother, a mentor, you know? Don't be working out your insecurities on me. Do that on your own time. I don't care how difficult I am for you, I'm still your junior. You're my senior. You've got years on me. That's a responsibility. When children lose their families, shouldn't they be treated with more Love, not less?" Cielo put his arm around Shonto and offered him a swig of some mysterious drink.

"Lake, you don't speak much, girl," Maricela noted. "What's going on in that pretty head of yours?"

Lake laughed blushingly. "To me, it seems like I'm talking all the time. In my head, I guess. When I was little, children used to mess with me a lot. Tied me up to trees and stuff like that. Don't know why. Then, when I got moved, it was even more bad attention. So, I figured, give them less to notice. I tried to fold into nothing. With my clothes, hair... the way I walked. And I went silent."

"Did it work?"

"To a point. Eventually they started riding me about being a silent ghost. Can't win. If people want to tag you for hunting, it's not like you can tell them you're not in season. Once they're drooling over you, you're marked."

"Okay, so why are you still so quiet?"

"Feels good not to have vibrations running through my head. I get enough from the outside world. Why add to that? I like the peace that comes from being away from human presence. Even my own."

"Hey, Lake," Ivory said. "Can you tell us about your thing with water? I mean, I'm trying to understand how you make it appear."

"It's not a superpower," Lake answered, calmly. "I'm not a mutant. It's... an attraction. You know, bees to flowers."

"Mosquitoes to humans," Balanta chimed in. "Those things Love me and Mende."

Binda thrilled to the kinship of silence she was discovering with Lake. She remembered the family stories about her great grandmother and her sister being snatched one day from along the rabbit proof fence line and taken to a boarding school where they were promptly stripped naked, dragged into the shower, and scrubbed so hard with stiff bristled brushes that their skin bled. They were told it was to get the top layers of their darkness off and begin their rehabilitation into being civilized.

The people there cut off her great grandmother's hair, then her language, her identity, and her habits. When her great grandmother refused to stop speaking her language, they cut off her tongue. A big scandal broke out. Staff were fired. Her great grandmother's tongue, however, did not grow back.

Now Binda felt as though she may have inherited her great grandmother's muteness. Especially in the presence of loud, boisterous types who seemed to have a strange inability to coexist with other human beings. They were like dump trucks, blaring their noise wherever they arrived, grinding their gears and rolling over everything small in their path, finally spewing out their garbage and leaving it behind. People like that, she preferred to stay quiet around, in case they got any ideas to cut off her tongue.

As darkness became complete, the moon assumed its sky throne, pushing up into the schools of stars that bowed and surrendered their light. "Look, Binda said. "The moon is down to just less than half now. Looks like a pool of dark ink is slowly spilling over it. In a few days, it will be gone."

"The moon looks like Ivory smiling at night," Pikea joked.

Ivory's face mocked. "Ha. Single ha. Still out on the street, begging for jokes, Pikea." He Loved the attention.

"The moon is walking over the water," Lake said. "That's how my Masaani used to say it." The sea rippled gently, a white carpet ribboning down its center, from the horizon to the shore. Lake fantasized about getting up and walking that carpet to a place beyond sight, all the way until she could smell lamb stew and happiness inside a home.

"Most of the homes I was in, they kept the fridge locked," Shonto recalled. "Made me feel like I was a criminal in lockup. Like, whose food is it? What am I doing here anyways? A lock on the fridge doesn't exactly make you feel like you belong. Not exactly trusted, Loved. You know? I used to dream at night about taking a sledgehammer to those locks and eating everything in one sitting. Still do.

"I have trouble with portions. Either eat way too much, out of fear there won't be enough or I won't find more later, or I eat too little because I'm trying not to eat too much. Man, going from child to adult means you gotta learn how to walk all kinds of tight ropes, get balanced on things that keep slipping away and getting slicked in the rain. I think that's what growing up is all about. Learning how to balance things out. Even if it means you lose your passion for anything at all."

"People liked to put me in the basement, for some reason," Maricela said. "I don't know how many times I ended up in some makeshift room that was just a cleared out basement space. Felt like I was buried underground. I can't stand that feeling. I want to live in a high rise when I can afford it. Highest floor in the place.

"I'm trying real hard to remember my original state," Maricela continued. "The one I was born with. Or maybe my nine months in the womb weren't so great, and I was already getting traumatized. If that's the case, do I even have an original state? Maybe I need to borrow someone else's."

"Break me off some of that fish jerky, Loni," Mende said. "That stuff smells good."

"When my brother was born," Lake said, staring into the fire, "his spirit brought a mystery into our lives. He came out with a distant face. Like a mime. He grew deeper into that state, not out of it. Masaani used to find him napping a lot out by the sheep. Sheep didn't seem to care. Masaani carried him back inside the hogan. I remember the white smoke coming from the hogan smoke hole. Ten minutes later my brother was curled up again back by the sheep.

"He tapped on wood a lot. And bobbled his head back and forth constantly. After Masaani passed, no one else was left to tolerate him, so he got moved by the state. Therapeutic foster care. Then institutions. People started looking at me strange, like they were thinking, *Don't get too comfortable, girl. You're next.*"

The air grew silent. Eloni dug his hands deep into his pockets, his shoulders hunching over like a prime Hawai'ian wave. "Well... I just want to say, I miss my dad.

"He's up for 17 years for aggravated manslaughter. I already haven't seen him in like eight." The words out in the open made them more real than he could take. Tears rose up and covered his face like marsh water.

Firelight flickered in his eyes as everyone grew motionless. "It's not like I have issues or anything. I just wish I could hear his voice. Seems like the sky is missing without that. And I miss his scent. I used to take his shirts out of the laundry basket and smell them before I left for school and after I got back home. You might think that's weird and you'll probably get on me about it, but that smell, it made me feel stronger. It was a potion for me. Made him feel present, like I could breathe his life inside me.

"That's about it..." Sobbing. His. Theirs. Promise stood and embraced him, all silent compassion and sturdiness. The proud Samoan let himself collapse into her arms, a little boy who had just let out his secret. Fire hissed, flames catching sap, popping a subtle punctuation.

Balanta stood with his spear, looking to the sky. "Everywhere I went, people always had papers on me. It was like this one file was passed around to every adult, and they had read it before they met me. Except the file listed all my bad things. Everything bad that happened to me, or that I had done.

"I'm telling you man, I learned to tell when someone had read my *dirt file*. They looked at me like you look at a criminal through the glass in some scared straight program. Or like you look at someone you feel so sorry for. No one actually looked at me. They were glassy eyed, phased out. It's because they were looking at an idea in their head, and trying to pretend they were actually paying attention to me."

"What would you do, Balanta," Ashia asked, "if you were running things and you had a chance to make changes?"

"I would make up a new law that says every adult has to read a list of my good things first, before they ever meet me. Before they get to make decisions about me. I wouldn't mind them reading about my bad things if it wasn't the first thing they learned about me, or if they didn't take some ink on a page to represent the truth of who I am. I'm not 1D, or even 3D. I'm 4D."

"What?" Cielo asked.

"I'm not one dimensional. I'm four dimensional: Mind, body, heart, and spirit. I'm a person. I'm tired of people reading some report and then coming at me like they know me, like they know just what I need. Just once, I want someone to admit, 'I don't know the first thing about you. But I care to. Can we start there?' I'd say, 'I thought you'd never ask.'"

Bad. A word that had draped itself over Binda's life with a totality and varied texture that snuffed out most of the light. A word that fell like dark snow even on bright days, and piled up over all the entrances and exits for Peace during her days. Often, it was a mountain before her, casting its shadow over her, chilling her marrow. Rarely, she was at the mountain's peak, looking down, feeling her power. Feeling triumphant. Binda thought about Balanta's words, how someone seemingly so self-assured and admired as him could be caught in the same cage of negative labels and ideas. The thought left her feeling even more vulnerable.

"Natives, we're not real to people, said Shonto." "We're like unicorns. Or leprechauns. Mist and myth. Even when people meet one of us, they don't think of it as a human encounter. They react like it's an archaeological dig. Like they just found an ancient arrowhead or some pottery. It's a date at the museum for them. They start asking us academic questions like we're their museum guide."

"It's even worse being Aboriginal," Pikea shared. We're not tokens of fascination. We're seen as a blight on the land, dark monsters who don't know better than to put on some clothes and drop our spears and flutes."

"That's what happens when you're a reminder of what someone spends their whole life working to deny," said Promise. "You get a sky full of arrows shot at you daily, at best. At worst, they go ahead and take you out. Basically, the world needs you to not exist, except in vapors that resemble them. Better to be a story told in a book of myths and legends than to dare being an actual human."

Shonto cracked a stone against the trunk of an old oak. "We always joke that Indigenous doesn't mean *First People*. It means, first people, each and every time."

"What do you mean?" asked Cielo.

"First people, each and every time, to get our butts kicked off our own land."

"You funny," said Promise. "I like your humor."

"Native humor is survival medicine," Shonto said. "If you're Native and aren't joking all the time, you're doomed. Too much pain. Fill that soul space with jokes, even bad ones, or pain will come flooding in. And our humor is dry. Like sage. We burn it when we speak, kind of a talk-cleansing for our reality. If you aren't tuned in to the dryness, you miss the humor. It's a private ceremony."

Pikea's mind began to swim in sour memories. "How would you feel being locked up with hard core violent offenders when all you did was get busted with a joint? That, and having been expelled from school for fighting that you didn't even start. Y'all know that kids jump on you when they know you've had to change schools a bunch of times. They sense it on you, like a scent. The scent of rejection and hard times."

She remembered the plague of harshness she encountered when she first arrived at the level four compound. The sounds of lockdown at night pureed Pikea's stomach contents in a blender of anxiety. *This cannot be happening.* Everything was cold to the touch. The toilet and sink. The floor to her bare feet. The walls, door, and even the quality of lighting from the fluorescent bulbs in the ceiling. Most of all, the stares of the other *residents.* Cold, inward stares. Cold, hostile outward glaring. Food, cold. Showers, cold. Somehow, on the exercise yard, even the sun felt cold. Pikea wondered sincerely whether, there in that squalid, humming no man's land in the midst of a scorching summer, she might actually freeze to death.

"Man, we could really be having a good time right now if we had some brew or something," Pikea said.

"Does it always have to be like that?" Maricela asked.

"Don't go getting high and mighty," Pikea said, shooting Maricela a sharp look.

"Don't get your rash up," Maricela said. "I didn't mean anything by it. Just that I don't think drinking is the only way to have a good time. Not judging."

"You sure about that?"

"What do you mean?"

"I mean, you seem to talk a lot about getting away from bad influences, and you seem to time it around things that we say and do here," Pikea said.

"Maybe," Maricela replied, "because a lot of what we say and do here reminds me of just how much we've all been polluted. Me as much as anyone else."

"Okaaay..." Pikea's voice trailed off, doubtful and weary.

Eloni drank the tension with a thirst. "Everybody's trying too hard to show out," he said. "It doesn't have to be that difficult. Just take a breath and figure out if you even know who you are."

Ashia intervened. "Look, we're all learning how to be free here. It's not cool being haunted, and no one taught us how to separate from our pain, and maybe we're not supposed to, because we've been dealing with enough separation. I don't see why we can't learn to hang onto our stuff in a way that helps us, instead of trying to magically make it go away. I vote for what's realistic over fantasy any day."

"Or, how about those so-called youth events where all the sessions are designed for adults?" Ivory asked, blissfully and entirely missing Ashia's point.

"Yeah!" Mende seconded. "Or those youth *empowerment* events where all they do is scold you or try to scare you straight? Where's the empowerment?"

Binda, attempting to return to Ashia's thought, yawned and sighed. "Birth and dying in the ocean, they aren't noticed so much, unless you're living in the water. My friends, they're not living in my water, so they don't notice the emotions that live and die in me, much less understand them.

"Even my own biological family, they don't get what it's like being so sensitive *and* going through living on the streets. I mean, sure, they get pains in their gut from the smell of restaurant food they can't have, or someone's lunch thrown in the trash. But me, hurt flowers inside me every time a child gets yelled at by a parent, even if I'm eight blocks away. I swear, I can feel lemonade sulking as it warms in a glass. And they wonder why my moods are all over the place. Come see what's happening in my ocean."

Binda went on. "I feel safer at night than during the day. At least at night on the streets the darkness protects you from *the stare*. You know, the one people give you. A mixture of hatred, fear, disgust. Like you're less than an animal. That stare haunts my soul. At night, I fold myself into the darkness, wrapping its security blanket around me, and, invisible, I sing myself to sleep.

"Y'all probably know about this one," Promise said. "One time, I came home from school and my foster parents asked me to sit down on the couch. Their eyes were nervous. They were acting all meek. I knew what was coming. I had dreamt it the night before.

"They said, 'Promise, we're so sorry but we just feel we don't have the capacity to meet your needs.'"

—A knowing chorus of "Um hmmm's."

"'Our younger children are uncomfortable with your anger and sullenness. We feel it's time for you to move onto a home that can support you better.'"

"They had already boxed up all my stuff. One box. No flaps, no labels. Just a blank brown box. They didn't ask me what I wanted or how I felt. It wasn't a conversation. It was a conviction and a sentencing. They got up and went to their room. I sat there on the couch, lava rising in my chest. I hadn't even set down my backpack yet from school."

"Man, I feel you! said Pikea. "How about, I came home from school one time and my stuff was in a trash bag! No tie-off, just an open trash bag on the porch, sitting in the rain. No one was even home. They didn't want to have to face me, so they made it comfortable for themselves."

"Yeah, why is their comfort always what comes first?" Mende asked.

"What kind of trash bag?" Pikea asked. "Mine are usually the big black ones. Seems fitting. Colors for a funeral."

Cielo said, "I got one once that had the scented powder on the inside, so all my stuff smelled afterward and reminded me of that home."

Eloni said, "I got a note once on my bag. It said: 'Know that you can always reach out to us.' I did want to reach out. With a fist."

"It's the fact that your whole life can fit in one cardboard box that messes you up," Ashia reflected. "Makes you feel like less than nothing. Like you could easily disappear, your body just blip out of existence, and no one would even blink, much less gossip about you. I'd take gossip over not a single person in the whole world even caring you're gone."

Mood heavy, Lake lifted it tenderly: "They put a candy cane in my bag once. Felt like my first Christmas stocking."

"Nahhh!" the whole group shouted. "That's messed up!"

"How many of you have been told you need to be grateful for what others have done to help you out?" Eloni asked. Every hand shot up, an instant forest of raised arms.

"You know it!"

"Just about every day!"

"I'm so tired of hearing that..."

"How many of you have been told you are ungrateful for daring to express your struggle out loud?" Again, instant forest, bodies electrified with currents of acknowledgement.

"Right here!"

"So many times I can't count!"

"Amen, girl! I'm with you on that!"

Ungrateful. A beetle boring its way repeatedly into Eloni's persona. *Ungrateful.* Stamps of identification filling a passport packed with evidence of sour ventures and unkind destinations. Ungrateful for not being happy, even though he had been placed in good homes. Ungrateful for not grieving his father's incarceration quickly enough. Ungrateful for not getting his emotions together tidily enough. Ungrateful for the way he strained to trust, for his tendency to scowl when the intensity around him became threatening. Ungrateful for participating in panel presentations where he told the truth about his family, and all the forever families he had passed through. Or, more accurately, that had passed through his unforgiving territory.

"So, if I hide my anger, that's supposed to mean I'm grateful?" Eloni asked, rhetorically. "If I just don't do anything but shuck and jive to the beat of people who don't get me, don't feel me, don't want to really know me, that means I'm grateful?"

"Yeah, like we're the only ones that need to be grateful, because after all, what would have happened to us if so and so didn't save us?" Maricela said.

"You mean, 'didn't *slave* us,'" added Pikea.

"I know y'all had some bad times at the places you were," Ivory said. "I have to say that I had some good placements. Two foster parents of mine that were like angels for me. They were older, and retired. My foster mom, she used to take me to card games at her friends' houses. All these older ladies cussing and slapping down bones."

"Slapping what?" Binda asked.

"Slapping bones. You know? Dominoes? I couldn't believe the way they acted when they were alone like that. I Loved it, man. I brought my comics with me and just pretended to read, but really I was watching them like a hawk. It tripped me out how happy they were. I wanted to learn to be like that."

"Ivory, you were just born slap happy," Maricela said.

"No, really, I actually was going through a lot of anger then. For real, I was getting tired of being angry. It was exhausting. I knew it was how people knew me and expected me to be. In some strange way, I woke up every day feeling like I needed to perform being angry all over again or I was gonna let everyone down."

"You, Ivory? Never would have guessed," Promise said, laughing.

"Yup. But those ladies, I'm telling you, they would laugh so hard they would fall on the floor, wet themselves, cry, all of that. And the stories! Man, I never knew ladies like that could be so... raw.

"I knew if I kept on being angry, I was going to blow a circuit before I hit 20. I think it stunted my growth, too. I put so much energy into being angry, I didn't have any left for just being alive. One thing I noticed about those ladies: They talked about their troubles all the time, but they weren't complaining or being heavy. They talked that stuff with a... a lightness. Like they were talking about the clouds passing over in the sky.

"That's when I figured out that I can tame my troubles. It's all about the story. However you tell it, that is what you become. They were telling their stories like they had more important things to do than to fuss and bother with troubles. They made fun of their stuff. Laughed at the most painful, hurtful things. I'm telling you, they laughed it off, just passed around the laughter bowl, taking turns picking up one lady's troubles, holding it in their hands, and laughing their old asses off. For me, that was the beginning of the end of anger."

"Hey, Cielo, you know any Caribbean beats?" Promise asked.

"As I was saying before, I'm free," Cielo replied, pausing from his bongos. "I play all species. Whatever moves me."

"Okay… can you please be moved by some island spirit right now? That sad stuff you're banging is bringing me down. How bout something smooth to cool me out?"

"As she requests, so do I fulfill. And I agree with you, Promise. All this negativity. I wouldn't be alive today if not for a guy on staff who looked after me. I acted like I didn't hear a word he said, but deep down I was lapping up every syllable like maple syrup."

"Why did you trust him?" Ashia asked.

"He wasn't trying to teach me. He was trying to learn me. I could feel it. Hadn't had that before."

"Here's a life skill for you," said Mende. "I can tell which way the wind is likely to blow just before sunrise, and just after. And how long an animal has been dead, based on the smell. And whether someone's going to give you some change or punch you out when you're begging to get some French fries in your stomach."

"Maybe my great grandmother's kidnapping was the start of our family losing the memory of how to be whole," Binda said, her voice just above a whisper.

"Why do some people feel the need to round up other humans like cattle or sheep?" Pikea asked, the warrior in her riled. "Internment camp. Concentration camp. Boarding school. Reservation. Rehabilitation camp. It's all the same. You're trying to squeeze a group to death, like ants. Just wipe them away. What's up with that?"

"Sounds like a crazy amount of fear, to me," Cielo offered. "Why else would you seek to destroy everything?"

"Or like an allergy to the world itself," Ashia said. "Can you imagine? Being allergic to the very environment that you have to live in?"

Pikea threw a thick piece of hardwood on the fire. Her memory found a trail, which she voiced mid-thought: "The chairs in that place were nasty. Things must have been 20 years old. Rusted, dented metal folding chairs. Hurt your butt as soon as you sat on them. And that's all they had for us in the whole group home: In the Cafeteria. bedrooms. Even the Chapel. One guy, Rudy, he went about 300 pounds. Good guy. He had these diabetic nutrition bars that he sold to all of us. Made good bucks, too. Ol' Rudy, he went to sit in one of those chairs during group, and the thing completely blew out underneath him.

His feet did that cartoon peddling thing as they went up in the air. He landed on his can and was cracking up before the rest of us. They had to cancel group cause we couldn't stop busting up. Turns out Rudy had fractured his tailbone. Finally, a group of us had had it. We revolted. We staged a sit-in in the rec center. On our backs, all our feet straight up in the air, like Rudy. Finally, they brought in some new chairs. Padded and clean. I'm telling you, behavior improved overnight. Therapist asked me about it. I told her, 'It's not magic. You treat people decently, they won't act like animals. It's the little things. Paint the damn walls. Fix the light bulbs. Get some windows that let the natural light in. Make the place at least feel like you guys care about us. And have music playing over the sound system. You aren't using it for anything else, except to terrorize us with your Doomsday announcements. Why are adults so afraid of young people having their music? You would have to prescribe half the amount of meds if you just gave us that natural sedative. Our tunes cool us out. Use that.'"

"You were giving her the whole program, weren't you? asked Eloni."

"You know I was, boy. Some stuff is too obvious. Stop trying to control us. Leave us alone so we can heal. I'm so tired of the system." With the phrase, Pikea was sent spiraling into a hole that smelled like concentrated suffering:

The system. A montage of agencies still in the dawning stages of realizing that, territorial as they may have always been, they actually serve the same children and families. A slow light bulb going on, popping and sizzling toward full incandescence. *The system*. Finally realizing that a child does not magically become an adult at 18. That society's responsibility does not end at that arbitrary denomination. And that, believe it or not, actively shepherding and supporting a person into and through the early, shallow water shelf of adulthood actually benefits society with, of all things, productive citizens who *become* that society. Who become that capable population who not only tread water but *swim*. Swim mightily once the shallow ocean shelf of adulthood suddenly drops off into an uninstructed deepness with canyons and abyssal plains so unspoken of, so untranslated, that only whole human beings have a chance of navigating that domain, and staying afloat. Not to mention, reach shore.

No. Such genius insights into the needs of transitioning youth only began to emerge when the voices of these very children began, by an act of God apparently, to be unmuzzled. Air now reaching their lungs, they experienced the very first stirrings of finding their tongues. And of all things to speak of, they spoke of their own lives. They cared nothing for the rhetoric of adults emotionally dependent upon pretty pictures of salvation for children like them. They only cared to roar and bellow their hot, humid, authentic truth. Regardless of how it might wreck the tidy paradigms and ideals so uninspiringly constructed. Regardless of how their truth might sting the skin of the experts and blow down their precious statistically validated fences and enclosures behind which adults seem to hide and crouch and hope all the messy things in the lives of others will have the decency to go away. Or, at least, not blow down their fence.

System. Somebody needing to take explosives and detonate them inside the system. Until all the walls come down and all that is left is a face to face with *them*: Real lives. The kind that defy seminar handouts and slide presentations and demand that people care enough to feel the abject discomfort of empathically *feeling* these children's lives. Feel the need and bruising and possibility. Sensate education, force fed understanding by way of escaping the tranquilizing spaces of intellect and evacuating academic masturbations until, until a child's life could be felt, searing and without conceptual comfort.

Pikea's chest burned. The wetness on her cheeks brought her attention back to the fire. "Okay, people. Can somebody please give me a hug?"

"I've been thinking," Shonto said.

"Uh oh," Lake jabbed.

Shonto ignored the comment. "I know of at least four generations of my family that have been messed up. I heard that my great grandfather drank like a dog in the desert after he was forced onto the reservation. Then, my grandfather tried so hard to deal with life without drinking that he blew a gasket in another direction and beat on my grandma.

"My mom, she grew up seeing that violence and now she shakes like a leaf 24/7 out of pure anxiety. It could be all peace and sunshine and she's still shaking, ready for the sky to fall. Now, here comes me. Don't even know what to call my stuff. Just a ball of anger, distrust, confusion. I guess pain just falls down through generations until it finds a way out. These days here on this island... I'm starting to see that maybe I have a responsibility to my ancestors. Who knows how far back they were messed up. I'm starting to feel that if they couldn't get well, then I'm the next one up in line. Being that I'm currently alive. I feel like I'm supposed to be the way out for the pain. Someone needs to break the cycle."

As the stories continued, Maricela found herself missing her father. Now, *he* was a great storyteller. Manuel "Manos de Cristal" (Hands of Crystal) Dos Santos, whose surname meant *Two Saints*, was really more like half of a saint. One and a half on a good day. This was more than good enough for his precious baby Maricela. Manuel came into his nickname as the unfortunate result of having hands that shattered like glass when he landed a blow in the boxing ring. This was not a good thing for an aspiring middleweight champion.

Manuel, *Manos*, grew up in deep admiration of the legendary Panamanian boxer Roberto "Manos de Piedra" (Hands of Stone) Durán, who hailed from Manuel's family's ancestral town of El Chorrillo. Though Manuel's people had long since left El Chorrillo for various parts of Mexico, eventually settling in the U.S., Manuel retained a deep pride in his connections with

Durán, basking both in their shared Panamanian roots and in the fact that Durán's own father was of Mexican descent, from Arizona.

One early October day, after Maricela came home from school, Manos sat his daughter down on the couch, and with glistening eyes, he did his fatherly best.

"Mi'ja, I know you have a lot of women in your life who are raising you to have a certain idea of what a woman is. But, mira, mi'ja. I'm your father. I am responsible for raising you to be a lady. You know the difference between a woman and a lady?" Maricela was already deep into an uncomfortable heart palpitation, wondering where this was going.

Not waiting for her answer, Manos continued. "Many women serve men and their male ideas of a woman. But a lady honors herself and her Godly sacredness. And as a man, I have to tell you, mi'ja, before I die, the one thing I care about achieving is to raise you to be a lady. Me comprendes?" No, she did not comprehend. But she listened. She always listened to her father. Didn't talk back, roll her eyes, dare to cut off the conversation. She carried a deeply embedded deference to this man, this bull chested, brawny armed, intense eyed, soft-hearted warrior poet who had once seduced her mother with Love lyrics written on the back side of fortune cookie paper strips. Maricela always listened.

"You know what, Maricela? My greatest prayer from this point out, for the rest of my life, is that my baby girl, mi pajarita, grow up to walk in the world in such a way that when people see her they say: *There goes Grace.* That's it. I don't want nothing else. God's been good to me. More than I can say. But this last prayer, if my daughter becomes Grace, I'll spend eternity praising His Holy name. This is about you treating yourself like the greatest treasure on earth. And letting the world see the *person* you are. Not the flesh. Whoever comes to you for your flesh will not Love or honor you, mi'ja. This I swear to you. I want my baby to be bathed in Love, and polished in honor, for the length of her life, and ever so long after I am gone. So Love yourself this way, mi'ja. Don't be just another person passing on the lie of what a female is. That would break my heart. Be the moon, baby girl. Be the precious places of the universe. Let the Light know your name."

Maricela, listening to her father speak in words and spirit with which she was not familiar, was quieter now than the absence of noise. Quieter. Knees drawn close, hands firmly on her thighs, elbows locked. Looking deeply into his eyes. Hot. So hot. Yet another kind of feeling, too. A warm tidal movement. Aware that this, what this intense, sweating, nervous man is speaking to her now, no matter how raw or imperfect or rambling, this is Love.

"Let's dance." Ashia was lifting her long, billowing white cotton skirt, already toeing the sand to an internal beat. "Hold on. Ladies, follow me." They followed her into her cabin. The cabin, even with only six souls inside of it, sounded like a marketplace. Teeming conversation. Laughter. Hooting and squealing.

"What are they doing in there?" Mende asked.

"Learning how to be women." Cielo answered.

When the six of them returned, they were wearing Ivory's handmade jacaranda pod chains around their waists or ankles. "Don't worry, Ivory," Maricela said. "We shared. We have plenty for now." Ivory's smile popped out, a floodlight.

Shonto had them all chew yarrow blossoms and roots like the Zuni do before fire dancing. Mende, Balanta, Promise, Pikea, Shonto, and Cielo all began taking turns drumming and dancing. Ashia, Binda, Maricela, Ivory, and Eloni let down their daytime composure and broke free into dance. Ashia moved her hips so fluidly, it was hypnotizing. The jacaranda pods around her waist clattered their approval, creating a transfixing blend of motion and sound. The sound of jacaranda pods on the others mixed with drumbeat, creating a soul elixir. A musical matrix from way back before way back. Their faces wore the fire, and were streaked and smoldering. Limbs swayed, hands reaching for starlight, for the candling crust of moon. Eloni lost his shirt. Ivory lost his mind, braying out a strange spiritual of sorts, tears painting his face in glistening element. Drumbeat grew louder. Became a lion. Became the entire pride.

Lake danced, too, her feet bare and joyful as they landed on the earth, feeling its warm chest, drumming its broad skin. Though this was for her a ceremonial dance, it wasn't complete, like the green corn dance of the feast days. For it to be complete, you needed your people with you, your relations, in order to give dance to the earth properly. People who knew the old ways, even as they increasingly ridiculed them, deeply insecure to be seen and accepted as modern. As human. So, though this was ceremonial, it was also Lake getting down. Her grin stretching its boundaries, she sang an old song inside her chest, a strong vibration of medicine words. Celebration words.

"I hear you there, Lake," Ivory said, out of breath as he moved. "What are you chanting?"

"We don't chant. We sing. Just like you. Actual words. With meaning and everything."

"Sorry. You know what I meant. It's just good to see you do your thing."

Lake was lost inside her thing, the group's voices drowned out, as if under water. Lake drummed the earth, bringing back her pueblo to her as she circled the fire, bringing back the reservation and its contradictory elements of sacredness and sacrilege. She danced fiercely, her thighs pistoning and pumping, her calves lifting. Her body curved into the posture of Kokopelli, her back slightly hunched, as though she were tending the earth, and she was. Tending the source of her emotions. The place of her emergence. Lake danced, her arms not moving randomly but with practiced purpose, picking blessings from on High, placing them in her hand-woven spirit basket. Her arms shaking gourd-painted rattles present only in spirit. Her arms reaching low to pull up the next generations from their roiling creation bath. Pulling down ancestral blankets and memories and stories from the sky. Lake danced.

And she was night, bold and silent and cathedral. And she was day, drawn and musical and naked. And she was the perfect rhythm for this perfect moment by fire and sea singing its pitch and fall, its howl and roar. Syncopated and synthesized. All glory and chaos siphoned into a precise channel of motion and sound. To call up the law of *being*. To punctuate this moment's dawning existence. Sealing the clear glass bottle of this memory so that it might withstand endless tumbling in an ocean's natural turmoil, a young life's unnatural spiraling and jagged stepping. She was Love determined to succeed itself, against so many failures in her atmosphere. She was a prism of light, pushed out of the mouth of Spirit, looking to land on a patch of deadness and bring it to life. She was giving, not taking. *Giving*. Lake danced.

Not wanting to retreat from the warmth of the fire, Ivory fetched a large log and tossed it onto the glowing mound of wood and embers.

"Okay, Ivory," Maricela said. "Now you get to stay up all night watching over the fire. You ever heard of building a fire for warmth, not so it can blind a space satellite?"

After they broke from the fire, they drifted, some to their cabins, some back down to the beach. Pikea noticed Cielo's eyes misting. She caught up to him as he moved toward the water. "Cielo, can I teach you something from my people?" Pikea asked.

"Sure, what is it?"

"It's a way we greet each other, especially two people who are close. It's a way of connecting, and showing honor. It's called *hongi*. Here, stand up. Now, we lean our foreheads toward each other, sort of like a bow. Good, and we go all the way until our foreheads touch. Yes, and close your eyes. Let our noses touch, too."

"Okay. Now what?"

"Now, you take in a deep breath of my spirit, my *ha*, and I take in yours the same way. In that inhale, we connect, all the way back to our ancestors. It is a merging of your essence and mine. Then, we gently let the breath back out, except in our minds we are exhaling good spirit, peace, back into each other.

"And now, we release. See? simple."

"That was cool."

"Yeah, something from the old days. It helps me feel grounded. Seems like everything in life makes you float up in the air, no roots. I don't like that feeling of separation."

"What makes me feel grounded is running the palms of my hands over surfaces," Cielo said. "Especially trees and rocks, or walls and anything that has some texture to it."

"So, sounds like what you do with nature is like what we just did. A form of hongi."

"I guess you're right. What you're saying makes me realize that I like to be in touch with things. And then, again, I like to have my space, too."

"A butterfly isn't always landing," said Pikea. "It has to take off, too, and be up in the air so it can land each time."

"I Love monarch butterflies. I used to read about them all the time," Cielo shared. "You know, they migrate over 2,500 miles from Mexico just to get all the way to some milkweed. It takes generations for the entire trip to be made.

"I read recently that because the milkweed is being destroyed, the monarch migration is being threatened. I wonder, at what point does the will to go away and come back home get overtaken by the pain of the journey? If I were a monarch, once I got to the milkweed, I might just stay. Find a warm spot somewhere to ride out the winter, and not go back down South."

"Then again," said Pikea, "you might just decide to stay in Mexico and not go through the trouble of 2,500 miles."

"That, too," Cielo smiled.

"Hey, Cielo? Promise me that when you're an adult you're not going to go zombie, okay? That would break my heart, seeing you on cruise control, afraid to take risks or think for yourself."

"Don't worry, sister. No stable for this wild stallion. If you find me living like a donkey, pulling a wheel around and around, put me out of my misery. I'm not built for that."

"I hope not. I wonder how many people start off saying the same thing, then the years settle in, and before they know it, padow! Zombified."

Ashia found Balanta sitting up the beach. She could tell he was far away. "Do you mind if I sit with you?" Ashia asked.

Balanta looked up, his spirit coming back into his eyes. "Yes. I mean, no. Please, sit," he said, scooting over on the sand. They were quiet, mostly.

"Why are we drawn to sundown over the ocean even more than over land?" Ashia asked, unsure about speaking into the quietude.

"Light and water have always made us feel closer to heaven," Balanta said. "Especially when they touch." The way Balanta spoke the words made Ashia swallow softly. Her locs were tied high on her head. She unwrapped the indigo cloth and shook her hair free. It covered her shoulders.

"Why have you been limping?" Balanta asked. He glanced at her for one of the few times since she had joined him.

Ashia flushed at hearing he had noticed. "I stepped on a thorn or something," she said, her tone dismissing any concern.

"Come here. Let me look at that." Balanta's voice was soft. The words poured over his lips like warm water. Ashia was taken aback by the effect this had on her. She looked into Balanta's eyes. She was unsure.

He took her foot in his large hands. His long fingers cupped her foot like a flower blossom. Ashia's stomach turned nervously. *Oh man. His touch feels sooo good.*

"That must hurt," Balanta said as he inspected the small but deep incision marking the bottom of her foot. "I'm just going to press a little, I'll be careful."

Ashia braced herself and groaned as the tenderness was touched into a sharper pain. "Sorry. I think you may still have something in there. Do you mind if I try and suck it out?"

"Okaaay..." was Ashia's yielding reply. She wasn't enthused to feel more pain, though she was intoxicated by the way it felt to have Balanta so close to her. So attentive. And his hands felt like strength pulsing against her skin. Her mind took her to the lagoon, and a vision of Balanta and her naked and swimming close in the night. She almost gasped audibly before shaking her head free of the thought. *Girl...*

Pikea and Promise washed their hands and faces in the brook behind camp before getting ready for bed. "Shonto seems to be up on you," Promise said. "You feeling him?"

Pikea laughed. "He's cute, in a shrubby kind of way. But no, it's not like that. I feel like we have potential to be good friends."

"Oh! Friend zoned!"

"Stop it. I really like his heart. He's cool to talk to. Plus, he makes a good pillow."

"Pikea, you're a mess."

"That's right. And don't you dare try to clean it up."

"Hey, Ivory, hold up." Maricela called out, jogging over to him. "I wanted to thank you again for the waist and ankle chains. That was so sweet of you. I can't wait to dance in those again."

"You're welcome," Ivory said. "I like making things like that. This place, she has so much to work with."

"How do you know the island is a she?"

"Feels like a she."

"How so?"

"My gramma used to hold me a certain way in her lap when I came home from school. Like she was squeezing the story of my day out of me, and putting back inside some comfort to soothe whatever hadn't felt good since I left home that morning. I feel the island holding me the same way."

After a pause, Ivory said, "I'm trying to figure out what this is."

"What do you mean?"

"This place. Our time here. Either this is the beginning of sunshine, or this is the beginning of rain."

"Ivory, stop dancing on graves."

"What do you mean?"

"It's best not to get too good at calling up the bad stuff. Least that's what I've learned. Leave it buried. Not that you shouldn't deal with it. Just don't start scheduling meetings with it when you should be dancing to beautiful music."

"I like how you put that. I guess I got a thing about that, huh?"

"Yes, you got a thing about that. Sleep well tonight, Ivory."

Ivory hugged her, kissing her on the cheek. "You too, Maricela."

Balanta, Eloni, and Mende settled quickly into their cabins, each of them weary. Soon, Balanta and Eloni noticed Mende jerk back and forth in his sleep, his skin wet, eyes clenched tightly just like his fists. He spasmed once, and again, his gut contracting inward as though we was being punched. His words were mostly lost in a slur of dream language, but Eloni could make out the gist: "I left that for you already. Didn't you see it? Why can't you see it? I left it last time. I keep leaving it for you. Why don't you see it?"

"When he has nightmares like that," Balanta shared, "I call it Mende writing letters to ghosts."

Cielo and Ivory entered their cabin, kicking off their shoes and stripping down. Cielo lit a match. Quickly, the cabin filled with the sweet fragrance of Nag Champa incense, ribbons of smoke dancing up the ceiling, draping it in clouds washed in word.

Ivory stood up from his crouch and slowly pulled his shirt off over his head, grimacing. As he stretched and lifted, Cielo noticed, even in the darkness, the skin, puffed like dark pink caterpillars crawling all over his back, pulling tightly against his unscarred territory. The scars looked to Cielo like a bonsai tree.

Shonto stood outside, facing the water, giving his offering before sleep. The day ran through him. The dunes. Lagoon. The stories and dancing. The way the water spirit came to Lake. Gratitude swelled his chest in unusual places. As though an aneurism was ballooning in an artery. He wasn't sure what to make of the emotion. He ended his prayers in his usual way: "...All my relations."

All my relations. Three words echoing inside of Shonto all his life. Sometimes they visited him as a taunt, as if to say, *You will forever be separated from all your relations.* Sometimes the words were a security blanket. A reminder of spirit companionship. A reassurance that he would never truly be alone. Now, for the first time, the words activated the truth of all Creation inside of him. And all around him. Instantaneous reverberation of all things. A web. He, a strand in the matrix. *All my relations.* A tingling erupted into quaking and rippled his cells, his flesh, his being. Sensation climaxed. He was aloft in the Great Tension. His body ceased to be. He was sacred smoke. Mist. The imagination of rain. *I am all of this.* More than a thought. A manifestation. From the farthest tree, the most distant mountain, to the nearest molecule of air. *I am all things. All things are me.* The strong son of struggle released his waters and became a flood.

Lake could feel the familiar tightness and tenderness in her body, as she changed for bed. It made her sleepy. *Great. Cramps.* She wondered if the other girls, sleeping together in close quarters and being around each other all day, would synchronize so quickly that they would start their moon times, too. When Lake's first moon time came, the summer before she turned 13, she was at the park with some friends, arcing high on a swing. When she slid off, she felt a strange wetness on the underside of her thighs and bottom. Fortunately, her Masaani had told her many times that when her first river came, she must not be ashamed, for she would now be in possession of the sacred gift of generations. Still, this did not entirely take the sting away when the younger boys who of course walked by just in that moment, saw her offering, still glistening on the swing seat, and commenced to theatrically voice their disgust and revulsion.

Lake simply turned from them and walked home. There, she stripped down in the bathroom, and looking at her face and body in the mirror sufficed herself by saying, "Well, at least I'm not bleeding to death, and I wasn't in class," which was her greatest fear for the previous two years as she anxiously anticipated the arrival of what older females were calling her womanhood.

Lake wondered if maybe manhood was a simpler thing. In the years to follow, she came to believe that life is a mystery, no matter how your body and mind are wired. She stopped stressing herself out so much in attempting to understand. Her friends thought she was strangely calm. Lake wondered why so many people chose to be anything but that.

Binda felt as though her soul's baggage, so stuffed away, had been exhumed, laid out on a butcher's block, and banged at with a tenderizing hammer. Quickly, she fell into a pronounced sleep. The kind that blooms with visceral dreams. Sometimes, Binda dreamed of being a rabbit. Panicked and sweating, dashing alongside the rabbit-proof fence, dying to find a hole. Her heart beating so far beyond its capacity, she tasted blood in her throat. Felt the shredding of her arteries. Her eyes welling up, causing her vision to perceive water level rising, her going under. Scampering, darting, looking for that hole in the fence. If only I can find that hole, I can get away, we can escape. I can bring great grandma back. And great great grandma. It's up to me. Need to find that hole in the fence. That hole in the force that oppresses us. The mountain that keeps dropping from the sky, squashing us out of existence. She is a rabbit. Coat matted and wet. Breath exhausted. Muscles trembling. Then a gunshot obliterates her hearing. Someone is shooting at me. She darts left. Then right. Another gun blast. Now, she is a rabbit looking for a hole in a fence and being shot at. Why can't they leave us alone? Her dream won't end. She is a rabbit, running, and there is no more fence. Just wide open prairie. Is this freedom? Panting and soaked, she considers the taste of freedom, and while she is tasting, she comes upon a cave. No, it is a mouth. Mouth of a gigantic beast. Drooling and retched and rotting inside. It wants to eat her. And all she can do… is sit there, paralyzed and soaking, considering the taste of freedom that now is retreating from her tongue, evaporating in the air of a malicious sky. Binda is a rabbit, wishing the fence had truly been rabbit proof, that she had never found the hole, and that she had never tasted freedom.

Night at 3 a.m. was dire dark. Like it was squeezing its eyes closed against any possibility of light. Eloni stirred, noticing a light around Balanta's head under the covers. "Why are you always up all night, Balanta?" Eloni whispered in a deep, sleepy rasp.

"Sorry," Balanta responded. "Nocturnal, man. Always been like that. I used to sneak and read comics under the sheets with a flashlight, after lights-out. Staff would catch me and act like I had just been busted building a bomb. But I felt safe under those covers, and actually happy flying inside of those comic pages, like a bird. I was free."

"Don't you get tired being up so late?"

"Exhausted. I've been wiped out all my life, especially at school. But I can't help it. No matter how tired I am during the day, around nine or 10 at night, my spirit seems to come alive. It opens up and all these other worlds come through. It's like… when I'm most alive."

Mende was awake, listening to the conversation. He stared at his brother with an intense sibling intimacy. Mende noticed how Balanta's eyes were nocturnal. Dark and searching. Not stealthy, but sharply alert. At first glance, calm appeared from Balanta's glance. Look close enough, and you could glimpse a frothing. Balanta was a redwood among less solid yet more fluid trees. He stood well in the wind. Mende sometimes felt his brother reaching the point where pressure might break him, only because Balanta refused to bend. Being brothers with such a tree was like walking with a giant through a maze that sometimes required contortion to get through. Mende had always been afraid that the giant would bust through the maze and leave him behind. More often, lately, Mende squirmed to avoid another fear: that it was he who would get through the maze, and be faced with a decision to leave the giant behind.

Balanta was haunted by whispers in his head of others scorning his family, shunning them as unclean, filthy, inhuman. From that first night in the shelter, with its aggressive smell of cleaning products mixed with the scent of human fear and body odor, to the revolving door of foster placements, and most of all at school. The worse rejection is always from your peers. And even though he was well regarded, admired, he was lost inside his own horror movie in which he and his family played the dirty, pitiable street urchins. And in this movie, he was sure that his schoolmates thought one thing alone when they looked at him: untouchable.

And so, Balanta became obsessed with making himself, and by extension his family, touchable. He hitched onto cleanliness in the extreme. He brushed his teeth too often and too hard, regressing his gums. He showered repeatedly, drying and rubbing raw his skin. His nails were too clean. His hair, too clean. His body scent, erased. He scrubbed his classroom grades all the way to straight A's. Whatever possessions he was afforded, he cleaned to a shine. Wherever he slept could never be found unmade, even while he was sleeping there. Sheets tucked tight and tense.

Balanta cleaned his language, his behavior, even the way he walked, all to effect an image of cleanliness, praying to counter the noxious ideas circulating about his family. He cleansed himself to the point of becoming a sanitized persona, sealing away the textures of his soul from public exposure.

And he made sure to cleanse Mende, too. That's how Mende felt about it, all the prodding and scolding and reminders to tidy up this and wipe up that. Mende felt like contaminated ground, with his brother called in for the cleanup project. He failed to see the Loving desire of his brother that Mende be embraced positively by the world, in spite of their family's struggles. Little brother could only see self-serving control in these impulses. It left him feeling dirty. And it hurt. It made him want their parents.

Yara Akushan was born in Sierra Leone, raised in Guinea Bissau, and schooled on the university level in the States, which is where she met the boys' father, Shanté Absolom, a schoolteacher with visions of leading an African-centered educational revolution. They relocated to Ghana, to a small peach-colored home at the outskirts of Accra. When Yara became with child the first time, she and Shanté decided—or rather, he decided and she followed—that they would name the baby in honor of her tribal heritage. Yara's family was from both the Balanta tribe of Guinea Bissau, and the Mende tribe of Sierra Leone.

Balanta was born in an apricot orchard, quite suddenly, interrupting a picnic Yara and Shanté were having. The story goes, Balanta's first sight was of a plump apricot falling directly toward his face as he stared up, wet and wailing, into the leafy canopy. Yara moved swiftly, the apricot just barely missing Balanta's face.

By the time Mende was born, only 10 months later, Shanté was already deep into a significant mental illness, which had cost him his job, and the family their means of provision. Yara poured herself as much into caring for Shanté as she did for her two babies. Shanté could be quarrelsome and brusque with authorities, and as a large dark skinned man, the combination did not bode well for the way the family was treated by the various social systems on which they increasingly depended.

On Balanta's third birthday, with Mende just having belatedly learned to walk with a degree of stability, the family found themselves huddled at the door of a shelter at 8:00pm on a cold evening. Yara and Shanté were silent, shocked and ashamed. Balanta was angry at having had to leave his bedroom and belongings behind. Secretly, he was also horribly scared.

Mende was bouncing excitedly at this apparent new adventure, tugging on his big brother's shirt and asking an endless train of questions about whose house they were visiting and did Balanta think they had a lot of toys. Through Grace, and the goodness of their community, they gathered the money to gain passage on a ship to their new hopeful nation. Within a week, they were back in a shelter, and Shanté Absolom's size and Blackness were an even greater threat in their new and hopeful nation.

Maricela turned over, waking as she noticed a light from within Ashia's sleeping bag. "What are you doing up so late?" she whispered.

"Sorry if I woke you. Just reading."

"You didn't wake me. Woke myself. What are you reading?"

"Just an old book about female rites of passage among the Ashanti. Reading relaxes me. Mind's been restless."

Ashia read books like many people ate popcorn. With an obsessive-compulsive gluttony. She devoured biographies. Tubman. Truth. Che Guevara. Gandhi. Toussaint. Patrice Lumumba. Steven Biko. Johnson Sirleaf. She had a thing for revolutionaries. Was drawn to lives of sacrifice. Those who gave away privacy for the public blender of passionate hate and idolization. Gave for a greater purpose. And suffered, along with their families, great pain in return. She wanted to know how Jesus felt on the cross. Really know. When she was a little girl, in church, she would see Jesus up on that cross on the sanctuary wall, and she wanted to climb up there and just hold him tight. And she wanted to whisper a question in his ear: "Will they do this to me, too, one day, if I choose to be like you?"

Ashia's dad fed her books like porridge. Old, tattered paperbacks. Stained library hardcovers. He believed that if he could pour enough of the world into her, somehow she would develop a homing beacon that led her to travel and experience the world. His was a navigational motivation. He was trying to set his little girl to sail, to breach the limitations and boundaries of his own life, escaping the oppressive tethers of his generations. He only let Ashia stay up late past her bedtime if she was reading. If she was, he even replaced the batteries on her flashlight so she could remain lost between the pages until sunrise.

Ashia Loved physical books that you could hold in your hands. The way they so graciously received fingerprints, sweat, blood smears, even sand grains and dirt, flower petals drifted down on that particular day, pollen and dust. Real books were repositories of the days and moments in which they were touched. Read. Integrated into Ashia's being. The pages smelled of glue and organic matter. Wood, its pulp somehow still alive and telling stories. With each book she began, her ritual was to place her nose in the crannies of the pages, close her eyes and inhale. It was for Ashia like falling into a new dream. Or relationship. Books had their scents, like people. She grew bound to them easily. They were one of her few nostalgias that had survived the journey from girlhood.

"I'm sure your mind *is* restless," Maricela poked.

"What do you mean?"

"Don't think I haven't noticed the way you look at Balanta. And don't think I haven't seen how he looks at you. You two might as well get on with it."

"Sush. Okay, so, he is kind of..."

"Hot? It's not illegal to say it."

"Stop. Okay, this might sound typical, but he's mysterious. Not like unknown. More like, I feel an urge to know him."

"Oooh... you're already slippin'. You two would make a good couple. Seem to have good chemistry. Go 'head, Ashia. Days are short here. No time to waste."

"You really feel like he might be attracted to me?"

"Don't be coy. You must have noticed."

"I feel him looking sometimes. But then, he seems to be looking at everything. All the time. And what about you, miss nosy? I see you and Eloni fussing, pretending you can't stand each other."

"You say. He's brutish. Anyway, I'm not sure I can be in a healthy relationship. That's too wide open. I like to have walls on three sides, so I know I'm protected while I focus on what's ahead. In a relationship, it's no walls. All four sides to the wind. I've tried to get in that, and stay in that. It feels so naked, it hurts."

"One day you'll have to get over that," Ashia said, "unless you want to spend your days like an old dusty cobweb in a barn."

"Stop reading that book. Get you some sleep. And tomorrow, be about it. Good night." Maricela rolled back over and pulled her bag over her head.

"Good night, guru." Ashia's heart was thrumming. Sleep for her was nowhere near.

DAY THREE

Something piercing and alien shocked the silence. "Ants! Ants in my pants!"

Ivory's hollering woke up the camp with a jolt of alarm. Most of them made it outside in time to see Ivory bolt out of his cabin with his shorts down to his knees, buck naked except for his tighty whities which were hosting some furious hand action as Ivory desperately brushed away his assaulters.

"Ivory! Man up! Get 'em, boy!" Balanta, Mende, and Maricela were already on the ground, crying laughter. Pikea and Lake were folded over at the waist. Only Binda registered a modicum of compassion, but even she was grinning hard.

"Run to water, Ivory!" Eloni was already rushing at him with a full bucket of sea water, on hand for putting out the fire.

Ivory hot danced toward Eloni, knees high kicking, hands still burrowed in underwear, screaming and exclaiming. "Get them out! Please!"

Just before Balanta and the rest died of laughter, Eloni swamped Ivory in the crotch with the water, which only caused Ivory to squeal in pain. "Ow! You bruised my stuff!"

A quick pause to assess the clearance situation, then panic resumed. "The ants survived the flood!" Ivory's voice was hoarse by this point, his scream the texture of grain on gravel.

"Get your black butt back in the cabin, strip down, and stop playing, Ivory!" Maricela was a natural field marshal, Ivory her willing subject. Realizing he was just about naked before the others, embarrassment shot up inside of him like mercury in a boiling thermometer. Humiliation propelled him back inside his cabin. By the time he reemerged in fresh clothes, head held lower than low, order had resumed in camp, out of sheer exhaustion more than anything else.

"Ivory, one thing about you," offered Balanta, "you're rock solid for some laugh medicine. And that's what we all need right here." Unspoken in the group was the instant recognition that wounds need certain alternate energy in order to heal. And that laughter resides atop the list.

It was early in the day. Early enough for the sight of the sun to still be but a hoped-for thing. Frost decorated sagebrush and willow crowns. Large blue birds and small finches clamored and jounced, children released from night's curfew.

"You want to go to the dunes with me?" Eloni asked Maricela.

"No, you go on ahead," Maricela said. "I'm sure some of the others will go with you. I don't feel like setting my legs and lungs on fire. Or picking sand out of my ears." It wasn't about the sand. What she really felt was a sort of dislocation. Not in a troubling way. She wanted to stay in this feeling. This feeling... new.

New. These were souls used to dealing with new. New placement. New peers. New rules and regulations. And yet, theirs was a world of the same old expectations: disappointment, threat, uphill climbs. Feeding on crumbs of belonging and beauty while it seemed as though the whole world was feasting on a meal.

Breakfast was fried potatoes with sautéed onions, tomatoes, chopped garlic, and red peppers. Seared bass with black pepper and caramelized watercress. Fresh cut melon. Dried apples dipped in maple syrup. Tortillas sprinkled with cinnamon and nutmeg, browned in almond butter. And fresh squeezed peach and orange juice with lemon zest. Ivory finished before the rest, growled loudly in satisfaction, and started pacing, anxiously. "Today, I am a panther," he announced to a null audience.

The others ate eagerly, quietly, savoring the bites. Everything tasted fresher, more acutely sweet, tart, rich. Flavors lingered, coated throats pleasurably. Binda and Lake shared some of their food with the birds who were learning who to approach and who not to. Strong black coffee and fragrant jasmine tea painted the air with their brush quills of steam. Morning sang a song of stillness and peace.

After eating, Lake found a stick the length of her forearm and walked out to the sand. She sat and placed the stick in the sand, letting it move to its own mood. She wielded the stick as a calligrapher's brush, parting grains with a slow, rhythmic crawl. The sand's blank expression became swirls, circles, symbols. Outlines of mountains emerged. Shapes of people. Some in groups. Others singular. The sand's face grew larger until it was twice as large around as Lake was tall. One pattern kept showing up in the sand. Lake didn't want it to. But it did. "Stick, you're not amusing me," she said, putting it down on the ground. "I see enough for now." She walked away, wondering if the ocean would come up high enough to claim this story in the sand.

Cielo followed the faint wisps of clouds as they curled in the sky. Down by the shore he found Ivory, who was sitting with his legs crossed, his eyes closed tightly, repeating a phrase over and again. "Oh, Manny! Pod my own..." Ivory chanted, his voice reverent and full of vibrato.

"What are you doing there, 'migo?" Cielo asked, his face warming in amusement.

Ivory opened his eyes and released a deep breath. "I'm meditating. You know, reciting the classic Buddhist mantra."

Cielo smiled, politely. "You know, I believe the actual words are, *Om Mani Padma Hum...*"

"You sure about that? I learned the street version. It goes, *Oh, Manny! Pod my own...*"

"So, who is Manny?" Cielo's tone was respectful, without judgment. "And what does *Pod my own* mean?"

"I figure Manny was an OG from back in the day, over in India. A Robin Hood kind of dude. Spiritually benevolent. That's why they meditate to him. *Pod my own*, don't know what that means. Something about self-containment."

"Yeah. I guess I've heard it both ways," said Cielo, turning to conceal a smile. As he walked away, he added, "Keep practicing, hermano. Keep on the path."

Balanta, Mende, Eloni, and Promise had set out for the dunes not long after the sun began to announce its intentions over the horizon. They knew the sand was a sponge for solar heat and they wanted to get into it while the air was still cooperative.

They entered the woods. Water coating the foliage hadn't quite become frost overnight. It was sluggish dew, cloudy, on the verge of metamorphosis. The drops' tensile surfaces vibrated to the leaves' microscopic movements. Each time someone brushed against the leaves, the drops broke into cold fine mist.

Balanta led the way. Promise kept right up. "You're strong, Promise. Where'd you get those hiking legs and lungs?"

"I used to live in this one home where the only bedroom window was up so high, and was so small, I couldn't hardly see out of it. I'd spend all night jumping up and down, just so I could see the moon, the stars, anything outside of that place so I could keep from losing it."

"How long were you there?"

"Almost two years. Two years of hundreds of squats and jumps a day. Thousands a week."

"Man, I bet you had springs. Think you could dunk?"

"Don't know about all that. Just know I'm not trying to live in a home with small windows when I get my own place. My place is going to have windows wall to wall, floor to ceiling, like a glass house. I want to see what's coming. What's out there. And what I'm missing."

They reached the dunes around the time when the sun was one hand above the horizon. The sand was already defrosting, summoning heat swiftly.

"Okay, let's head on up." Balanta's calves and thighs powered into the sand, pistons working against shifting terrain.

"Wait up," Mende called out, already huffing against the steep slope. "Stop trying to drop me, Balanta."

Promise kept a steady pace, not far behind Balanta and Eloni. They stopped for a rest in the whispering morning air. The ocean shimmered in the distance. Breeze song swirled in the crisp atmosphere. They gathered their breath and moved on.

Eloni Loved this place. It was like walking on water. He felt heroic. Triumphant. The sand made him miss Samoa, and Hawai'i. Maybe his soul was a palm tree. Or a bowl of poi. Laughing, he broke into as much of a sprint as he could up the steep dune incline. Words came. *Climbing the backs of dunes... Feet drumming sand like Samoans drum tunes...* His leg trunks powered up the sand, arms swinging for leverage. *Honu*, the sea turtle on his back, turned wet with perspiration and slipped into the ocean of Eloni's resurgent soul. Higher, he pushed, his heart working double shifts. His body dropped into the sand and rose up again, spraying grains behind him. At last, he hit the wall, falling out onto the slope, laughing, spread-eagle against the sky. Sand coated his Honu as he got back up and hoofed onward, step by step. He reached the pinnacle and performed *haka*, the war dance Pikea had taught him. He was free of all authority except the chaperone of breeze and totem of sun. He was a sea turtle conquering dunes. Enormous. Multi-climatic. Diversified in his supremacy. Eloni's celebration only down-shifted as he caught sight of the distant sea and imagined the sea turtles traveling there, wealthy in their companionship, swimming their own element collectively.

Promise liked the feeling of the warm sand tingling the soles of her bare feet. *Every step I take up this dune, I'm sliding partway back down. Just like my life, I guess. Displaced and slip sliding all over the place. Some people get to race across flat ground. Some get to climb mountains. I get to sink into and then scale quicksand that's been pushed into a pile by the wind.*

To Mende, the sand felt like an angry sea of fire ants swarming his soles. He leaped his way upward, trying to maximize air time so his feet would cool for an instant before landing back on the skillet.

Forty minutes later, Balanta and Eloni summited the highest point in the dunes. They savored the quiet moment of solitude before Promise joined them. "Here, drink some water," Balanta offered. Promise poured the first water over her head, releasing steam from her scalp that rose from her in ribbons. She offered some water to the dunes in the way that Lake had taught her. Then she drank.

"There you are," Promise said to Mende, who was grinning at his climbing achievement even as his thighs raged.

"That... was... cool..." he rationed out, one word for every three desperate breaths. "Now, give me some of that water."

Maricela took off on her own, heading for the deep woods. She had seen some rolling hills during yesterday's hike to the dunes and wanted to check them out. They had seemed like ocean waves, so smooth and inviting. She was feeling tender hearted. It hurt to be the centerpiece of a libelous legend being told repeatedly. No matter how Maricela tried to rewrite the story, her life was cast by foreigners who only cared to imagine her. It was as though she was a movie script possessed by a studio that wanted her to fill its quota of horror movies. She wanted to be an independent film. She wanted to have a soul, and to be told soulfully.

She came to the familiar waves of land. It ebbed and swelled, its surface so smooth. She imagined the sky polishing it. Sprinting up one hill, then another, she felt air rush inside her and lighten her spirit. The next hillside was terraced. Loamy. A band of deer nuzzled grass in the distance. Sky was proud and exultant. *This is a good moment*, she thought. *I want to gather more of these.*

She crossed an open space with little vegetation or ground cover. The dirt was rich and dark, with determined shocks of dandelions scattered about. Maricela noticed a glint on the ground, coming from between two rocks. She kneeled to look closer. The sunlight was reflecting off a wide clay jar half buried beneath the rocks. Maricela dislodged the jar from the earth and pried open the top. The small treasure chest held much more than it first appeared. An arrowhead. Three small geodes. Dried flowers. A sand dollar, chipped at the edges. A strange animal effigy. And a small parchment scroll fastened with twine. Maricela took off the twine and unspooled the scroll. She carefully smoothed out the brittle paper, which seemed to be papyrus, and focused on the words etched upon it in rudimentary handwriting. *This ink's so old, it must be from the biblical days*, she thought. She read the words. What the biblical ink spelled out made her heart contract painfully and her every cell cry out for comfort.

Lunch brought them all back together. The dune hikers were the most famished. They all joined Eloni in whipping up a fruit salad, taro chips, and avocado sandwiches. Camp fell into the sound of animals at a trough.

"What... is that, Cielo?" Promise asked, frowning.

"Kelp taco. You don't know what you're missing. Gathered the kelp just now. Fresh from the sea. I threw in some fresh dandelion, mint, and lavender. Wrap it up in a whole grain tortilla and you're good to go."

"Boy, you're going to have actual crabs crawling in your gut. You know? Microscopic parasites?"

"Nah. Boiled the kelp first. All good." Cielo chowed down the tacos with gusto, moaning and licking his fingers like they were candy canes.

After lunch, it was down to the lagoon to cool off. They continued baiting Ivory into jumping off the waterfall. Each time they did, he started murmuring, "I walk through the valley..." and swam out to find refuge in the lagoon.

Mende kept chasing Binda and Lake off the ledge. They fell, squealing and screaming, delighted and holding hands.

Promise and Maricela had taken to diving off the waterfall, articulating their bodies into graceful arrows. The water applauded in soft ripples as they entered.

Shonto, Pikea, and Eloni raced from one side of the lagoon to the other, and back, over and again. With each race, they collapsed more completely at the shore, panting and laughing.

Balanta followed Ashia down into the hot spring plume at the lagoon's center, and rose with her. The spring mouth expelled slivers of something that shone like mercury even at this depth. Ashia was a mermaid dressed in the effervescence of a long, ribboning crystal chandelier. Balanta treaded beneath the surface, beholding her.

Cielo let his belly brown as he backstroked languidly in circles and random patterns. A docile heron came to the edge of the foliage and watched the activity. Air continued to warm. Sun looked down, smiling generously.

"Hey, y'all," Eloni called out. "Let's all go up to that cave Promise found yesterday."

"How far did you say it is?" Ivory asked. He was playing with hibiscus blossoms that had blown into the water.

"Not too far. More about the climb." Promise answered. They left the lagoon and went back to camp to grab torches and food. It was still early, in the time of no shadows.

After taking turns pulling Ivory up the slope, they reached the cave. "Y'all must be chewing too many herbs if you think I'm going in that black pit," Ivory said.

"Then why'd you come up here, Ivory?" Maricela said.

"I was dragged! Bamboozled! I didn't set out to the cave. The cave got set upon me!"

They entered. The initial darkness swallowed them ominously. The cooler air felt good against their sweat and skin. Still huffing from the climb, the group's breathing became a soundtrack in the cave, which was quiet and still.

"You smell that?" Binda asked. "Moss. Minerals. Things that grow in the dark." As they penetrated, a stream emerged at the low point of the ground. It trickled as it showed itself, disappeared underground, and reemerged. The cavern was furnished in sparse clusters of mud stumps on the floor and weeping pillars of glistening quartz on the ceiling. The air in here was dry, and tasted stale on Maricela's tongue. The cave's walls were blackened by the ash of generations of fire. They moved in deeper. The cave floor dropped gently. The space opened up. Blackness grew.

Binda leaned to stretch her calves, putting her hand against a wall. Suddenly, the wall lit up, a light emerald glow spreading quickly across the wall like an instant moss. The rock of the wall seemed to be illuminated. Binda looked more closely. It wasn't the rock that was glowing. Nearly microscopic creatures teemed over the rock's surface, each a bright lantern scrambling. *What caused them to ignite*? she wondered.

More than once, Binda noticed Promise wheezing slightly. Especially late in the day. "Scarred lungs from Valley Fever," Promise explained in a casual tone when Binda asked if she had asthma. "It's kind of like tuberculosis except not contagious. Messed up my cool factor, though. You try dancing with a boy while you're sounding like an old hound dog climbing a hill."

"Do you have to do anything for it?" Binda asked.

"Nothing I can do. It mostly flares up when I get tired. My lungs start getting tight and I can't get enough oxygen. At that point, it's just a matter of getting through until I can lie down and rest."

The passageway narrowed and turned. Torchlight crept over the walls, making it seem alive. Rounding the bend, they moved into an expanded space. Balanta noticed an opening in the wall to the right and checked it out. "Come over here!" he called. They moved into a smaller space. Its floor was flat, almost graded. A circular opening was at the center of the floor, and dropped down into another space. An old timber ladder leaned against the rim of the hole, beckoning them down. After bartering with Ivory, and finally dragging him, they all descended the ladder, which creaked and gave against its loose rope bindings.

"This place smells," Binda noted.

"Say it plain, girl," Ivory said. "People been pissing up in here. For a looong time."

This underground chamber was just large enough to fit all 12. It had a central fire pit. A few partially burned sticks were scattered inside it. They flashed their torches against the darkness. And saw. Ancient drawings, chalk white and simple, covered the walls. Twelve figures were etched into a high point along one stretch. They were hardly more than stick figures, pictured standing in a circle. No one noticed that Maricela's face had gone entirely pale and that her lips were trembling.

"Those are some cool petroglyphs," Cielo said.

"What is this place?" Binda asked. Ivory was silent, his lips trembling.

"Must be a kiva," Shonto said, his tone matter of fact.

"What's that?" Promise asked.

"The heart of a ceremonial cave. It's where the ancient ones went for their ceremonies."

"Why all the way down here?"

"Maybe they felt that since earth was their mother, the womb from which they came, they would find the most spiritual power back in the womb."

The walls here were thickly blackened. Charred many layers deep. The ureic air also smelled like soot. A trickling of water made its way along the kiva floor, pooling in spots, gurgling along in others. Promise suddenly sang out in a high, lush octave, "I've been needing you... my sweet dark beginning... Here I am again... take me..."

"Wow, that was beautiful," said Ashia. "Your voice echoed so amazingly in here."

"This is the perfect amphitheater," marveled Cielo. "We could have a legendary jam session in here."

"Is everyone's torch in good shape?" Balanta asked. "Let's climb up out of here, keep going and see how far back this cave goes."

They climbed out of the kiva and moved back into the main cavern passage. A ribbon of breeze came through, dragging a few dried leaves with it that fell into the meager central stream and boated further into the cavern. The group followed the sound of the water around the contours of stalagmites, stalactites, and the cavern walls. The air grew cooler as they progressed along a slight descent. Shonto's skin felt clammy. Binda noticed groundwater creeping toward Lake, who acted unaware.

"The dark is getting darker, if that's even possible," said Cielo.

"Just keep your torch dry," said Balanta, his voice stern and focused.

Notches appeared along the walls. Straight lines. In groups of 12. Then 10. Eventually, three notches remained. "Seems like someone was counting something," said Promise.

"Yeah, like bodies dropping," Ivory said. "Y'all can keep playing explorer. Brothers like me, we take warning signs for what they are. Time to roll, y'all."

"Maricela, you haven't said much since we came into the cave," noted Ashia. "You all right?"

"Yeah. I'm good. Just trying not to stumble and break my leg." Maricela was not good. The notches were making her heart race, especially as their number decreased. She thought of the 12 figures on the kiva wall. And of the clay jar, the scroll, and its words. *Dios mio, why am I even in this cave?* she asked herself, choking down the dread that kept trying to climb up her throat.

Binda felt it first. A sick murmur in the cavern's heart. Then, a mountainous aneurysm. "Avalanche!" Balanta shouted. A rain of boulders echoed inside a curtain of dust as the entire roof of the cavern seemed to collapse. Balanta dove to cover Lake and Ashia, pulling them down beneath him as he crouched. Mende did the same with Pikea, who pushed back at him and crouched into her own shelter. The rest flattened themselves on the ground and covered their heads. Jade Mountain thundered horribly. The sound amplified in the cavern. Promise wondered about the Rapture. Cielo took the opportunity to meditate on the cycle of birth and death.

Ivory howled and wailed and kicked Maricela so hard in the thigh that she spanked him with all her force. He whelped in Lake's ear, who slapped him. "Ouch, Ivory! That hurt my eardrum!"

For a very long time, the entire world fell apart around and beneath them. Shockwaves. Fractures. Booming. *Had the sun fallen into the ocean?* Binda wondered. The thunder receded. The world began to feel solid beneath them again. Thick dust had filled the cavern.

"I'm blind!" Ivory screamed.

"Ivory, stop being a—" Eloni started, but was cut off by Ashia who swiftly covered his mouth.

Mende choked on the thick dust still billowing from the cave-in. He wiped his eyes with his shirt, itself caked in dust, only worsening the burning sensation.

Lake saw Promise doubled over, her fist on her mouth, hacking violently. "Are you going to be okay, Promise? I'm worried about you."

Promise's voice was faint, distant. "I need to get out of here. I need fresh air."

"You guys, we need to get out of here, now!" Lake yelled, her own voice dust clogged and muffled.

Circles of light jumped all around the cave walls as Cielo and Maricela scanned with their torches. Coughing and retching echoed in the darkness and dust.

"Look! Over here!" yelled Cielo. "I found something." A clammy draft poured over Mende's skin and a howl emerged from the depths.

"What was that?" Ivory whimpered. They stood still for just a moment. Listening. Claustrophobia pressed on them. They rushed for the cave entrance, only to see, after breaking through to the other side of the dust cloud, that the way was blocked. Muddy clay was piled to the ceiling. No way through.

Just before Ivory started crying for real, Cielo called out again. "Come on! Over here! I think I found a way out!" They moved back through the dust cloud and found Cielo crouched up on a large ledge. "Come on up! Jade Mountain is being compassionate to us, I believe!" As they climbed up onto the ledge they noticed the scatter of bones, animal, hopefully. And the fluttering of breeze that gave them hope. They followed Cielo through a curtain of glistening moss into a smaller passage about four feet high. Crawling for a ways, they muddied their hands and knees in the sludgy ground. Pikea in particular felt the vice grip of imagined suffocation. Her breath was loud, labored. Her eyes glared fiercely. They felt the passage dilate. The darkness brightened. Then, they were out. On another hillside between two folds of the mountain. Taking desperate gulps of fresh air. Crying. Laughing. They had emerged as mummies, swaddled in a cake of dust. Hair, faces, eyelashes, skin, and clothes. Dust had invaded their ear canals, nasal passages, and lungs.

Ashia noticed how the craggy trees along this slope had their hair blown back in the direction of the onslaught of ocean breeze. *We are shaped by the forces of our lives.* The thought slipped through, mundane and brief.

"I have dust in my brain," Ivory said.

"Ivory, you're too easy," Maricela replied, forgoing the several jokes in her mind.

"I'm so thirsty," Shonto said. "Lake, do you think you can make us some water?"

"It doesn't work like that. I can't just summon water to appear. I'm not a magician. It's more like an allergy. My body reacts to energy and mood in the world. Water comes, like some people get rashes."

They worried over Promise, whose face, even after they found a stream and washed, was ashen. Her voice had faded to a bleak whisper. She could barely walk. As they reached camp, they ran for the security box, frantic to get to the satellite phones and flare gun. Ashia inserted the box's key and turned.

Nothing. She gripped the lid and base, straining to open the box. "I can't get it open," she said, alarmed.

"Here," Balanta said, taking the box. He applied all his force. The box would not give. Maricela took the box from Balanta and gave it to Eloni, who kneeled for leverage. He placed the box on the ground and pried, grimacing and determined. The phones inside clattered against each other. The lid remained stuck.

Ivory was jumping up and down like a child who has to pee. "What is this? Some sword in the stone madness? Maybe it takes the right person to open the box. Give it to me."

They did not give it to Ivory. "This is not good," said Ashia stating the obvious. I hope this isn't part of the whole mysticism thing. Cause this is dangerous. I hope everyone's okay, but what if something worse happens? We need to get this box open. And what the heck happened to the lookout boat? Antonia must have lost her mind, leaving us hanging out here." They tried for the rest of that day and into the night. In the end, fatigue and adrenaline burnout encouraged them to consider the jammed box a fateful, meant-to-be kind of thing.

It was late afternoon when they departed camp again to find solace in the lagoon. Its lucid water was the antithesis of dust. This time, they were there to bathe and cleanse more than anything else. It was a mostly silent time, except for Ivory's rampant narrative about them almost being buried alive.

After their water therapy, they went on a walk to explore more of the island. This time, on the other side of camp. Promise was feeling much better and joined along. They lost themselves in a dense revelry of willows. The willows' lithe crowns danced in the breeze. It felt to Binda as though the group was being brushed by the sky. After that, a convening of almond trees. Shonto raced to one and plopped down. The tree trunk was curved outward near to the ground, offering a lumbar convenience to Shonto as he sat and consumed handfuls of almonds he had freshly liberated from their shells. The others did the same with pistachios and cashews.

They also came upon a rambutan tree, sagging with its hairy fruit. They picked some, intending to cook the seeds later for snacking. Nearby, calla lilies stretched their slender necks 10 feet into the sky, their faces blushing orange and yellow, a dazzling of embarrassed suns. The island kept giving. After jumping a few shallow brooks, a field that looked like a painter's pallet. Honeysuckle bushes had convened a powwow. They were clustered in large, thick masses everywhere. The air dripped with their sweet scent. It made Promise want to lick her lips. Bluebells stood thick like chimes. A fig tree grew near yet another brook. Eloni felt the tree beckon him. Figs, obese and molasses-dark, sagged in their husks on the tree. An overpopulated resource that Eloni was all too happy to put to use in some mad recipe.

A kinship of olive trees huddled at the foot of the hillside. Promise had the arm reach to access the ripest olives. She picked them swiftly, handing them to Binda, who sat each one gently in her basket, as though they were swaddled newborn babies she was bringing to cradle. Soon, they had hundreds of large ripe olives, some pale green, others cloudy black. They walked back, buoyed with achievement.

They moved into a neighborhood of angel oaks, their long, thick arms extending like octopus tentacles, the weight of the branches bringing them low, some to crawl along the ground and reach back up for the sky. Promise marveled at a particularly grand angel oak. Shonto came and stood next to its trunk, looking up. "That's no junior varsity tree. That's varsity. All-Star."

"Trees do better when you plant them in the ground instead of keeping them in pots," Promise said. "What's that called when the pot gets too small? Root bound. That's it. That's how I feel in most relationships. Root bound. Give me some space to breathe and grow."

Binda and Lake wanted to spend time in the meadow before dinner. They made their way, arriving to a warm playground of flowers, insects, and breeze. Lying down, they made wild grass angels with their arms and legs, letting the ground and its energy soothe their anxiety from the cave.

"The feather grass is dreaming," Lake said.

"What do you mean?" Binda asked.

"It's moving while it sleeps. Must be a good dream."

A dragonfly appeared, daring toward Binda, away and back again. The dragonfly's wings, diaphanous and stained in a light auburn, caught sunlight, reflecting it into Binda's eyes, briefly blinding her. She could feel the wind lapping at her skin. Sheets of it, touching down, lifting, flapping against her body, cooling her sublimely. She found Lake. "Hey, a dragonfly just came and played with me. It was so cool."

Just then another bright red dragonfly, or maybe the same, appeared just above Lake's head. She followed its flight as it cut the air precisely, painting a rouge streak over the sweetgrass and blue mohawk grass. "Hmmm... I wonder what that means," Lake said.

Binda saw soberness in Lake's eyes. "What do you think it means?"

"A red dragonfly symbolizes the coming of fire. Not destruction, but change. What fire does. What it leaves behind. Among Native people, it is a sign of happiness, and speed. And Purity. Purity because the dragonfly eats from the wind itself. Do you think that's the same one you saw?"

"I don't know. Why?"

"Just... I wonder if it has to do with our friendship. Or, something else. Either way, I've always Loved those things. They come from a time before dinosaurs and when I see them, I feel like they are trying to take me back to the world before humans. When things were in balance even if they were imperfect."

The dragonfly circled Lake and Binda from above. It repeatedly came close enough that they could see the segments of its eyes. Lake fell into those eyes and heard a voice: *Awaken. Open your eyes. Join this limitless vision.* "Wow. I think it's hypnotizing me."

Binda smiled. "Eternal Love. That's what we say dragonflies are. Or, what they bring. A mature Love that goes far beneath the water's surface and is profoundly deep."

Lake extended her arm. The dragonfly hovered, then landed briefly on her skin before alighting again. "I Love the way they move. Such power and poise. They can move in all directions, instantly. And they hover so gracefully, like a nymph or a fairy or something. I like to think that this one being here with us means that a goodness is coming. Maybe while we're on the island."

Binda giggled as the dragonfly touched down on the soft bed of her hair and darted away. "One teacher I had when I was very young took our class out on a field trip. It was by a river with all these cattails. Dragonflies were everywhere. My teacher said they symbolize the defeat of self-created illusions. The way there's an iridescence to their wings and body that changes color depending on your angle of viewing. Reflecting and refracting light. My teacher said that a dragonfly's realm is of the light."

"That's what I mean," Lake said. "I feel some kind of new light coming." Just as Lake had the thought, the flutter of butterflies banked sharply in the air, in her direction, as though they had heard her mind. Though she was not aware, a bright cloud was approaching her and Binda. They bathed in the pleasure of the moment as their new friend played with them like a puppy with wings.

They went walking up into the sparse woods along the back perimeter of the meadow. Binda bent down to smell the leaves of a plant that looked stained in milk.

"That's white sage," Lake said. "My Masaani took me to gather it with her at dawn in the springtime. It grows high up in places like this. Masaani told me that white sage gets its color because it is an elder among the sage people.

"My cousin Lonny told me a different story, though. He said, a long time ago, when the land was still quiet and free, sage only grew green. Its seeds would gather each circle moon and go out on the wind. Sage people had an agreement with each other that their seeds would only ride the wind that stayed down in the valleys, because higher up in the mountains was a mysterious place where the sage people were afraid to go.

"Well, this one group of sage was curious and restless. They whispered to each other, Don't you want to see what it's like growing on the mountains? They planned that they would release their seeds to the mountain winds one night, under the Clear Moon, which is when you can't see the moon at all. That way, the other sage wouldn't see them breaking the agreement. Once their seed started to grow up in the mountains, they could finally discover the mysteries they had always dreamed about.

"So, this group of sage waited until the Clear Moon. That night brought a darkness that swallowed up everything. It was like swimming in ink and trying to see beneath the surface. Just after midnight, when the night birds and owls sounded off, a strong, cold wind came running up the valley. It howled and huffed. The sage crouched low, opened their bellies, and all at once, released their seed.

"Now, as soon as they started growing up on the mountain sides and passes, they sensed that the air was different up there. And they felt a new presence. Some say it was creatures from a faraway land, soulless and with eyes like dust. Others say it was the spirit of change, come to foretell the future. Whatever they saw, it turned them from green to white. They have been colored that way ever since."

Lake stirred some fallen leaves at her feet. "I like my cousin's version better." She plucked and chewed a long blade of sweetgrass, and handed one to Binda, whose mind and spirit had drifted from in the forest.

For Binda, grief was its own blade. It had left thin keloid scars across her heart. The scar tissue made her wheeze sometimes, but it wasn't her lungs that were tight. She believed that people possessed a gland that produced chemicals allowing them to Love themselves. And she knew the valve of her gland was blocked with centuries of adhesion.

Among her memories of Aboriginal childhood, Binda seemed to retrieve certain scrolls more often. Like the one of sunburned 'roo shooters pulling up to the petrol stations in their hunting trucks ornamented with roll bars and flood lights. The 'roo carcasses stacked over each other in the truck beds. Some dressed, some fat and swelling in the heat.

Or the parking spaces everywhere demarcated by old rubber tires buried halfway in the dirt. Older children pouring boiling water on anthills so the babies could be set down outside to play. The scat and scoundrel whining of wild dogs and dingoes.

Or the whispers. The ones that forever followed *dark breeds* like her. In the school hallways. Inside of stores. Wherever the superior ones were inconvenienced with the sight of her. And the reminder she posed of what they really were.

She preferred the sweeter memories. Harder to retrieve. The ones of loitering old fellas dropped around old card tables like potato sacks, watching the footie on the telly, maneuvering for the seat closest to the fan that thankfully drowned out their conversation from Binda's ears. For the old fellas, bellies swollen like toads in croak, were inevitably oiled up on *amber*, and telling fabricated stories for the umpteenth time.

Or the shielas passing each other on the street, performing their polished shiela rituals. Lathering each other with their inimitable phrasing, such as, "How are you going, dear?" and, "We should have a feed sometime," and, "Keep this dark, but did you hear about so and so? You know, she belongs to so and so…"

Inevitably though, Binda's reach into the past was a net that drew up those 'roo carcasses, their eyes as large as entire night skies and just as solemn. Their eyes like the mouths of caves. Their eyes accusatory and acute.

This is where Binda went when she journeyed backward. To slaughter. Stacks upon stacks of slaughter.

Lake and Binda headed out of the woods and back to the meadow to head toward camp. As they reached the meadow, they saw Ashia and Maricela cutting into the opening from the side toward camp. "There you two are," Ashia called out as they approached.

"Where's Promise?" Lake asked. "Is she okay?"

"She's resting," Maricela said. "Pikea, Balanta, and them are taking good care of her. She says she just needs to rest."

A strong breeze shook the woods surrounding the meadow. A rustling reverberated across the open space. Binda felt her skin flush. She looked into the tree line and saw something out of place. Snowflakes in the air. Dancing and lifting in eddies as they moved from the trees out over the meadow. Binda ran toward the advancing snow, Maricela and Ashia following after her. The first snowflake landed on Binda's cheek. It was not wet or cold. It was dry and light as... cotton. *The cottonwoods!* The meadow was awash in a blizzard of white. Cottonwood seeds had dislodged from their tree crowns along the streams. Now they filled the air in dense flocks, drifting sideways, a summer snow. Binda and the others raced through the sweeping whiteness, laughing deliriously, thrilled as children, skipping and reaching out for the nearly weightless fluff. Binda could barely see the others, the snow was so heavy. Whiteness clung to the sweetgrass, building in clumps on the blades. The meadow was filling with snow, deeper and deeper. They somersaulted. Swam the grass. Whiteness obliterating sky. Blinding their way forward. Whiteness clung to their hair, their lashes and clothes. Silent and falling. Silent and falling. A dream come undone from the netherworlds, now upon them, feathery and sublime.

Eloni came over to Maricela back by her cabin, the familiar slight hitch in his step. Though something about Eloni's energy made Maricela uneasy, she had to admit to herself that he possessed a few scattered traits she found attractive. The cinnamon kindness of his eyes. His full body laughter that took his head back and often ended in tears of completion. The cuddly plumpness of his ears. And, of course, his flat out ridiculous cooking skills. Boy had game, seasoned and spiced like nobody's business. "Did you always have that limp?" Maricela asked him.

"Nah. I stepped on some glass chasing these guys behind my school. They were calling me street sweeper, and shelter boy. I popped. Didn't stop chasing them, even when they bolted through a restaurant. I know they saw fire in my eyes and they were scared to death.

"Cops threw cuffs on all three of us, right there on the main street, with about half the school driving by after being picked up after classes got out."

Maricela saw the unsettledness in Eloni's eyes. "How are you doing, for real, hermano?"

"If I'da known it was going to be like this, I don't know if I would have come. I didn't sign up for this."

"You could have fooled me. You seem to be having a good time. And, actually, you did sign up for this."

"Very funny. Just because I'm enjoying some of it doesn't mean I'm feeling all of it. You mean to tell me that this has played out like you imagined?"

"No, but what in my life, or yours, has? That's part of what we become, people like us here. We become mist walkers. We don't walk on solid ground, able to predict things securely. We walk on mist, never knowing when it's going to open up and we'll fall through."

"Yeah," Eloni concurred. "Walking over minefields."

"Don't know if that's a skill," Maricela went on, "being able to live in limbo, levitated, really. Up in the air. But has to be a way we can use that. Everyone else seems to need to be able to predict what comes next. They freak out if the script gets flipped in the slightest. Somehow, I feel stronger than people like that. At least in that way."

"Yeah... I guess."

"Eloni, do you ever wish you could have had a different father?"

"Yeah, all the time. I wish it all the time, just cause he was never around. But then a deeper wish takes over and I end up feeling guilty that I ever wished for a different father."

"What's the deeper wish?"

"That my father could have had a different father."

Maricela considered the backward rippling that ran through generations, just as it ran forward. She wondered about the kind of father Eloni might come to be.

"If I see Cielo do any more yoga poses, I'm going to lose it," said Eloni, averting the subject.

"Why are you threatened by that?" Maricela asked.

"I'm not threatened," Eloni snapped, his sap rising.

"Then why does it bother you so much? What are you associating it with?"

Eloni thought about that. *Association.* A shadow of a thought flashed through. He shook it away. Something about a position. Of his body. Eloni clamped down on that thought angrily. A frigid, clammy river crept through his interior. If Eloni was angry, it was only because people had been pouring their miasmic hostility into him since birth. He would have been happy to be one of those fortunate souls for whom the world only seems to have Aloha spirit. Wasn't his fate. He was the sea into which a festering volcano expelled its molten guts. And what was he supposed to do with that? He wasn't fireproof. He scalded so many times over that the scar tissue had scar tissue. No cosmetic surgery was going to fix that.

"Eloni," Maricela beckoned softly. "Will you please do me a favor and massage my calves? I've been cramping up since yesterday in the dunes."

Eloni blushed. Saying nothing, he approached Maricela and kneeled down. Taking her leg in his hands, he began to rub and press, searching for the contours of her muscle. "Like this?"

"Um hmm... That feels good." She felt his strength, and a little too much friction against her skin.

"I know what you need," Eloni said, standing up.

"Oh yeah?"

"Yeah, give me a minute." Eloni was gone and back in less than a minute. He had a sliced half of a mango in his hands. "Here, try this." He rubbed his hands together, coating them with the mango pulp, its juices glistening on the back of his hands and forearms. This time, his hands moved smoothly over her calves, her skin cooing and purring. "I think maybe the compounds in the mango might even help with your cramping."

"Oh, yeah? Never heard of that. Hey, you're the chef. I trust your recipe, hombre."

Afterward, Maricela's calves felt so tenderized, she could hardly walk. In fact, she melted. Right down onto a hammock strung between two towering eucalyptus trees. The last thing she was aware of was the way the eucalyptus leaves rustled lightly far above her, and the wisps of white clouds beyond that, moving over inside an invisible stream. Then she was out and dreaming in a language reserved for the tranquilized.

When she woke, Eloni was smiling at her. And the sunlight had shifted.

"Here, let me return the favor, hombre." Maricela stood behind Eloni and began kneading his bare shoulders with all the strength in her hands and fingers. His muscle was thick, dense. Knotted tightly. "Hey, man, you have to learn to let some of this stuff out. Feels like marbles in here."

Eloni was quiet. Mostly because he was nervous and thrilled to have Maricela touching him like this. And, he didn't want to be thinking about his tension and its source, or the way he held it. He just wanted to close his eyes, stifle his urge to moan, and let himself feel good inside for once.

As Promise rested, the group checked in on her, especially Ivory, who brought lemonade, and fanned her with palm fronds, and serenaded her with made-up songs. Ivory blew on the cottonwood seed clouds he had in his cupped hands. The clouds littered the cabin in their confetti. Finally, Promise smiled, and asked Ivory to please let her truly rest. The others meandered and dithered, still working off their stress from the cave-in. Pikea decided she needed to go on her own mini vision quest, so she grabbed a spear and hoped to be back in time for dinner. The air was in the mature part of its daily phase, holding plenty of heat, though not showing off with it the way midday does.

Pikea found a groove of fairly clear ground running between clusters of stately, large Indian laurel fig trees, their massive crowns a rich green, their trunks powder white. The trees gave off an energy that made Pikea think of monks meditating. Following the groove, she walked on, not having any particular vision quest-like dramatics in mind. She moved through a grove of Mexican weeping bamboo, running her fingers along the soft, slender leaves. The culms reached several feet above her head, and swallowed her. Pikea looked behind her, in the direction from which she had come. Nothing but bamboo, smiling at her. Their lush green crowns rustled softly. She moved deeper, sunlight showering around her in thin ribbons, framing the bamboo stalks in fiery gold. The leaves felt feathery against her skin and face. A massage of a million supple fingers.

Soon, Pikea noticed the bamboo stalks change from olive green to a robust black. The stalks were taller, too. Towering. Timber bamboo. The leaves were wider and firmer now, but still soft. All around here, nothing but leaves and stalks. Dried leaves lay inches deep on the ground, a soft bed beneath her feet. Crisp breakage sounded as she stepped. The air inside this bamboo kingdom was rich with oxygen. And clean. Pikea took deep breaths, pleasuring to the cool air billowing in her lungs.

The bamboo began to thin out. Sunlight grew more dominant. Looking ahead, Pikea made out what seemed to be a manmade structure. Moving closer, she saw it. The well stood in a bright clearing. Its walls were old stones, dusty but intact. Pikea lowered the wooden bucket by its thick rope down the well. A butterfly landed on a nearby rock and fanned its wings casually. Pikea raised the bucket, retrieving the rope hand over hand. She dipped a large wooden ladle into the bucket, filling its bowl. The water was the sweetest Pikea had ever tasted. She drank to bursting, and gave thanks for water.

Water. Pikea's father was named Moana, which for the Maori means *wide expanse of water*, or *deep sea*. As a boy he had been known to exhibit wanderlust, roaming the wilderness at every opportunity. Sometimes with adult supervision, often alone. As a young man, he lost the wander, and just exhibited lust. He seeded the conception of many children. Fathered very few of them. This was not the Maori way. It was the way of a man-ghost soaked in depression, a descendant of ancient ways that had been blasted to shards like dynamite eating a mountain. But they were still mountainous, the Maori, and so the community did all it could for Moana, meaning that it scalded his failures in their cultural reprobation. Pikea had heard the rumors. That Moana, *her* father, had been dragged by 10 men up a mountain and had the manhood drummed back into him. No one knew what happened on that mountain. But it was something strong enough that the shroud who had walked the earth until that moment now became a *tangata*, a human being, again. Pikea had heard the rumors. Whether she chose to believe them, chose to even consider traveling those thousands of miles to look for him, to repair the existential tear, that was another question. She spent many moments weighing the possible benefits and downsides of a reunion. Or really, of a first encounter with the deafening vibration in her life others called *a father*.

Lake's heart hurt. She was thinking about her brother, and how he would have Loved it here on the island. All this solitude. Just him and the island creatures, keeping time and rhythm together, their own special jazz ensemble. Her brother was a musician, really, she realized the more she thought about it. His curse was that he had been gifted to hear a music that no other human could conceive.

Balanta noticed Lake's expression. "What's in your heart, friend? The cave-in shake you up?"

Lake didn't feel like talking, but Balanta had a way of making his voice sound... like it didn't come from a person, but from something safer.

"Just missing my brother. You're lucky you and Mende have stayed together."

Balanta didn't respond.

Lake sighed. "My little brother is what you would call autistic."

"You don't call him that?" Balanta asked.

"My family calls him *wonderfully focused*. He can count all the stars in the sky. Every single one. My poor brain can't count my shoelaces."

Balanta sat close to Lake. "I believe that we have a tether connecting us to all the souls we Love," he said. "We can tug on that tether whenever we wish, and the other person will feel it. And when the season comes for us to be near to each other, we won't have to do a thing. Togetherness is not ours. It is our Maker's."

"Thanks, Balanta. I guess I feel guilty that I didn't do more to protect him. You know? Stand up for him. Even now, I feel guilty that I'm having a great time while he's somewhere suffering."

"I feel you, Lake. I also keep getting taught a crucial lesson. Although Suffering is lonely for company, Peace has been to visit Suffering, and knows better than to return."

Balanta observed that it had not rained since they had arrived. Something in the air made him wonder if they would know this island's particular cloud water touch.

A few of them had gone on a hike to some cliffs before dinner. When they got there, Shonto climbed a bluff, wanting to get a better view. He stood on the bluff and gazed out over the canyon. The wind tossed his hair as he reached into his pouch for the cuttings of cedar and sage to make his offering. He scattered cedar out into the wind, in all four directions. "To my four teachers. To the four elements. To the past time. The future time. This time. To the All of time." Brushing hair from his eyes, he offered gratitude. "For the blessings of Creation. For the plant people, the animal people, the human people, and the spirit people." The music of the canyon echoed around him, strumming his heart. "For all that you have given us, Island. For all that we take. May we leave you well. Ahó." The last cedar he tossed was for his family, which remained unspoken in this solitary and sacred conversation between warrior and wind. He concluded with, "All my relations," and waited until he felt the familiar tether and tremble of coexistence move through him. Shonto put his pouch back in his front jeans pocket, took one last inhale of the crisp air, and imagined a world of buffaloes down on the canyon floor as he turned and descended the hill.

They came to a scratch of rocks thick with small sand colored lizards scrambling in and out of the jumble. Eloni saw one lizard doing pronounced pushups on a stone. Eloni dropped down with military quickness and assumed the pose. Grinning, he faced off with the lizard, his face close enough to the vertebrate that their breaths could meet. The lizard, its face emotionless, continued undeterred. Up. Down. Eloni dropped into the lizard's rhythm. Up. Down. "Me and you, buddy!" he shouted. Any normal lizard would have scooted at such a loud bluster. This one kept at its labor. Up. Down. One hundred twenty reps later, Eloni's arms were trembling, his spine and belly, no longer erect and tight, bowed and sagged. Eloni pressed his lips, eyes wide open and manic. The lizard pressed on. Up. Down. Finally, another smaller lizard saved face for Eloni by rushing up to its kin, nudging its tail. The larger lizard broke formation and chased after its pest, both of them darting into a black mouth of shadow in the rocks. "Man," Eloni exuded, his strained breath a haranguing punishment. "That lizard must work out all day."

Ashia stared at Eloni, disbelieving. "Eloni, something broke in you, boy. You just went at it with a lizard."

"A win's a win," Eloni crowed, still bent over at the knees, gasping his pride asthmatically.

The group was sitting around the sleeping fire pit, Ivory whittling, Cielo chewing sugarcane, when Eloni came out of his cabin and quickly moved to the fire circle. Ashia noticed the look on Eloni's face. "What's going on?" she asked. Just then, yelling voices rose up from inside the cabin.

"Balanta and Mende are getting heated up in there," Eloni said.

"About what?" Ashia asked.

"We told Mende that we are going on a vision quest in the morning. Stay out in the wilderness for maybe a day or two."

"You can't take Mende with you?"

"It's not like we're going shopping. This is what we've been feeling called to do. Mende, he's just not ready."

"But he's the same age as you and Balanta."

"He's nearly a full sun cycle younger. Makes a difference with stuff like this."

"Is that Spirit talking, or ego?"

"It just feels right between Balanta and me. It was Balanta's idea."

The yelling in the cabin grew louder, creasing the air with a discomforting tonal energy. The group remained quiet, not sure what to do. Binda dropped tears that felt like hot sparks as they landed on her arms. Hurt spread from one to another as they beheld a breaking of bonds between brothers.

117

Balanta's eyes flashed. He stepped up into Mende, his face just an inch from his little brother's. "Don't make me, man."

"Go ahead. You know you've always wanted to. Especially since we got here. Do it."

Balanta visualized his forearm slammed against his brother's neck, up under his chin, pinning his head back against the cabin wall. He saw the whole thing in a microsecond. The hurt it caused him to see that, to see what he was *this close* to doing to his brother, and the sleet of pain in Mende's eyes—made Balanta draw back. Mende was shaking, but steeled with conviction. "Maybe you would have been better off without a brother. *Brother*." The last word broke Mende, his voice crumbling into emotion, tears stampeding.

"I can't be your dad. I can't replace him," Balanta said.

"I don't need you to be my dad. That's your problem. Back off and stop hating me for reminding you of mom."

Balanta clenched his jaw tightly, his chest ballooning in and out. His shoulders turned inward, like an eagle's wings in perch. He turned and was gone.

Mende burst out of the cabin soon after, kicking the sand and spitting angrily. His eyes were on fire. Cielo approached Mende, placing his hand on Mende's shoulder. "Calmaté, 'migo. Here's what we're going to do. We're going to go on our own quest, okay? Probably be even better than what those two grizzly bears are likely to stumble into." Mende's face did not break loose of pain. Without acknowledging Cielo's attempt at compassion, Mende turned and ran into the woods. His scent was furious and broken.

The spirit of the fight traveled quicker than the island wind. Everyone felt the sickening sensation of dread and alarm. When two so close come to such violence, peace seems so much more fragile, thought Maricela. Is the peace that holds days together and people in a stable state really just an illusion? Are we all doomed to suffering, with rare bouts of calm? She chewed licorice bark and tried to convince her mind to pause its despairing rampage.

"Es la hora que comer," Cielo said. "Tengo mucho hambre." It was time for dinner. Eloni boiled some sugarcane down into a cloudy syrup. He used this to sweeten the dandelion tea that was Cielo's request. Then Eloni pummeled pomegranate fruits against a large stone, kneading them into the rock patiently, the way a baker kneads dough, softening the pulp and seed inside. He sliced open the peel, scooping out the innards with his fingers, laying them on the stone, then pounding away with hand-sized stone until the pulp and seed were one. The juice had run down the natural funnel in the stone, dripping over the stone's lip into a hollowed-out gourd. He saved the juice for a future meal he had in mind.

He rubbed the insides of the fillets of cod and bass with almond shavings, garlic cloves, and basil leaves. Then he stuffed the fillets with the pulped pomegranate flesh, which was a deep wine color, fibrous, and sweetly aromatic. He wrapped the fillets closed with slender juvenile sprigs of willow, still pliant and green. After encasing the fillets in sea-soaked palm leaves, he laid them gently in the sand pit. He gave the fillets good company, positioning them around palm-wrapped sweet potatoes that he had perforated and soaked in blackberry juice. Eloni covered the food with a layer of fronds, and more sand. As the smoke from the fire rocks below penetrated upward through the sand, it quickly began to carry with it the scent of roasting potatoes and simmering fish. Eloni sat on the sand beside the pit, tuning himself to the cooking beneath the ground beside him. He was paternal, patrolling his precious nest.

Maricela and Balanta worked on the cornbread, Balanta picking and denuding cobs, Maricela cleaving free the kernels, then pounding them in the bowl of rock. They added coconut and almond milk, cane syrup, cinnamon, nutmeg, and eggs—Cielo called them caviar—that Eloni had found in one of the snappers he had filleted. After baking the batter in three gourds buried under a light layer of embers, they opened the shells, releasing perfectly browned cornbread, steaming and fragrant with still peaking spices.

They sat around the fire, their plates piled high. "I like the way we just grab our food and grub," Promise said with a full mouth. "I gotta tell you guys about this one foster family. Lovely people. But the dinner ritual was stupendous! Most of my foster families didn't ever eat at a table, so this was like an adventure for me. I was also nervous like crazy cause it was so... formal. I'm sitting there, trying to be on the sly watching what everyone else is doing so I can mimic their motions. Picking up the fork like this. Cutting like this. Putting the utensils down in this position, on this spot. Too many rules to keep track of, except I'm embarrassed that I don't know how to do this table thing. And I need to represent my family, cause I don't want this family thinking my family is ignorant, so I'm trying my hardest to play it off and go along.

"And their conversation. Strange, man. It felt like some kind of ritual. They spoke in turn and with this kind of automated rhythm, like it was a school play that they had rehearsed. I'm just wanting to get down to business and eat the food cause I'm starving. But it's like first I have to learn the dance steps: 'Thomas, how was school today?'

'Fine.'

'Didn't you have that history exam?'

'No, that's Thursday.'

'Raquel...'

Promise's eyes sparked as she spoke. "I'm trying to figure out when I'm supposed to jump in, or even if I'm supposed to jump in at all. It's like trying to get in on some double dutch in a new neighborhood and you don't know their style. You just know that if you come with something crazy that isn't how they do it, you just know you're going to get busted on. Or talked about behind your back. Those kind of whispers where you can feel them cutting into your skin even when you're nowhere near the ones doing the talking, you know what I mean?"

"Yeah, I feel you," Maricela said.

"So, I'm trying to jump in on this double dutch, and my stomach is saying, 'Do me first!' And I see the glass with water in it and no one's touching theirs but I'm thirsty, so do I grab a drink or do I hold off for a minute. And when is the right time to drink?

"TV is off. My family has never had the TV off when we eat. TV is like our condiments that we pour over our food. But here, it's just this weird silence, reminds me of when I went to church with this one foster family and the whole service was so quiet I got freaked out. I'm used to 'Praise the Lord!' and, 'Hallelujah!' and, 'Preach, Reverend, Preach!' I'm telling you, it was like being inside of a casket underwater. You couldn't just hear a pin drop, you could hear what the pin was thinking as it dropped: *Good Lord, no wonder Jesus nodded to sleep up on the cross on this sanctuary wall.*

"So everyone at the table is taking turns talking. It's a merry-go-round of small talk. I'm spying my food which by the way has been arranged on my plate like some kind of artwork. I'm afraid to touch it! We always just grabbed a plate and filled it up ourselves, piled everything on top of everything. Not like this. In this house, I guess one person does the serving and then you come sit at the table, except you don't just sit. It's a whole nother ritual. You all stand around the table, behind your chair. You wait for the mother and father to sit, then you quietly pull out your chair and sit down. No noise but the sound of chairs moving over the floor that shines too much. Feels like ballroom dancing, tight, rigid rituals and stiff movements.

"So, I was saying. My food has been positioned on my plate like shrubbery in a landscaped garden or something. I mean, precisely placed. Meat in the center, vegetables on one side of the circle, mashed potatoes on the other side. And salad in a bowl! Can you believe that? Separate accommodations for some lettuce!

"Anyways, I sit down and I'm ready to get to it, you know? I grab some bread and take me a big ol' bite. I sit back to wipe some crumbs off my mouth, and it's way too silent. I look up and the whole family is looking at me with a nervous smile, like they've just seen their first wild bobcat and don't know whether to try and pet it or get out the boom stick.

"'Promise,' the mom says, 'We always say a blessing over the food before we eat, dear.'

"*I'm thinking, 'My bad, the food was already blessing me.'* I shrink down close to nothing in my chair. Humiliated. Now they really think I come from swine. Worst first placement day ever.

"I recover enough to join in the dinner ritual. Eventually I figure out your supposed to say please and ask for what you want to be passed to you, rather than to reach over for it which seems quicker to me. No wonder dinner took a whole hour. Back home, we got the thing did in maybe 15 minutes.

"I figure out some other things, like you're supposed to smile sweetly and nod your head when someone talks. And you're supposed to look them in the eye for some reason. Me, I'm going into ADHD fits, bouncing back and forth looking at my food, looking at whoever speaks, looking back at my food, hoping it's still there after the latest exposition on soccer practice, or the car in the shop, or Muggy the pet dog's needing a haircut or whether it's time to lay down the mulch in the front yard.

"I'm feeling like I'm figuring out the double dutch small talk rhythm, so I get set to jump in. I want to be smooth and natural, so I try not to edit my stuff first. What comes out is, 'Ya'll hit that bootleg of the *Terminator Redundancy* movie yet?' Dead silence. No, disintegrated silence. Dust.

"I kid you not, this is what the mom said: 'Promise, dear, I hope you're not talking about drinking alcohol. We know you're smarter than that. Bootleg, or whatever you kids are calling it, can't possibly do anything but rot your brain. Thomas, tell Promise about the drunk driving video your class saw last semester.'

"'Mom!' Thomas yells out. Boy was horrified.

"By the time we got to everyone just about clearing their plate, I noticed folks finally taking a swig of their water. By now, it's all warm and nasty. I'm thick in the throat though, so I down my whole glass. Again with the nervous wild bobcat smiles and stares. *Lord, get me through this one.*

"Finally, fiiinally… folks start asking permission to be excused. When in Rome, right? I come with my own version: 'The meal has been delightful. May I go watch some TV now?' Again with the wild bobcat stares.

"Promise, dear." *Don't call me dear again, woman.* "We take turns doing the dishes, and the ones that don't cook are the ones who do the dishes for the night. Would you like to join your sister Hannah at the sink?"

"Arghhh! That right there tied a ribbon on it. I'm not slavin' for no one, at least not on the first night. And Hannah's *not* my sister. Don't be forcing your family labels on me. Just because you signed some papers and let me in your home, doesn't magically make us family.

The next day, I met with my caseworker. I just about lost it when she said, 'Promise, that must have been special for you last night, a nice dinner with your new family. I bet that made you feel like you belong!'"

Ivory cleared his throat. "I would like to cook the main course tomorrow."

"You cook the food too long," Ashia said, laughing.

Ivory laughed back at her. "I like it crisp. I don't do sushi."

"I don't do carcinogens," she said.

Ivory pursed his lips, chomping on some cornbread, crumbs falling from the corners of his mouth. "How come none of you got invaded? Not even Cielo, sleeping right next to me."

"Must be your special aroma, Ivory," Maricela cackled.

"No, really, we need to investigate," Ivory protested. "We need to be… how do they always say it? Preventative. I'm not trying to be had by no ants again. Those things were fire ants, I'm pretty sure."

"We know, Ivory. You already informed us at least five times of that. Even though fire ants only live in the Amazon."

"Well, I guess my briefs are the Amazon then. We all know they are amazing, after all."

Not a soul gave his corniness the decency of a reply.

"Do you think we should try and get Mende out of his cabin?" Binda asked. "Or at least bring him some food?" Mende had been in the cabin, stewing, since he returned from his stomp into the woods.

"He's grown," Balanta said, looking at the smoldering pit. "He can come feed himself if he's hungry."

"Man," Ivory said, "when your spirit goes underwater and no light gets through, and you feel that blanket come over you to where you can't breathe, that's what you call going dark. Mende done went dark."

Cielo was deep into his food. He had reached ecstasy. "Man, hermano. This is way past good." Eloni's face flushed with pride. Their dessert was yam pudding that Balanta had made. It was spiced with nutmeg and cinnamon, freshly picked and ground.

"I'm feeling too spoiled with all this food," Ashia said. "Like I'm on the other side of the fence for once. I feel almost guilty eating so well."

"Girl, let that go," Ivory said. "Just put one bite in front of the other. Soon, you'll be working out that *poor*."

Cielo's mind flashed with a roll call of painful hunger moments from the past. And the mental tricks he forged to get through. "Being poor in this country," he said, "is like being forced to sit at a dinner table piled with insane amounts of food and being told you can't have any, you aren't worth having any, and you have no hope of becoming worthy of having any, so just sit there, be content, be invisible, and don't disturb our meal."

As they continued to eat, Balanta's eyes focused on a space near to the ground next to the trunk of a flowering orchid tree. A shadow swelled, as though it was peeking from behind the trunk. A form emerged, straight from the ink, separating itself into a new shape. Balanta had noticed strange movement in the shadows the evening before. The shape became form. Dimensional. It approached Balanta, who walked toward it, away from the group.

The form had questions.

"When do you come from?" Its voice was subterranean. Dense. Its vibration thudded against Balanta's eardrums.

"What do you mean?" Balanta regarded the shape, which kept changing. Coyote. Fox. Shrub. Then, a humpbacked figure with a shock of hair extending from the back of its head.

"What time? What era? All souls come from a time before. That's why they have ways. Messages from the past for the ones in the now time. If you don't know when you come from, how can you know what to do in your now time? And if you don't know that, how can you know peace? Peace is a wind that fills a soul each time it delivers even a single grain of its message from the time before."

Balanta stared deep into the form, but could not quite fix on its appearance. It was a black hole. A quantum storm. A billowing of photons. "You don't do small talk, do you?" Balanta asked, sincerely. He was not afraid. The seer in him took over. Solemn. Reverent to the moment. "Who are you? Why do you come to me?"

"Why do you come to me?" the form asked in return. "I have been here all along. It is you who journeys."

"You have been watching us. Me."

"It seems that *you* are the watcher. You see into shadows and recognize spirit. And now, you evade the question. Your soul hovers over a canyon between two worlds."

"You speak in riddles."

"I speak in truth. To humans, who exist in illusion, truth makes very little sense."

Balanta considered the form. Its existence here on this island. "Are you lonely?" he asked. His eyes continued searching for something within the form to lock onto.

"Loneliness is a weather system that clings to those who have forgotten the part of them beyond form. Why do you ask?"

"You are welcome to wander around here with us, or whatever it is you do." Balanta wasn't sure where his words came from. Just that he was compelled.

"Thank you," the form replied. "Your gathering amuses me. You and your companions are flirting with this place. Maybe soon you will make your move. Remember, Pain is a strong warrior. It fights for Freedom. There isn't so much distance between the inside of a human heart and the sky where freedom roams." With that, the form winked, and receded back into the trees. Balanta came back into himself. Although he thought he had walked away from the fire, he saw that he was still seated there.

"You all right, brother?" Cielo asked. "Your eyes were far away there for a minute."

To Balanta, it felt as though hours had passed inside his encounter with the form. He did not answer Cielo. Nor even offer him a glance.

Most of the group made their way down to the beach after eating. The ocean assaulted the shore. Row upon row of swells building to angry foaming legions racing each other to land. Sun plummeted behind transient clouds, creating white smoke and bold orange fire in the sky.

"The water looks creamy," Pikea said. She took a deep breath of the salt air. The scent caused a tinge of sadness. So many friends with whom she had shared *hongi*, exchanging their sacred breaths and *ha*. She wished they could appear now from across the water to hongi with her.

Maricela's dark hair wrapped around her face in the strong breeze. Her thin white cotton pants billowed over her legs as she stood still, lost in thought. *What kind of arrangement does the ocean have with the sun that the sun comes back down to it every single day?*

Out in the deep, a family of *something* moved beneath the water, their dorsals cutting, dipping, rising. The waves swelled, peaked, hunched, and crashed down. Then they seemed to dart rapidly to the right like a frothing sea snake just before subduing into a flat sheet that rolled over the sand and finally retracted back into the ocean's mouth.

Balanta spotted a baby sea lion far up shore. When they got to it, it appeared beached and in terror. It barked a weak call of alarm. They stayed close by for a few moments before its mother appeared from the waves. They backed off quickly as she moved with startling speed for her size, closing in on her pup. She regarded them. Ivory thought it was a warning. Lake felt it was a thank you.

Another squadron of gulls swept over the coastline, easing effortlessly upward on warm currents, seeming to mock the earthbound people below.

"How do they do that?" Promise asked. She was feeling better, especially now, catching extended breaths of the sea air.

"What?" Eloni asked.

"Fly in formation like that? Doesn't make any sense. Too perfect."

"Don't know," Eloni said. "A part of their instincts, I guess. They were born knowing how to move together."

"Wonder what would happen if you broke them apart, separated them?" Ivory asked.

Ashia's gaze followed the airshow. "I'm sure they would find their way back together. It's what they're wired for."

"I heard you can move pythons 100 miles from one location and they will find their way back." Ivory said. Seems like most animals have a magnet inside, pulling them toward what they come from. Like, how do turtle hatchlings know to head for the water at birth? I'd be stumbling like a drunk in the wrong direction, for sure."

"Hey, Ivory. When was the last time you read a book?" Ashia asked, rumbling with laughter.

"Outside of class? Don't remember," said Ivory.

"Did it ever occur to you that your game might be as thin as your reading habits, and that it's not a coincidence?"

"How so?"

"People are attracted to what adds to what they already are. It helps if you actually know something about... anything."

Ivory laughed off the comment. "I know this: when I flash this here smooth seal of approval, all the pretties lean my way."

"Probably trying to be sure they're seeing what they think they're seeing: a freakishly large forehead," Ashia said, Lovingly slapping that very plot of face.

"Ivory, pull your pants up." Promise said, piling on.

"You pull your pants down."

"Did you get that registered?" Promise asked.

"What?" Ivory said.

"Your sense of humor. It's a deadly weapon."

"Ivory," Ashia said, "maybe if you soak your words before speaking them, they'd turn out better. You know? Like rice or beans before you cook them. Just an observation."

"Ever notice how dolphin fins are the same shape as the ocean waves?" Cielo asked. "It's like they are camouflaged to blend in."

"We all do things to blend in." Ashia said under her breath.

Eloni rolled his eyes. "Every day we say we're not going to keep talking about bad stuff that night at the fire. And every night, we end up right back where we were, talking about the bad stuff."

"Maybe that's because it's not bad stuff," said Maricela. "Maybe it's just a part of our stuff, period. Bad, good, there is no such thing. It's just us working out our stuff."

"Blood flows toward a wound," added Cielo, munching on a carrot dipped in pureed olives. "That's what carries the white cells and plasma to the wound, where they can do their healing work."

"What?" asked Eloni, his face wearier than his voice. Both were sharp and hard.

"I'm saying, when we come to the fire, we are drawn toward what we need to talk about. It's not our choice, really."

"Buddha, please..."

Cielo said, "That's the third time you've taken a shot at me. What's your issue?" His placid aura switched. He was a dark moon now, his voice crumbling into a nervous vibrato.

"What's real, Cielo! What's real?" Eloni taunted. He pushed Cielo's chest. Cielo fell back but not down. The group was confused and shocked at the sudden change in energy.

"Eloni just went dark," Ivory announced. "Keep your distance. That's one strong Samoan."

"Control your cortisol, Eloni," Promise said. "Your anger herd's loose."

Cielo was scorching mad, too. He felt his blood cells swell. Wasn't hearing anything but the river surge of hot blood gushing through his head. His eyes were primal, watered and red.

"Cielo, step off. I'm not playing," Eloni said. Cielo swung wildly. Eloni shifted, averting easily. A dust cloud obscured their movement.

"There it is, boy!" Eloni mocked. "I knew you had that beast in you. Go ahead, let it out!" Cielo was quivering, his eyes hot and primal, the potent mist of Eloni's spit and dominance all up in Cielo's face. Cielo threw an awkward and disembodied blow. Eloni stepped back, his head moving away, out of reach like Ali in his prime, a phantom, there one moment, tauntingly out of range the next. In a single meditative movement, Eloni grabbed Cielo's wrist, using the forward momentum of Cielo's whiffed punch, pulled Cielo's arm down and behind his back, and brought Cielo facedown in the sand, pressing his knee forcefully on Cielo's back like in a steer roping contest. Cielo's face heaved in its disgrace of sand and snot, puffing for air, crying. Lost in something beyond anger. His body surrendered, spirit shamed.

"Please!" screamed Ashia. "Stop! Eloni, you're hurting him! Stop, you guys!"

Ashia's tearful voice filled everyone with a piquant terror. Even as he subdued Cielo, a river of ripe pain opened deep in Eloni, a self-hatred and disappointment that set off a vomit reflex. He barely held it down as he remained fixed in on what was now more performance than calculation, flooded with adrenaline and all the inflammation of his lifetime.

Cielo had been inside of a pain like this before. He was barely ten, his wafer body still only sniffing muscularity. His own padre had just smashed Cielo's cherished guitar against a coffee table. A guitar that Cielo had polished for hundreds of hours with the oils of his own hands. His padre spoke only a few words in that moment. But the hell in his eyes, and the precision of the words, were enough. *Bastante*. His padre said to his 10-year-old son, "I will never stop regretting that I let you into this world." The words and their meaning landed on Cielo's heart like a bunker-busting missile and bore into his tenderness violently. The pain was so unbearable, Cielo felt willing to do anything to end it. Even the ultimate thing. In the piercing, boiling torture of that moment, that place, a splinter of a thought entered him. That splinter would change his life the way spring changes winter.

Maricela was in pain. She couldn't believe what Eloni had just done to Cielo. No one else could either. Everyone just went silent and retreated back to camp. Maricela needed to cool off, she was so upset. She waded into the calm sea, the light turquoise water rising to her waist. "Madre mia..." she whispered, plaintively. Her hands circled in the water, stirring eddy currents that performed and vanished. Her white skirt floated to the water's surface, a jellyfish around her waist. A light breeze moved her hair over her shoulders, and back again. Her eyes, still releasing tears, closed to the sound of seabirds. She smiled. Tilting her head back, she faced the sky as she dropped down under the waves. *Madre...* She ascended to the surface and lay on her back, the water bobbing her up and down gently. Her body weight disappeared. She was no longer on earth. She was a flower floating in the palm of Grace. Sanctified.

Eloni tried to touch Maricela's arm. He had waded out after her. Startled, Maricela opened her eyes and stood up urgently out of her back float. She pushed Eloni's hand away forcefully. Her dark eyes were ignited. "You could have killed that boy, Loni. You had to pick the sweetest soul to hurt and humiliate?"

"I'm sorry. I..."

"I'm not the one you need to apologize to. Que pasa? What got into you? Don't tell me Cielo threatens you somehow."

Eloni dropped down until the water was at his neck. His face was a valley of shame. "It's not his fault. I snapped. Too much pressure." He started hitting the side of his head.

"Don't do that!" Maricela shouted. "What pressure? We couldn't be in a more relaxed, drama-free situation out here, and you're talking about pressure?"

"You wouldn't understand. I'm dealing with stuff you can't imagine."

"Oooh..." Maricela sounded in warning. "Don't give me that, 'you wouldn't understand' bull. Everyone here is dealing with stuff. No excuse for you to get violent. For no reason but your mood went rancid!"

Eloni backed away from Maricela. "I shouldn't have come out here to you. Sorry."

"Yeah, man. I was trying to get my peace on. I was so upset with you. Still am."

"Cela... Look. I'll go talk to him. But please don't give up on me. I can't take any more rejection right now. Can you please give me another chance?"

Maricela turned away from Eloni and looked out to sea. "Dominating everyone and everything isn't what makes a man," she said, calmly. "You got all that Samoan pride. Want to know what will make Samoa proud? Learn to be at peace with the world. And with your own heart. That's the Samoan way, right? That's what you've been telling me, in your own words."

"It's hard for me," Eloni said. "I know that's not an excuse. Some stuff out here is bringing up some of my issues."

"You and Balanta need to go on ahead and do your little quest thing and get it out of your system. Hopefully you'll get some of that anger out, too." Maricela resumed her back float, closed her eyes, and listened to the sound of Eloni swimming back to shore.

At camp, people were looking for conversation that would help them feel more comfortable. Eloni's violence left adrenaline flooding through their bodies, still.

Lake looked into the trees, scanning. "Where are the firefly people tonight? I haven't seen one so far."

"I bet they're all over in the meadow," Ivory said.

Lake, Binda, and a few others ran over to the meadow for a brief visit, just to catch the light show that started at dusk. They arrived right on time. The meadow sparked with fireflies. Clouds of them condensed, then dispersed. Their bright bobbing briefly scripted thin lines of light against the darkness. The glowing orbs decorated the trees. Mimicked the stars. Illuminated the tall grasses. They scripted radiant fonts on the paper of night. As if they were trying to communicate. Something. Starlight in the heavens had a soul mating of starlight on earth.

For Lake, this display was like being in an art gallery. "At the group home," Lake said, "they kept taking my art supplies away. They said I was too antisocial and lost inside myself. For me, being in my art was the same as finding myself again, returning to a private place in the woods where I am safe and home.

"*Antisocial*... When grown folks say they want you to develop socially, I can feel their own fear of loneliness. But alone is not the same thing as lonely. There's a difference. I'm okay in silence. I know it won't touch me wrong or scream at me because I pointed out how something feels against my heart. I would rather have an absence of words than the presence of a hurtful tongue.

"I learned to paint the air with my fingers. It wasn't just about the colors. It was also the sensation of my heart expressed through my body, touching the world and changing it. Feeling that power to change the air soothed me. Made me feel I could roll over in the blanket of being alive and relieve whatever pressure had built up.

"Air is an endless canvas. Imagination never runs out of paint. And no one can stop me from painting the sky."

"Will you walk with me?" Ashia asked. She extended her hand. Balanta took it and they walked along the shoreline until they reached the estuary. Balanta kneeled and scooped some rich, white clay into his hands. "The word *Balanta* means, *Those who resist*. Our people fiercely resisted colonization and slavery when it came to our lands. We were known and even resented by other West Africans for not cooperating with that evil machinery."

"Well, then you sure are true to your name, Balanta," said Ashia, "because you are stubborn as a mule stuck in the mud. Resist might just be your middle name."

"*Ashé*. Anyway, our Balanta people have an initiation ceremony for boys who aspire to be true men," Balanta shared reverently. It is called *Fanado*, and takes place in sacred woods. The woods here remind me of such places." He thought of his Mende culture's Poro and Sande societies and the way boys and girls were socialized into them, achieving their adulthood authentically. The white clay in his hands reminded Balanta of *Hojo*, the sparkling white clay Sande society women used to pronounce their territory, and their initiative membership. *Hojo* was sacred and exclaimed sacredness. Balanta rubbed the clay between his palms. A pang of yearning needled through his heart.

Ashia saw the way his lips briefly pursed. Those lips. She felt they were blessed by God, lined and filled out to perfection.

Balanta's face grew unusually bothered. Ashia noticed him clench his left fist repeatedly, as though he was trying to work out a kink. Moisture beaded on his forehead. "It's good to just be able to have room to breathe right now," Balanta said, his voice dropping, "without having to constantly be the big brother."

"Are you looking for a way to excuse your behavior toward your brother? Ashia asked. "Because if that's what you're doing, I've got news for you, brother. There is no excuse."

Balanta's silence barely held behind taut lips.

"I was taught that this world is a canvas we've been given to paint," Ashia said. "No matter what we do, think, or feel, we continuously and forever leave a mark. There's no such thing as do-overs and erasing our footprints. We are artists using permanent paint, so we need to take care with each and every stroke."

"Is that why you walk the way you do?" asked Balanta, his tone warming only slightly.

Ashia laughed. "I've always been given grief over that. I never thought about it, I just walked the way that felt right. I like being as close to the sun as I can get, so I stretch out my spine."

"But I mean the way you move slowly, too, as though you're performing. Reminds me of tai chi."

Ashia thought for a moment. "I remember swinging on the playground in elementary school, watching the other children running around like jacked-up monkeys. There was almost a panic in their excitement. Their eyes bulged too much, and their energy was desperate. I sat there, swinging. It felt so good to feel the air rush through my hair and over my face and body the higher I went. It was only a brief moment, but I had this thought: Don't live like that. Don't be panicked. Move the way a giraffe moves. Like you have no troubles, just finding leaves."

"Even giraffes freak out now and then," said Balanta.

"Yes, but it isn't their default setting, you know? I get tired sometimes just being around so many panicked young people, and grown folks in crisis mode. I don't think humans were made to exist like that. So, I guess I stroll when I walk. Just trying to own my own Peace."

They moved on from the estuary, back into the privacy of the woods. Dusk was just beginning to creep down through the canopy. Balanta stopped at a eucalyptus trunk and ran his palm over its smoothness. As they moved deeper into the trees, he cleared vines and branches from around his head, and from around Ashia's waist. They came to an opening where tall grass took over. "Let's stop here," said Ashia, softly. Will you lie down with me for a while?"

They lay on their backs on the soft mattress of grass, its blades still holding the day's heat. Crickets were already announcing the coming night. Staring up at the sky, they watched the sparse clouds turn from white to gray in the changing light, nebulous shapes drifting, chasing each other, merging. Ashia nestled her head between Balanta's chest and arm, his hand engulfing her shoulder. She closed her eyes, nuzzled his neck with her nose, and inhaled his scent deeply. He smelled of garlic, of sweat that was like sweet water, and of a hormonal richness that made her whole body tremble.

The trees around the clearing were becoming silhouette people. Jacaranda pods clattered in the light breeze. Willows sashayed. Ashia and Balanta lay closely, their contours finding each other. The sky above roofed their privacy, invited their intimacy to leave the mundaneness of earth and swirl up and into a realm with no boundary, no concern, no inconvenience of time.

Eloni walked, a scolded child, over to where Cielo sat, soothing himself with his palms against his bongos. Eloni's shoulders slumped nearly to his belly, his bull chest concave.

"I like those walking sticks you whittled, Cielo." "Will you make me one?" Eloni asked, timidly.

Cielo wanted to be hard and cruel, but those were spirits foreign to him. He slid into his nature. "Sure. You want one waist high, or chest high?"

"Listen, man," Eloni cut to the issue. "I feel badly for coming at you like that. I'm... sorry."

"I don't know about floating like a butterfly, but you sure can sting like a bee!" Cielo stretched for humor, uncomfortable with the tension.

"Man, I'm sorry. You actually remind me of who I want to be in a lot of ways. It hurts being reminded of your failure. I took it out on you."

"How have you possibly failed? Everyone here looks up to you. Even Balanta."

"My competitiveness isn't a trait. It's a wound that hasn't healed. Pops didn't think enough of me to stay. I've been living ever since then to become a king, so he would have to come and bow to me one day. Takes a lot of energy. I'd rather be like you."

"A pauper? A beggar? A peasant?" Cielo tried to smooth the way toward a lighter moment.

"Huh... yeah, I guess. Just a regular guy, free from proving points. I'm too consumed with auditioning for acceptance from a mythical man who doesn't exist. Skip that. I want to just be. That's all. Just be."

Cielo looked at Eloni with eyes of forgiveness. Eloni recognized the gesture for what it was, bringing tears just beneath Eloni's surface that he fought back down. Instead, he sat down next to Cielo. They both looked into the distance and drafted a treaty in their silence.

Darkness bloomed. The starry sky was perforated with a bright scallop of moonlight, a vanilla parenthesis silent and beckoning. "It's a quarter moon, now," Lake noted. "The moon is losing its belly. The giant is falling asleep. Soon he'll be dreaming all the way."

Pikea and Ivory fed the fire. Pikea out of a spirit of industry, Ivory out of fear. That, and his addiction to flame. He found himself craving flames in strange moments. Like while watching romantic movies by himself. Or during late night study groups.

Mende appeared from his cabin for the first time since before dinner, and approached Cielo, sitting down next to him. Cielo could see that Mende's spirit had returned to his eyes. "I know what we can do for a quest," said

Mende. His voice hoarse, subdued. "We can circumnavigate the island. By canoe."

Cielo looked out at the ocean, its territory so boundless and anonymous. "You mean go all the way around the island? Sounds good to me." Cielo was down for anything, before even knowing any details, especially if an adventure was involved. He was a wild horse, fated for a life in a domesticated human herd, but he himself would always jump at any wind. "I guess we should get right to planning?"

They told the group of their plans. "You two can't be going out into the ocean in that canoe," cautioned Ashia. "Let's be real. We don't need any drownings."

"We already thought about that," said Mende. "We'll stay inside the barrier reef, where the water is calm."

"And what if the reef doesn't wrap around the entire island?" Ashia asked.

"Then we'll just turn around and head back," said Cielo. "But something tells me this whole island is protected by that reef."

"Does the canoe even float? Have you tested it?"

"About to," said Cielo. "Shonto? Ivory? Anyone else want to come?"

Ivory waved Cielo off. "No way, Columbus. I was given legs, not flippers. No way I'm trusting a piece of wood on the whole ocean. You do know there's sharks, right?"

"Not likely inside the reef," said Cielo.

"You never heard of reef-jumping sharks?" Ivory asked.

Maricela stood up, wiping sweetgrass strands off her lap from the basket she was weaving. "I'll go with you two jokers. We're not having any segregation, me comprendes?"

"That will be great!" Mende exclaimed.

Cielo flipped a twig onto the sand and brushed back his bangs. "I'm sure there'll be some amazing coves out there. We can explore them and bring back news, like a scouting party."

"Like Conquistadors?" asked Shonto.

"No," answered Cielo. "Nor like missionaries. Just... pollen following the wind."

"Pollen gets stuck," Ashia observed. "Make sure that's not you."

"Claro, claro," said Cielo. "We'll be sure to get back to the hive. We can leave early in the morning. Probably be back the same day."

They went to the shore and tested the canoe there in the darkness. It was waterproof. The hull, carved from the trunk of a large sinker cypress from a river at the island's interior, was thick and stained black and rustic along the waterside with a generous application of eucalyptus sap. Twenty feet in length, the main challenge had been getting the canoe from its storage spot up by the cabins, down to the water.

Darkness congealed. Bonfire stretched and sparked. Stories began.

"Ivory, when you had ants in your pants, I seriously thought I was going to die," Lake said, cracking up again. "I could not breathe, I tell you, and at least three of my ribs darn near broke."

"Who you telling? Ivory said. If that wasn't a come to Jesus moment for me, it was at least a come to Moses. Y'all had your jokes at my expense, but that was crazy. And how come I'm the only one who got attacked?"

Maricela laughed. "You just have it like that, Ivory."

Ivory was already onto another tangent. "Moms was always running dudes through her bedroom," he shared. "I wasn't having that though. I wasn't gonna let no one hurt her. I felt like she was the only thing I had in the world. The only thing to hold onto.

"When I heard fussin and arguing going on behind her bedroom door, it set off my blood, man. I kept my ear to the door, trying to decide whether I needed to bust in. I was a straight up ant soldier, protecting the Queen.

"One time, dude started to get rough with Moms. I heard him barking, through the door. A child knows the qualities of his mother's voice. I was learning Moms' since the womb. She was a strong woman, but I could tell when her voice broke into fear. That one time, I heard it break. I busted in, went and got the shotgun she kept under the bed. Pointed that bad boy straight at dude's chest. Tears were burning my eyes. Hands shaking. "You ain't laying another hand on my moms," I said. "I ain't afraid to light off this here match."

"Dude's eyes went from surprise to smugness to fear in a hot second. He saw what was in my eyes and must've thought: *This little punk is desperate. He's ready to kill.*

"I was six years old. Moms died when I was nine. AIDS. Gramma stepped in and became the next *only thing* I had in the world. I had one piece of wood in the ocean to keep afloat. Lost it. Then took hold of the only other piece of wood that floated by.

"I posted up outside of Gramma's bedroom door just like I did with Moms. Always with my ear to the door. Grown folks reveal it all when the door is closed. They think doors are soundproof, that a home is soundproof, that their thoughts are soundproof. Eventually, whatever is in their soul, it all comes out for a child to hear."

Ivory's face saddened, his gaze dropping. "I had an auntie once, but... she got took out by some dude trying to pimp her. The murder made my gramma more religious. It made my Moms not believe in God."

With their silence, the group affirmed Ivory for several beats of time. Ivory looked at Ashia, her face noble in the firelight. "I admire you, Ashia. You must have it easy, being so popular and all," he said.

Ashia frowned. "Was that a compliment or a putdown? You think being *popular*, as you call it, is easy? I bet you fantasize about how good I have it. Let me tell you, I used to hate myself privately. Thought I was the ugliest person in the world. I didn't even notice what you call being popular. I couldn't believe anyone could truly like me. Just because I liked everyone didn't mean I felt so popular.

"People are always assuming that I'm conceited, all because they see people drawn to me. That's so judgmental and ugly. I can feel them resenting me. I don't want attention. I just want someone to make me feel like I'm a human being. And that I belong. Anywhere. You can have your popularity. Be careful what you ask for. Those bright lights can burn, baby. Anyways, there's a big difference between people knowing you, and people *knowing you*, feel me?

Ashia ran her fingers through her locs. "In high school, at the end of each year, I stapled some pages together that I had torn out of my class notebook. I used that in place of a yearbook cause I could never afford a real one. I went around asking people I didn't even know to sign my so-called *yearbook*."

"Man, how did that feel?" Mende asked.

"Embarrassing as could be. Some people thought I was joking at first and laughed with me. Some took the opportunity to laugh at me. Some just looked at me with pity and signed their name nervously. That hurt the worst."

"Why did you ask people who weren't your friends?" Binda asked.

"I don't know... I just... wanted to feel like I knew people. You know?" as Ashia spoke, she was hit with a cold realization of just how isolated she had been.

"We had cheese samiches about twice a day, five days a week." Ivory said, already moving on.

"Cheese sandwiches?" Cielo asked.

"Nah, man. *Samiches*. And not Swiss or brie or whatever. Straight-up processed cheese. Still not sure what the percentage of rubber content is on that stuff."

"What about juice?" Mende asked.

"Wasn't no orange juice or apple juice. It was red, orange, pink, and purple. That's it. And Moms used to keep refilling the milk jug with water all week to replace the milk as it went down. By day three, that joint was two percent alright. Two percent milk and 98 percent water. She thought she was fooling us. We felt bad, so we didn't say anything. Y'all ever had milk flavored water?"

Mende slapped his thigh and bounced up. "That's what I'm talking about!"

Pikea stood up. "Y'all check this out. We used to have this thing we would say: *Troll on the bridge*! Those group home staff, man, I don't know, I had a few that were aright, but a lot of them seemed like people who had no power growing up, so give them some power over some young people and they go crazy with it.

"They would do things that made no sense, like make you go back to the end of the hallway and walk down it again, only this time 'quieter.' Man, if I repeat the walk, it doesn't make the noise I just made not exist. What are you even talking about?

"Or the adults, anywhere, that you have to deal with because they have *authority*. You ask them if you can do something and you can feel their brain start rattling, looking for some dusty policy or procedure that they can quote just so they can tell you *No*. Just straight set on shutting you down, before you even approach them.

"When they power tripped on us like that, over little things, there was only so much we could do—"

"Cause we had no power!" They called out in harmony.

"So we just relieved our pressure by making fun of the situation. *Troll on the bridge*! would be our warning call when one of the power-tripping staff was coming. It was also our way of supporting another teenager when they had just been scolded, or put down. *Troll on the bridge*! Like handing out candy at the dentist's office. Just trying to make the pain and tears go away."

Cielo held forth on the metaphysical meaning of being recycled through various families. Promise took his point in a different direction. "My friends and I call it *regifting*," she said. "Like when people get gifts they don't like. They just rewrap it and give it to someone else. That's what these families do with children like us. Regift us on to the next home. Done deal. Wash your hands. Sleep tight. And not just with foster care. Happens all the time with adoption, too. Merchandise returned. Failure to thrive. Bad match. Unfortunate outcome. And it's never the family who's blamed. Always the child. Failed to bond. Failed to fit in. Couldn't get it together. You know how when a small space craft docks with a large one in those sci fi movies? That's what it feels like. You're trying to dock, but there's too much turbulence. The linking mechanism fails and you just blow away into space."

"People treat us like lepers," Pikea said. "First you get separated from your family. Then you get separated from humanity for the crime of being separated from your family."

"Don't try too hard to be normal," Ivory said. "It's not all it seems to be. I prefer the freedom of being a freak."

Promise tossed a birch log onto the fire. As its sap heated, a sweet scent saturated the smoke. "Don't tell me how much you Love me," she said, "Show me that you care to learn me. I've had it up to here with parents thinking that they can use *I Love you* to tidy up and end every conversation. If I have issues with you, deal with my issues. Don't run away from them by saying, 'I Love you.' What a cop-out."

Eloni shared a Samoan legend of *the Turtle and the Shark*, about a blind grandmother and granddaughter banished by their family during a famine. The two threw themselves into the ocean to avoid starvation, were transformed into a turtle and shark, and traveled far. Arriving at Vaitogi, they were transformed back into their human form and greeted and cared for by a hospitable people. Eventually, they returned to the sea. By the time he finished his story, he was so animated from portraying the figures that he broke into dance. He was a boy again. Light and inspired. "Go, Loni!" the group shouted, encouraging him on as he smiled and danced with an emancipated heart around the fire.

Pikea felt something hard come up inside her throat. She spat it out with as much civility as she could. "My father came back from combat a whole different spirit. When he came through the door the first time, I hid behind my mother's leg. I was only six.

"He's large, so he blotted out the outdoor light as he stepped into the living room. His energy was... absent. Like a ghost who had put on my father's clothes. I was looking for some warmth in his eyes, cause I missed him and wanted to run into his arms. I saw nothing but absence in those eyes. It made me want to hold onto something I could feel. So I grabbed my mother's leg real tight and closed my eyes. I was hoping the ghost had come to the wrong address and would leave."

"Maricela, tell us about La Llorona," Pikea asked. Maricela had shared part of the story with Pikea when they went out to gather wild berries the morning before.

"You all sure you want to hear that story?" Maricela asked, deferentially.

"Yeah!" The response was collective and eager.

"Mi abuela told us children that when her grandparents first came to this country, they had to leave most of their life behind. But that one of the few precious belongings they were able to preserve was their cultural stories. Abuela grew up hanging around her grandparents' sides like squirrels around an acorn tree."

"You mean oak tree?" Mende asked.

"I call it acorn tree. One of Abuela's favorite stories to listen to was the legend of La Llorona. La Llorona means *Weeping Woman*."

Ivory and Eloni leaned forward, eyes wide, rapt and enchanted. Firelight sashayed over everyone's faces, making them lanterns circling the center flames. Sap popped in the fire, dramatizing the scene with its staccato cadence. Maricela introduced them to the woman who wept for her lost children, which turned out to be a story they all knew too well.

The conversation came around to the issue of incarceration. Pikea jumped in. "When you're inside, it's not like you think. Whatever you imagine about it is magnified once you're inside. The bad stuff is blown up worse than you can believe. And there is good stuff, too. Not that it's a reason to be there. But I finally stopped running, racing in my mind, searching with my behavior for some kind of safety. A place to land. When you land that hard, it can shut up your mind. After years of yelling for attention, you finally shut up. From the pure shock. *Wow, I can't believe I'm here. Is this real?*

"The other thought is, *When am I gonna get jumped?* You just know that's a part of it, like three square-and-a-cot. Or steel toilets and lights out at 10 flat. When my mind shut up like that, first it was frightening, to be honest. I was used to noise. Mine. Everyone else's. Now, it was only this strange buzzing of silence. Felt like its own noise, really, except that it was like a wind or something empty. And it filled up all the corners and spaces inside my brain. Mind you, it was actually loud as could be in the joint. But in my head, those sounds were muffled all the way down.

"I fought that mental silence like it was to the death. I did feel like I was dying. I clawed to get some noise back. I got into it with the other cons, caused trouble over nothing. I just needed some noise *inside*. But the silence kept creeping back. It was like a moss growing on the cell bars, in the cracks of the cement floors and walls, and on the fluorescent bulbs on the ceiling. Especially after lights out. Just kept creeping back at me. Like it had a mind and I was on its Most Wanted list.

"At some point, I began to crave that silence. Almost like I had gone through withdrawal from the noise from my life, the shakes and sweats and delirium. And now I was cooling out on the other side. I began to look forward to lights out, and real silence. I slept like a champion."

"Not like a baby?" Ivory asked.

"Babies don't sleep so well where I'm from. I was all peace at night, and in the morning, just before all the hollering and conflict started up again, I was full on Zen inside my cell. Taking deep breaths with my eyes closed so I could hold onto that silence through the day. However being locked up messed me up, and I'm sure it did, at least it introduced me to inner silence. I wish I didn't have to go there to meet it, though."

Pikea tossed a pitch knot full of sap, onto the fire. She looked up at the stars, then said, "My advocate kept asking me, 'What does it feel like being you?' I said, 'It's like being walled off from your own existence, trapped behind drywall, having to chip away at a breathing hole, desperate to create a hole large enough so you can break into your own self. And the whole time you're behind the wall, you're screaming for someone to notice you there. People pass by all the time. Sometimes they lean against the wall, right on the spot that you're behind. Sometimes they even think they hear a whisper. They knock on the wall, listening for a response. And you're yelling until your throat bleeds. No one ever does find you back there. Years go by, with you stuck and suffocating behind a wall."

Shonto told a story about one time when his math teacher pitched a fit at him because Shonto had drawn eyeballs inside of all the multiple choice bubbles on his exam. "My teacher almost pulled his hair out," Shonto said. "He was screaming something terrible. I thought he was going to stroke out. This was the same guy that always glared at me in the hallway because he thought I wasn't going to end up anywhere but prison."

"How do you know he thought that?" Ivory asked.

"Because he told me. Anyway… after he blew his top, I just looked at him and said, 'Now who's really incarcerated here? You judge me. I know you do. I can feel it in your eyes when you look at me. You see all the labels: Convict. Criminal. Thug. Monster. At least I have my rage under control. From that display you just put on, I would say you're the one who's imprisoned.'"

Pikea shook her head in disgust. "It's all a joke. How's locking me up supposed to prepare me to be a better citizen? I did what I did. I get that. But it doesn't matter how many times I beat myself up over it. I can't figure out how putting me in a cage, with other people in a cage, makes me better. Where's the healing part?"

Eloni agreed. "When your family and friends are on the outside, living their lives, and you're on the inside, eventually you start to see yourself as a ghost, not really alive. And you can feel them moving away from you. All the ones still living. You can feel them burying you before you're even dead, cause they can't stand the pain of thinking of you all the time. Thinking of you shriveling up like a fruit dropped to the ground and left to rot in the sun.

"You ever been buried alive? I have. That's what lockup does for you. Tell me how that benefits society. Cause once I'm out, now you have a situation on your hands. You're dealing with the dead come back to life. And no one has the program to handle that."

Ashia stood and danced a few circles around the fire, just to get her blood flowing. "Some of these placement homes and shelters can be a form of incarceration, too," she noted.

She was thinking of one place in particular. An experience that had seared into her a disdain for institutions. No, Ashia would not be returning to that group home, with its hard, squeaking flame-retardant mattresses, and its sulfurous tap water. Its showers that turned your hair green if it was naturally light, and your naturally dark hair a dull puke-cardboard brown. Its AWOL alarms blaring as frequently as classroom period bells. Its *no razors* policy because, we can't have you cutting yourself, not that you would, honey, just to be safe, you know? Its carpeted room for after you threw a fit (what about rug burns?), carpeted walls and floors, carpet stained with urine and vomit and blood and sour tears. All washed so insufficiently, leaving terrible tattoos, reminders of concentrated suffering burst forth like an adolescent acne uprising. Burst forth like a bloated whale two weeks on the beach, scalding beneath July's ferocious solar offering. And its fetid daily schedule that drained any righteous soul of a will, not to live, but to even breathe with full intent to take on oxygen, or anything that might be renewing for a worn out pre-adult. Its hallways like petulant coroner's rooms. Hallways not content with being lifeless, gray, and frigid. No, having also to belch out assaultive language on harsh colored posters warning of the dangers of drugs, alcohol, twerking, self-mutilation, pregnancy, anger, violence, violating personal space, slouching, hanging your pants too low, listening to your music too loudly, refusing or stashing your meds, gambling, frowning, not using your inside voice, not obeying authority, using too much toilet paper, hiding candy in the rare private spaces of your room, not participating in group stuff, not taking advantage of alone time, grieving your past too much, caring about your relationships too deeply (we're your family for now). And its mortician staff, drained of blood and sensitivity, empowered by coursework and certificates and licenses. Its turpentine and vinegar building odor. Its spider webs left unremoved from light fixtures so that when you stare up at the ceiling, which you inevitably and often will, you are left with staring at ceiling tiles that make you wonder about the dangers of mold and asbestos. Along with the gusty drapery of webs letting you know that while you sleep it is more than a numerical possibility that a spider will drop onto your face, or in your mouth or ear, and that you might therefore wake up in an ambulance, swollen and mercurial of temperature as the emergency attendants in their too bright white uniforms smile at you through gleaming grills and reassure you with, "Let's get you fixed up so you can get back *home* as soon as possible." No, Ashia would not be returning to that desolate, vermin infested, asylum of a group home ever again. Nor any other home where they dump you because you aren't suitable to have a real life. And anyone who tried to put her back in one of those places was subject to lose their reproductive jewelry right quick.

"I know where you're coming from, Ashia," Eloni said. "I can't stand it when you get to a family's home for the first time and they sit you right down in the living room to go over the rules, before you've even had a chance to use the bathroom. Makes me feel like I'm a violent felon in their eyes. Why you got to hit me with the rules straight from the jump? Is this prison or something? We can't grow into the relationship and let it come natural? Why are you so nervous with me you got to lay down the law before I get a chance to put my clothes away? Is that how you do your own children? Come at them all corporate and controlling, soon as they come out the womb? If that's what I wanted, I could have stayed in group for that.

"You want me to feel like I belong, but you treat me at a distance, all nervous and uncomfortable with me. I'm supposed to feel secure inside of that?" Eloni was now lost in his rant, imagining his intended audience as being right in front of him. "How about if I sat you down, parents, right from the get go, and laid out my rules to you? How would that make you feel?"

Eloni pounded his chest, apelike, and stretched out his arms. "But I have to admit, y'all. My last group home finally gave me a place to feel like I belonged. Like it wasn't just keeping me for a minute before passing me on. I felt safe. The staff was down to earth. Most of them actually listened when I tried to explain something. Without that place, I would not have made it.

Looking back, I see that my family wasn't even close to being able to handle me. And no other family would have been able to either.

"I felt secure being surrounded by so many other youth like me. I didn't have to explain or hide anything. Just be about it. A whole campus dedicated to my particular needs? Felt like insulation against the world."

Promise broke into a grin. "Look at Loni, contributing a positive spin to the group!"

Cielo smiled at a memory. "I stayed under this one overpass onetime where, I kid you not, I woke up with some dude pissing on my face while his two-year-old in his Huggies stood their laughing at me. The baby was saying, 'Make it rain, daddy! Make it rain!' And pops was saying, 'Daddy's making it rain!' I promise you, on my own grave."

"*On your own grave*? What does that even mean?" Promise asked.

"Who knows? I'm just saying, it's probably why I don't get too ruffled here on the island over every little inconvenience."

Balanta shot Cielo a sharp look that Mende and Ashia both noticed.

"We need to treat each other better," Ashia said, staring at Balanta. "We don't know who is in this circle, do we?"

"What do you mean?" Lake asked.

"Imagine if your classmate was, I don't know… some future world changing humanitarian. You would treat them differently in class if you knew that. But we don't. We don't know until we know. So we better decide to assume that each of us right here is something worth being good to. Even if we don't see them clearly yet."

"There's this ancient place I got to go to one time," Maricela said, wearing a faraway gaze. "It's called the Convento de San Gabriel monastery, down in Puebla, Mexico. You get all that?" she joked. "We were able to go into this sanctuary there that the monks use for some kind of special ceremony. The floors were dirt, the walls, adobe. I went in with a group of about 20. All of a sudden, I felt something weird come over me. I got dizzy."

"Did you start speaking in tongues?" Ivory joked.

"Ivory, stop," Ashia scolded.

Maricela's eyes were distant, lost in the memory. "The dirt floor smelled so strong, but not in a bad way. It smelled like fresh air. Looking back on it, I feel that I was somehow wavering between the present and the past. Like I could smell the dirt from when the monastery was built.

"When I came to my senses, the group had moved on and left me. I was the only one in the sanctuary. I sat down on the floor. More like collapsed. And I cried the happiest cry I've ever had. That was the most peace I have felt in my life. And I was alone. On a dirt floor. On a tour. What does that say?"

Maricela continued. "My family is obsessed with being good Catholics. Dropped me at this Catholic boarding school one year. Nuns there were either mean as badgers or sweet as cherry pie that grandma forgot and put double the sugar in. No in-between.

"This one nun, Sister Henrietta, we called her Sister Henry on account of her beard, she come from Pittsburgh and had trouble telling apart Mexicans from Indians, so she lumped us all together. Thought we were all pagans doomed to hell. That didn't go over too well. One night, we put on ski masks and when she was out walking in the garden, we tied her to an old tree and made up a fake Indian dance. We stomped and hollered and war cried in a circle around that poor woman until she peed her pants and cried out to the Lord Himself, 'Oh, why have you forsaken me?'

"Most of us developed a guilt complex about it after that. And when she was transferred to a monastery up North in the mountains two weeks later, we were actually sad. Strange how you miss someone's presence, just out of habit, even if they took you through the blender.

"Yeah...," Maricela said wistfully as she returned to her thoughts. "But most of the nuns weren't that bad, just a little drowsy in the head, like an allergic reaction to pollen or something. Except their pollen was spiritual. You know? Like they were sleep walking through a performance of being saintly. I just wanted to shake them sometimes and say, 'Put on some jeans, woman, and come join the rest of us here on earth and eat some pizza. It's not that serious.'

"If I invented a nun-slapping machine, would that be blasphemy? Nah, just playing. Maybe I'm still a little angry. I never been so condescended to other than that year. One of my favorite people was one of those nuns, though. Sister Roberta. She stole apples with us from the orchard on the next property over, and she even took us to the R-rated movies in the Pope Mobile. That's what we called the old school van.

"Then there was Sister Angelica, not aptly named either. She stole drags on these fat Cuban cigars and smelled of it, too. Drank lite beers like there was about to be a prohibition. I mean, she pounded those things. Never saw here tipsy, either. And she swore worse than any of us kids. She tried to play it off that she had Tourette's, but we noticed how strategic she was about cursing the male superiors when they were around. She cursed God plenty, too. Wasn't scared of retribution. But then, she was always the first one to go for confession. You could hear her laughing and swearing up in the confessional. She was a hot mess."

Eloni bounced up and grabbed an ankle, stretching out his thigh, then the other.

"You getting ready to run, Kunta?" Promise asked.

"Pikea taught me this," said Eloni, his spine erect, shoulders pulled back, hands on his crouched thighs, poised for the *haka* war dance.

"Can't be taught," Pikea replied. "Have to have it in you already. You must be Maori somehow. You know how we Polynesians are. Only so much island space. People come together."

Something old rose from the earth and surged into Eloni through his bare feet, which sprouted roots that sank into the soil. Eloni's muscles clenched and swelled with blood. His eyes misted. Sweat broke on his skin. A mountain's voice boomed from Eloni's chest, waking troops of drums from within. He began to lift his thighs, pistoning them back down, stomping his feet into the dirt with impossible force, oaks landing from the sky. With his open palms, he pounded his chest, mountain voice bellowing in cadence. He was no longer a boy. He was warrior spirit unleashed.

Ivory regaled the group with a litany of fire-starting exploits. Enough of a roster that Promise wasn't the only one looking at the others with concern. "I was setting everything on fire," Ivory testified. "Ants. Dolls. Grass. Pine needles. Leaves. For some reason, I was fascinated by seeing things melt. I looked through those flames at whatever they were melting, and a current ran through me."

Ivory's eyes opened wide. "Hey! I figured it out, just now. I was thinking about something you said to me this morning, Binda. I think what it was about for me, seeing things burn and melt... it was about witnessing transformation. That did something to me. I detest things not changing. I have this need to see change happening. Maybe because it's always happening *to* me. Seeing it around me makes me feel that it's going to be alright, because then that means change is normal. Even if I'm not."

"I see where you're going with that, brother," Promise said, "but just in case you start getting that old familiar itch around here, you be sure to wake us up from sleep first, bet?" Ivory's head dropped.

Maricela jabbed at the coals, creating a cloud of smoke. Shonto, eyes closed, waved the new smoke over his face, smudging himself clean in its spirit.

"I feel like we're, like we're more... saturated... than most people our age," Maricela said. "Like something down inside has been penetrated and brought up."

"Like magma?" Ashia asked.

"Yeah, or like with a geyser," Maricela said.

This inspired Ivory to freestyle:

"Pain is a drill. Brings up another deal, but at least it brings up the real. I pain, I feel, my soul gets drilled, my core gets filled, I spout what comes out, I spray, I pray, I soak the day, I broke the day, I sculpt the clay. Masterpiece, I, release, I, cease this piece, I, lease this piece, I, crown myself: Peace, say Peace, say Peace..."

As the applause died down, and Mende finished banging the drum, Ashia held up her hand. "We do need to check ourselves though. We can't have it both ways. We can't say we're somehow deeper, that we have a story, and then complain when people ask us to tell it."

"Hold up though," Pikea interjected. "Having your story honored is one thing. Being weaseled into having your story prostituted is another thing. *Youth Voice.* What does that even mean, *youth voice*? Just another tag line to get funding. They don't really want to hear from us. They just want to drag us into their events like pets and have us posted up in there, grinning. Soon as we get back to the group home, or shelter, or the streets, where are all those professionals with their clean suits?

"I'm still eating Spam and crackers, and they're still at home eating steak and potatoes. They're sleeping in their comfortable beds and wasting toilet paper like it's going out of style.

"You know what I want to see? I want to see all these advocates spend a day and a night with me, doing what I do, going where I go, dealing with what I deal with.

"They have those job shadow programs. They should have a youth-shadow program where they have to live in our world before they ever get to sit in on a policy meeting, making decisions about lives they can't comprehend."

"Say it, girl!" Promise shouted, snapping with both hands. "Got you lathered up and all that! Take 'em to school!"

"I'm just glad I'm finally *finished* with school," Ivory said, triggered by the word. "I wish I could sandpaper the stigma off my forehead. It's not cool when you're trying to be cool on the yard at school with your friends, or you're up in the classroom all anonymous, and here comes CPS with the po-po, marching up in the place about as covert as a hurricane.

"That actually happened, man. I mean, they couldn't wait until I was away from school? They branded me for life. I could literally feel the gossip kick off. And I don't think it's a coincidence that I couldn't get a girl to go with me to prom."

"Could be. Could also be that no one wanted to be seen on your spaghetti arm!" Eloni couldn't help himself. "But seriously," he went on, "School was no joke for me, either. None of the staff ever understood why I was bouncing from school to school. They just assumed I was a bad case. I had one teacher admit to me after I graduated that at the beginning of the school year, the teachers fought over who was going to have to have me in class. How's that supposed to make me feel?

"My mood swings were making it hard to concentrate in school. Instead of trying to understand what I was dealing with, they punished me. After school probation. Suspension. Expulsion. First person who actually tried to help me instead of criminalize me was a substitute teacher who noticed how I was acting in class. The regular teachers probably gave her hell for showing me any sensitivity. It was like they wanted to railroad me right out of the school. Never mind figuring out what was going on with me. How come it took a substitute to care enough to stop and look? It's not that I wasn't interested in school. It's that I had other fires to put out. Like how to put my family back together, and keeping myself from falling apart."

"And now we get to look forward to the joys of college," Pikea added. "Either that, or the so-called real world. Schools look at college applications from institutionalized youth the way employers look at applications from felons. They don't care what caused you to bounce from school to school, or why your grades are all over the place. They'd rather get quick to labeling you as an application risk so they don't have to be associated with transcripts like yours. Get to know who you really are? What? Forget it."

Maricela absentmindedly fidgeted with Lake's hair, and sighed. "Sometimes you want to get away from all this *being in the system* talk. I feel like I've spent my life being paraded around by these people, pushed to tell my story. Over and over. Except they don't really want you to tell your story. They want you to tell *their* story. The story that makes their program look good. They stuff you with their proprietary keywords and phrases, and push you out under the bright lights, all so they can say that they are child-centered or some such garbage."

Eloni let out an exasperated roar. "Can we please just not spend every single moment talking about this stuff? Can we enjoy the island and let off some steam?"

"I hear you, Loni. I don't know if it's that simple though," Balanta said. He was still feeling the after-draft of his encounter with the shape shifting form. "We seem to keep coming back to this stuff even when we don't mean to."

Ashia stretched out her legs and moaned at the release. "When your life has been dominated by something, that's how you color everything. Hard not to talk about air when that's all you've been breathing."

Hyenas were in the trees. Small, winged ones with beaks. They performed taunting vocal quirks that chilled Maricela's bones. Foxes were busy squelching rumors among their tribe, ranting and lamenting in their squeaky sopranos and irritant falsettos.

Cielo sliced open a regal cucumber from the garden, revealing its pale jade flesh. It was the size of his forearm. He sucked some of its juice, then sliced the two halves into half-moons. He munched the crisp pieces as he paced, tossing offerings to the ground for the birds. It was good to be blessed and to offer blessings, he thought, and all with the same succulence in his possession.

"I've been couch surfing and garage slipping all my life," said Cielo. "That ought to count for a life skill."

"What's garage slipping?" asked Mende.

Cielo laughed. "You just hide outside of any house with a garage, preferably where someone you know lives. Then, when they pull out their garage to take off for the day or whatever, you slip in under the garage door before it closes. Have to be fast. Had more than one door slam down on me. Protect your family stuff, for sure."

"So you just sleep there? What about when the people come back home?"

"It's all about choosing garages with the right cover. I treat it like a paint ball game. If the garage has enough stuff to hide under, go for it. Camouflage yourself real good. Cover up completely. Leave just a breathing hole. It's risky business, but you're out of the elements. Some of those garages are so full of junk, they're warmer than a bedroom.

"One time, I found an old record player in this one garage, buried under a pile of clothes. They even had a stack of cool jazz records. I kicked back, pounded me some goji berries, and listened to the sweetest tunes all day long until the family came home. Man... you know, those old cats," Cielo reminisced. "Miles and Monk. McCoy and Bird. Sonny Rollins. Coltrane. Those cats, sometimes they caught a spiritual high greater than any preacher I've seen."

They went on like this long enough for the sky's full womb of stars to be born. Cloistered in the amphitheater of night, they debated the accumulated evidence of their lifetimes. Passion, both jaundiced and clear, leapt like flames from their bodies, equaling the bonfire's intensity. They were a sequestered jury of 12, strident, erupted, justified. And certifiably engaged in their incomparable truth.

It grew late. They grew sleepy. Ivory, who tended to fall out during fire talk, startled himself awake as Balanta and Pikea doused the flames with sea water. The pit hissed and popped and coughed up smoky phlegm. Balanta thought he saw a shadow move in the tree line. The moon's sliver still gave off enough light, along with the stars, that visibility was manageable around camp. They gathered their loose clothes and their spears and headed into their cabins.

"You and Ashia are vibing," Eloni said to Balanta as they settled under their blankets.

"Yeah." Balanta kept his eyes away from Mende, who was silent and turned away on his cot.

"Like, real strong," Eloni continued. "What do you think is going to happen after?"

"Who can know? I don't want to think about it right now."

"That cave-in was crazy, though," Eloni said. "I guess if we were looking for adventure, we got it. Wasn't sure if we were going to get out of there. How about you?"

Balanta's eyes were closed, his voice already fading. "Cielo was right. The mountain was being kind to us. I actually felt as though it was protecting us. Creating a cocoon."

Eloni rolled over onto his stomach. "Hadn't thought about that. I figured it was trying to take us out."

In the other cabin, Cielo, Ivory, and Shonto settled into their sleep. Cielo hummed a Spanish song. Ivory was already faded. Shonto thought about being buried alive.

"You have any tats?"" Shonto asked Cielo.

"Nah. Never been into that. You?"

"No. I've been wanting to get one someday though. I don't want to be erased by this world. I want to be a graffiti that can't be washed away. Why are you so laid back, man?"

Cielo kept humming. "I decided at some point to empty myself of what didn't serve me, and to fill myself with what does."

"That simple, huh?"

"I hope so. Then again, I feel extra... wide awake here in this place. Maybe it's the water. It tastes so good, I've been drinking it like crazy. I feel like it's doing something to me. I feel so much more lucid. But calmer. Everything looks more vivid, like I have on special glasses. Makes me feel like I've been blind to beauty."

"Maricela, are you okay?" Binda asked. Maricela sat against an outside wall of her cabin, tapping on her knees.

"I wonder what Antonia was thinking, having us come here," Maricela said.

Binda wasn't sure what the comment meant, or where it came from. "You seemed kind of off when we were in the cavern, even before the cave-in. What's going on?"

Maricela thought of the stick figures etched into the kiva walls, and the lines on the cave walls. The way there were less of them as the group moved along the walls. Her eyes teared. "Can't anyone understand? I don't care how messed up my family is. I still want my family. Just like anyone else. *Its. My. Family*. Is that so hard to get through their skulls? Sorry, Binda. I don't want to go inside the cabin yet. I... hope we're going to be alright here."

"Alright?" Binda asked, perplexed.

"I just hope nothing bad happens to us."

Binda sat close to Maricela, who dropped her head onto Binda's shoulder. A gust rattled the trees. Ocean scent mixed with the island's endless flower blossom fragrance and streamed through camp.

Binda touched Maricela's chest, just beneath her collarbone. Warmth spurted from Maricela's skin deeper into her body, deeper than her bones. She felt stones come loose. Stones that had been stuck inside her being like tumors as long as she could remember. Maybe the stones were in her ancestors and had been passed down to her. A petrified inheritance. The old obstructions shuddered, then disassembled in her, as though they were soldiers at attention for years, now finally dismissed. Stones so old and hard and weary that they had changed the texture and territory around Maricela's heart. Stones that had blocked her breath, her peace, her affection. She was released.

"How did you do that?" Maricela asked in a hushed voice. "*What* did you just do?"

"I'm not so sure myself," Binda answered. "It's still something new for me. I began to notice, or rather, friends began to notice that sometimes when I touched them, something would shift inside them. Then they would feel better. I played it off at first, but it's been happening more and more the last couple of years.

"You know," Binda continued, "for Aboriginals, we always used to live together according to gifts, or roles. We each had a purpose in the community. Could seem like something small, or it could draw a lot of attention. Thing about it though, if a person was lost and didn't know their purpose, it was seen as a threat to the whole community. I've always been confused about what my role is."

"Clearly, you're some kind of healer, Binda."

"Maybe. I think I've run away from that idea."

"Why?"

After a long pause, Binda said, "When people start seeing you as something like that, the line can grow long. There's a lot of hurting in the world. It gets overwhelming for me. I mean, look at me. I come from brokenness and shame. Who am I to be the one others turn to in brokenness and shame?"

"I think you just answered your own question, girl," Maricela said, smiling. "Who better than you? Besides, if you can do for others what you just did for me, who are you to hold onto it? Really. Don't be a hoarder, girl!" Maricela said, turning gleeful.

"Stop," Binda blushed. Maricela's words fell on her with the force of truth. Like the way sunrise calls upon a new day.

The women gathered in Ashia's cabin. She lit the four candles positioned in the corners on the ground. Her heart was feeling tender. The truth was, Ashia's emotional terrain was not smooth. It was serrated. She often stumbled on its teeth and edges as she aspired for tranquility. Even when the moments should have presented ample serenity.

Though they each carried too many cuts from their fathers, their words fell into a grievance over mothers.

"Listen," Maricela said, "with my mom, even when I was little I got that burn of annoyance in my chest if she asked me more than one question at any time. She got a one-question quota to pry into my life, and I was able to respond with a decent tone of voice. Every question she asked after that, my tone got tighter, colder. It was my way of managing how much I open my heart to her."

"When I was five, my mom bought me a full-length mirror for my room," Binda said. "The kind that makes you look fatter than you are. I kept telling her the mirror distorted things. She denied it, until I finally got her to admit that she bought it on purpose. She felt I needed to lose weight. Thanks, mom. So much for a healthy relationship with my body."

Lake huffed. "My mom wouldn't let me eat butter in wintertime. She thought I gained weight when it was cold."

Ashia shook her head. "My aunties used to tell me, 'Every size up in clothing you go, your chances decrease to land a good man.'"

"You think you two will keep it going after we leave?" Ashia asked, looking at Maricela.

"Hmmm…" Maricela pondered. "Been thinking about it more like a summer romance kind of thing. What about you and B.?"

"Hope so," Ashia said. "You wonder how much of it is the island, and how much of it is real. I do feel like he's a kind of medicine for me. Balanta has a way of listening that heals you if you give yourself into it."

"Into what?" Promise asked.

"Into his listening."

"Pikea," Ashia asked. "how about Shonto? He's so sweet."

"He is," Pikea said. "He's just not my genre."

"Your what?" Maricela asked.

"My genre. You know. My type. He's more like a brother."

"Wow, girl," Maricela teased. "Aren't you upper crust with your language. All exclusive class an' that."

"You ever notice that Ivory smells like the lagoon?" Binda asked the others.

"What do you mean?" Pikea responded.

"I don't know. Somehow he just smells like the lagoon water."

"Oh, please." Pikea could feel the aura that seemed to always cloak Binda. A radiance that moved with her. Atmospheric peace. It was hard to penetrate that with anger, and Pikea was ashamed by her impulse to try. Envy was a painful rash inside Pikea's chest. She found her breath and tried to calm it out of its shallows. "Sorry, Binda. I'm tired. You didn't do anything to deserve that. I'm just having issues right now. I'm sorry I'm so dysfunctional."

"It's okay," Binda said. "If people keep shooting arrows at you, eventually you're going to put up a shield. I don't call that dysfunctional. I call it wisdom." Still, the sharpness of Pikea's tone was even then cutting its way through Binda's heart.

Ashia wiped wetness from beneath her eyes. "Sometimes, I wake feeling so fragile, it feels that even sunlight can break me. And then there are those mornings when the warrior in me has been stirred in the night. On those days, I put down my armor, strengthened by something older than bravado. I wish that when I needed to, I could scratch those days out from the dust, and summon the warrior at will."

Promise nodded her head and looked up at the sky. "I am not a nightingale. I'm not that delicate. I'm not a barn owl, either. I like open spaces.

Where I can breathe air that travels, and see what's coming from a long ways away."

Pikea chewed her lip and frowned. "They either pity you, or they blame you. For real though, I think most of the time they do both. People act so confused and conflicted with me. I can feel their energy coming off of them in waves. Because they can't deal with me normally, they get stuck in these places of guilt, discomfort, judgment, and feeling sorry for me. Too much stuff, like a tar pit. So they can't get out."

"Like a stick stuck in an eddy current?" Lake asked.

"Yeah, like that. Except I'm waiting at the shore, just wanting them to get there. Not to do anything. Just get there. They never do."

"Promise, what's your middle name?" Ashia asked.

"Ananda."

"*Ananda*. I like that name. It's pretty. What does it mean?"

"It's Sanskrit for *Supreme bliss*."

"Sanskrit. What's that?"

"Ancient language from India."

"You give yourself that name?" Maricela asked.

"Nope. Recognized it. I believe it's my truest name. As I began to discover myself, the name started coming to me. In my dreams. At school. In my cereal bowl," she said laughing. "Finally, I figured it wanted something with me. Once I grew still enough to begin to have a relationship with my own spirit, it made the truth clear. Ananda was right there waiting for me all along."

Ashia's eyes grew bright. "That's amazing. My middle name is Jaan. Jaan is Sanskrit and Persian for *Life,* or, *Dear One*. Except you spell it J-a-a-n."

"So, John spelled the other way comes from the same thing?" Promise asked.

"Don't know. Probably."

"I thought John was Hebrew." Maricela said.

"Maybe it came through Hebrew after it passed through Sanskrit. Sanskrit is older. All languages have mothers."

"Do all languages lose their mothers?" Promise asked.

Maricela patted Promise's thigh. "Only if people let it happen."

"Girl, I Love your hair," Ashia said to Promise, adoringly. Those summoning words, and it was on. Ashia ran her fingers through Promise's lush texture, massaging as much as admiring. Promise purred silently and smiled.

"I Love your hair, too," Promise reciprocated, stroking Ashia's thick soft locs, so starkly black, framing her majestic face in African pricelessness. "Can I braid it?" And with that, a mutual admiration society convened its inaugural gathering. Fingers stroked and plied and separated. Essential oils were applied, filling the cabin with scent baths of amber, sassafras, lilac, sandalwood, and jasmine.

After Promise had braided Ashia's locs, Ashia oiled Promise's scalp and corkscrewed her hair. Promise brushed Binda's hair tenderly, running one hand over Binda's hair just after a stroke of the brush, nurturing her own natural oils into Binda's lacey cotton candy texture, waking it, bringing it to fullness. Binda curled up blissfully inside her heart as warm tingling ran through her scalp and down her neck, all the way to the bottoms of her feet and toes. Binda braided Pikea's loose black curls into large plaits. Pikea brushed Maricela's licorice river of hair until it shone like a galaxy. Lake melted to Maricela's touch, the warm fingers lifting Lake's hair over and over, fluffing until Lake felt she was possessed of nothing but sky growing from her head. Woman circle was drawn, bodies close, harbored in a cove of intimacy. Moon swelled in their tender wombs. Caregivers shifted, traded places, switched. Silently. In harmony. Braids and plaits undone. New parts brushed into black waves, new designs, creative and unencumbered of fads and ethnocentric fears. Freedom. In their hair. In their hands. In their hearts.

A rhythm liberated itself, breaking forth, emerging out of an unseen eggshell of instinct and social shaping. The rhythm was old, deeply generational, sacred. Voices spilled into that rhythm. Soft, easy voices. Safe voices, speaking from deep down inside the breast of safety. Voices spilled into laughter, gossip, and inappropriateness. Voices spilled and were cleaned up, into the silence of hands moving through hair, like children running through golden fields of grain, brushing their hands against the miracle of life growing, in touch with their nature of growing, gaining, yearning for sunlight to breach its sky nest and spill down onto their aching stalks, dripping and coating and blessing their tender places, their girlhood visions, filling those empty wells with drinkable water, delivering songbirds, whole skies of songbirds to settle in their braids, plaits, afros, in their curls and locs and spaghetti strands, settle and commence to do what songbirds do: Sing. Sing. Sing.

DAY FOUR

Eloni and Balanta set out early, while darkness was still savoring itself, more than two hours from sunup. They had only an idea of where they were headed. Balanta imagined that by traversing the island they would encounter the greatest range of its environments and challenges. They would have to do hard climbing, with no guarantee of not getting lost, or injured. The honest truth was that they both relished the idea of an old school spirit quest, a 40 days in the desert kind of thing, condensed into one or two days of hardship. They would require at least one night. One night away from the group, and the security and comfort it offered. A chance to depend on catching their own food, or starving. Well, okay, maybe not starving, but at least having to sleep on a surly stomach. They would take their spears and not much else. Water, they trusted they could get along the way. It would be a revival of warriorhood, or rather, an initiation into it. Neither had slept that night, anxious and boyish for their imagination of manhood.

They walked into the woods at the back of camp, penetrating the brush quietly, holding their conversation until they were farther from camp. They had each crafted special spears for the occasion, stocky ones that had been carved into blades on one end and spear points on the other. They anticipated having to machete their way through thick undergrowth at many points. They were right. Soon enough, the pathless path grew abrasive and grabby, with vines and thorns reaching from everywhere for their clothes and skin. Reaching from the ground, at waist level, and down from the trees. They cut and cleared their way forward, and by the time sun breached horizon's lowest point, they were soaked and blessed in a sense of rarified achievement. Even if they had only covered two miles. An unknown forest, mountain, and more still lay ahead.

Balanta stopped by a eucalyptus tree, moving his palm over its body. Viscous sap oozed from the trunk, ruddy black, tarlike. Eloni came over, knelt and rubbed some of the sap between his fingers. "We better take some of this with us," he said. "We can use it to help start a fire." They spent 15 minutes searching for a suitable container.

Balanta found a hard gourd shell from an opo squash. "Calabash," he said to himself. They broke open the dried bronze *long melon* shell with a rock, doing their best to crack it in half.

Eloni scooped up sap using one of the half-shells, until the other half was filled. "You never know. This stuff, plus the oil from the leaves, can burn down a whole forest. I've seen burning eucalyptus trees explode. But the sap can also save your life. It'll stop blood flow. My grandmother told me it puts poisons to sleep. It's old medicine, from way back."

Eloni placed his hands on the eucalyptus' trunk. The smooth bark was soothing, even stimulating as he moved over it. His palms were chalk white when he brought them back from the tree. *War paint*. He massaged the eucalyptus powder into his face, mystified as he felt old spirits stir inside.

"Balanta, you and Mende couldn't be more different," Eloni said as he strode forward with a warrior's gait.

"Who you telling?"

"You sure you come from the same mamma?"

"Now... don't start talking about my mamma."

"No, seriously, remember what you were telling me about taking on your cow name when you come of age?"

"Yeah."

"You said your favorite cow was solitary, and you wanted to live just like that. Mende told me he can't stand cows and wants to live like a seagull, always surrounded by people and flapping his gums all day long."

"Ha! You got that right."

They moved over a hill, walking at an eager pace. A rancorous community of trumpet vine blossoms spilled out over the hillside, turning their nearly neon faces giddily to the sun. A small family of aspens had assumed squatter's rights along a tendril of water running through a shallow crevasse. The aspens' papery white bark contrasted with their rich, dark leaves. Eloni thought he saw a slight trail of tears on Balanta's cheekbone. He wondered how the brothers' argument the day before was weighing on Balanta now.

Back at camp, the woods exploded with noise at the first touch of sunlight. Burdensome, quarreling birds. Yapping winged malcontents thinking their branch on the tree to be the prized heirloom, the sole space worthy of their precious feathered bottom, not realizing that as they spend their energy on meaningless debates, they could be using it to find food or build a nest or mate or at least to fly. Something more productive than this absurd theater of squeaky, shrill social contagion. Like doomsday preachers on street corners. Or drunken, overly loud male arguments at street parties. Or the whining metallic grilling of middle-aged gossip girls oiled up on mimosas, their voices sharp and nasal, as though their teeth, corralled into preternatural order by unnecessary braces, are caught against one another, sparking off another mewing rumor, bleaching their brains further in the process.

Morning's disciples lifted their heads to the fresh sunlight and smiled. African violets, morning glories, calla lilies. Hydrangea and salvia with their white tubular blossoms. All saluted and preened, stretching like felines post nap. A fat cluster of hibiscus had freshly bloomed to morning's serenade. Star jasmine and fruit tree fragrance danced with the aroma of fish bacon, popping on the fire. Small lizards with maniacal grins were doing pushups on cool rocks in sunlight. Praying mantis pairs bowed to each other on palm leaves.

151

Lake woke to the scent of coffee and peppermint. *Cielo*, she smiled to herself. Sitting up, she ran her hands through her hair. *What a mess*. She stretched her spine, raising her hands high above her head, then shook her whole body, rustling warmth back into her bones.

Stepping out of the cabin, her eyes were assaulted by sunlight and fire smoke. Squinting, she called out, "Ya'ah'teh" to whomever was present. *Good Morning*.

"Morning, Lake," Cielo called back. He was sitting on a log, legs crossed, drinking his coffee with high-minded effect as though he were royalty.

"Where is everybody?"

"We're the first ones up. Guess we're the early birds in the group."

"Not usually," said Lake. "Your coffee got up my nose. You put peppermint candy in it?"

"How'd you know?" Cielo asked, excited.

"Hard to miss. What, you used half the candy bag?"

"I like my coffee sweet," Cielo said, laughing sleepily.

"I like my stomach full," said Lake. "Would you like some eggs and bacon?"

"Mighty kind of you, Señorita. Don't mind if I do."

Lake, dressed in plaid pajama bottoms and a pullover fleece, blessed her face with palms of fresh water from the nearby jug, then set to the joyful task of making her stomach say amen.

Ivory greeted the day with a spontaneous headstand, then walked out of the cabin on his hands. "Who's coming with me up the mountain?" he asked. "I want to find out what was making that noise all night."

Promise shook her head. "What are you going to do if you find it? Ask if it would please be quiet between the hours of 11 and 7?"

"Just curious. Don't expect to find it. Just want to go look. Plus, I got my walking stick sharpened. I'm ready to spear something."

"Like your foot," Maricela mumbled.

Breakfast was quiet as they processed the absence of Balanta and Eloni. "I hope those two don't end up falling into a hole somewhere," Ashia said. "They took their whistles, right?"

"Let's hope so," Pikea said. "We don't need to be spending the day conducting a search party."

Cielo was stripping down willow branches to use the bark for some type of shade structure for the canoe. "Anybody else want to join Mende, Maricela, and me for the adventure of a lifetime? We might discover a hidden pyramid in the jungle or something."

"You're more likely to stumble on a root and break your toe," Pikea cackled. "Or get your canoe grounded on a sandbar. Get ready to swim your way home, y'all."

Maricela called Pikea over to a corner of camp where Cielo had set up his hammock. The spot was shaded most of the day. Maricela pointed Pikea's attention to the ground. "I planted that bell pepper seed three days ago," Maricela said, her voice disbelieving. The stalk was nearly two feet high, with a full skirt of leaves. Pale fruit was visible. "How does that happen?"

Pikea looked at the plant for a long moment, her fingers playing with her short waves of hair. Her relaxed face was that of a person for whom time has suddenly become only a legend. "I'm telling you," Pikea said, "this place has some crazy *Hau* going on. Some epic essence. It's like the island is drugging us. Last night, I could have sworn that banana tree over by the cabins was over here by the hammock."

As morning's moments ticked by, they heated. Lake felt the beach sand's temperature beneath her bare feet. "Today wants to be hot," she said. Binda, who was walking behind her, leaping into Lake's footprints, felt moisture in the depressions, and wondered if Lake might actually be able to make it rain.

Maricela, Mende, and Cielo paddled out toward the reef, which grew at an epochal pace nearly 100 yards away. As the water went from pale powdery blue to a darker sanctioning of color, the ocean floor disappeared from view. Soon, they were at the reef. The coral peaked not far beneath the surface. Its granular families were afire. Sunset red. Sangria red. Salmon red. Ancient colonies of it grew as a broad plateau, buttressing the island against the ocean's hammering palpitations. The canoe hull scraped for a moment against the coral, prompting Maricela to command a course correction. Cielo and Mende both paddled furiously on the canoe's right side, turning them back toward the island. "Let's just try and keep it in the middle, boys," Maricela said. "Where the water runs deep. We don't need to get hung up on the reef, wondering if we can make the swim back to shore."

After a while, Cielo leaned back at the stern of the canoe, his feet in flip flops, swinging out and back delightedly. He erected his willow bark umbrella, opining "Should hold up *bueno*." He munched on plantain chips dipped in apricot syrup as he observed the scarce clouds above passing vaporously like the breath of heaven. He trailed a hand in the water, drawing schools of minnows that crowded close to his fingers and fell back in the canoe's turbulence.

"Most cultures around the world were far better mariners and navigators than Columbus," Cielo noted. "Micronesians, Polynesians, Africans, Asians, Indigenous people everywhere. It's in the archaeological records. Earth tells the truth. Humans have always been migratory. We're no different than birds, butterflies, and blue whales."

"Hey, Cielo," said Maricela, "you want to pitch in on the paddling for a minute?"

"Sure. Let me powder my palms."

"What?"

"I'm already getting blisters. Hand me some of that corn powder, please."

"Boy... you aren't exactly making your ancestors proud. Weren't they Amazon River folks? Come on now."

Cielo laughed and joined Mende on the paddle. Mende was searching the island bank for a hidden cove to explore. The last one they found had been covered at its mouth by a dense party of mangrove, their thick roots lacing above the waterline. They would have missed it if not for Cielo deciding to go for a nude swim at the right moment. As Maricela and Mende did their best to look in the opposite direction, Cielo, bare and bearish, dove into the calm waters and breast-stroked beneath the surface toward the island. Underwater, he could see clearly how the shoreline disappeared at one point. He surfaced and swam closer. After he swam back to the canoe and reported the hidden cay to Maricela and Mende, the three of them docked, and spent the next two hours diving and swimming in the cove whose belly of azure water was deep and teeming with brilliantly colored fish. The humans chased the submarining comets to a point beyond exhaustion.

Lying on the white sand letting evaporation cool their skin, Cielo, a beard nearly achieved after four days sans shaving, watched clusters of meek bright clouds flow by in the upper atmosphere. "I used to swim a lot when I was little," he said. "I wanted to be an Olympic swimmer. Or cross an ocean channel somewhere covered in grease, full on naked. Anyhow, my dad put the kibosh on the competitive swimming career. He said, 'No son of mine is going to traipse around in a miniature butt band wasting his time going in circles in the water. Your ancestors didn't die conquering jungles so you could splash around in puddles.'"

"For real? Mende asked. "Those were his actual words?"

"Yeah. *La verdad*. So needless to say, I said adios to swimming. Haven't really done it so freely again until now."

"I used to read children's books to this man in his nineties whose light was fading, only because he had lived so long. He'd fall asleep smiling in the twilight of the room as I read him stories that he first heard as a child. Funny how life takes us in circles. Maybe that's why it causes so much damage when circles are broken."

Mende listened to this with a cramp in his side. He wondered for the millionth time what his and Balanta's lives would have been like if their family had stayed together. How could something like *potential* exist if it never came true? Forget about dreams drying up like raisins in the sun. What if they never got to become raisins in the first place?

The cove kept them feeling adventurous for a while, especially with the giant blue herons that kept peeking at them from the waterline at the edge of the mangroves. And the flying fish leaping in high arcs that kissed the water like silver rainbows.

Four hours into the great island circumnavigation, Cielo announced an unbearable cramp by howling and grabbing his hamstring. Relieved of rowing duties, he lay in the canoe, rambling on about the history of global exploration and the ecological ramifications of human and continental drift. By the time he arrived at the epoch of first contact with the Galapagos, both Maricela and

Mende had begun privately pining for a return to camp, and the priceless benefits of silence.

Shonto and Ivory went pig hunting, which, since there were no pigs on the island, meant they took off to go throw their spears at shadows and make-believe creatures.

"You ever dream about being invisible?" Ivory asked.

"You mean like we already are?" Shonto replied.

"No, I mean actually being magically invisible. You spend your whole life yelling and screaming to get people's attention, but no one even notices.

"Being invisible doesn't mean you're mute. If you're yelling, people are going to notice."

"Oh yeah."

"Sometimes... I don't know about you."

"Nobody knows about me," Ivory responded. "I'm what you call an enigma."

"More like an ignoramus," Shonto laughed. "Just playing, bro."

"Yeah, yeah. You all just don't recognize my brilliance. I'm afraid to let it out, on account of the sun might get jealous. Here's a trivia question for y'all: In the whole history of humankind, has anyone ever gone all day without blinking?"

Shonto cracked up. "Ivory, sometime between when you open your mouth and when words come out, do you bang your head?"

Before Ivory could come up with a comeback, Shonto had taken a swipe at a gnarl of honeysuckle vines growing all over a large bush. With the honeysuckle removed, a stone statue stood revealed before them. About six feet high, the statue was a bust, an intricately sculpted human face. "Man! That reminds me of those giant statue faces from ancient Mexico!" Ivory shouted.

"Yeah," Shonto said. "The Olmec. I think that's what the statue people were called."

"It looks African," Ivory observed. "See how it has my magnificent nose and lips?"

Shonto playfully shoved Ivory, sending his wispy body nearly to the ground. "Son," Shonto said, "I don't know about magnificent. You're about a centimeter here or there away from looking like a gerbil."

"Oh. Okay. Jokes guy."

Maybe we should do something reverent here," Shonto said.

"Yeah, rub it with your belly," Ivory said.

"I'm serious, fool."

At which point, Ivory assumed a fencing pose and began to lunge at the stone face with his spear, jabbing it repeatedly. "That's not exactly what I had in mind," Shonto said. "Let's sit ourselves down and see why Spirit brought us here."

Shonto fell down onto a large bed of star jasmine, its fragrance rising up and over him like a blanket. As he lay there, the jasmine blossoms took to the air, rose on invisible strings into a high perch in the distant sky, and became stars, visible even in the brightness of day sky. Shonto wasn't sure if such a thing was possible. He didn't care. It was happening. *The likelihood of things* was less a consideration for him than ever before.

After Ivory burned off some energy by racing around the statue whooping and menacing with his spear, he sat down not far from Shonto and made peace with silence. For a moment.

"My favorite part of going on a trip is coming home," Ivory said. "I Love that feeling of coming through the door, smelling the familiar scent of your place, being able to shower in your shower, raid your fridge, get lazy on your couch, sleep in your bed. I feel like I'm melting in that first moment. All the tension running out of my body cause I can finally relax and be me."

"You feeling homesick, Captain Courageous?" Shonto's eyes were closed, his fingers drumming his belly.

"Nah. Just thinking. We're already four days deep into this."

"You're anxious. Admit it."

"No, I'm cool. Really."

"What do you think of Promise?" Shonto asked.

"Plush."

"What do you mean?"

"You know how when you fall on a nice soft bed, you feel like you're falling into a cloud? She seems like that, like she would be a nice place to land. Not literally, but... emotionally I guess. She seems gentle. Like she cares how you feel around her. I wouldn't mind landing in a place like that."

Shonto opened his eyes and looked at Ivory. "When you want to, you can be deep, Shaka."

"Shaka?"

"Shaka Zulu. I see the leader in you. The visionary. You just hide it. Most of us here seem to be hiding our gift. I guess that's what trouble does. Flips your stuff upside down. You show your B-side to the world. Not you're A-side."

Ivory grunted. "People always talking to me about my calling. Saying I need not just do enough to get by. That I need to thrive. What if I don't want to thrive? Seems like a lot of work."

"Yeah, but how much work is misery?" Shonto asked.

"Point. I guess my approach is, let me just settle down with God in this here puddle that is my life and see if it turns into a lake or dries up and blows away. Either way, I'm cool. Cause I'm settled down with God."

"Except that I think God probably wants you to make some kind of effort. Not just sit in a puddle."

Ivory stared at the monument. Butterflies kept landing on its nose. Bright yellow ones. "Hey, Shonto, are you feeling Pikea? You two seem to have some kind of energy between you."

"Really? You noticed something?"

"Yeah, your jolly-place getting lit up when she's around."

"You're a fool. I think we're just friends. I mean, I like her, yeah. But not like that, I don't think. She reminds me of... of my mother, I guess."

"What! Shonto be freakin' on his own mother!" This earned Ivory a punch to the gut.

"No, man. Pikea's on fire, you know? Not just the anger. I mean the fire for justice. She's not having the world the way it is. My mom was like that. Then life happened, and she couldn't get that need for justice met. She opened her mouth a lot about it, but no one ever taught her how to go and get it. Or fight for it in a way that works. It burned her out. If you have fire on the inside, you gotta get it out, or it just burns your inner forest down."

"Hey, Shonto, man. I think I just saw that statue move."

"That's no kinda good. You need to stop smoking that stuff and start smoking some peace. You're tripping."

"I'm not playing, man!" Ivory was shouting and had already sprung up and back, his spear in thrust position.

Shonto lifted himself from his jasmine cloud and stood. "Coyotes can be polymorphs," he said.

"What?"

"Shape shifters. Tricksters. Maybe what we got here is a trickster." Shonto moved closer to the stone face, scrutinizing its granularity. Ivory reached to touch the giant face. "Don't do that, man," Shonto warned. "If it is a shape shifter, it might grab your hand and pull you in."

"In to what?"

"Its world. I don't know." As they backed away from the jasmine garden and the stone bust, Shonto wiped his eyes at what he was seeing. The statue's face began to ripple, become fluid. Then, no lie, the sculpture smiled.

With everyone else doing their thing, Ashia and Promise decided to go for a long hike inland. Maybe they would find yet another amazing part of the island. Or maybe they would just lose themselves in the moment. Good enough for them. Promise slathered her skin in cocoa butter as they headed into a kingdom of towering timber bamboo. The stalks were as big around as their waists. Promise looked closely at what looked like a red trickle flowing down the stalks. Ladybugs. Thousands of them. A river of ladybugs flowing up and down the dark green bamboo. Looking up into the canopy, Promise saw red clouds lifting from the leaves and spreading out as a faint mist. These ladybugs are having themselves a house party, Promise marveled. She placed her hand on a stalk and let the red river course over her fingers. The tickle made her laugh as she walked forward, bracelets of ladybugs circling her wrists.

They sat for a while. Ashia brushed through Promise's deep crop of hair with her fingertips. "Promise, can I braid your hair?" Ashia asked.

"Sure. That would feel relaxing."

157

Ashia sat behind Promise and began to separate the strands. Ashia wove a succession of designs, taking one out, creating a new one in its place. She took Promise's hair from plaits to rows, from spirals to circles. Her fingers worked quickly, with the nimbleness and fluidity of someone who had worked with hair since she was a little girl. Promise closed her eyes and melted.

They talked of mothers.

"I want to swim in the milk of my mother," Promise said, her voice a serene purr. "Smell her scent on my face. I want my recurring dream of her as perfect, whole, and happy... and *alive*. I want that dream to come true."

Ashia hummed her understanding. "You know that pain when someone you Love has died, then you dream of them alive, and in the dream you feel such happiness, but then you wake up and realize they are gone, and it hits you just like they've died all over again, and you just want to go back into the dream again and never wake up? You know that pain? That's where I live. And I can't get out."

"Never would have guessed it," Promise said.

"I have mastered the masks I wear," Ashia said. "You're on a whole 'nother level though. Promise, do you ever stop smiling?" Ashia asked.

"Why should I? I learned early on, I can't control how much heaviness people throw at me. But I can do something about how I'm feeling the moment.

"I see you," Ashia responded. "Better than going super nova."

"What?"

"Galaxies contracting and expanding, eventually blowing up. That's how it is with hurt," Ashia reasoned. "That much force. If you don't give the expansion or contraction somewhere to go, you implode."

Promise was still watching ladybugs on her skin. Maybe they were digging the cocoa butter. "Having fun is so crucial. This world is too serious. I want to start a community center for young people and have it be all about having a good time, even if you're learning something. I should say, especially because you're learning something.

"I went to this youth advocacy camp where they train you to advocate for changes in the systems that we all came up through. The whole time they were pushing us through this nonstop agenda, 7am until we went to bed. And a lot of it was cool, it's just that it felt too much like..."

"Work?" Ashia asked.

"I don't mind working. This felt like adults who spent too many years on the job in a depressing way and can't remember how to gather in a group and have it be fun. And then they put together this advocacy camp for us and made it the same way. It was all about acting like a professional, which apparently means being stressed and zombied out. I'm not with that. I don't have to be grim to prove I'm working hard."

They got up and started walking again. They passed under towering banyan trees, their massive, sprawling trunks like octopus tentacles. They moved through flowering Plumeria and chestnut trees, dragon trees with their dagger-like leaves, and silk floss trees shedding their fruit seed fluff like dandruff.

Soon, Ashia noticed something strange about the ground ahead just as Promise, distracted by ladybugs and soapboxing, stepped onto it. Promise's foot landed and kept sinking. The ground made a noise like a baby slurping at a bottle. "What the?" Promise blurted right before her leg was swallowed up to the thigh. "Oh no!" she yelled. She was already sunken up to her butt.

Ashia dove for her. In midflight, Ashia realized: *Quicksand!* She managed to flatten out into a horizontal plane before she hit the ground. She landed on the edge of the quicksand and felt her torso sink as she frantically pulled herself back until she felt solid earth beneath her.

Promise was looking at Ashia with fear. "What do I do?" She was still registering that whatever she had fallen into was not about to let her go. And that this pit had no apparent bottom. The muck pulled at her waist. "I can't move, Ashia! This is crazy!"

"Don't move! You're making it worse. Try to be still." Ashia focused on her own heartbeat, telling herself to take a breath. The breath didn't come. She was growing faint with panic, and made every effort to make her voice sound calm. Promise looked terrified. "Try to slowly reach your hand out to me." Ashia, lying as flat as she could, with her diaphragm just skirting the quicksand perimeter, stretched her arm toward Promise. Promise slowly extended her hand toward Ashia, but the tilting of her torso caused her to sink another few inches. Their fingers were still about a yard apart.

"Ashia, I'm scared! I'm really stuck! Maybe you better find a reed I can breathe through if I go under?" A stream of old movies with quicksand scenarios flashed through Promise's mind. She felt ridiculous at the thought of breathing through a reed while buried in quicksand.

"You're not going to go under, Promise," Ashia assured. "I'm going to find a stick or a vine or something."

"No! Don't leave me!"

"No, I'm not going anywhere. Let me just look close by here." Now kneeling, Ashia scanned the area. Sweating heavily, her hair felt like a 10-pound sack of rice on her head. "Please, try and stay still, Promise."

Promise's mind was a blizzard: *I can't go out like this. What will they say about me? Who will tell my mom's people? How will they find them? What was my last meal? The group is going to be so depressed. I ruined our whole trip. Stop tripping, Promise. Get it together. Ashia isn't going to let me die. So much for a nice walk. The sky is insanely blue.*

The moment ebbed into a slow flow for Ashia. Her heartbeat was loud in her head, even as she kept willing it to calm. She saw several dead bamboo stalks lying near the base of their tall cluster. They were just out of reach. She leapt over from her kneeling position and grabbed for a stalk. It was still connected to the earth. She pulled desperately, alarming a swarm of ants whose cover she had just removed. In her heightened alertness she also noticed what looked like an iguana peering out from the bush. Its gaze seemed to suggest befuddlement at the sight of this human drama. Or maybe, Ashia thought, it was anticipating a meal. The bamboo stalk broke free, sending Ashia tumbling backward. Its length was several yards. More than enough. Ashia crawled back over to the edge of the pit. Promise was now up to her chest in the slog, its weight against her ribs stealing her breath.

"Here," Ashia said, "Take a hold of the bamboo. Don't move too quickly." Ashia noticed that Promise's face was contorted with some kind of effort, as though she were fighting something back.

"I sure hope this works," Promise said, "or I'm about to start sucking mud." She grabbed the stalk with both hands so tightly that her nails dug into her palms. Blood came. Now her grip was slipping. "Hold on. Let me get ahold to it better."

Ashia wasn't waiting. She pulled from her prone position at first, then managed to sit up so she could dig her feet in for leverage. Sweat burned her eyes. The shadow of a bird passed over, as large as a jet plane. Ashia heard rustling in the bush, dry leaves being displaced. Fear painted a vision in her mind of the iguana-type creature, or something worse leaping onto her back. Her forearms burned as she pulled against Promise's weight and the suction force of the quicksand.

"Ashia?" Promise said.

"Yeah?" Ashia's voice was barely more than a groan.

"I hope you been working out, girl."

"Don't make me laugh!" Ashia could feel Promise's grip slipping repeatedly. *Lord, give me the strength for this. Don't let me fail.* It felt like her shoulders were popping out of their joints. Like her toes were breaking off against the ground. Her calves were cramping. Her thighs screamed for mercy.

Promise began to work out an upper body movement that seemed to help. She wriggled back and forth from the shoulders, fighting to keep her hips still as she did. A new kind of salsa up in here, she thought, trying not to crack up. Anytime she breathed too deeply, the quicksand seemed to reclaim her. The two of them grew wordless with effort and fell into a state of clarity and focus. Thoughts fell away. Promise was aware of each muscle in her body, which ones to move, which ones to deny. Ashia had taken to grunts and huffs to get even a few more molecules of oxygen. Her face looked like birthing.

As Ashia's hands began to slip over their own blood, the fulcrum between the parts of Promise above and below the quicksand perceptibly shifted. She kept writhing, rotating. The sludge line moved from her belly down to her hip bones. Then down her butt. As she gained more oxygen, she only grew fainter. Just as she thought she was about to pass out, Promise felt her entire body lifted up onto the surface of the quicksand. Through her fog, she heard Ashia urging her to carefully sidestroke herself over the surface toward Ashia. "Just be careful not to let go of the bamboo!" Ashia's voice croaked and strained.

Promise rolled over onto solid ground and onto her back. Ashia fell down beside her. They were too tired to hug. They barely touched fingers. For a long time, all they could hear was the sound of their ponderous breathing. Something kept stirring the dry leaves beneath the bushes nearby. The sky above them was quiet, as though it was listening in reverence to two souls breathing for their lives. The sky was also insanely blue.

Eloni and Balanta, still questing, came to a towering, sheer cliff face. A wall of black rock that shone against the sun, obsidian and daunting. Thick green vines draped themselves down the rock, emerging from somewhere up and over the cliff top. Eloni looked at Balanta with a glint in his eyes and a delinquent smile.

"Are you sure?" Balanta asked. But he already knew the answer. They climbed the first 20 feet quickly, their feet finding easy holds in the crevasses and shelves the cliff's face offered. Higher they went. A breeze fluttered over like a stray creature from the forest, investigating. It licked Balanta's skin. The cool was refreshing. Up here, sun rummaged through the canopy of the highest trees and lapped against the two climbers with increasing intensity. Then they ascended above the canopy line and sun bore down against the black rock, framing them in heat. Balanta reached for a vine to his left, to purchase leverage so he could swing over into a fold in the cliff that offered a thin strip of shade. Thin, but enough to cover his body for a moment. Balanta's pores were wide open, releasing curtains of sweat that soaked his shirt and jeans. He gathered his breath back to his body as he looked out over the canopy. He could see the distant ocean, and small black grains in the sky— seabirds roaming their territory.

Eloni was euphoric. Climbing vines up a cliff with another warrior. Out here in the freedom of nature, which never lied to him, never deceived. His palms and fingers ached from gripping the vines, which filled the circumference of his hands wrapped around their girth. His heart pounded a drumbeat of achievement as he gripped and pulled, lifting himself as much with his legs, entwined and pumping, as with his arms. Eloni came to a spot where the cliff grew bare and unblemished. No foothold or handhold. Eloni thrilled to the challenge. He looked for a vine he could jump to, and then swing over to a more cooperative rock face. Trusting. All along, he and Balanta were trusting that these vines would hold them. That these living things were well rooted beyond the cliff top, and could hold their significant weight. Eloni trusted the wisdom of nature, which spoke in parables that always held true. Either a thing was going to go one way, or it was going to go another. But there would be no misdirection. No subterfuge. Nature's laws could not care less about Eloni's criminal record, his grades in school, or how old or worn his shoes were. These laws here were truly indiscriminant, unlike the lie of human justice. Here, Eloni knew he would be judged by a jury of his actual peers. The elements, brave and bold that had their way on the island, so far away from society and its rhetorical bluster about fairness and equality. Eloni didn't care about equality. He cared about climbing this here cliff. And finding a vine to hold.

Eloni leapt. Letting his left hand release from the vine that was the only thing keeping him from falling 40 feet, he pushed with his feet against the black rock, recruiting all his muscle. For a moment he was airborne, angling his husky body toward a larger vine he spotted five feet to the right. He reached with his right hand, straining his shoulder, willing it to come out of its socket if need be, as long as he made it to the other vine. He felt the adrenaline surge in the microsecond of doubt in which he anticipated falling. Then his finger touched vine. His palm slid onto the organic rope, feeling its grainy skin. Adrenaline subsided as Eloni secured his grip, simultaneously completing his swing, his body finishing its momentum against root and rock. Eloni glanced to his right, looking for his next hand hold. As he worked his legs around the vine, the lengthy plant shed its skin. The green coating sloughed off from directly beneath Eloni's hand grip. Both hands. The sloughing gained beneath gravity, continuing downward along the vine until it reached the places where Eloni gripped with his thighs, knees, calves, and feet. The vine shed its skin and Eloni was holding nothing but a collapsing corpse of slickness. His body began to pitch back, away from the cliff. *This is how I die.* The thought was not complete when Eloni reflexively shot both hands up, as if to have God grab them and prevent his fall.

God sent Balanta. Eloni looked up to see Balanta's right hand closed around Eloni's thick wrist. Balanta's face was showering sweat, painful effort pronounced in an acute grimace. His eyes were locked on Eloni. So focused and burning that Eloni lost all doubt that Balanta would save him. What he saw in Balanta's eyes was a ferocity, a cold-blooded faceoff with death. A refusal to give up Eloni to that all-consuming eternal mouth. "I've got you," Balanta intoned in an eerily calm voice. The two of them hung there, suspended and sweating critically in the breeze. Balanta summoned unnatural strength, and still holding both himself and Eloni with his left hand on thick cusp of rock, with his right hand Balanta reeled Eloni up and in against the cliff. Both of them wondered if Balanta's right arm would tear loose from the shoulder and send Eloni plummeting. It did not. Eloni urgently found a hand hold, then wrapped his legs around a vine that appeared less inclined to shed. He yanked several times to test, then gave his trust back to the cliff. After several moments of reclaiming their breath and vanquishing thoughts of the event to which they had been so close, Eloni and Balanta kept climbing. Moments later they summited the cliff. They sat there, arms around their knees, looking out over the canopy and the far ocean whose sky was being grazed by herds of clouds. The few words shared in that moment atop the mesa traveled like a rich clay dust and scattered on the high wind.

Lake and Binda sat on a large tree root on the lagoon bank, swinging their legs in the warm water. The red dragonfly flew to them, darted away, and returned, a puppy playing go fetch with nothing but the air. It was late morning. Shadows were drawing up into themselves. Binda played with a lotus blossom floating loose on the water, gently swirling her foot around it, stirring it to dance. Lake took off her sweatshirt and let the sun reach her skin. A dream from the night before came back to her. The familiar sense of déjà vu it always brought was still with her. She had felt almost groggy so far today.

In the dream, the most vivid, recurring dream of her life, Lake moves silently along a seacoast. No humans. Just sea, shore, and cliffs. Then, she is inside a cave. The sea surges in and out. The sound of water washing. Her eyes adjust to the darkness. Images emerge. Her heart becomes a newborn planet as she realizes that she is in a cave of turtles. Turtles cover the entire floor of the cave. Are stacked up along the cave walls and on its shelves. Turtles swim in the tidal surge. Juvenile turtles waste their energy. Old turtles savor their own. Paternal turtles nuzzle hatchlings in the water. Small ones hitch rides on the backs of their elders. Turtles are everywhere. Lake swells with a joy beyond what she has known. Joy floods into virginal coves in her heart. Joy overflows her riverbanks, begins to fill the old trenches in her, generational holes, long so empty and waiting. Lake cannot believe her eyes, or her dream sense. She is in a cave. By the sea. And she is with her kind. No human presence. No human voices or anxiety. A peace for which Lake has prayed comes in with the tide. It carries salt on its breath, and seems to whisper: *Stay with me...*

Pikea, thinking of Maori food and New Zealand sunsets, explored the far side of the lagoon, beneath its surface, where she noticed schools of small yellow fish congregating. Swimming beside the lagoon bank, Pikea felt pressure on her face, like Jacuzzi jets against her skin. She followed the water current to a puckering of rock where the water rushed in. The opening was plenty big enough for her body. She powered through into a dark space that dilated, a tunnel stretching into the blackness. Light from the lagoon offered enough illumination that she could make out air pockets at the ceiling of the tunnel. She swam in deeper. Her body felt strong. Her legs pumped, her feet powering her along like flippers. She Loved the feeling of straining her arms against the water's resistance. Every few moments, she surfaced the several feet to the tunnel's ceiling to sip smaller air bubbles, or pop her head entirely into larger pockets. As long as she could see this trail of air behind her leading back to the opening into the lagoon, she felt it was safe to continue. With each breaststroke, she imagined the world of authority screaming at her to turn around. Screaming jeopardy. Screaming delinquency. She had no idea where this tunnel led. Liked that she did not know. She was forcing herself into a great, watery mystery. At points, the tunnel opened up into small caverns. Luminescent critters lined the floor and walls like miniature lanterns. She saw stalactite and stalagmite formations everywhere, teeth of a giant rock shark whose mouth she was swimming through. Endless shapes of calcium and lime belched out. Surreal artwork. Totems. She swam on. Silence. Echoes of water slapping. Magnified creaking and groaning of the island. She felt the capacity and boundary of her lungs in ways she hadn't before. *I can.* A chant rising from her old, desiccated earth. She claimed it. *I can*. Neon minnows and guppies came up beside her, minions at the side of a whale, now so tame, calmed by the hush of solitude and the ardency of water. The water was cooler here, migrated from sunlight. She felt the fine hair on her arms and legs raise. Felt the swelling of her lips. And she could see. See through water so clear it was a telescope, casting lines and forms precisely. She surfaced to a large air pocket, her head and neck above the water line. With her face so close to the wet rock ceiling, she smelled eons of mineral generations. Sharp. Assertive. Rich. She treaded water, letting oxygen renew itself in her cells and organs. Her legs and arms were beginning to ache. She Loved it. She wanted this violation of order, of red lines and fences that made her feel like cattle. Or sheep. This was her liftoff from earth. Her musical rebellion. So much treble down in this dark river. So much percussive bass as she fled. She dived down again, into the tunnel's marrow. Swimming over a rise in the floor, she saw that the tunnel narrowed ahead, grew darker. She took the invitation and entered. One last stretch of water. She saw a violet shaft of light penetrate the black a few yards ahead. Lifting up into the beam, she was swarmed with microscopic animals, highlighted and busy. Collectively, they looked to her like animated dust clouds. She smiled as they blanketed her. Looking up she saw a large bright plate of surface water rippling and shifting. She ascended. As her crown broke through the surface, what she saw held her heart for a beat. She was afloat inside of a giant natural amphitheater. The cavern towered over her, and spread its rock awning far beyond where she treaded. A large bright window that was the cavern's mouth dazzled her eyes, still used to darkness. She blinked and cleared her vision as she looked out into the lush forest with its splashes of green. The air inside the cavern was cool against her face. Birds flew in and out like a circus act, settling like trapeze artists into notches and hutches high in the aviary ceiling. Butterflies jounced outside of the cavern, remaining in sunlight. She let out a sigh and submerged herself in the opal water. Her world, beneath and above water, stretched out for a great distance all around her. *Space*. She took it in, as though it was a meal she would not be served again. Time became a thing with wings and left her. Her chest opened and kept opening as she dived and rose and splashed in the luxury of a place that she alone had dared to reach.

Hot gusts pulsated through the late morning air, slowing down the movement of most living things. Maricela fantasized a cold glass of horchata. Mende didn't satisfy himself with fantasies. He walked through groves of oaks and eucalyptus until he reached the tribe of lemon trees standing guard around a meager trickle of water. The trees each were heavy with 100 yellow suns hanging from their branches. The air was saturated with the scent of their citrus blossoms. Mende filled the apron of his shirt with a dozen fat lemons and came back to camp, looking like a dumpy miscreant up to no good.

He sliced the lemons with his pocketknife, serrating the bright, thick rinds down to the nearly clear flesh that burst forth in tart fountains of tears.

Mende sucked his fingers as he worked. Pursing his lips repeatedly. Soon, he had a basket full of sliced lemons, which he poured into the large pot he had already filled with spring water. Some raw sugar, nutmeg, and cardamom, and things were all good. Mende stirred his concoction over the low flames, just until the sugar dissolved.

He sat the pot in the cold stream, to let it chill. Unable to wait, he sampled his locally harvested, locally brewed, special recipe, fresh lemonade by the ladles full, drinking a quarter of the batch before he offered it to the others.

"Man, this is right on time, Mende," Maricela praised, smacking her lips dramatically.

"Bravo, Mende!" was all that Cielo offered before he was back to savoring his drink.

"Mende," Pikea said, "we need to commission you to make a batch of this stuff up every morning. You down?"

"Sure. As long as I can skip dishes."

"Okay, boy," Pikea ordained, "that's a bet."

"Where are Binda and Lake?"

"Out picking berries, I think," Mende answered, his fingers lightly tapping the drum.

"Mmm... I hope they bring back a whole bushel. I can't believe how good and fresh those things taste."

Most of the group gradually made their way back to camp as appetites returned. Other than the two spirit questors, only Ashia and Promise were missing. Plenty of food was left over from breakfast. Stacks of cornbread. Coconut halves. Jerked lobster. Piles of gigantic tomato and cucumber slices.

"Hey guys, try this sandwich I made," Cielo offered.

"I told you, bro. *Samich*, not sandwich," Ivory corrected.

"What's that?"

"You say, *samich*. *Sandwich* sounds all proper. You trying to go to uppity dinner parties all your life?"

Cielo grinned. "No. I just want to get invited at least, so I can politely turn them down. Try this."

Shonto was skeptical. "What's in it?"

"All the right stuff. Marmalade—"

"Stop right there," Pikea urged. "I've heard enough. Anything that sounds like marbles and lemonade doesn't belong on a samich."

Smiling, Cielo bragged, "No really. Pineapple marmalade, fish, and radish mush wrapped in wild greens."

Shonto looked like he was going to throw up. "That's gotta be no kinda good," he said, covering his mouth.

"Cielo, you eat the craziest foods. I can't believe some of the stuff you come up with," Maricela said.

"What can I say? What's good is good," Cielo replied, rocking back with his full body laughter. "I like to think of myself as a squirrel of sorts. I make do with what I find. I like combining things people wouldn't normally mix together. Kinda like jazz."

"Well, brother," Maricela said, "you can riff on that all on your own. I like my basics."

"You mean you don't like crackers and ketchup with wasabi?" Cielo cracked.

They ate lunch at a relaxed pace. The air was slightly more humid today, the breeze more alert. Leaves drifted the sky around them, landing in a scatter. Ocean scent carried better today, bringing with it whale song and bird calls. Lake thought she saw whale mothers and calves sounding and breeching, but at this distance, she could have just been seeing what she wanted. As they began finishing lunch, Ashia and Promise appeared, looking like mud mummies. Everyone followed them down to the ocean so the two could wash off. Promise told their adventure story with a big grin and a tone of pride in Ashia, as the group asked questions frantically. The way Promise told it, the quicksand pit was a mile wide, and Ashia had fought off gators and bears to save Promise. Dark red starfish gathered around Promise and Ashia in the water, listening in on the story. As adrenaline washed through all of them, the group paused for a beat as long as it took for drowsiness from lunch to come over them. Then each went their way, following drowsiness where it led.

As Pikea and Shonto cuddled close under a lone monkeypod tree at the corner of a meadow, the tree's crown, easily 200 feet in span, began to rain. Pikea felt soft patters of wetness on her bare shoulders and on her head. "What's that? Do you feel that?"

Shonto looked up and saw a fine mist falling, almost floating. His face was soon sprinkled in a mist that cooled him. Smiling, with his eyes closed, Shonto felt that life could not be any better than this. *The island has given us a tree that rains. I am no longer surprised by anything we find here.*

The two human people sat shoulder to shoulder against the trunk of the tree that rains and let its subtle shower bring them to a place of happiness they had no choice but to believe.

"I like being near you," Shonto said. "You're like a song that melts your spirit. Can I put you on repeat?"

"Don't get breezy, cousin." Pikea laughed inside.

As they stared up into the monkeypod's leafy underside, they heard a rustling. Pikea sat up and looked into the trees set deeper into the woods. A deer was looking directly at her, its large eyes reflecting light that seemed to transmit words.

"Shonto, look," Pikea said. "There's a deer back in there. I think it's watching us."

"Nothing to see here, Brah," Shonto said. The deer approached, a few tentative feet at a time. That's when both of them could see that the deer was missing a leg.

"Wow, poor thing," Pikea said. "I wonder what happened to him."

"How do you know it's a *him*?"

"See those antler buds? That's a boy toy, buddy."

The young buck began to stomp the ground with its front left hoof.

"He seems angry," noted Pikea.

"Maybe it's our Love musk," Shonto joked. "You know I got it like that."

"Shush, boy. You might be right, though. I wonder if he's bothered by our scent, or hormones. I've never seen a deer stomp before like that. You?"

"Just this one time when my friend's dad was driving us home from a concert one night and a deer came out of nowhere and jumped right through the windshield."

"Oh, no!" said Pikea. "That's horrible."

"Who you telling? Spilled my drink all over me. Deer was completely losing it. Braying in this high pitch that almost blew out our ears. It was stomping like crazy, too. Broke my nose, and my friend's dad got his arm busted up. Still can't use it right. My friend, he was in the back seat. Lucky bone sweeper. Slept through the whole thing."

"What's a bone sweeper?"

"Someone who comes behind when the buzzards and other scavengers have eaten all the carnage. They come and sweep up all the bones."

"For what?"

"Don't you know how many things you can use some good bones for? Tools. Games. Ceremonies. Artwork. Whatever you want, pretty much."

"So a bone sweeper is a real thing?"

"Don't know. That's my word for it."

Pikea watched the deer as it continued spying them from the bush. She thought of hormonal attraction. Bad choice of thoughts. It led her to a train of memory she had been trying to shake for years. Visions of people making her feel violated one way or another. *Try to be present, Pikea.* She feared that if she couldn't be at peace here on an island, eating like crazy and lazing around under a tree, she might not ever be free of the sickening yanking and pulling in her chest.

This one memory train, though, had worn deep grooves in her brain. *Violation.* Females seemed to be as licentious with Pikea as were the males. If it wasn't her body, it was her young energy they wanted. She was a commodity, but only because of her age and its presumed purity. And naiveté. What sick carnal impulse makes people want to desecrate what is pure? To make naiveté dance and shame itself? She clenched her jaw and looked at Shonto, who was *peacing out* with bliss on his face. She shoved his shoulder for no good reason. He looked at her strangely, shook his head, and closed his eyes again. A placental film obscured Pikea's vision, a watery rage she could not blink out of. An old darkness had returned.

Pikea held a certain secret so tightly that the stress had manifest as a nervous twitch. The right corner of her mouth jerked outward, like with a smirk, then back again. This happened increasingly when her nerves were restless. It would repeat itself seven, eight, 10 times within a minute if she was anxious enough.

The secret was planted in her when she was seven. She came out of her and her brother's room late one night, thirsty for some water. Moving from the darkness into the kitchen, her eyes were blinded by the ceiling light. That's what she had always told herself. That's how she explained to herself that she couldn't make out the adult form that was moving strangely over her brother. All that her psyche would allow was an awareness that her brother was in the kitchen that night, and he was silent and his eyes were raining. And a dark silhouette, a scarecrow or goblin or something was doing something to her brother. That's all she was willing to remember. That, plus that her brother never smiled again.

Pikea observed two crows cleaning each other on a high branch. Their intelligence was evident as they nuzzled and picked each other. One bird twitched its head, hearing or seeing something. It crouched, then lifted and flew away. Pikea wondered whether crows suffer when they separate and how they cope with that. *Loneliness*. The feeling landed on her more often than the thought. By the time she would notice, she usually was deep into one dysfunctional response or another. Sarcasm. Anger. Or pushing people away.

Staring at the sky from the cabin rooftop, Ashia decided to write a letter to her Ama. Ama was briefly Ashia's foster parent. Her actual name was Samjhana, which meant, *Remember* in Nepali. Ama had become so much more than that. Ama was a patient soul. She saw beyond Ashia's presentation, down to the core. The little girl grieving her mother. Determined to surpass her mother's life. Guilt ridden because she wanted that. For a time, when Ashia was about to turn 16, Ama was the glue as Ashia's emotional fabric fell apart. Her grades, always sterling, dropped off a cliff. Even her usual grooming and physical conditioning suffered. Ashia was no longer staying with Ama, but they met regularly for walks. Talks. They went to open mic nights. Sipped herbal tea at cafés and laughed Lovingly at the parade of human characters who passed by the windows.

Samjhana had a sister named Sulochana. Sulochana's name meant *beautiful vision*, or, *seeing the world as beautiful* in Sanskrit. The two sisters had been orphaned in India, and raised in Nepal by a family in Kathmandu from a small village in the Helambu region. The sisters possessed compassionate hearts, and opened them to anyone who radiated true beauty. Ashia was one of those. Now, Ashia recalled the time when Sulochana had fallen ill, and Samjhana had to leave her job as a nanny to care for her sister. Ashia had always depended on Samjhana for emotional support. Now, Samjhana was in need of the same, even from someone so young as Ashia. Ashia nursed her Ama with songs and books and laughter, as her Ama cared for her sister through frightening and uncertain months that took their toll. When Sulochana was blessed with recovery, Samjhana credited Ashia for being there for Sulochana, indirectly. Ashia always remembered Samjhana's soft yet strong voice, saying to her, "When we pour Love, who can know where it goes? What we may know is that it does go. And where it goes, there grows beauty."

Ashia drank juice from a coconut shell, and opened her journal. It was bound in saa paper, from mulberry trees, a Thai tradition. She Loved to run her fingers over the raised décor of the journal's cover. Ashia took a deep breath and began to write to her Ama. She was once more looking for guidance in the ways of Love.

"Binda, you smell like water lilies," Cielo said, his voice quiet.

"Is that a good thing?" Binda asked.

"It just is. I like it."

The sun was just beginning its slow slide down from the peak of the sky, grabbing up handfuls of heat as it went. A cool breeze picked up over the water as Binda and Cielo sat on the edge of the lagoon, all four feet dancing under the surface.

They were talking group homes. Cielo popped figs in his mouth as he commenced to reminisce. "I spent eight months at this one place, they had a whole campus not far from the ocean. It was surrounded by these amazing mountains. It was the kind of place people would pay a lot of money to vacation at, if it weren't a group home.

"Sounds like a dream," Binda said.

"They had this therapy dog named Scuba. I guess he was there to calm down youth with their anxieties and emotions. All he did was go around and hang his big 'ol tongue out. Everyone petted him. He was irresistible."

"What breed?" Binda asked.

"Saint Bernard. Scuba was basically the mascot. A day didn't feel right if you hadn't seen his goofy face. Loved that dog."

"Binda, what's it like down under?" Cielo asked.

"I don't come from the Outback, you know. I grew up in a suburb, just like you."

"For real? But, I guess what I mean is, what does it feel like inside to have the kind of ancestors you do?"

Binda felt Cielo's sincerity, otherwise she would have been way past offended. Not because he had said anything wrong. She was just way past through with people imagining her as some kind of wild animal. "It feels like having an old world move through your blood and be rejected by all things new," she answered.

Binda rolled some poppy petals in her pocket, biding time and strengthening her resolve. She felt acid in her throat. Her ears were buzzing. "I... cut myself," Binda said, barely putting the words out on the air.

"When?" Cielo asked.

"No, I mean I cut myself sometimes."

After a vibrating silence, Cielo wanted to offer some token of support. "I... I appreciate you trusting me with that. How often do you do it?"

"I don't know. Whenever things get too tense. I feel things so deeply. It cuts the intensity, no pun intended."

"Have you shared this with anyone else here?"

"I would tell Lake, or Ashia, but I guess I'm judging myself too much."

Cielo's usual casual expression grew attentive. "*Mira*, Binda, you know you're safe here. What's going on?"

"I just feel like I need to stop pretending that I'm so in control. Truth is, I feel completely out of control. Always have. That's why I cut myself. Makes me feel like in that moment I have a say over my pain. When to start it. When to stop it. What a joke that is."

"I feel you. When did you start doing it?"

"Back when we first had to go out on the street. My *wiyanga*, my mom, she called it downsizing. She was embarrassed like the rest of us. I just wanted to scream, like that was the last straw.

"It's not like I made a plan to cut myself the first time. I just remember feeling like screaming, and behind that a curtain of the most horrible fear for my family. Then, things went slow mo, and I saw this hand holding a razor blade. A river started running down my forearm that reminded me of happiness for some reason. Warm. Free. Quiet."

"Wow. How many scars do you have?"

"I stopped counting scars when people started counting everything for my family. Food stamps. Shelter vouchers. School day absences. Bad checks."

After sharing her secret with Cielo, Binda felt so light. But drained, too. She dipped into the water and swam for an hour in and out of the lagoon spring's warm funnel, delighted at the sensation against her body. She wanted to laugh, but was able to avoid opening her mouth and swallowing water. As she swam, the mineral-rich water seemed to infiltrate her pores and join with her bones, making them feel less like hard skeletal structures and more like a fine silt. She lost sense of any separation between her body and the water. She was fluidity. Self-determined and reposed in wholeness.

Pikea, chewing a strand of her hair and wiggling her toes, was writing in her journal. After her solo discovery of the underwater cavern, she was feeling... poured into. Memories of the day. She wrote:

Binda is the kind of person who speaks at the end of a conversation, after everyone else, and when she does, her words make everyone else's seem foolish.

I think I noticed the turtle birthmark in her eye the first time we all went swimming. She slipped into the water like something born from water. No hitch, just fluid movement, then gone, down beneath the surface. She came up, bobbing and smiling. She didn't like to be caught smiling. It was like she was betraying her image when she smiled.

Ivory called us all over to a spot out in the lagoon, about 20 strokes from shore. We formed a circle, dog paddling and panting. Ivory said, "Look down." That's when we saw the bubbles and light for the first time.

I happened to look over at Binda, and saw it. She was close, otherwise I would have missed it. About the size of an old memory, maybe a quarter of an inch... less. It was light turquoise, swimming in the dark brown iris of her right eye. She didn't notice me staring. Everyone was tripping on the mystery coming up from down deep in the lake. It took me a while to break away from her birthmark. I sort of fell into it... swimming in the dark water with a mystic creature, and it felt... unreal.

Eloni and Balanta, sharing Samoan and West African stories, arrived at an overlook where they paused to replenish. "Every time we eat and drink," Balanta said, "our load gets lighter. I like that about hiking." They both watched as two hawks rose up from the canyon and regarded them briefly before banking away and resting on the wind. One of the hawks had an animal in its talons. "Life is real out here," Balanta said.

Eloni coughed and reached down to rub his calves. His arm ink glistened beneath sweat. "I used to keep a private list of all the things wrong with me," he said. "All the bad things. I picked up what my mom used to say about me when she was "blessing herself." That's what she called it when she drank. She was real good at coming up with things for my list.

"I also got real good at paying attention to what the world was calling me, out loud to my face or just thinking it so loud I had to turn the volume down. By 15 my list was so long I was having trouble hiding all the pages. I couldn't keep it written down because every time I moved or was on punishment I would have lost access. So eventually I decided to memorize it. My list started growing like a tapeworm inside my intestines. I could feel it squirm every time a new segment was added to its body. My tapeworm got fed up with my guts, so it did the natural thing and traveled to my brain. It kept growing there, fed by all those thoughts.

"Finally, my tapeworm laid eggs in my heart. And that's when I went off on some dude in the park one day who looked at me a second too long. Truth is, I'm not sure he was even looking at me. He might have been spacing out or something. Didn't matter. By then my tapeworm was looking for a way out. Feel me?"

Balanta felt him. They swatted at small bushes with their machete spears whenever they could, and kept onward. The quality of sunlight was melancholy now. The part of day that feels like the beginning of its goodbye.

Eloni pulled himself up onto a small plateau pocked with mohawk grass and bluebells. Heat shimmered above the ground. Eloni's legs felt shredded, in a good way. This was the test he had been craving. He couldn't stand school subjects. Math, science, English... all that stuff intimidated him. He needed to touch and know reality from that touch. He needed to be touched and have a clarity about what was touching him. He stood erect, stretching his spine, lifting and circling his shoulders backward, loosening muscle. Balanta followed soon, one hand and then another grasping the stony escarpment, pulling his body up onto flat ground. He sat there for a moment, leaning back on his hands, surveying. To his left, Balanta saw a gymnastic arrangement of rocks piled into a triangle. Getting up, he moved over to the rocks. Strange. Clearly something a person did. He kicked the stones, less than conscious that he preferred the stones in a more natural order. Eloni turned at the sound of the rocks scraping over each other, tumbling to the ground. He turned just in time to see Balanta jump back suddenly, and to hear him yell in an unusual pitch.

The snake was large. Twice as thick as a garden hose. As long as Eloni was tall. Its skin was a white and brown merengue, with a neon red stripe running its full length. It moved quickly, its shelter having been obliterated by the strange tall animal. Before Eloni could cross from the plateau's rim and reach Balanta, the snake was gone. Balanta was on the ground, gripping his right leg, moaning. Eloni knelt and placed his hand on Balanta's shin, which was perforated just above the ankle by two dark red bite holes. The area was swelling. Balanta looked into Eloni's eyes. Searching.

Eloni moved fast. He tore off both sleeves from his shirt, knotted them end-to-end and tied the tourniquet tightly around the base of Balanta's calf, inches above the bite wound. "This is going to hurt. Gotta do it," Eloni said, as he pulled out his buck knife, rubbing down the blade with pungent leaves he had retrieved from his backpack.

"What's that?" Balanta asked, his eyes growing distant.

"Witch hazel. Got it from the garden. Good sterilizer." Eloni picked up a nearby stick, thick and sturdy, gave it to Balanta, and told him to clamp down on it with his teeth. Balanta turned his face to the sky and huffed, his breath coming rapidly. Eloni placed his hand on Balanta's chest. "Easy, brother. Slow that breathing. You need to hold off the toxin." Balanta took one deep breath, and Eloni sliced open the wound, directly between the two bite holes. Balanta released a muffled scream into the wood, his fingers digging into stones and pebbles. His eyes rolled up and Balanta's upper body fell to the ground.

Eloni pulled the small gourd from his pack and separated the two halves that he had bound with river reed fibers. He cupped two fingers into the tarry eucalyptus sap. With his other hand, he parted Balanta's flesh where it had been cut open. He spread the sap into the cut, pressing it down as deeply as it would go. Eloni tore the rest of his shirt into one long piece, and wrapped it over the sap application.

Balanta stirred. "We gotta get you to a fire, man. Bed down for the night," said Eloni.

"I'm all right. I can make it back to camp." Balanta's eyes were drifting in another world.

"Nah. We can't move the toxin. You gotta stay as still as possible. Let the sap do what it does. Here, I'm going to carry you."

Balanta had never been carried in his life. "No! I can make it. Where's Mende? Go get him and we'll all make the hike."

"Bro, you're not making any sense. You're delirious. Mende's back at camp. I need you to downshift." Eloni put his hand back on Balanta's chest, ushering Balanta's heartbeat back into a calmer mood. Balanta's eyes closed again, his body falling slack. Eloni strained to lift Balanta's deceptive weight. Finally, Eloni lay on his side on the hard terrain, positioning himself up against Balanta. Eloni reach behind himself, pulled Balanta onto his own side, and then over partially onto Eloni. With Balanta now mostly lying on Eloni's back, Eloni struggled to a kneeling position. Hefting Balanta more squarely onto Eloni's back, Eloni squatted and thrust upward into a standing position. Balanta, half-conscious, put his arms around Eloni's neck. Eloni wrapped both arms beneath Balanta's knees. Eloni strained back into a crouch, grabbed both packs in one hand, and both spears in another. He took a deep breath and carried Balanta off the plateau.

Bellies growled back at camp. With Eloni gone, they realized how spoiled they had been. After staring at each other blankly, and after Cielo offered to make up something special, the group was motivated to hop quick to making up a decent meal. Ivory started the night's fire, feeding thick maple logs into the flames, which perfumed camp with a sweet aroma. Ashia and Lake tossed a salad that swelled as they added to it. Spinach and collards. Radishes, tomatoes, onions. Basil and thyme. Melon, red bell peppers, berries. All drizzled in a dressing of orange peel oil, pressed olives, and browned apple nectar.

"I like artists like Jacob Lawrence, Jonathan Green. Francois Cauvin, too." Lake said, absentmindedly. "A lot of soul comes through their stuff. It's like Nina Simone singing barefoot through paint."

Ashia smiled. "I like your words, girl. This planet doesn't exactly speak your language, does it?"

"No. But I'm learning its tongue the best I can."

The others came over and conversation got around to philosophical matters. "If ever we were free, life made us slaves," Ashia said. "Now, we have to kill the slaves."

"What are you talking about?" Mende asked.

"There's a part in each of us that is destroying our chance for happiness," Ashia explained. "It's a slave, chained to pain and negativity and fear. Won't leave the plantation even when we try to go Harriet Tubman on it. Sometimes, we get it to stand up straight, like when we're dancing to some good music. Most of the time though, it wants to crouch and shuffle and *yessir, yesma'am*.

So we have to kill it. We don't want to, because it's a part of us, and we actually have feelings for it. But I say you can't be free if you have a slave roaming around in the plantation of your mind."

"It's like my man Marley sang, *Emancipate yourselves from mental slavery...*" Cielo crooned.

Ivory bit his lip and looked inside himself, wrestling.

Maricela went on with the theme. "Don't you all see what's happening here? Our situation's made us slaves... to everything. Slaves to other people's ideas of us. Slaves to authority. Slaves to our fears. One thing my popi Manuel taught me was, he said, 'It is a rare creature that will still live free even when it is caged. Takes an unexplainable spirit to do that.'

"I look around and I don't see one of us having the courage to tear our pain out from our hearts, right here and now, and throw it on the fire. Maybe we're afraid of losing something we've been a part of so long. Whatever... I just know I'm ready to kill this slave inside of me. I want to live free, me comprendes?" Maricela's eyes were glistening. Her voice wavering with determination.

Mende, and Maricela handled preparing the crab cakes and clam and mussel gumbo. Shonto brought over redfish and croakers to Ivory, who was tending the cooking rock. Cielo had polished it almost to a shine by now with a hand-sized stone and much patience. Anytime they needed to grill fish on it now, a little oil was all it took to keep the fish from sticking. They also soaked willow branches and used them as a grill atop the cooking rock.

"My friend, you are wealthy in your... rotundity," said Ivory, patting Shonto on the shoulder.

"And you are blessed in your boniness," said Shonto, returning the Love.

"Lay that fish down right here on this rock," Ivory said. "I got it nice and hot." The sweet scent lifted up from the wet sticks right on beat with the sizzling.

"Make sure you turn it over every few minutes," Shonto said. "Who's got the first serving?"

Promise looked up. "Make mine well done, please."

"Fish doesn't come well done," Ivory cracked. "This isn't burgers. You get what you get."

"That doesn't even make any sense," Promise retorted. "Of course fish comes well done. I'm not for sushi today. Go ahead and crisp mine up."

Cielo passed around a calabash filled with a special brew he had been boiling and adding to since the day before. He called it *roots beer*.

Ivory heartily drank from the coconut shell he used for a cup. "Mmm! This is primo!" he declared. "What's up in it?"

"Let's see," Cielo said, encouraged by the positive feedback of lips smacking. "Cinnamon, black pepper, cayenne, cloves, ginger, nutmeg, pimento berries, balsam, wintergreen, cassia, sweet birch, molasses, spearmint... and blackberries. Yeah, I think that's everything."

"I don't even know what half those things are or how you identified what plants to pick," Ivory croaked, "I just know it kicks like a kangaroo. It's the stuff, man."

"Gracias, hermano. It's all in the art of seeing the spirit of a plant. It wants you to know how to use it."

"Okaaay..." Promise said, still licking her lips. "I think this stuff is making me spacey."

"It may have some, shall we say, visionary qualities to it," Cielo said, laughing.

"Oh great!" Binda said, "Cielo got us all sideways. Gonna be a long night!"

Shonto entertained them during dinner with stories of Native legends. He rolled out character after character, each of whose tales served to connect their tribal people back to their origins. To their nature and reason. One-legged roadrunner birds pogoing away from coyotes. Women warriors who claimed great victories. Some of the stories were stereotypical, involving drunkenness and dysfunction. These made Lake wince, and Binda wince at Lake's wincing. Other tales broke stigmas over brave rocks of intelligence, familial vibrancy, and spiritual wealth. Shonto's natural staccato cadence made his story even funnier. Dry, understated spaces like canyons between words that punctuated his meaning. Ivory claimed to have burst a lung and strained a spleen laughing so hard. For Mende, the shared laughter was good medicine for his still bruised heart.

They decided that after dinner they would help Ivory face one of his many fears. He was going to jump off the waterfall. Ivory started off agreeing to the proposition, even boasting about the world-class dives he was going to perform. But as they headed to the lagoon, Ivory reverted to Ivory. They had to drag him the rest of the way. At the lagoon, Mende, Promise, and Pikea forced Ivory up the embankment and onto the waterfall ledge, where Ivory stood shivering in the knee-high water even in the heat. They formed a semicircle behind him, blocking any attempted escape.

"Go on, Ivory. Kill the slave!" they yelled, with all the supportive energy they could gather.

Pikea was less patient. "Try not to fill your pants, Ivory. It's just some water and the jump isn't that high."

Ivory was repeating his private mantra under his breath: "Walk through the valley... Walk through the valley..." He sucked in a massive gulp of air, which ballooned his belly and bulged his eyes like a bullfrog. Clenching his fists and squeezing his eyes closed tightly, he crouched, exploded up, lifting onto his toes, onto air, out over the cliff side.

"Go, Ivory!" the group shouted, proudly. Ivory's slender body was a tree branch aloft and falling. His grin blazed as his eyes poured out fear water. He felt sensations that could not be real. So intense. Alive.

He hit the water with a face plant to rival all face plants. "Oooh!"

"Ouch!"

"Man!"

"Whoa!"

"That's gonna leave a mark!"

"Man down!" The group's barrage was merciless even as it was concerned.

For too long, nothing broke up to the water's surface. Then, Ivory's black moss crown rocketed into view, a bubbling sponge. His bullfrog eyes followed, then his mouth, which had already started exclaiming underwater. "No way! I'm alive! I'm aliiive! I killed that bad boy!"

"Ivory! You did the thang!"

"I knew you had it in you!"

"I'll never doubt you again. You better check your private parts, my man."

They washed off the heat and tensions of the day in the waterfall and lagoon. Promise swam out to the center of the water, to the spring, and descended alongside the effervescent shaft of bubbles. Down farther she went, yearning to reach the mouth of the spring. She still couldn't believe the water could be this color, or so clear.

The pressure built in her head. Her lungs burned. On the way back to the surface she laughed at herself. *Like I was really going to reach the bottom.*

When the first crickets sounded, most of the group headed back to camp. Shonto and Pikea remained at the lagoon, hanging out on shore.

Shonto kicked a smooth stone as he sat on a log and rocked side to side on his hands, elbows locked. "I want to be an engineer. Or a geophysicist. Or an archaeologist."

"That's some deep stuff. Why all that?"

"I like figuring out how to put things together after they've fallen apart." He thought most naturally of his community whenever he heard those words: *fallen apart.* His Love for them, and the generations of hurting, brought up a strong spurt of sharp pain in him. He wondered just about daily where the line is across which a people cannot return once they cross it.

Then he thought of the jump shot he missed to lose the league championship game. He still hadn't forgiven himself, even though he had scored 27 points and his teammates were long since lost in more consequential travails.

This thought made him hungry. He could taste Eloni's conch fritters topped with coconut shavings. And fry bread for dessert.

Pikea tossed a bunch of flat stones across the water. They each bounced several times before sinking.

"You got a major league arm there," Shonto said. "Why do you like skipping stones so much?"

"I don't know," Pikea answered. "Something about the way the rocks are suspended for that brief moment over the water before smacking down and taking off again. It seems like a dream. Rocks flying. You know that once their momentum slows, they'll plunge down in the water. It's freedom. That's what it is. To feel something freed by your own power.

Pikea slung another stone. "I've been living that way, trying to run fast enough to stay above the water."

"How's that working for you?" Shonto asked.

"Ha! You see me drowning, don't you? And that's a rhetorical question, so don't bother."

After several beats of silence, Pikea said, "I'm afraid. Afraid of healing. What if it means that I lose the person I've been for so long?"

"Isn't that the point?"

"Yeah, but after so much time, it's scary to lose yourself, even if it's your bad self."

Shonto shifted his sitting position and brushed back his bangs. "I'm forgetting what I was like when I was little. What joy felt like. Then again, I've never felt stronger. Like I can catch the moon if it falls. Is that what it means to be an adult? To lose your childhood heart and have it replaced by something duller, that doesn't feel so much, so you can take more pain?"

Pikea looked at Shonto. Her eyes far away. And stewing. "Whatever an adult is supposed to be, I'm clearly failing miserably so far."

"Why are you always so hard on yourself?" Shonto asked. "That's no kinda good."

Pikea frowned. "I refuse to be like my mother. She took no responsibility for how she affected others."

"So, by beating yourself up, that's taking responsibility? Seems like a strange form of domestic violence to me. Self-battering."

"Look, I get it," Pikea said. "I know it doesn't help to dig myself into a dark hole at every little incident. It's a hard habit to break. Then again, those dark holes feel safe in a strange way. Familiar. I get confused as to what direction I should go for Peace. I feel so inflamed."

"That's probably what you are, for real. Inflamed on the inside. Your actual tissues and organs and brain. From all the trauma and shame. No wonder our health falls apart. We're burning up. Only way to put the fire out is to get some dignity."

The setting sun drenched the sky in rich, placental tones, foretelling the birthing of night. The sun wavered behind thin mist and heat ribbons, taking on the geometric appearance of a pyramid. Soon it drowned, leaving a darkening sky to mourn.

The stories began as the fire grew obscene, thanks to Ivory's repeated tossing of maple logs. "Hey, Ivory, you better give up the matches, amigo," Cielo playfully said.

"Haha. Just because I liked to burn things back in the day doesn't mean I would do anything dumb like that here. I'm a conservationist now."

"A conservationist?" Shonto asked.

"Yeah, I like to conserve the earth. But I do have to say, sometimes you need to burn something down before it can grow up the right way."

"O...kay," Promise said. "You're scaring me now."

"Don't worry, you'll smell the fire long before you feel it. Just playing."

"I'm not so sure."

"Ivory, that *guwiyang* is gonna set the sky on fire if you're not careful," Binda joshed.

"Gooey what?"

"Guwiyang. Means *fire*.

Ashia slapped her palms together loudly and puffed out some air. "Shonto, you tell a story, please? Yours are good."

"I don't know," Shonto shrugged. "I guess I could tell you about the Gila Monster."

"The helium what?" Ivory asked.

"The gila monster. It's this lizard out in the desert that has skin covered in dark colored beads. Its skin looks like Indian corn, if you've ever seen that."

"How big is this thing?" Ivory queried, as Lake and Binda giggled.

Shonto ignored the question and told a story of how the gila monster came to be known amongst the Diné people, and how they learned to appreciate its unique features, even weaving their blankets in its color patterns, honoring its peculiar beauty. Shonto's tale was a story of how we make our monsters, and then our monsters make us.

Balanta awoke to the warmth of a small fire on his face. Darkness was coming. Eloni was pitching small branches onto the fire. "Good to see you coming around," Eloni said, handing Balanta a soft flask of water.

Balanta took a long, urgent drink, the water spilling down his chin. The water hitting his stomach seemed to light a fire inside his leg. He looked down at the wounded area. Eloni had rewrapped it after soaking the cloth in boiling water. "You use that eucalyptus sap to start the fire?" Balanta asked.

"Yep. That stuff is like lighter fluid. Reliable. Fire likes it."

"How did you know how to do all of this, with the bite and all that?"

"Don't know. Been around enough snakes and stuff, I guess. Island life, you know?"

Balanta stared at the flames for a long moment. He rubbed his thigh, which was aching painfully all the way down to his knee, now swollen badly. "I've never seen a snake like that before," Balanta said. "You?"

"Nope. That one looked like it came from another planet. That stripe on its back freaked me out, to be honest."

"We don't know how poisonous that thing was. You think I'll make it?"

Eloni looked Balanta in his eyes, pausing. "By the way you're reacting now, I'm hoping you're going to be all right. We need to hold the toxin down. The more your blood flows, the worse it gets. Keep your leg down lower than your waist at all times, too. You feel like eating?"

Balanta was sweating profusely. Lightheaded. Weak. Still, it had been since morning that he had eaten anything, and the exertion of the hike and climbing had left him with an appetite. "What do we have? I don't suppose you also caught our dinner."

"I did manage to gather some fruit, once we got back down to a lower altitude."

"You carried me," Balanta said, dawning to the practical implication of his body weight on Eloni's back. "How far did you walk?"

Eloni cast his eyes downward, tossing another stick at the flames. "Don't know. Maybe a couple of miles." Eloni got up to get some fruit together for Balanta. Before Balanta felt a swooning of sickness, and vomited, he noticed Eloni limping badly on his left leg.

They ate apricots, olives, plums, and some leftover snapper jerky courtesy of Cielo's forethought. Eloni tried not to look too often at Balanta. Tried not to worry. He found a suitable nervous tick, throwing twigs at the fire, watching them flare and pop and disintegrate in the blaze. He imagined himself leaping from star to star in the black sky moving glacially through the hours. Balanta moved in and out of sleep, cold sweats, and fire that consumed his skin. Night wrapped around them. The meager fire did its part, warming bones enough and keeping away anything that might have a taste for the blood Balanta's wound offered acridly throughout the night.

Nascent night was indigo. Trees were indigo. Sand, stones, stars. Everything was indigo, its inky milk waiting to be suckled by those who dared to dream.

Shonto massaged his hand drum. A damsel fly landed on his shoulder, and, content with the touch, departed. "The Native drumbeat," he shared casually, "is mostly calmer and slower than the African beat. Its cadence doesn't rise and fall as much. It is seeking something. An equilibrium, I think."

"The African beat seeks the marrow of movement," said Mende, playing a slow seduction on his djembe.

Cielo dipped into his cabin and brought out his bongos. Hopping up onto a stump, he nodded his head a few times to an internal beat, wiped back his thick bangs and drummed quick staccato haikus that floated into sky's absorbing acres.

Lake had been listening to the stories and fire talk while weaving sweetgrass strands, patiently, her eyes lost in the hypnotic movement. As she wove, a basket emerged in pencil thin rolls atop one another, bound and tethered just tight enough to cancel out the light between layers.

The moon now was a suggestion of closure, a thinning crest now less dominant within the burgeoning starlight. "The giant is very drowsy," Lake said, her face to the sky. "Almost there, to sleep. I like the way it makes me feel."

"Like what?" Promise asked.

"Like whatever is on earth is becoming something again."

Mende had run to his cabin to retrieve his drum and now was working up a good sweat over it.

"Mende," Ashia asked, "I notice that you go get your drum when you're upset or nervous. Does it calm you down?"

"More like it builds me up," Mende said. "When I touch its skin, I feel old power. When I start calling for the beat, I can feel my ancestors come to me."

"That's pretty cool. How come Balanta doesn't play more?"

"I don't know. I think maybe he's fighting himself right now. He actually makes the sky listen when he plays. You should see it."

They danced and drank Cielo's roots beer as they swapped stories about fools and clowns and rabid ravens and rarified romances. The ladies couldn't get enough of the sound of the jacaranda pods clattering as they moved their hips in waves and jounced their ankles.

Ashia taught the other women a traditional Ga womanhood initiation dance. Lake showed them the green corn dance. Maricela, a sassy Panamanian number.

Pikea laughed at all of it, even as she tried to get the dances down. Finally, she broke into a house party freestyle.

Ivory did a line dance. By himself. While spitting out a story about a neighborhood pit bull he claimed to have tamed by telepathy.

Through it all, the drumbeats, rapid at the drama points, somber when someone put their pain on a totem pole and painted it fiercely.

Promise looked around the fire at the glowing faces. Almost dying had broken apart something feeble in her. A kind of fascia in her being. Scar tissue. She felt something warm in her chest. An odd emotion for her. She named it pride. "The thing I like about this group," she said when the drums were whispering, "is we just tell our stories and it's no big deal. With adults, you tell your story and they pretty much freak out. It's either the fountain of tears, or the red face of major discomfort. Or, major condescension and pity. They can't just listen and honor what you share. They have to make it like you're having a crisis just because you're sharing some bad things. People, you asked me to share, okay? It's like they think you need a therapist with a bottle of meds after every panel presentation or even if you're just in a mad mood.

"Here, we can just tell our truth, talk story together, and everyone stays calm and normal. They think we can't handle traumatic stuff coming up. Where do they think it stays in us when we're not talking about it? In a nice, safe fire resistant security box? It's boiling in us all the time. Talking about it is how we deal. How we release the steam. And we're not feeling sorry for ourselves or ungrateful when we talk. We're not trying to get back at someone or to be nasty. Stop projecting all that crap onto us. That's your stuff. Your guilt and discomfort. We're just telling our story. That's what humans do. It's pretty much common knowledge.

"Everyone wants to be a voice for young people like us," Promise continued. "They don't even notice when we're trying to be our own voice. It's just more imposition. Someone needs to be an *ear* for us. Commit to humbling yourself and listen."

"Anyway, I lost my point. Sorry. I appreciate that this group has created a space where we can put our stuff in the fire and poke it with a stick. And if the stick catches on fire, so be it. Drop the stick. Or use it for a torch. I don't know. But it feels good to stir the coals. You know?"

"Some of the most supportive, honoring spaces I've been in have been group conversations in residential care. When we're left alone to be ourselves. We don't always talk about heavy stuff, but whatever we're talking about, it's not put on us. It's not an assignment. And people don't bully people and make fun of them. They are genuinely supportive. I haven't felt safe like that anywhere else."

"I've got one," Maricela said. She was used to scavenging hard for good memories. It was a life skill, she figured, being able to rearrange reality in her mind with such strident repetition and determination that it became truth. *Constructing truth.* She figured she could list that one on her résumé under Work Experience.

Tonight, she was in need of wrapping herself in good memories. She chose one that actually was good, so that she could magnify it into great. "My quince was one of my best nights ever," she shared, filling the silence.

"What's a quince?" asked Binda.

"It's kind of like your fairytale moment. Mexican girls, when we turn 15, our family throws us a huge party, a *quinceañera*."

"Like a graduation party?"

"No, no. This is a rite of passage. It's part ritual and tradition, and part straight out bash. I think the adults end up partying harder than the children.

"My tio Ernesto, he always thought he was like a reincarnation of Che Guevara, even told people that. So, he liked to think he was a revolutionary. Well, at some point he got it into his head that he was going to make a grand gesture to The Man and use my quince as the staging ground. He came up with a scheme to rent out a hotel ballroom for my quince. His genius idea was to invite the city council members. In the middle of the whole thing, there I am in my dream dress that I started sketching when I was six, with all my family and friends dancing and happy, and my uncle stands and taps his spoon against his cerveza glass to call for attention.

"The whole place goes quiet, which was quite the feat with about 200 people in fiesta mode. My tio clears his throat and turns to the table where the city council members were huddled up and nervous, and he announces that this is what immigration is all about. Look around, he says, tell me you have seen a collection of better human beings.

"Then he goes bolder. He says, anyone here who thinks that immigrants don't improve this country can get up and say so in front of everyone. By this point, the council members have each turned red as a crayon and slid halfway to the floor.

"Tio was lathered up that night, and everyone knew it. My dad and two other uncles and some cousins tried to get him to sit down and shut up. Then they tried to pull the microphone away from him. Someone finally pulled the mic plug, but not before Tio squeezed in, It's time for the people to rise up and seize our dignity! At which point he turned his back to the council members, pulled down his pants, and mooned them in all his dignity.

"Some revolutionary. Half the people fell out laughing. The other half didn't know what to do, so they kept drinking and dancing. The hotel banned my family, and my uncle hightailed it before the cops could get there.

"Not many people remember my quince dress. They do remember the drunken moon that shone that night."

"That's crazy, Cela," Pikea said. "Sounds like my kind of party."

"I'm just glad I got to have a quince," Maricela said. "Mi hermanita Isabella's quinceañera was looking to be legendary, until her mother had to use the money she had saved 10 years for Isa's quince to bail her father out of jail after he beat the living blood out of Isa.

"Your little sister?" Promise asked, confused.

"She's that to me. We're not blood, just amigas from the word go."

"I wish I could have had people care enough to hold a whole quince for me," Pikea said. Maricela noticed the honest pain pronounced on Pikea's face. She also noticed the corner of Pikea's mouth twitch. Maricela felt a needle point stab her heart. With that sharp sting, an idea came.

Cielo deliberately picked at the willow bark he had attached to the side of his bongo heads, as though he were working to summon something. He stopped and stared absentmindedly at the sky. "My patron," Cielo began, "he told me about how he lived out of his rusted white van when he was my age, driving from town to town to find whatever work he could. He said one time these two brothers approached him coming out of a library and asked him if he liked to read.

"He told them yes even though he had only been in the library to take a piss. He figured, if they're so impressed that someone like me can even read, why not play along and see where this goes?

"They took him to an old folk's home and introduced him to their 87-year-old mother who was blind and feisty as a rabid squirrel. They told my patron that their mother couldn't fall asleep unless someone read to her, but they couldn't be there all the time because they were about to get fired from work.

"They gave my patron a stack full of old travel books and children's fables and sat him down near their mother's bedside. 'Good luck, kid,' they joshed him. 'Try not to let her trick you into giving her cigarettes or candy. And duck when she starts grumbling deep in her throat. Means she's about to huck her mashed potatoes at you.'

'Why would she do that?' he asked.

'She likes the sound it makes when it hits your face,' one brother said.

'And she likes the sound of your anger after you get hit even more,' the other brother laughed.

"My patron came over and read to that woman about five nights a week for a whole summer. She liked the way his voice quavered and released certain words gently, like a tree dropping leaves. His voice was still changing at that age, so I guess it had a feminine pitch, and that calmed her.

"Well, after that summer ended, the two brothers were real grateful to my patron. They gave him a collection of old books as a gift. My patron doesn't think they realized the value of the collection, because he had it appraised for $10,000. He sold those books and used the money to start his first business: a program that brought children and youth into nursing homes and rehab centers and had them read to residents.

The conversation swirled like chocolate syrup in milk until it condensed over the subject of adulthood: the season they all felt racing at them with a speed that made no sense.

Shonto stood up on a large rock and twirled his spear over his head. "Transitional living programs? I'm not clueless. I can eventually figure out how to open a bank account or apply for a job. I need help with actual life, man. Like, how to be in a healthy relationship. Not take my anger out on someone. Communicate right. That kind of stuff. I need someone to show me how to be human. Why didn't we get that in school?"

School. The word puckered Pikea's tranquility. School was for her an endless birth. *Pushing.* Pushing young ones through their masticating machinery, until they came out on the other end, graduated, which meant primed to participate in the soullessness of being civil. Schools. Places where children went to learn to be adults. Not to be fierce. No. Timid, flaccid, crouching servants in a feudal system disguised as modern illumination. Pikea despised the whole act. Felt that at least in the Middle Ages, people were honest about their miserable stations and castes in life. Pikea wanted revolution. Tear this whole clown show down. Burn the circus tent. Schoolwork? The meaningless tent pegs that circus hands spend their pitiful lives pounding into interminable dirt.

"My favorite foster parent was this retired military guy with a prosthetic arm," said Maricela. She was still dancing. Soaked and twirling herself into a trance.

Fire for a poncho and starlight in her hair. "He was married and his wife was a nice person, but it was Arturo who was my favorite. He took me and my sisters to baseball games. Pro games. He had a big ol' belly that extended out like a bullfrog's neck when he sat in the bleachers. He called for the vendor moving up and down the aisles, and had the vendor bring me and my sisters a hot dog every inning. That's nine hot dogs and we ate every one. He made us promise not to tell his wife, even though I'm sure she was onto the gig. We only came home from every game with stomachaches and not touching our dinner.

"The thing I liked about him most was how he was always laughing. That calmed my nerves, which were shot from all the abuse. I needed to be around an adult who wasn't wound tight. He laughed from his big ol' gut and didn't care who noticed. And he laughed easily, at just about anything. And every time he got to rolling, it's like I released whatever was balled up in me. I felt like I had landed and could stop beating my wings. That's what I Loved about Arturo. That and the way he smelled. Same aftershave every single day. I liked the consistency."

Ashia stroked her locs and stretched her back. "We're all looking for our tribe to belong to, that's all. No one wants to be outside the fire, freezing and looking in while everyone else is sitting close and warm."

Pikea stood and bounced on her toes. "I like being on my own. I need to breathe."

"Yeah, but what makes you feel happy, at peace?" Cielo asked.

"Just breathing, being in touch with myself and my spirit."

Promise joined in. "Isn't that still a form of company? Of belonging? And besides, if you're so solitary, why are you here with us?"

"I didn't say that I don't enjoy company. I just don't stalk it, or freak out if I'm by myself."

Cielo played raindrops on his bongos with his fingertips. "I'm with Pikea," he said, "in the sense that I would rather be a lone wolf at peace than a sheep in a herd of predators, which is what people become when they are busted up inside. They become predatory."

Shonto saw the white fire ash clinging to Ivory's brows and lashes and laughed. "Having a busted up family," Shonto said, "means you get to hear everybody else talking about the good things in life that they take for granted but that you're missing out on. Then, you're expected to shut up and not disturb their happiness by pointing out that you missed out on what they got to experience. And on top of that, you have to show no signs of unhappiness with your life of missing out on things, because people get uncomfortable with your unhappiness and you get banished from the tribe."

"Most relationships are fraudulent," Pikea opined. She was holding her hair to her nose, smelling the maple in the smoke. "People perpetrate to create joint agreements. They want comfort, not truth. What I've been through, I'm beyond comfort. Boycott all the manipulative presentations. Strip down and burn your clothes. Give me your marrow. I'll give you mine. How you like those chips, Lake?" Pikea nudged Lake playfully. Lake blushed, lost for words. Water formed on the leaf of a nearby fern and fell to another leaf, leaving a tensile window of water between the two worlds.

Pikea wasn't done. She rubbed her eyes, waving away the smoke. "Everybody wants you to kill off your first family, in your heart. In your mind and memories. No room for your roots in the replacement family. The culture can't handle coexistence. It's a conqueror's spirit. All or nothing. 'Die for us if you want to live with us.' I know a bunch of young people who go along with that. A part of them dies. Problem is, the dying doesn't stop there, with their origins. It spreads like an oil spill and consumes their spirit. Spirit death is worse than anything. That's no kind of life. I don't care what kind of privileges you receive that you should be grateful for. I'm not joining no gang that makes me kill my own soul before I can be jumped in. That's too high a price.

"*Permanency*. You know who Loves that word? The system people who get tired of carrying my sorry behind. They want to put me down, *permanently*. They want someone to pick up and carry me, *permanently*.

"I don't think I even want that kind of arrangement. No matter what, my family is my family. Doesn't mean I have to stay with them. And I sure don't need to accept another family to feel secure. That's just sales pitch mumbo jumbo. I mean, don't get me wrong, I'll take any positive relationship I can get. I just don't see why everyone has to obsess over the labels. Forever Family. Permanency. Mentor. Guardian. Resource Family. Please! Can someone simply be normal with me, and try to hang around for a while? Thank you!"

"Preach!"

"Teach!"

"You put a label on it and it starts feeling too official to me. Too formal and corporate. Who wants that with the people closest to them?"

"It's simple. To me, at least. Take my relationship with cops," Ivory said, breaking into spontaneous wordplay:

Cops come when I get in trouble... On the double... They spend time with me... I'm looking for time, not crime, but seems like crime's the way to get the time, so I crime, drop sin like dimes... I detest the rest, them grown up mimes, I test their minds, digest the way they look at me, move their rook at me, I move back with my king, my groove thing, my true bling, they can't hang, I swing through, I swing, I'm too... tired, take my wings... Just take my wings.

"Snaps all around!" said Promise.

"Man, Ivory, you were up, but then you came down," said Mende. "I feel you though. Inspired, but then too tired to be inspired. So you retired."

"Aright, brother," Ivory concurred. "Aright."

A large owl perched on a tree branch that looked like a broken elbow, and twitched its head, staring at Ivory. At least that's what Ivory thought. He moved closer to Binda and leaned his head on her shoulder.

The group fell into a listing of *Nevers*:

"I never had a birthday party."

"I've never had any baby pictures of myself."

"I never went to prom."

"I've never had any friendships longer than three years."

"I never had a bedroom to myself."

"I never got to know any of my teachers."

"I've never felt safe."

"I've never landed in this world. I'm still floating."

"I've never seen myself in another human face."

Ashia kept thinking about Balanta and Eloni. She was feeling what everyone else was avoiding: the camp and night fire felt empty without them. "Shelters aren't to protect the people who stay in them," Ashia said. "They are to protect the world from the people who stay in them. The world works hard to shelter itself from people like us. We scare it, so it needs to herd us together so it can sleep at night, knowing where we are. They know that if we're in a shelter, we're invisible. They won't have the inconvenience of coming across us in their routine."

"Speaking of shelter," Cielo said, "This world has so many empty spaces that could be filled with people who need shelter. All those ski resorts that just sit empty all summer while the people who own the condos there are off vacationing. Foreclosed homes sitting empty for months, years. I used to fantasize about all those empty cabins and houses to get me through the cold nights. It's not about a lack of space. It's about a lack of compassion. Too much self-obsession. And too much fear."

Cielo saw Ivory looking at the owl. He saw the fear in Ivory's eyes. "Being homeless," Cielo said, "used to make me fear the dark something terrible. By about noon, I started to sense the darkness coming and it horrified me. Then after a while being homeless made me fear the day. The way people treat you, you wind up to where you can't wait until it gets dark so you can be invisible again." Ivory smiled at Cielo with eyes wet with gratitude.

Promise stood and stretched, raising up on her calves. "When people wear uniforms for their jobs, it seems like it makes them feel superior," she said. "Maybe people who work with children and teens should have to wear regular clothes. That might reduce the ego and power tripping."

Suddenly, Promise felt a potent wave of emotion rise up and fill her chest. *Gratitude*. She had almost died today. Ashia was there for her. I am still alive to live this night. To feel this cooling air. To exist. "I'm still here," she shouted. Her eyes watered. Her mouth opened. Her whole body heaved and trembled. *Grateful* came out. In song. A voice that could not belong to her, so ethereal and haunting. So celestial. And yet it was. Her voice. And the trees cried. And the people, their hardness crumbled. "Still here!" she sang. And when song left her, her spirit came back into her body. She collapsed back to a seated position and panted. Everyone was staring.

"Wow," Ashia said. "I didn't know you could sing like that."

"It's a good moon tonight," Promise said, still winded. "Does something to my spirit."

"Apparently."

Mende started telling a story about a song lost in the world until it found the little girl who it belonged to.

"Put some meat on those bones," said Pikea, interrupting.

"What do you mean?" Mende asked.

"I'm saying, tell the story. Facts aren't story. Soul is story. Where's the soul, you know, the part of what you're saying that is alive. Okay... story is human spirit in motion. Without the motion, you just have dead spirit."

"Oooh, you so deep, Pikea!" Ivory shouted.

"Seriously, you have to speak life into story, to bring your story into this life. Otherwise, you don't change the world. And that's the whole point of telling a story, right? I mean, we're trying to change things here. Change the map, the terrain, the journey. If not for us, for the next ones."

"Yeah boy..." Ivory bleated.

"Let's just let Mende tell his story," Maricela urged. Her voice carried a tone that sparked tension around the fire. Even after Mende finished his story, the air felt tight.

"We're all here for the same reason, right?" Binda said. "To come together for each other. To find ourselves through each other's journey as much as through our own."

"I'm not so sure about that," Pikea said.

"What do you mean?" Ashia asked.

"Just because we all wanted to come here, doesn't mean we all want to be here. And I for one have to wonder about some people's motives. I've noticed more than a few signs of folks running away from themselves."

"Like you, Pikea?" Promise asked, respectfully.

"Maybe so. I don't know. Just seems thick up in here a lot of the time. I mean, we're running around the island pretending to be happy, but seems like every time the carousel pauses, people's pain comes to the surface again."

"Isn't that how healing works?" Binda replied. Binda's voice swept up into a higher pitch. She sounds like a finch, Lake thought.

"I don't mean to be the group cheerleader here," Binda continued, "but if we thought that by coming out to paradise we got to bypass all the ugliness that comes with dealing with our lives, we were naïve. This island means nothing if we don't use it to break open the scars and walls we've built just to get by."

"Use it, how?" Ivory asked.

Binda stood up, buoyed by a surge of spirit strength. "I don't know. Maybe we use this place to remind us that beauty is real. Not just a dream. That we too can be beautiful, and deserve beauty in our lives."

"Too poetic," Pikea shrugged out.

"C'mon, man," Mende responded. "I feel what she's saying. I for one don't expect this to be a joy ride. If we get ugly with each other, then that's the thing."

"What thing?" Pikea queried.

"The thing. Whatever happens is the thing. What's supposed to be. Like, when you throw up—"

"Eeewww!" protested half the group.

"No but seriously, when you throw up, it's not pretty, but it's how your body is getting rid of something foul, that's making it sick. We feel better afterward, but how often are we grateful for spewing in the middle of the spew?"

"Eeewww! Stop, Mende!"

"Aright. I'm just saying that I didn't come here expecting us to walk off the island 100-percent whole, each of us. I came knowing that storms may blow on the island, and that we may have some mess to clean up before we leave."

Ashia jumped in on the double dutch. "Maybe it's just me. I feel like we're already cleaning up something together here. Friction is just part of any ride. It's like we're all consonants, trying to make up words together. Some of us need to be vowels. Someone has to be the soft air between stones. Then we'll get our own language going."

The fire died down. Stars grew brilliant. The group slouched down to the water, hands in their pockets, feet skidding and scuffing over the sand. Binda felt as though the island were scolding them. For something. The sky by the ocean was full of feathers. Errant and willful, the young egrets darted downward, perhaps chasing dragonflies, causing a more mature bird to bank back to the left and corral the wayward souls back into flight formation.

Ivory broke the heavy spell by chasing everyone with an overflowing handful of cold seaweed, trying to stuff it down their shirts. Between the squealing and the threats to knock Ivory out, seabirds arrived, curious and hungry. A particular squawking of gulls assembled above them and, seemingly on cue, emptied their bowels. More shrieking as the humans dove for cover and Ivory ran in circles, joy and fright pumping through his veins. He tripped over the seaweed tendrils he was still clutching and fell on his face.

Beneath the crowd of gulls, Cielo saw a flurry in the water. A spray of brightness fanned out across the surface. Several dolphin fins lifted from below like instant islands, then were gone. "Come and look at the dolphins!" Cielo called out. "There's a whole family of them!" Out in the depths, a pod of dolphins broke the ocean surface with their curved backs, undulating in and out of sight gracefully. A mob of sea lions gave chase.

"The ocean waves are creamy," Lake said. "Like lemon merengue."

Shonto rubbed his belly. "Now I'm hungry."

Ashia saw Lake over by herself, sitting and doing something with a stick. "Lake, you drawing in the sand again?" she asked.

"Yup."

"What's that?"

"Sand painting."

"Like a mandala?"

"Yeah. A way to pray in the sand. It's kind of like recruiting the earth and nature to help you out with stuff."

Promise and Maricela lay near to each other on the beach like a greater than sign, their heads touching as they star gazed. "You sure you're doing okay after just about drowning in sand?" Maricela asked. She tried to give her tone levity, but her concern poured through.

"Thanks, yeah. I'm okay. Wasn't the first time I've had a close call. Just the latest. You start to expect it. Like it's your birthright. Or a birthmark."

Maricela crossed herself. "You ever seen stars like this?"

"Not sure I've ever really seen stars," Promise said. "I mean, I've seen them, but the sky is usually so polluted, the stars look like faint patches. Easy to miss. These here, it's like I'm being stabbed in the eyeballs with light. It's cool. Kind of unreal."

"Yeah. Unreal."

Back at camp, Ashia came over to Cielo and sat by him as he caressed his bongos. "Cielo, drum me some of that romantic stuff you're always drumming when you think no one hears you," she requested.

Cielo was an unrepentant Lothario. Couldn't help but fall into sensual fits over anything that hinted at beauty. "Sure, amiga. I'll play you a beat from deep in the Amazon. A wedding song. You might need it sooner rather than later," he said, smiling.

"Stop playing, and just play, boy." Cielo found his rhythm and followed it for a good stretch of time. Through the Amazon. The Andes. Patagonia. Machu Picchu. La Paz. And back. Ashia closed her eyes and went with it. Hips and hands. Feet and torso. The speeding and slowing of the beat hypnotized her. Relaxed her enough to voice a question. "Cielo, how'd your family end up on the streets?"

Cielo, his own eyes closed, kept drumming as he responded. "My little sister was on a school bus for a field trip when a truck slammed into the bus. Everything blew up into flames. Only ones who survived were twins who managed to break open a window with a hammer that was under their seat for some reason. Bus driver was found lying on top of three children, with her arms around them. Like she was trying to protect them from the flames.

"After that, my dad bottled up so tight he blew a gasket. He started hanging out down at the red light district. Then he lost his job, we lost our house, and my parents lost their wedding vows.

"Dad split, mom had a stroke from working two jobs plus overtime, and that, ladies and gentlemen, is how you go from a home with a washer and dryer to living mobile—we don't call it homeless, we call it *mobile*—living mobile every day and getting warmed up inside of laundromats.

"When you find yourself painful cold, go find yourself a laundromat dryer and huddle up next to it until they kick you out. When you're homeless, you get real good at finding one or two extra degrees of heat. If you drop me at the North Pole, I'm going to find me some heat. Promise you that."

Ashia was looking at Cielo with a warm expression. "I memorized something my Ama once wrote me in a letter: *Trauma is a hosting of ghosts. The ghosts come to our mental ballroom and dance, smashing the chandelier and furniture, tearing up the floor. We invite moments that no longer exist to inhabit our existence.*"

"I like that," Cielo said. "I have one for you: *I keep getting conquered back and forth by armies of competing pain. I am Jerusalem.*"

"Nice," Ashia said, snapping her fingers. "We struggle with letting go of what has been ours for so long. Even the terrible things."

Cielo let out a forceful exhale. "I've been feeling like I'm walking on air across a deep, wide canyon. I'm saying, there's nothing under my feet. Only Grace is holding me up. I'm scared to death, but I'm stepping, right? And each step I take, Grace is laying down another piece of a bridge for me. Now I'm getting close to the other side of the canyon. I'm carrying my whole family and all my ancestors on my back. Still scared to death and trying to stay faithful. To take those steps. And you know what? I'm beginning to feel that any minute now, I'll be taking that last step, and Grace will lay down that last piece of bridge, and I'll be stretching out my legs and I'll come down on land. No more air. I'll be on the other side, and Grace will have delivered me, and mi familia. But the bridge wouldn't have been laid without me taking each step. Cause that's what causes Grace to do its part, you know? Least that's how I see it."

"Generational cycles are shackled in supernatural chains," Ashia said. "That's what my Ama said to me. *Supernatural chains*. It must take supernatural effort to break chains like that. That, my friend, is why I pray."

Cielo's warm smile touched Ashia. He blessed his drum and said, "And that, my friend, is why I *Namasté*."

Ashia couldn't sleep. Her spirit was with Balanta and Eloni, hoping they were keeping each other safe. She imagined it was cold where they were. She began to speak to Balanta: "I keep tasting you on the breeze. What happens, do you turn to pollen at night and take flight? That's okay, as long as you return to your body with sunrise and make it back here in one piece."

Ashia got up and sat by Maricela, who was still visiting with the other girls. "Why does Love hurt so much?" Ashia asked.

"Looks like the boys aren't the only ones hot in the pants," Maricela said. "Someone better go cool off in the lagoon."

Ashia dropped her gaze shyly and grinned. "Come on…"

"You feeling split wide open?" Maricela answered. "*Mira…* It's like birth. That's the most pain a women ever feels, and it's because something unbelievable is coming through. Love is like that. When we Love, we are open as wide as we can ever be, and something greater than we can imagine is coming through. When I tell myself that, it helps me to remember why I don't just give up on Love, and why it's worth all the pain."

Lake made herself speak. "Love hurts the worst because there's nothing better."

"That's too sappy and simple," Pikea said.

"Okay, Pikea, then what's your grand thesis?" Binda asked, trying to soften the effect of Pikea's retort on Lake.

"Love hurts because the effort it takes to burrow down into it is basically a waste when you get blasted out of that place in an instant. The hurt is because you realize you're a fool for ever digging in the first place. Plus, you couldn't be more humiliated. You feel like the whole world knows what a loser you are, the gossip party is on full tilt, and you're not invited."

"How cheerful," Maricela said, smiling.

Ashia found herself inhabited by Balanta. Her grounds increasingly effused with his scent, his presence growing inside her like thick patches of wild grass, nearer to the sun with each pumping of her heart:

Sun is a cream on your skin,
so bright is your aura.
I dance in the ellipsis of your lips.
Wake me gently.
Dreams like this
should not end abruptly.
The hurt is too great.
The scar that grows over
seals the door through which
future Love is meant to pass.

Moon was now a delicate, eroding shoreline, giving way to the tide of a swiftly blackening sea.

DAY FIVE

The thick scent of salt in the air mixed with that of morning blossoms as Balanta opened his eyes. He had to blink several times to clear the haze in his vision. The throb in his ankle announced that it wasn't going anywhere soon. Eloni was by the fire, stirring ashes as hibiscus and dandelion tea and poi porridge cooked in their mango wood bowls.

"Made it through the night, huh?" Eloni asked, smiling. His voice was hoarse. His black hair matted and disassembled. The skin on his legs was dry and ashy, and the blue-black tattoos on his bare torso and shoulder were blotched with grim.

"Yeah," Balanta said weakly. He coughed to clear his throat, which tasted like battery acid and was swollen. So were his eyes, ears, fingers, and feet. "Feel like I went 20 rounds with a jacked up gorilla."

Eloni laughed. "From the sounds of your moaning and groaning, I figured you were having some delirious fantasies, so I left you to your pleasure. You got an appetite?"

They ate their porridge and drank as much tea as they could to get their hydration up.

Balanta stood, testing his balance, and his leg.

"Don't fall out on me again," Eloni said.

Balanta took a few hop steps, and figured he could walk well enough. Eloni helped him over to the nearby stream, so they could wash out their clothes. Morning mist was thinning out already. Star jasmine were showing their snowy faces to the sky.

Delirium. Balanta chewed on the word. He had always struggled to keep an old, shameful fear contained where it couldn't touch him. He knew mental illness could be congenital. Often, the spirit of his father's mental descent brushed by him like a large bird, and Balanta feared what that bird might leave behind in him. He wondered if something like a snakebite, and its poison, could be enough to send him over some kind of edge.

"That's deep what you said last night, Eloni," Balanta said. The cold water soothed Balanta's still feverish skin. He soaked his wounded leg in the current. "About learning to be free. You would think that we're born knowing how to be free, but maybe getting your life torn up kills your freedom impulse. Maybe it puts you on crisis mode. But where's the button for turning that off?"

"I didn't think you were coherent enough to hear me," Eloni said. I was just rambling. Tired of feeling so caged up, though. That's why being out here feels so good to me."

"Loni, if you could go back to the past, what one thing would you change?"

"My father."

"You mean you would make your father different, or you would have a different father?"

Eloni's frown and silence exposed his conflict. Balanta thought about the idea of souls choosing the parents through which they come into the world. *Must be a whole lot of confused souls*, he said to himself.

"Hey," Eloni said, "let me put some more eucalyptus sap and clay on that bite. If we're going to walk all the way back to camp, you can't be leaking oil."

Without saying so, both of them figured they had endured enough hardship for this experience to qualify as a certified vision quest. Eloni had fashioned crutches for Balanta out of birch branches. They ate figs and apples as they hiked, shirtless and weary, out of the canyon and into the day.

Cielo woke to the sun's first dose of heat gaining atop the cabin roof. He sat up and wiped his eyes, looking for the shadow form, and then at the tree that had been a family. *I need me some naked time in the water*, he said to himself. He jumped down to the ground and scurried off to the lagoon for a quick solo swim.

Cielo dove into the water and swam out into the expanse. The lagoon's microscopic organisms fired into their bioluminescent charms. Cielo's body glowed with a neon aura that trailed in his wake, a dimming comet. He treaded water, his hands flaring into torches. Light bloomed and faded at his feet as he kicked. He closed his eyes and dropped down into the depths, plunging inside a chrysalis of luminous bubbles. He came to the bottom, paddled into a sitting position and recited a new mantra that came with the moment: *Cloak of light and Grace... Cloak of light and Grace... Cloak of light and Grace...*

Ivory got the morning fire started. Shonto and Lake gave offerings to the morning with cedar and freshwater from the brook behind the cabins. As the others came out of their cabins, slowly and sluggish with sleep, Cielo dripped back into camp. "You already been to the lagoon, amigo?" Maricela asked.

"You should feel the water this time of day," Cielo said. "So cool and soft. It was amazing."

Lake and Binda helped Ashia bring food from the garden over to the fire circle, where they got to peeling and slicing.

"I'm not so sure that all these fruits and vegetables on the island were already here," said Ivory. His fro was matted on one side and picked out on the other.

"What do you mean?" asked Ashia, still in her pajamas with panda prints.

"Something doesn't add up," Ivory said. "Some of this food he prepares, any of you see him make it? I've seen him make some of it, but it's almost like he..."

"Waves a magic wand?" Cielo said, whipping his long hair like a dog to dry it off.

"Well... he was the first one to the garden when we got to the island," Ivory continued. "Remember that? How do we know it was already there?"

"I don't know, man," said Mende. "That's a little far out, what you're talking about."

"Hasn't everything here been far out?" Ivory said. "That boy has some kind of... gift. He's not just a good cook."

"Well, he's not here right now," Ashia said, "so come help us out with these fruits and vegetables, Ivory. Let's get belly full."

"I sure could use a leprechaun siting," Ivory mentioned, out of nowhere.

"What in the world are you talking about?" Shonto settled in for a whopper.

"There's everything else here. Why not a leprechaun colony? Liven things up."

"Oh, now it's a colony?"

"It'd be more interesting that way. Then we could exchange in commerce with them."

"I'll pretend that this conversation is normal. What would we trade with them?"

"Don't know. I could make some more seed pod jewelry. Cielo can carve something. We could barter skills, too. Binda and Pikea could sing. Lake could dance. You could shake your belly."

"Funny. And what would we get from them, besides nightmares?"

"They'd have to let us in on the secret to making those sultan shoes and top hats. I'd Love to have a set."

"You've been sniffing the moss around here again, haven't you? Or, I know... you found some wild mushrooms."

"Warlocks need a union," Ivory proffered.

"I give," said Shonto. "What are you talking about now?"

"Think about it. Everybody's always talking about witches. They get all the screentime in movies and shows. Warlocks don't get any Love. They need representation. Better PR."

"Are you in a fictional world right now?" Shonto said, rhetorically. "I can never tell."

"Here's another thing," Ivory said, skipping right along. "If you think about it from the perspective of a monkey, or a fish, humans are pretty ugly. No disrespect."

"No disrespect to me? Are you not human?"

"Yeah, but I'm stable in my identity. I *know* I look good. Must be a genetic mutation."

"Got that right." Shonto shook his head, completely dumfounded and awed.

Breakfast was fast and quiet. They each drank a good deal of orange and grapefruit and coconut juices to get hydrated for the day. The ocean bay was smooth. Still waking, Lake thought.

Ashia went to her cabin to change out of her pajamas. Ivory looked at Mende. "Hey. You want to go roll some boulders?"

"Sure," Mende said. They ran off to find a suitable hillside low on Jade Mountain.

The three-legged deer was showing up at the campsite more often now. Three times since the morning before. "Maybe it's trying to tell us something," wondered Maricela.

"Maybe it wants to jump in the pot and let us eat it," Cielo deadpanned.

"You're sick, Cielo," Ashia said.

"As long as the death is honorable," he responded.

"Pikea, you or anyone been feeding it?" Ashia asked.

"Why?" Shonto spoke up. "It has all the food it wants around here. The ground on this island is pretty much covered in fruits and nuts, alone."

"Something must be attracting it," Ashia said. The deer nuzzled into a patch of honeysuckle drenched in sunlight and nibbled away without a care. Soon it had its fill and hopped back into the bush, out of sight.

"Hey, Shonto," Cielo said. "You want to try some of this?" He was holding something slimy in his palm that dripped down between his fingers.

"What is that?" Shonto asked.

"I marinated some squid overnight in coconut juice with kale and spinach cuttings. I put it in a calabash and lodged it inside a ring of rocks in the brook to keep it chilled until morning. This might be the best squid you've had. I hear it's an aphrodisiac."

Promise made a gagging noise. Several others contorted their faces in disgust. Shonto though, was game. "Sure, let me try some of that. Just so I can say I didn't punk out like the rest of them." He took a few tentacles and slurped them into his mouth. "Feels like rubber noodles," he said.

Mende slapped his own forehead, his eyes wide. "You are either very brave or... nah, that's not brave, Shonto. Don't be experimenting with that boy. Cielo's guts are probably evolved to a whole 'nother level than yours."

Shonto made a funny face as he swallowed the rubbery mouthful. "No turning back now. Tasted... sandy. A little sweet."

Cielo nodded and downed the remaining squid. He wiped his hands on his shorts and dropped to the ground to do some yoga poses. Maricela wondered what Eloni would be saying about Cielo's yoga if he had been there. She still felt something tugging at her about how Eloni had reacted before.

"Where are Ivory and Mende?" Ashia asked. She had come back out dressed in a mudcloth skirt and a sleeveless yellow cotton top. She was running oils through her locs, massaging the remainder into her arms and legs.

"They went to go roll boulders," Cielo said. "Pikea ran after to join them."

Mende found a boulder as tall as he was. It sat on an incline of scree and psychedelic agates, along with other bright gemstones. "This one should give way with a good push," said Mende.

Ivory ran over, slipping and sliding down the slope as he came. "Cool. What's our strategy?"

Just then, Pikea caught up. "Y'all thought you'd leave me out? I'm down for some mayhem." She was panting from her long sprint. Sweat held her bangs against her forehead. She took off her hair tie and ran her fingers through her hair, then pulled her hair back into a ponytail before reapplying the tie. "Okay, set. How about Mende, you push from directly behind, and Ivory and I will be on each side of you, pushing more from the side?"

"Sounds good," said Mende. He moved directly behind and uphill from the boulder. He put both hands on the jagged granite, felt its warmth. The air up here was summer heat diluted with breeze.

"You sure it's all clear down below?" asked Ivory. "We can't be having anyone out traipsing around down there."

"I checked it," said Mende, which meant that he had glanced downhill to the gully and saw no movement or people. The three of them leaned into the rock and pushed. The rock did not give, but Ivory's footing did. His feet managed to slip uphill, and he fell flat on his face, busting his lower lip on a small rock.

"Rock's revenge," said Pikea, inspecting the bloody cut.

Ivory was emboldened by his battle scar. They resumed pushing. The rock seemed to have roots. "I know," Ivory said. "I'll move a smaller boulder over here behind this big one, and I'll get up on it so I can push with more leverage from up top."

"Sounds risky," said Pikea.

Mende went to find a long thick hardwood branch to use for a pole. He returned in a quick moment, satisfied. "This will give us some real leverage," he said. He jammed one end of the pole as far under the boulder as it would go. Then he put a small stone under the pole, about a foot from where the pole head was jammed under the boulder. Now the other end of the pole was up in the air, just above Mende's head. "When I give the signal, I'm going to pull down on the pole with all my weight. You two push at the same time as I pull down."

Mende never did explain what the signal was. He shouted as he reached up and grabbed the pole head. At the same time as he pulled and dropped his body weight, Pikea grunted and pushed. Ivory did the same, causing the rock on which he was standing to slide backward and uphill. Ivory's body fell parallel to the ground, suspended between the large boulder and the sliding smaller rock. They felt the boulder give. The great rock lifted up from its soil bed. Ivory completed his fall, his head nearly scraping against the boulder as it slowly turned. Mende's face poured sweat as he pulled down on the pole, its length bending. The boulder reached its pivotal point and gravity carried it past its inertia. "Zoo's loose!" Ivory yelled, as the boulder picked up momentum, crushing rocks beneath it. Then it was moving downhill with a roar, bouncing and smashing. They saw it reach a spread of scrubs, where it decimated the bushes in its path. The rock disappeared into denser growth. A moment after, they heard the unmistakable explosion of boulder against tree. "Zoo's loose!" Ivory kept yelling, blood dripping from his lip. "I tell ya, that was the show!"

They kept rolling boulders until their hands were raw and blistered, their arms trembled, and their legs hollered for mercy.

Maricela sat alone behind her cabin with the clay jar. She wiped old dirt from its surface. She opened the jar and took out the stained brown papyrus carrying the inscription. She unfolded the paper and forced her eyes to trace the words:

One day a tribe will come. As it is written inside the great mouth of this earth. And they shall die of fire. And begin as light. Their shadows to be released like crows to the sky, as the mountain of water crushes their false seeds. Forever.

Maricela's skin chilled. Who wrote this? Maricela wondered. Why did they leave it buried in the dirt? Who was the tribe? It has to be us, right? But what in the world does all this code mean? Shadows released like crows? False seeds? Maricela was lost and frightened. Especially after having seen the stick figures in the cave dwindle in number from 12 down to... one. Who's the one? Cold crawled through her. She hunched her shoulders against the fear. She put the scroll back into the jar and slid the jar back down under her cot. She sighed. Her breath was an icicle, vaporous in her chest.

Shonto felt squeamish just as he and Lake reached the estuary. Then a sharp pang in the gut. He kneeled and promptly uploaded his breakfast onto the sand. He laughed post-chuck, satisfied with his efficiency and hopeful of a quick return to feeling better. *No more of Cielo's concoctions*, he chuckled to himself. *Especially anything raw and from the sea.*

"You okay?" Lake asked.

"Ugh. Not so much," Shonto replied. "Give me a minute though." He sat back on his butt, propping himself up with his hands behind him in the sand. After a few deep breaths, the nausea passed. His bangs were wet and dripping into his eyes. Wiping them away, he saw how the reeds around this part of the estuary were filled with damselflies and dragonflies, perched in the nooks of the stalks.

A spider web belly danced in the slight breeze, its form reminding Shonto of a dreamcatcher. He bowed to the brown spider with long legs that had appeared at the web's perimeter, checking out its handiwork. Shonto admired such industry, and often thought about which of his own desires he might finally land if he were ever able to persist in the labor. Biblical Job, he was not.

And if patience truly was a virtue, he knew he had far to go to even begin to taste virtuosity.

Lake sat down next to Shonto. She lifted her face to the sky and closed her eyes. The breeze made her smile. "You miss going to the gatherings back on the rez?" she asked.

Shonto kept one hand on his stomach and chewed some peppermint leaves from a patch right beside him. "I got mixed feelings about the gatherings. On the one hand, you get to hang with your buddies and soak up the old ways and the tired-out stories. On the other hand... being there makes me two spirits."

"How's that?" Lake asked.

"I feel a lot of pride with everyone dancing and drumming, don't get me wrong. But I get sad looking into the faces. We got so much brokenness, Lake." Shonto's face grew pained. "I don't like looking at our old people and seeing what I see in their eyes. They got so much grieving. They look around at their people and they must see a bunch of lost folks. Then again I know they must feel good seeing everyone together at least."

Lake bit her lip. A spider was tickling her on her knee. She gently picked it up and set it in the grass. "One thing about the gatherings," Lake said, "whatever we are after all we've been through... whatever we are, comes out times 10."

Ashia and Maricela went for a walk, just to feel the woods around them. It was turning into a lazy morning. "I can feel us all getting tired," Ashia said as they moved through shafts of sunlight.

"Yup," Maricela said. She was still feeling anxious about the old scroll, and about saying something to Ashia.

"The time is passing so quickly," Ashia said. But the days are so full. It's weird. I'm feeling a bunch of energy that I haven't before. And I'm tired at the same time."

The spirit of Shuraa Solomon kept invading Ashia's tranquility. *Am I feeling guilty for feeling so good?* she asked herself. She wondered about genetic inheritance. Was it a tide pool that overflowed into a person's spiritual self? Would her mother's soul-crushing guilt at losing—no, *choosing to lose*—her daughter, become Ashia's own propensity for self-punishment? She thought about the nature of happiness and the fragility of a cliff that crumbles clod by clod into the ocean; or the fragility of anything, for that matter, that stands so close to majestic instability.

"Cela, do you want to have children?" Ashia asked.

Maricela stopped and gazed at the ground. "I wouldn't bring a child into this world."

"But what about you?" Ashia asked. "You were brought into this world. Are you saying you don't want to exist?"

Maricela looked at Ashia wryly. "I hope you're not trying to tell me something. Y'all better keep your stuff on ice, girl."

"Ha ha," Ashia replied. "No but seriously, I'm going in another direction with that *bringing a child into this cold world* thing. I want to have as many children as possible one day, and be there for them like nobody's business. The more happy children I can put in the world, the more distance I'll put between myself and what I went through. And I'm going to be a social worker or a teacher."

"Go 'head with that," Maricela said. "I'm getting as far away from that stuff as I can. Even if I end up working a rice paddy on the other side of the world."

"You say that now, when you're young and your back is strong," Ashia laughed, slapping Maricela on the shoulder. "You wait until you've put on a few years and all your joints ache. Then you'll be looking for that plush desk job."

"Please," Maricela said. "If you ever see me in a desk job, please, put me out of my misery. I'll even leave you something in my will."

"Okay, woman. We'll see about that."

Maricela tried to mention the scroll to Ashia, but instead took a different path and shared about her relationship with her father, Manos. "I can tell you been through it with him," Ashia said. "When you told me before how he would whup you... that was hard to hear."

"Yeah," Maricela sighed. "I guess I folded the abuse up into a strange kind of origami and tossed it into my bag of mental tricks. I tell myself it wasn't so bad. I excuse him a million ways. In the end, I just want my life to be a beautiful story, so I remake the ugliness."

"Maricela? What did it feel like? I mean, when he whupped you? What was going through your mind?"

Maricela took a deep breath and stopped walking. "A familiar warmth spread over my back with each lashing," Maricela shared. "A strangely comforting warmth. Like when you can't stand a classmate, but you somehow feel back on track when you see them at the start of the school year? The warmth was like someone pouring hot syrup on my back. I could even tell the direction it was going to spread. Like continents blooming on my skin. People say the scars look like trees. To me, they're just lines in the shape of my childhood. Like a family seal. At least I know I come from a legacy."

"Rough legacy," Ashia said. "I admire you. I hope you know that."

"Thanks... I'm trying to Love myself, but you can't Love yourself if you don't Love what you come from," said Maricela. "I'm ashamed of my family. I'm always obsessing about what other people think of us. Why can't we get our act together?"

As they crested a treeless hill, Maricela tugged on Ashia's elbow. "I need to tell you something," she said."

Ashia stopped. She could see the gravity in Maricela's face. "Go ahead, please."

"You remember the day after we all went to the dunes, when I went off on my own to go find some hills? Well, I found this old clay jar buried in the ground. It had some junk in it, like a sand dollar and some other stuff. But there was this old scroll, and when I opened it and read it, it really freaked me out."

"What did it say?"

"You're going to think I'm overreacting, but it's messing with my spirit. It was a handwritten note, and it said something about a tribe and how the tribe was going to die in fire. I'm not trying to be gloomy, but I feel afraid that the note is about us. I'm seriously tripping, right?"

"Oh, girl," Ashia said. "I wish you would have told me sooner. Is this why you've been acting so funny?"

"Well, I was trying to be cool, but then when we saw those 12 stick figures in the cave, and they started disappearing one by one, then I lost it."

"Yeah!" Ashia said. "I remember how you all of a sudden went mute. Now I get it."

"Can I show you the note when we get back? I don't know if we should say something to everyone."

"Well, I'm not trying to believe that those words are about us, of course," Ashia said. "Let me check it out with you, and then we'll go from there. Someone was probably drinking out here years ago and started hallucinating or something. It can't have anything to do with us."

"I hope not," Maricela exhaled. "I feel better just telling you. I should have sooner. Sorry. I get insecure sometimes."

"I wasn't going to judge you regardless," Ashia said. "I'm just glad you told me. I hope you can let it go and enjoy yourself the rest of the time." The sky darkened instantly as Ashia spoke. They both looked up and saw the largest bird they had ever seen.

Pikea and Shonto managed to get lost in the woods. It started as a simple venture: find as many other rain trees as they could. Half an hour in, after detouring to chase a goat through the underbrush, they were deep in the woods, with only a vague sense of direction. It didn't help that Shonto kept stopping at every fruit tree to "sample the local goods," as he put it.

There were so many lemon trees on this part of the island, they seemed to be following them as they headed beyond the meadow to the deeper inner forest he had dreamt of. *You shouldn't be doing this, brother*, Shonto scolded himself with no heart in the effort. If he could just see the buck, with its one surviving antler and white patches shaped like snowflakes. Deeper they forged into the substance of the woods, their steps on dry leaves and twigs sounding a rhythm of earnest calling.

A throttling of cicadas, their mating calls sounding like rocks raining on hollow wood, caused Shonto to look up into the trees. A heavyweight hawk perched on a high branch looked back at him. Its neck twitched forward nervously. The down on its chest was mottled, its wing feathers streaked amber and white. Shonto wondered what hope the hawk held in a potential meal such as himself. *Not today, brother.* Shonto and Pikea continued on, following the stream up into a slot canyon whose serpentine roof was broken through by fat pillars of sunlight. The beams breached the canyon like strobe lights, revealing dense populations of dust particles, all scattering for their own plot of air. Pikea took off her shoes and stepped into the clear stream. She extended her arms and turned in circles, smiling in wonder at the colorful striations of the canyon's walls.

Pikea noticed a slender scar on Shonto's bicep. Its surface was smooth, running about four inches along the muscle's horizon. "Where'd you get that scar from?" Pikea asked.

"Notching trees."

"What do you mean?"

"We used to notch trees on the rez. With knives. One notch for every death. 'Specially for the young ones. Me and my friends—I think it was Nelson who came up with it—we decided we were gonna leave evidence of all the deaths in our community. Trees seemed like a good place, only there were too many deaths, so by the time we were in 10th grade, the notches were up so high on the trees, we had to start climbing so we could put in new notches.

"What grade were you when you started?"

"Fourth, I think. This one time, I got picked to climb this big cottonwood. Those things are rough. I got up on this branch, hung upside down like a bat, and reached down to put in a new notch. Being upside down, blood rushed into my head and I got faint real quick. But I wanted to get the notch in, cause I wasn't gonna climb that cottonwood again. So, I chipped away with the knife harder than usual. I rushed too much. Knife slipped off the trunk and cut through my other arm. Saw the blood before I felt the pain."

"How'd you guys even come up with something like that?"

"Sometimes you need traditions in your life. Even if they don't make sense. To us, our notches did make sense. It was our way of saying to the world, 'You're going to have to notice what you did to us one day. Have to account for all the deaths.' We knew the trees would be around, breathing and living, long after we would."

"That's a sad reality."

"Just life on the rez. Ahó."

"Did you just call me a *ho*?" Pikea asked, her dander up.

"No! Sorry. I said, Ahó. I was sealing the sacred words that we just spoke together."

"Ohhh... Like Amen?"

"Something like that."

Pikea's skin was starting to feel sensitive against her clothes. Her clothes felt tight. Her womb gurgled. "Can I rest my head on your stomach?" Pikea asked.

"Sure." Shonto flashed back to the flood in the arroyo. *Random,* he thought. "You okay?"

201

"Yeah. Just my cycle coming around."

"Don't know how you do it."

"Maori culture traditionally teaches that it is an honor. We say a warrior is one who sacrifices herself for her people. A woman gives her body over and over to the fire of generations. She bleeds humankind forward. She is the ultimate warrior."

They lay there for many heartbeats, until their breathing grew calm like the breeze. So many heartbeats that Pikea fell into a trance inside their cadence. She dreamt of her great aunt, Pania, walking a field of dry tall grass in a prairie. And a sky of butterflies and dragonflies that followed her.

Ivory dared himself to go on a hike alone. A mini-quest, he called it. Two hours maximum. So as not to miss lunch. He loaded himself down with so much food and water, he was exhausted 100 yards from camp. To his credit, though, the group would acknowledge later, instead of giving up, Ivory sat down and promptly feasted. Plums and bananas. Perch jerky. And about a quart of Mende's lemonade. Having lightened his load, Ivory sloshed forward. Half an hour later, he found himself in completely unfamiliar territory. Something moved in the brush. Ivory gripped his whistle. Sweat pooled in the nooks between his forearms and biceps. His Jimi Hendrix t-shirt was soaked. The sun was nearly peaked. "I should have packed for a desert crossing," Ivory mumbled.

This part of the island felt Cretaceous to Ivory. Ancient species of conifers, ferns, all supersized and thriving. The air smelled rich with nitrogen. He saw a lizard the size of an iguana, its radish red tongue forking the air habitually. Ivory half expected a brontosaurus or stegosaurus to come sauntering through the brush. Then the vision of a Tyrannosaurus flashed through his mind, and he quickly changed mental tracks. He turned and jumped clumsily over a creek bank and lost his balance, falling onto a soft mat of emerald moss. He rolled over as though he was inspecting a plush new mattress. It felt too good to get up. He turned onto one side, with his head propped up on an elbow. Before him, the moss extended out, an entire meadow. Ivory crawled forward on his belly, inhaling the sweet pungent fumes lifting from the soft carpet. He stroked his hands over the dark green pelt, its cool face massaging his skin. The moss strands gave easily beneath Ivory's touch, then bounced back, springy and resilient. He looked around to assure no one else was in sight. "Okay, I'm about to do this," he said under his breath. Then he stripped off his clothes and rolled naked over the entire moss bed like a child over new fallen snow.

"Hey, Ivory! Can we join you?" It was Mende. Ivory flipped onto his stomach in a flash and scrambled for his clothes. Most of the group was on the other side of the clearing, fallen out on the ground busting up.

"If you saw me rolling, it was only because I heard it's good therapy for the back," Ivory said, stretching his torso backward, as if to relieve pain. "They say it's better to let your skin move against the ground to soak up the healing properties." His face was stone serious.

"Whatever, Ivory," Pikea said, grinning broadly. "It's okay to have a fetish."

"Hey, Ivory," Maricela called out. "I didn't think your skin could blush like that."

Ivory was still zipping up his pants as the group approached. "Hold up!" he yelled. "Don't come closer until I give the go ahead. I gotta get my stuff straightened out."

"Sorry, Ivory," Ashia said softly. "We were worried about you coming out here on your solo mission. Hope we didn't cramp your thing, but we felt it safer to keep track of you."

Promise was at the back of the group, pausing to drink some coconut milk. Suddenly, she felt a chill in her skin and the fine hair on her arms raise up. Her mind was trying to process what she was seeing. On the vague dirt path not 50 feet behind her, an animal. That's a big fox, she thought. She knew it wasn't a fox. Coyote? Can't be. Then, Promise heard herself screaming and tasted blood in her throat. "Wolf!"

The next moment passed in a flood of adrenaline. Ivory boogied so fast and so far, it took them half an hour to find him. Everyone else jumped into a huddle, moving back away from the animal slowly. "That can't be a wolf," Promise whispered.

"Don't turn your backs," Mende said in a hushed voice. "Just keep backing up."

Maricela's face was wet with tears. Was this it? *They shall die of fire...* Was this the dying? How could Antonia do this to them? She prayed to God, her patron saint, the Holy Mother, and all her ancestors. "Dios mio. Dios mio. Dios mio..."

The animal was acting strangely, seeming not to even notice the humans. Its coat was thick with brown-gray hair. Muscles rippled along its shoulders and back. It sniffed the ground and turned in circles. Then it backed off the path and crouched under the leaves of a large sweetgum bush.

Promise heard the bleating first. A small fat goat came from around the bend of the path and walked right past where the animal, its eyes black and cold, was hidden. Promise could not believe the goat couldn't sense danger. The predator appeared to not believe it, either. It remained crouched and tensed under cover. The goat moved farther along on the path, circling to the far perimeter of the clearing. Just when Promise thought the goat might actually get away, the predator sprang for the goat before anyone could push out a sound. It closed the distance by air, in a fraction of a second, a missile of fur, musk, and burning eyes. No time for even a single bleating. Primal instinct and relentless practice brought the gates of teeth, weeping saliva, down on the prey's throat. A crunch, a violent twist, and a canine huff to seal the death. The animal, its muzzle bloodied and dripping, dragged the carcass into the trees and disappeared. Leaves crunched and branches snapped beyond view.

"That's flagrant, man," Shonto whispered. "Horror movie stuff."

Most of the group was crying quietly and shaking. Pikea scratched her forearms so hard she broke skin. Her mouth twitched rapidly. They backed away from the scene so far that they ended up out of the clearing entirely, in the shade of birches and elms. They stared at each other, their eyes dilated. Heavy breathing was their only conversation for several minutes.

"Wow," Mende muttered. "We just saw that. Did we just see that? Hey, Shonto?"

"Yeah?"

"How fast can you run?"

They ate lunch on the cabin rooftops. Ivory sat in the center of a circle made by Pikea, Ashia, and Cielo. He was still shaking. Pikea rubbed his back. "Come on now, Ivory," she said. "You need to dismiss that panic. You're just working yourself up."

The others were beginning to get over their fright, even questioning what it was they saw. "Could that have been a collective hallucination?" Maricela asked.

"All I know is," Ivory said, "when God's on the line, don't put him on hold, man."

"What?" Promise snapped.

"Signs, man. That was some kind of message."

"Could have been a rabid, supersized fox," Shonto said.

"That didn't look like a wolf to me," Mende said. "More like a strange looking dog, except... did you see it... change sizes?"

"That's exactly what I saw!" Promise shouted. "I knew I wasn't crazy. When I first saw it, it was small enough I thought it was a fox."

They talked about what they had seen until the story became an imagination in each of their minds. Inside those imaginations, they worked hard to make themselves feel safe again.

Pikea stood on the roof and sang an old Maori *waiata*, a traditional song. Her voice wasn't hers. It was the sound of a people laboring together. Her voice was haunting. Pure. Beautiful. Cielo, Lake, and Binda, shoulder to shoulder, rocked side to side with the melody. When Pikea finished, the rooftop held a calmer tribe.

"Didn't know you had it in you," Promise said, fighting back tears.

Pikea dropped her gaze shyly. "Promise, I know you know what it feels like when Spirit splits you wide open and has its way with you. Inspiration pours through like a supernatural newborn species. That's how it is for me when my ancestors come through."

"Promise," Ashia said, "I see you holding back tears. I can't believe you didn't cry when you saw that animal attack the goat either, as loud as you screamed."

"What day is it?" Promise asked.

"Wednesday. Why?" Ashia was perplexed.

"Okay, I guess I could have cried. But I don't cry on Thursdays," Promise said.

"What? Why?"

"I was born on a Thursday. I've cried enough in my life. I figured I'll at least reserve one day a week when I don't cry, except in happiness or from laughing so hard. My day of birth seems like the right day to make tear free."

"How do you manage that?"

"How does a woman manage the pain of childbirth? You don't manage anything, really, you just determine to do it, then you move through it. On Thursdays, no matter what, I move through it." Truth was, every single Thursday, Promise felt the most shattering grief knowing her mother was no longer in the world.

They talked about the animal and the killing long after they had eaten. They stayed on the cabin roofs for a stretch after that. Talk turned to lighter subjects. Crushes. Things they missed back in civilization. They got on to wondering what Eloni and Balanta were up to, and when they would return. No one said it, but they all would have felt a little more comfortable with those two around.

"Binda, are you going to try and reconnect with your family after this trip?" Pikea asked.

Binda was silent for a moment, her eyes searching the ground in contemplation. "I want to say *No*," she answered, "but that's like saying you're going to stay away from your next breath. I don't want to suffocate myself by trying to protect myself. It's more up to them, anyway."

"What about you, Cielo?"

"I have this dream," Cielo said, "where I'm on tour playing music, and after this one show I'm in my backstage room, cooling off. And there's a knock on the door. I'm talking with my manager and some other people I can't really make out in the dream, so I'm not paying much attention to the knocking.

"Someone opens the door and my dad comes in. Everybody goes quiet. I stand up, just knowing I'm about to get a hug and have my dad tell me how proud he is. In my mind, I even see his machismo break down in tears.

"I step forward to my dad and he steps toward me. Now about 30 people are somehow in the room, all of them eating popcorn and transfixed, like they're watching a movie. It's hot, man. Sweltering. And my dad, my dad opens his mouth and says to me, 'I didn't pay all that money for your lessons so that you could give a half-assed effort like you did out there tonight, mi'jo. You represent the family. Never forget that.'

"Now there's about 100 people in the room, old classmates, strangers, people from the streets. And they're all covering their mouths, their eyes bulging. And I just want to go drown myself in the toilet."

Ivory, valiantly working to shake his nervousness, started cutting on Mende, playfully taking verbal shots at him. Soon, they were all playing the dozens.

"Ivory, your lower lip is so big, we don't need a flotation device out on the lagoon. We could all jump in and still have room for snacks."

"Whatever, Mende. Your ears are so small, word on the street is your mom must have mated with a lizard."

"Talkin bout my mom? Your mom is so greasy, when she eats French fries, even the fries say, 'Man, that's a lot of grease!'"

Lake fell out, all the way to the ground, spasming in soundless laughter. When she caught her breath, she joined in, targeting Promise: "Promise, yo mamma is so simple, she thinks ketchup comes from spaghetti sauce!"

"Oh no you didn't!" Promise cracked. "Talking about my momma! Your momma is so slow, tortoises be honking at her behind to get a move on!"

They kept on like this, making the rounds, cracking, cutting, each rip pumping good medicine through their veins, flushing adrenaline and calming nerves.

"Your group home is so nasty, even the rats say, That's all right. We'll pass."

"Your group home is so nasty, when they turn the lights out, the tiles on the floor say, Time to make a break for it!"

"Your group home is so nasty, when someone goes AWOL, it stands for Another Warrior OD'd on Lice."

"Your group home is so nasty, when the cleaning crew comes on shift and sees the situation, they phone home to tell their families to go on without them."

"Your group home is so nasty, when you open a window there, all the air runs away."

"Your group home is so nasty, the walls are wet all the time from crying in misery."

"Your group home is so nasty, when the state inspectors show up, they're wearing hazmat suits. Two pair each."

The clowning and small talk left Cielo, Pikea, and Shonto hungry again. They still had piles of fruits and vegetables on the rooftops. Cielo munched a large yellow onion from the garden.

"That's nasty!" said Promise.

"Hermana, these things are sweet as apples," Cielo responded. "You don't know what you're missing. Come smell my breath."

"Um. That's a dee-cline."

"One of my favorite snacks is a Cheetos and peanut butter sandwich. On whole grain bread," said Cielo, wistfully.

"Hmmm. Not so sure about that," said Promise. "Why whole grain?"

"Concerned about my cholesterol," answered Cielo.

"You pound Cheetos but get picky with your bread? You, brother, are what they call an enigma," Promise said, laughing as she slapped Cielo's back and walked away.

Cielo chewed a wad of basil, offering some to Ashia and Maricela. "This will freshen your breath real good. Especially if you add in some peppermint leaves." They obliged, proceeding in small steps, one leaf each. They blew their breath at each other and laughed as first Ashia, then the others jumped down from the rooftops and went to change for the lagoon.

They kept together the rest of the afternoon. When the shadows began to stretch, they gravitated back to camp. Some took naps in the coolness of their cabins. Others hung by the fire ring, messing around.

White smoke poured from Shonto's cabin. A pungent air billowed out over camp. "Shonto's burning that white sage again," Ivory said. "You think he's scared about the wolf or whatever that was?"

"You think?" Promise asked sarcastically.

"That's why he burns that stuff, right?" Ivory asked. "To keep evil spirits away?"

"I wouldn't say it exactly like that," Lake offered. "It's more about purification. Bringing sacred spirit back into the cabin. Pollution doesn't have to be evil. Even something you think is harmless, like confusion, can be enough to keep a space from being clean."

Binda saw Promise scribbling in her journal. "What are you writing?" she asked.

"Just some stuff in my journal. A story, I guess."

"You write stories? That's pretty amazing. I wish I could write like that. I used to write little kid stuff back when I was little."

"What happened? Why did you stop?"

Binda blushed and grinned. "Why do we ever stop? People took the joy out of it for me, putting rules and judgments down on it. Before, I was free. It's not the same creating something with shackles on you."

"Promise, pleeease, read your story for us," Binda begged.

"Aright, aright." Promise read a story about two Lovers banned from seeing each other by their bitterly rivaling families, so they drank a potion and turned into two vines. Freed from their human forms, they grew together, interlocked around a sacred oak tree that grew for 1,000 years. She titled her story, *A Thousand Year Embrace*.

"Now, that's spinning a yarn, P.!" Ivory shouted. He scratched his temple and wiped sweat from his forearms as he tapped his spear tip nervously on the ground. "Who's got next?"

"Y'all heard about Anansi the Spider?" Mende asked to no response. "That's one crazy boy. Me and Balanta grew up on those stories. Can't believe none of you have heard any of them. Let me clue you in." Mende spent the next hour spooling out a web of Anansi stories, from the Ashanti people, each wilder than the next. By the time Mende finished, the web had caught more than imaginations. It had imprinted itself in their sense of Africa, and therefore of the world.

"I'm afraid that I'm losing the memory of our tribal traditions," Mende admitted. "I don't want to be a hungry ghost, always looking to other people's cultures to fill my plate. I want to eat my own stuff."

Ashia shifted her locs over her shoulder. She was feeling the first flutter of cramps. "Ama told me, 'What's in, comes out.' She said it's that simple. We all need to be eating our own stuff."

Lake felt a pang in her heart. Her voice was solemn, a canyon song: "My Masaani used to tell me that there are grains of fire in every soul. Stored pain. That a big part of life is to keep going on quests to find those grains of fire and release them. She said that if you don't do that work, the grains grow, like cancer. The grains find each other inside of you, and combine. Become bigger grains. Masaani said that she knew people who weren't human any more. They had been consumed by their grains of fire. Nothing remained of their true soul."

"I'm ready for a nap," Pikea said, yawning.

"Me, too," said Lake. Some others followed suit. Mende took his djembe and walked a short ways into the woods. The attack on the goat hadn't frightened him as much as it had fascinated him. He had the feeling that even that event was somehow meant for them to see and be shaped by. The creature didn't seem to have any interest in or fear of them, which was strange to Mende. It was almost as though the whole thing was some kind of test.

He found a log to sit on. A high wall of scotch broom towered at his back. The bright yellow blossoms gave off a sweet fragrance that relaxed Mende. He positioned the djembe between his knees and began to look for a mood between his palms and the drumhead. A hushed, irregular beat came first. It grew more solid. Searching. Mende grinded his teeth when stressed, and had been grinding away since two days before, after his fight with Balanta. His heartbeat slowed as he revisited the hurt of what Balanta said to him. Guilt came after. *I'm tired of feeling like a burden to him*, Mende thought. *It's my fault he can't breathe. I'm always suffocating him. I need to stop being so insecure and let him enjoy his space for once. It's not all about me. I wish people admired me the way they do him, though. Just once I want to feel that kind of Love.* These thoughts brought more guilt and conflict. Mende's palms and drum had left the island. They were back in Sierra Leone, in Guinea Bissau, and the drumbeat was a peaceful one. Yarrow cooked in a pot. Steam rose that smelled like the earth. Women in brightly colored wraps and dresses and headdresses moved around naturally in the courtyard. People were themselves, not chasing ghosts of acceptance that could never be caught. Not fighting a deadly amnesia of who they used to be. Mende's palms and drum were one prayer, filling the sky with soul substance. Men were sitting in a circle around Mende's prayer, splitting open their chests and adding their scars and pain to the prayer. Adding what they had gathered from the woods and dug from the soil and captured from the rain. And Mende's palms grew raw then red then bloodied, as Balanta came and sat with the men. Mende's djembe head became a shallow pool of blood as Mende kept pounding, the beat rising, turning, performing sacred dance. Balanta's proud face surrendered something. Tears. Water fell on the face of Mende's big brother. Their parents, Yara and Shanté, walked from the woods and sat with the people. The circle grew. Wider. Deeper. The woods filled with relatives and friends. People were themselves. Shanté and Yara were themselves. Balanta, his face of water, was himself. The people drank from the sacral offering spilling from Mende's djembe. His palms were the cup. Anansi, the Spider, spun a web that held the moon in place so that night was now a forever land. People were themselves.

Ashia and Maricela went down by the water to sunbathe for a bit. They rubbed their skin down in cocoa butter they had made from fresh picked cocoa and turned over on their stomachs. "My cycle is starting," Ashia said, sleepily. "This warm sand on my belly feels good."

"Yeah, it's early for me, but I can tell it's coming. I figured you ladies would reset my clock," Maricela said, smiling. She smacked Ashia on the butt. "Thanks for the gift."

"You think that Loni is bangin'?" Ashia asked.

"I don't know," Maricela replied. "He acts covert about it. If he is, that's on him. I'm not *for* that. I wasn't born for that, and I won't be used for that. Not gonna be a widow or raise someone's children on my own all because a boy can't break free and be a man."

"Keep talking that," Ashia said, her voice muffled against her blanket. "You and Loni act so hard, like you're afraid to show any Love to each other, but you know you're feeling him."

"Cozy for you to say. You and Balanta are like chocolate syrup. Melting all over each other."

"No you didn't!" Ashia shouted, grinning. Maricela jumped up and ran into the surf, squealing. Ashia raced in after her. Waist deep in the bay, they had a water fight until they were out of breath and fell into back floating. Buoyant in the sea water, they bobbed and drifted in suspended tranquility. Maricela lost herself in the blue sky above and hoped she would live to feel such joy and ease again.

Cielo was swinging in the hammock in the late afternoon, freestyle humming an impromptu folk tune when he saw two figures break through the tree line down shore, moving toward camp. His eyes focused and he recognized the two shapes. "Hey, people! They're back!" Everyone came over to Cielo and looked down the beach. Balanta's arm was around Eloni's neck. Both of them were limping, ragged. The group ran to meet them, a buzz of questions and comments. They moved down to the ocean so the two warriors could bathe.

Balanta's ankle was more swollen now, from the hike back. He was weak and dizzy. Questions flew at him like mosquitos. Eloni was dehydrated and not in much better shape than Balanta. They both tried to process the barrage of questions and shouts about a goat killing and a vicious predator. Nothing made sense. The ocean took them. Made them sleepy. The others spoke in voices captured by surf song and sea breeze.

It was only after the initial energy of reunion receded that Ashia called for the group's attention, and asked, "Where is Mende?"

"I saw him walking into the woods a while back," Shonto said. "Haven't seen him since."

Balanta heard this and filled with sorrow, even in his exhaustion.

"You guys made it just in time for dinner," Cielo said.

They helped Balanta up to his cabin. He was growing feverish again. "Where's Mende?" he kept asking. "Should we search for him?"

"Rest," Ashia said softly.

An accretion had flared on Balanta's leg at the site of the snake bite. The lump was purple and pusing. "You need some more witch hazel," Eloni observed. "I'll go get you some." For the next half hour, Eloni lanced and evacuated the wound, and flushed it with serum from the witch hazel leaves. He made a poultice of yarrow flower, cottonwood bark and leaves, and cottony fluff from a silk floss tree for gauze, mixed with clay from the lagoon, and wrapped Balanta's leg once more with aloe leaves. Binda knelt behind Balanta the whole time, holding his shoulders in her hands, her eyes closed, spirit traveling to Balanta's body where it spread like a rain cloud through his cells, touching Balanta in a mitochondrial place, her compassion swelling into his molecules, pools of rainwater overflowing their banks on a scorched savannah. Binda would fall into bed dearly exhausted that night, sleeping deeply and dreamless, and waking with her mouth dry as desolation.

While Balanta slept in his cabin, Eloni staved off sleep and jumped in with the others, preparing the meal. He had missed this ritual while they were gone. He came up behind Maricela, who was making a sauce for the fish, and put his arms around her waist. "Can I help?" he asked.

Maricela stirred the almond butter sauce gently, her eyes following the swirling lines. "Just don't make me lose my focus, hombre. I'll burn the sauce." She was relieved Eloni was back. Now she anticipated her and Ashia telling everyone about the jar and the scroll.

"More thyme," Eloni said, moving his hands down her forearms from behind.

"You need to put your Samoan butt to bed and get some rest," Maricela said, smiling.

"Not alone," Eloni responded. His thick fingers pulled her closer at the waist.

"Git, boy," Maricela said, stirring without breaking rhythm.

In the twilight, a dark shape came to sit with Shonto for a while. Shonto was down by the water, singing a traditional Diné song to the movement of the tide. He felt a presence. When he turned, the shape was next to him. Shonto could see through the figure, even though it was coal black.

The shape spoke. "You afraid of drowning?" it asked. Its voice seemed to come from down in the earth's crust.

Shonto thought of the flash flood back in the arroyo. "Almost did drown. Are you Kokopelli?"

The shape did not answer. Instead, it said, "Your name... Shonto. Means, *the light that shines on spirit water*. You should not be afraid. You cannot drown."

"I miss my brothers and sisters," Shonto said. Even as he tried to tighten the burlap around his heart, he felt his heart opening. Sadness coming through. He recited his sisters' names. "Chooli. Kai. Nascha. My sisters were always playing tricks on me. And my brothers, Tahoma and Atsa, they were older. They showed me the way."

The obsidian cloud beside Shonto billowed, its outline rolling, expanding, contracting. "You should not be afraid. What is light cannot drown." Then the cloud called Shonto by his spirit name, known only to Shonto and the healer who had revealed it to Shonto.

The shape grew taller, more slender. Its form moved over Shonto's shoulder. Not a touch. A misting. As Shonto kept staring at the bay, its turquoise body, and the white ruffle breaking out at the reef, he felt the shape depart. Shonto felt an arrowhead, lodged in his heart since the old days, break free. The river there began to run again.

By the time dinner was ready, Balanta had made a miraculous recovery. Everyone credited Binda, who waved them off. Eloni asked for just a little credit. After all, he had only drawn out the poison, carried the giant over great distance and perilous terrain, applied his medicinal talents, and stood watch through that long night. Okay, Eloni, they conceded, you get a little skin.

"What did you use on Balanta's bite wound?" Shonto asked.

"Mostly yarrow, clay, and eucalyptus sap," Eloni said.

"Yarrow? We call that *plumajillo* in New Mexico. Means *Little Feather* in Spanish," Lake said.

"Diné call yarrow *Life Medicine*," Shonto said. "We chew it for toothaches. Use it for earaches, too. Strong medicine, that little flower. The Chippewa inhale it as steam for their headaches. Cherokee drink it as tea. Reduces fever that way, and puts you to good sleep."

They feasted on a giant fruit salad, and a mountain of grilled and earth-baked fish: sturgeon, grouper, mullet, flounder, croaker, shell cracker, perch, yellowtail, and sea bass. Fat green olives and star anise had been wrapped up with the baked fish. The resulting taste and aroma was fruity, with a licorice

211

tint. More yam pudding for dessert. All washed down with Mende's lemonade. Ashia had found Mende in the woods, still drumming by the light saffron wall of scotch broom, and appealed to his ego, urging that everyone was begging for his lemonade brew.

"Are you going to eat your bones?" Ivory asked Mende through a mouthful. "I'll take them."

"Nasty," Promise said.

"Good minerals," Ivory said. "How do you think I got this body?"

"Are you going to finish your plate?" Pikea asked Promise, who still had plenty of baked fish left.

"Nope. You can have it. You must have two stomachs."

"Nah. It's just two lifetimes running around inside me."

Talk got around to music. Cielo listed his influences: Ruben Blades. Antonio Carlos Jobim. Santana. Leadbelly. Blind Lemon Jefferson. Burning Spear. Black Uhuru. Marley.

"You better throw some Bessie Smith and Ma Rainey in there," Ashia said.

"And don't forget Nina!" Lake said, laughing.

"Man, Cielo, I never would have figured you for a reggae guy," Balanta said.

"Maybe you shouldn't be figuring me at all," Cielo replied benignly. "Any sound that has good spirit to it, I'm on it. I've been into Marley and Tosh and all those way back cats for a long time."

Cielo stuffed his mouth with baked fish and moaned. "All this needs is some grits," he said, muffled.

"What'cho know about grits?" Balanta asked Cielo in a weak, sarcastic voice.

Cielo smiled, his cheeks still stuffed. "My older cousin used to cook them for me for breakfast when I went to visit familia down South. Love those things. With some black pepper and melted butter? Man…"

"What I could use," Balanta countered, "is some more of those tortillas please, Cielo, to sop up these fish juices. They're thick as gravy."

"What do you know about tortillas?" Cielo cracked.

Balanta laughed weakly. "I'm the most tortilla eating brother you'll meet. Tortillas for breakfast, quick-browned in butter on a skillet, with sugar and cinnamon sprinkled on top. Wrapped around whatever you got for lunch. Y con frijoles y pollo for dinner."

"Look at you talkin that Español!" Maricela shouted.

Balanta wrapped another corn tortilla around his fixings of fish and mango slices, his eyes gleaming. "Ha. You got jokes. You never know though, do you? Back in the day, Mende and I got free food for a week from this hole in the wall Mexican place in exchange for helping them repaint and do some repairs. We ate enchiladas and tacos on the daily. It was my first time eating Mexican food. I was set. Now, Mende thinks we might have different mothers after all. He can't eat ketchup without sweating." Balanta looked at Mende, who kept his eyes to the ground, sipping lemonade and tapping his feet against the ground.

Balanta had lost his breath and grown weaker, just from that last effort to speak. He took deep breaths and bowed his head, his elbows resting on his knees.

"Let's get you back to the cabin to rest for a beat," Ashia said. Balanta obliged.

Ashia sat on the edge of Balanta's cot. She wiped his forehead with a wet cloth. In the dark of the cabin, she couldn't make out Balanta's face well enough. She lit a candle. Vanilla and amber scented the air. "You need to talk to your brother," Ashia said, her hand on Balanta's thigh. "He's been hurting the whole time you were gone."

"I know," Balanta said. "It's been weighing on me. Can you please go and get him?"

"Sure. I'll let you two have your privacy." Ashia asked Mende to come talk with his brother. Mende kept his sad face on, but didn't hesitate to go to the cabin.

Balanta counted the hours between when he and Eloni had left camp, and the time of their return. They had been away 40 hours. It felt like four days, easily. Mende came in and sat down on the opposite cot. He kept his gaze to the floor, shuffling his feet.

"I'm sorry, man," Balanta said. His voice was hoarse.

Mende stared at the ground for a beat. Finally, he said, "Are you feeling okay?"

"Yeah, thanks. Not good to get snake poison in you. I would advise against it. Don't change the subject, though. You know I didn't mean what I said, right?"

"But you should mean it. I'm sorry you're always having to carry me. I know you put too much pressure on yourself."

"That's on me, brother. It's not an excuse to go off on you."

Mende smiled. "Yeah, I appreciate you setting me straight. Next time I bother you, though, you don't have to go all volcano about it." They both laughed. Balanta sat up and hugged his brother.

"You think we'll ever be capable of healing?" Mende asked. "I mean, really getting to a place of being whole again?"

"Again? I'm not sure I ever was whole," Balanta responded. "The older I get, the more I forget what I was like inside when I was younger. I'm afraid that I might be wishfully creating a false version of my past self in my mind."

"I need to share something with you," Balanta said, his face becoming serious again. "A big part of why I try too hard to be too perfect... I'm... afraid. Afraid of having what happened to dad happen to me. I don't want to lose myself, become mentally sick, and have people think about me the way they do dad."

Mende stared at his brother. Balanta wiped his mouth and his forehead of perspiration. "It's hard for me to admit, but I must be addicted or something to people thinking highly of me. If the look in their eyes changes from... admiration to pity... I can't handle that."

"I never knew you were afraid of becoming ill, like dad," said Mende. "I've been alone with that fear. I've been scared to death of the same thing happening to me. I'm always looking for the slightest sign that I'm losing it. It never occurred to me... You just seem... better than that. I feel like the weak one."

Balanta stared at his brother, whose eyes had misted. He pulled Mende to his chest. Mende sobbed. For their father. For what was lost. And for this new comfort of a shared fear that had instantly grown smaller. Balanta held Mende close and said in a low rumble, "You aren't weak. In some ways, you've always been stronger than I am. You carry me home sometimes."

Eloni made nutmeg butter from the fruit of the trees that were scattered among the more dominant olives in a grove they had found. He slathered some over the cornbread cakes and offered them to Lake and Binda, who were meandering around camp like flower petals in the wind. "Mmm..." said Lake. "This isn't even fair, 'Eloni. I can eat these all day."

Later, Maricela didn't let Eloni live down his legacy, purring to him, "Oh, Loni, won't you please come home with me? Oh, and you'll need to bring all your cooking supplies." She mocked him all night with adulation. Eloni smiled and kept feeding her cornbread cakes.

Night gathered its hue. Ivory and Pikea built a bonfire. The second Pikea turned away from the flames, she heard Ivory whelp. She turned and saw Ivory jumping up and down. White strings of ash fanned out from his eyelids. "Ivory burnt his eyelashes, y'all!" Pikea shouted.

"Oh no!" Ashia lamented. "Ivory's gorgeous lashes! Are you kidding? Boy, get over here. Let me see." She sat Ivory down and checked him. The front of Ivory's afro was also singed white. "You're looking like an old man right now, son," Ashia said.

"You think I can get some seniority points around here now?" Ivory said. He was rubbing his fingers against his thumbs nervously. "Will they grow back?"

"Your eyelashes?" Yeah. "Just don't be sticking your face in the fire again. Tends to end poorly."

Lake scanned the skies. The moon was a parenthetical glint. Emancipated of its fuller bosom and free to swim less conspicuously with the stars. Lake liked this part of the moon cycle. She could feel everything in nature emptying itself, cleansing, including her own body.

"The stars stripped naked tonight," Cielo said. "Look how bright they are." Constellations flared above them. Comets drew bright mascara on the face of the universe.

The chubby-faced owl appeared again, this time perched on a corner of the rooftop of one of the cabins. Its pillow of a head ticking back and forth robotically. *I just want to squeeze it*, Binda thought. *Does it even have a body under all those feathers, or is it just feathers down to the bone?*

Maricela, Cielo, and Ashia got the spirit flowing, leading everyone through a passionate montage of Latin dances: Rumba and Mambo. Bachata. Merengue. Salsa and Sambo. Sweating bodies painted in flame light moved around the fire ring, calling out, howling, scatting.

By the time they had exhausted themselves, Balanta had joined them again, wrapped in a heavy blanket. Ashia and Balanta sat closely, their extended legs touching between them, Ashia's foot nuzzling Balanta's calf.

Lake and Binda leaned against each other on a log, wrapped together in a cotton blanket dyed in dark blues and reds. Fire talk got to popping. Souls jumped into words and fled out from their repressive caves like a great burning flock of truth. Scars came up in the conversation.

"I got this scar from falling out of a treehouse," Pikea said, lifting up her shirt and baring her side. "Wasn't our treehouse. Just came across it and wanted to climb up into it. Landed on some rose bushes. Might have broken some ribs, but I couldn't tell anybody, so I tried to play it off. Could barely breathe for a month."

"This scar was a bad one," Eloni said, showing the bottom of his foot. "Glass bottle that bit me like a rattlesnake when I stepped on it. Sorry, B. Don't mean to bring up snakes."

Shonto pointed to a round mark on the underside of his chin. "My older brothers used to drag me around the house on my stomach. They pretended I was a prize winning trout or something... that they were dragging to shore. I scraped my chin on the carpet, down to the bone."

"This fool at a group home gave me this," Balanta said, lifting up his shirt to reveal a large keloid in the shape of a star. "He was trying to be the man, said I had taken his food off his plate. Man, that food wasn't fit for a stray dog, much less a pet one. He could have had his food, for all I cared. He raised up on me with a hanger rod from one of the bedroom closets. He got me a good one. Once. Then I caught hold of the rod, broke it off and threw it out of the way. He didn't want to go at it with fists, so he backed down. I was cool with that, cause I didn't want to be getting listed again, so I just pushed him. I guess I didn't realize how mad I was, cause I pushed him hard enough that he went flying through a glass divider in the cafeteria. Cut up his back and hand real bad. Sure enough, I got listed. Again. Can't win."

"And over some food, huh?" said Shonto. "That stuff's the worst. We had something called Wildcard Wednesday at this lockdown I was at. We kids called it Russian Roulette Day, cause you were seriously playing with your life by daring to eat what they served. The cook was this dude from another joint, who claimed to have been some kind of five star chef. He liked trying out new recipes on us. I was convinced he was trying to poison us. I lay awake many a night imagining him laughing at us back in the kitchen, watching from around the corner to see who would gag first.

"You ever had group home food so bad to where you went on a hunger strike? Me and some guys went on a hunger strike one time. They just laughed us off. I guess they knew we didn't have much of a choice. I lasted the longest, two and a half days. Then this guy just in from another home. He lasted two days. Once the cramps start kicking in, you start to reimagine the same old awful food as darn near delicious."

"I like what you said about turning your pain into power," Eloni said to Promise. "It's like grapes into wine, isn't it? It takes time and patience, and the right conditions. That's what I didn't get about my life before. I thought that if I wanted my pain to stop badly enough, it should happen right away. I wanted it on my time. When it didn't happen, I just got angrier."

"And that's why we need to start believing that we even have a future," Promise said gently. "Most of us, we don't believe much in tomorrow, I guess because today is a handful enough. And we've been shown that the rug can get pulled out from under us at any time."

"The rug and the floor, and the foundation," added Eloni.

"Yeah, but the thing is, we're stuck in a Catch-22, because we want our pain to end, but we won't believe in the one thing that has to happen for us to get there: time."

"Time is what faith and patience graze on, I guess," said Eloni.

"Now you're speaking my language, brother. Trauma makes for the most impatient souls. When you hurt, you don't want nothing to do with time, you just want to put out the fire with a quickness. Trouble is, treating your whole life with urgency guarantees you'll miss out on what happens slowly, gradually. Which is all the best things, in my view."

"Like relationships?" Eloni grinned.

"Like relationships, you clown." Promise laughed.

"Okay, here's something y'all don't know about me," Balanta said, standing up. His legs trembled, and the bite area throbbed, so he sat back down. "You're going to crack on me forever on this. Whatever. I'm into opera."

Sure enough, the whoops and jokes came flying, led off by none other than Lake, while Mende grinned sheepishly and stayed out of the way.

"Y'all are just a bunch of uncultured heathens. You don't know nothing about this." Balanta cleared his throat, feinting as though he was about to launch into a soaring arietta. "Man, something about the vibration in their voices," he said. "I can't believe you can do that with your body."

Eloni cleared his throat, shifting his feet and scooting closer on the log. "I feel like a prisoner inside of my own fear. You notice those turtles in the estuary, poking their heads out of their shells just far enough to take a look? I don't feel like I can get even that far."

The group listened quietly, their faces reflecting the flickering firelight. Somewhere in the black distance, a night bird warbled a lamenting lullaby.

Eloni continued, his eyes locked in on the flames. "I'm afraid. It's hard for me to say that, as a male, from my culture. But I'm afraid. Afraid of choosing, failing, shaming my family. I'm terrified of being rejected."

"I'm with you on that, Eloni," Promise said in a quiet voice.

"I need someone to help me learn to be free. Like you, Balanta, the way you go charging forward in situations. Or like you, Ashia, so at peace with how things go, however they go. Or... and I mean this sincerely, Ivory... like you. You're free in a crazy way that feels so foreign to me."

"Understandable," Ivory joked.

"But I don't feel that it is supposed to be so foreign to me. Freedom, I mean. It might have something to do with all these adults who have controlled every breath of my life, thinking that they are protecting me. It's belittling to me, really. Like I'm this defective creature that can't do life the right way, so they have to chaperone me through wiping my ass and eating cereal. I mean, damn."

Pikea was in a mood for revolution and protest. She commenced to get on her soapbox. "You know how businesses hire landscapers to come in and clean up the trees and bushes around their building? Be clear, those landscapers often aren't people who Love trees and plants. They are people who Love putting food on the table for their families. So, if you aren't very specific with them about what you want done, they aren't gonna come in and just neatly trim your trees. No, they want to feel like they've accomplished something. You could have the most beautiful, healthy, full tree in blossom. By the time they're done, that tree has been violated, massacred, denuded. Whole main branches gone for no reason. Thing looks like a survivor from a nuclear bomb. Destroyed for no reason at all, other than you figured just because you hired someone to trim up your trees... that meant that they Loved trees.

"Systems for children and youth are like that. Everyone assumes that just because some person with a degree got hired to do a job, that they must Love young people. No, they Love putting food on the table. They Love getting paid. But Loving young people? That's a very big assumption. I can't tell you how many young people I know, by the time some professional got done with them, they looked just like one of those landscaped trees. All raw and naked and exposed, bark shredded, branches chopped off, their sap running everywhere. Halfway on their way to dying. Having a real Love for young people should be a credential if you're gonna be trusted to serve them."

Ashia pulled Balanta closer to her. Beneath their shared blanket, she could feel his body heat. She was sitting beside two fires.

"A child in foster care is a professional immigrant," Ashia said. "A chronic exile. Whatever language you come with, you're forced to learn a new one. No one cares about your roots. Just fit in. Fake a smile. Be grateful. Tell our family that *we're* your home. Make *us* feel secure in the relationship. Never mind that you, the child, are the one who's juggling fireballs and who's suspended over a bottomless canyon. Make *us,* the family, feel secure with you."

"Foster care?" Maricela mocked. "A better name for it is Barely There. Family? Barely there. Sensitivity to your situation? Barely there. Stability? Barely there. Peace? Barely there. School support? Barely there. Long relationships? Barely there."

"Or how about Foster Snare?" Ivory said. "Or Foster Blare? Foster Dare!"

"Okay, Ivory," Promise said. "We get your point."

Mende opened up on the subject. "The way my foster families have dealt with me has always made me feel like taffy being pulled in two directions. It's like I'm not supposed to have any feelings for my biological family, like that's disloyal or something. So I keep what I'm dealing with to myself."

Shonto concurred. "It's not cool when the family you're with is threatened by the family you come from. And then the family you come from resents you for caring about the family that helped raise you."

"Can't win, Baby," Promise affirmed. "Can't win."

"Cut folks some slack," Ashia said. "Humans, man. We need our fantasies and fables. We don't do well with the truth. "By the way though, why do you get penalized for being placed with your own relatives? Ashia asked in declaration. "You lose funding and all kinds of resources. Why are the incentives designed to draw you away from your family? Smells like more slavery techniques to me."

"I'm telling you," said Ivory, "Straight up oppression."

Eloni pitched on another log, then jabbed at the embers with his spear. "I'm tired of all of it," he said. "The world in general is too lazy to make an effort to understand anything outside of typical. I shouldn't have to explain and defend my life three times a day just because God didn't color inside the lines with my situation."

"Hey ya'll," Pikea said. I want to tell you about my PO. He has this limp when he walks. Makes him look like he's getting ready to high jump, every other step."

Just then, a line of pelicans traced the coastline, unperturbed by marauding egrets flirting with danger. Lake noticed and felt the urge to wade in the surf.

"What are you staring at, Lake?" Promise asked.

"Just spacing out. I don't think of this island as land surrounded by water," Lake said. "I think of it as water interrupted by land."

Pikea continued, "I asked my PO one time, 'Did you used to run track?' He said, 'No, but I used to run crack, and that's how I got this limp.' He said he broke a bone in his foot jumping out a window when a neighbor called the cops on him. Says every step he takes reminds him the way his life could have gone, and drives him to work with juvee offenders. I guess a person's walk holds their whole journey, from the tension and fear, to the triumph and peace."

Pikea had long wanted to be healed enough to introduce herself to others by saying, "My name is Pikea, and I come from the deep sea. My father is Moana. I am his daughter." She had stood before many mirrors and tried to get the words out, but they stuck in her teeth, embedded poisonous fibers. She was always left choking and pale.

"We're all looking for ways to stop being haunted," Cielo said. "I'm glad I went through foster care. I feel like I have more substance, less blinders. The people I went to school with, they mostly seem shallow. If your childhood is too smooth, it puts you to sleep and makes you majorly self-centered. My helping genes have been turned on, bright and hot. Cause I know what it's like to need help. To be desperate for it."

"Some fruit ripens on the tree," Ashia said. "Some only ripens after it falls. Like avocados."

"Avocado is a fruit?" Ivory asked.

"Yes, and you're missing my point. We've all taken one fall or another. Hopefully, we haven't seen our best days yet. Once you hit the ground, hard, maybe that jars something awake inside of you, and you're on your way."

"Or maybe you just start rotting away," Pikea said.

"Precious," Promise responded.

Promise looked at Pikea and spoke in a tender voice. "You got anger stuck to your heart like barnacles, girl. You better let that go. Stop being so diagonal."

"What are you talking about?"

"Counterposed. Oppositional, I'm saying. Your attitude needs a multivitamin."

"You funny, P." Pikea responded. "Don't forget, I hold the fire for my circle."

"Am I a sick person?" Pikea asked to no one in particular.

"Why do you ask that?" Promise said.

"I feel... relieved that I have no one left. It means I have nothing left to lose. Nothing worse to be afraid of."

"I don't blame you for feeling that way," Promise said.

Pikea groaned and pounded her fists against her thighs. "It feels like Paradise is sparring with Misery in my chest. It wears me out. I just want the sparring to stop. Maybe even if it means that Misery has to win."

Ivory got fidgety and started beatboxing.

"Go, Ivory."

"Last year—"

"—Uh huh..."

"Last year, I was seven—teen... This year, I'm eight... teen... Body so lean... Grill so clean... Game so mean, I *have* to be your sweetest dream..."

"—Uh oh!"

"Got more personality than a priest got prayers... than life got layers—"

"Go with it!"

"I may be young, but I seen a lot... People always trying to scheme and plot... but I see 'em quick with the eyes I got... Early on, I got shot a lot... got hot a lot... Then I got real... Learned to chill... Put ointment on my burns, and learned to heal—"

"Ivory!"

"Now, here's the real... Every time you cut me open, I use that blood and start to seal... I tighten up, go waterproof... Stand in the rain and can't be touched... I lived through much... I conquered such... I walk strong, and all the people say, that boy Ivory, he don't play! No, he don't play! No, he don't play!"

"Whooo! Ivory said the thing!"

"Nice, Ivory!"

"Frosty!"

Ivory was pumped. He raced down to the water for a quick saltwater dip. Before the others knew it, the dip was over.

"Stingray!" Ivory's shrill voice was a sonic squeal. Ivory bounded out of the surf, an obsidian dolphin leaping onto land. "Stingray!" he barked, running up to camp as Ashia took her sweet time walking over to him. He was rubbing his behind in the worst way, his smooth face contorted into a plum way past ripe. "I saw it move right past me, right before I felt the sting! That's what I get for listening to you people and trying to spend some time in the water!"

Eloni, having had plenty of experience with sea creatures, calmly queried, "Okay now, Ivory. What did this thing look like, exactly?"

"It was about this big," Ivory said, extending his two hands to about a foot apart. "And it had a tail, a stinger. It looked like a shadow in the water and it moved fast. That's the last thing I remember before the attack."

"Attack?" Promise didn't mean to be mocking. Yes she did. "Oh! Ivory!" She squealed, doubled over in tears already.

Cielo placed his hand, still messy with guacamole, on Ivory's shoulder. "Ivory, I believe what you saw was a jellyfish. I've seen plenty of 'em since we've been here. If it was a stingray, you wouldn't be so energetic, and you wouldn't just be rubbing your booty."

At this tentative identification, Ivory allowed himself an exhale. "What should I do? This thing stings like bejeezus. "

"Well," Eloni said, "I'm afraid it needs to be peed on, my brother."

"You said what?"

"We always used to pee on stings like that."

"I thought that was for sea urchins, not jellyfish."

"Pick your poison," Eloni said. "All I know is that's what we used to do."

The consideration didn't get any further. Ivory's eyes rolled up to the top of his head and his slim body collapsed like laundry blown off the clothesline.

Ivory, panting, turned toward Balanta. "You gonna jump me into this thing now?" he asked.

"Jump you into what?"

"Into you and Eloni's warriorhood? I think I earned it at this point. You got a snake bite. I got stingrayed."

"Brother, there is no warriorhood, and if there were, no one would be doing any jumping in. No gangs here. Just boys trying to be men. Girls working to be women. Right?" he said, patting Ivory on the back.

"Okay," Ivory said. "Just make sure if you do start up a warriorhood that you hit me up. Bet?"

"Bet." Balanta's smile was really all the inclusion Ivory needed. It was his best meal all day.

Mende was growing sleepy, the adrenaline of the day long since out of his system. "I used to have a hard time falling asleep when we came to this country," he said. "The smells were all wrong. The air at night wasn't sweet, like I was used to. It was sour, and... something strange about it. It felt distressed, like it was being strangled. Balanta started reading to me."

"Awww! How cute," Lake high pitched.

"Not like children's stories, Lake. Mostly books from home. History books. Novels. Cookbooks. Those really helped calm me down. I could smell the cassava, okra, and fish stew curling up between the words as Balanta read. Soon, I would be half dreaming myself over a bowl of steaming food. Then, I was asleep and licking my lips."

Balanta smiled. "Yeah, brother, you don't know how hard I cracked up at you licking your lips like that, fast asleep. You looked like a fat cat napping after it downed a mouse."

"You ever get afraid that you're forgetting what home looked like, or smelled like, Mende? It's like that for me," Pikea said.

"Most of the time, I feel like I'm on a boat drifting farther and farther away from shore, which is my homeland, and everyone I've known is standing on the shore, waving at me. Some of them are crying. Some are smiling, like they think I've won the lottery." Mende replied.

"At least you have your brother with you. That must help a lot."

"When he's being cool."

"Hey, man." Balanta said, biting his lower lip in an Ali-like threat.

"Just messin. Balanta's like my shelter, man. Don't know how I would stand in all this rain without him."

Pikea lamented, "A lot of the time, I feel like I don't want to grow up, because each day older I get feels more and more like I'm losing what I came from."

"I wish I could erase what I came from," Ivory spit out.

Night deepened. Eyes heavy, like twigs holding up shutters. No one wanted to leave the fire. Eloni leaned up against Maricela. Cielo tapped his bongos quietly. Promise picked up the verbal baton: "Usually I'm in a sprint to grow up, so I can have control over my life for once."

"I don't know, Promise," Eloni said, "I wonder whether we just keep on losing control the longer we live."

"Dour, man," Balanta, punctuated.

"Don't mean to be. I just wonder about the way human beings go about living. Seems like we tend to wander farther from our truth the more we experience life. So many adults I know seem to be on auto pilot, just downloading the same old tunes each day, never trying out any new stuff."

Promise stretched her arms and moaned satisfactorily. "Here's my plan. Get my edjamacation. Open my youth program. Pay my bills. Never have a boss telling me what to do. I'm through with authorities, rules, and policies. Tell me what I *can* do, not what I can't. That's my playlist from now on."

"We don't all have it like you and Ashia," Ivory said. "What'd you get, Ashia? Something like nine scholarships?"

Ashia sucked her teeth. "I got what I earned over 18 years, and what I made the effort to apply for, Ivory. That money isn't a gift or a handout. It's society banking on me. It's an investment the world makes in its own future. I plan on being a good investment."

"Here's the thing about education," Maricela said. "People treat being a student as though you're a peasant taking orders from royalty. You have to flip that script. A student has to be a revolutionary. An absolute fire-breathing agitator. If you're not challenging the system, from the classroom to the boardroom, to become what you need it to be, you're just feeding the status quo. The only kind of education that makes sense is when the peasants rise up and own their education."

Shonto recalled the generations of Native American boarding schools, and so many herds of long braids, cut and dying on the floor. "For me, education is all about who's telling your story: you, or some strangers. Students have to make school systems support them in telling their own story, or it's not education. It's subjugation."

Ivory cleared his throat, pulled out his 'fro with his fingertips, and commenced to rap on the subject:

Booking cemeteries, switching schools, records in the wind, no proof of me, asking for my Blood type, and family tree in the classroom, no class, just doom, putting my shame on display, calling it teaching, calling it learning, I call it burning. Grade to grade, freak parade, I burn. I Fade. You seek my finer light. I seek the kinder shade...

Mende read them an old school essay that he kept on hand because it was a moment of his life that he burned so hot it forced him into courage. It also earned him both an *A* and a scolding. The essay concluded like a blunt rainstorm:

If one third of the world hordes all the resources, aren't those people the Third World? If the rest of the world gets locked into one cage or another because it is determined to still be human and hold relationships as sacred and primary, isn't that the First World? Who is running the Lost World, and who will be alive to rebuild after the Last World? Who is being called civilized, and who actually *is* civilized? The bone I broke in my arm when I was seven is my reminder now of what it means to be whole. My arm throbs in that spot, not when it's humid, but when I'm not being a human being. Thank you, Teacher, for grading my essay with the human part of you.

Lake ran to her cabin for a blanket. Coming back out, Ashia was nearby, pacing uncomfortably. Holding her hands just beneath her belly.

"You too, huh?" Lake asked.

"Yeah, Lake. Bloated like crazy. You?"

"All of us are coming into our moon times together," Lake said. "When that happens, it brings strong medicine to all the women. Especially when it's during a circle moon, or a Clear Moon." Then Lake said something, almost as an afterthought: "We should probably take advantage of our power." Those words, and Lake's tone, stayed with Ashia, even while she slept that night.

The rest of the time before bed, Eloni and Balanta entertained the group with stories about their near-death experience on the cliff wall, Eloni's frantic efforts to save Balanta's life, and encounters with creatures and plants not identified by science. Promise called Eloni and Balanta out for telling fish tales, which the two storytellers firmly denied, not without horrible poker faces betraying their embellishments. Lake mentioned the fading moon, the diminishing tide, and her happiness at having the whole group back together again.

Promise approached Binda as they were leaving the fire for their cabins. The scent of the fire was strong. The night sky was brilliant.

"Hey, Binda. I appreciate what you shared about cutting yourself. I always thought I was the only one."

Binda paused, looking at Promise with a soft expression. "Yeah, I used to think that, too. You know, I've been learning that every time you open your mouth to tell the world about what it's like being you, the world is likely to round up someone who knows what it's like being you. I guess that's how I got over being so shy to speak, let alone share personal stuff."

"How are you doing with that, now?"

"Pretty good, I guess. I haven't done it in a while. I've been feeling more stable lately, like I don't have to take my emotions on a rollercoaster for every single thing that happens in my life."

"Yeah, I know what you mean. Like, you start to figure out that you can handle life just fine by staying calm, right?"

"Yeah. And you can actually handle life even better that way. I just get worried sometimes that I'm going to slip and hurt myself again if I get really stressed out."

"That's why I tell myself over and over that I'm the only one who can truly hurt myself," Binda said, "and if I want to be safe, I need to be Loving to myself. It helps remind me to focus on other ways to deal with my stress.

"This mentor of mine told me that I can think about it like planting seeds of sacredness," Binda continued. "Each time I tell myself a Loving thought, I am planting seeds that help me learn to treat myself sacredly."

"Thanks, Girl," said Promise. "You have a good night. I'm looking forward to catching some z's."

"Goodnight, Promise. See you in the morning."

The night air clung to its coolness, spreading it over the compound like a blanket, total and silent.

Binda pulled up her thick cotton socks, and wrapped her heavy blanket around her. "You want to share dreams tonight?" she asked Lake.

"Sure! That would be cool, Lake replied. Can you show me how to do it?"

"Sure. It's easy, actually. You just need to pay attention to each other's heart while you are going to sleep."

"What do you mean?"

"It's something my father taught me when I was young. He always said, 'Binda, in the times before, people knew how to pay attention to each other's hearts. That's why we could find each other by our dreams. Now, that is being lost. I want to teach it to you, so you can carry it forward, and hopefully that one torch light won't go out.'

"He taught me to listen for someone's heartbeat. Really, to feel it. Find its rhythm. Hearts are talking all the time, saying things about what a person is feeling, not feeling; what they're afraid of, or excited about. And what is on a person's heart before they fall asleep ends up in their dreams that night.

"So, if you can get in tune with someone's heart, and they can get in tune with yours, then you can both share your dreams that night."

"That sounds wild," Lake said. "Okay, now, show me what to do."

"Here, lie down and relax your breathing. Think about everything that happened today. How it made you feel. What you thought about it. Today was a journey you went on. Now, you are capturing it in your heart journal."

Lake closed her eyes, not able to help smiling with embarrassment. She thought about what Shonto said about the Diné being a returning people, and how she felt a strange tingling move up her spine as he spoke.

She remembered how the lagoon water felt so good during her morning swim, and the way the dragonflies hovered over the surface like swarms of drones with confused flight plans.

She followed a tribe of sea turtles along the sand, not knowing where they were leading her.

And then, she was sleeping. Her dreams broke open and a whole other world fell into her own. She could feel Binda's skin. Hear Binda's heart. And Binda was walking with her, holding hands, looking back at her with a smile. They moved across an endless meadow. Then, they were swimming through an ocean of genocides. So many millions of souls, indigenous faces, spirits humble enough to trust and be dominated, and the water grew thicker as entire families surfaced and sank. Lake felt Binda's pain, which was her own. The ocean they swam huddled itself into a puddle and now Binda was a leaf blowing across the puddle, and Lake was seed riding atop the leaf. The world tilted. Binda and Lake slid down a mountain that felt high as Everest and soft as silence. They landed in a pot of stew in a sacred woods in Africa. A pot that Balanta was stirring. Ashia was beside him, cradling something. And then, Lake and Binda were being born. Placental twins. All their heart scars had grown into a new skin that protected them as they moved, wet and fetal, out of a dark cave into a bright land of buffalo and koalas. And the land was peaceful and unblemished. And the descendants of genocide had gathered upon that land by the billions. And the reunion was so joyful that Lake's heart burst like a pomegranate in her sleep. She drowned in the sweetness.

Maricela turned over fitfully trying to sleep. These mama hips just don't fit on this precious little cot, she said to herself. She got up quietly and stepped out into the dormant air, feeling its coolness as a night cream on her face. The words from the inscription came back to her as she walked out toward the brightness by the beach: *One day a tribe will come. They shall die of fire. And begin as light.* A chill ran through her muscles. Those words... *They shall die of fire.* It was hard for her to shake the thought that the jar, the scroll, those words... were meant for this group. Ocean's face rippled in the black. Maricela felt dread. The sound of lapping water brought her to the surf's lip. She rubbed her hips and squatted down to be still for a moment. Sandy seawater ran over her feet. She recounted the rise and fall of the group's tension since they had arrived. Mende and Balanta's argument. Eloni's strange reactions to Cielo. Pikea's simmering. Lake and Binda's intuitive avoidance of drama. The way they seemed to always hover at the perimeter of conflict, two butterflies not trusting the unease enough to land on it. She envied them for this. Their lightness, with heavy air swirling around them. And the scroll. The words. Should she say something to the group, and not just Ashia? She already felt bad for keeping the secret. She didn't want to ruin the week, and maybe it was all just her imagination. Maybe she should tell them, so they could laugh it off and help cast away her foreboding feeling. Manos came through the doorway of her mind, not speaking, just crossing himself as he passed the religious shrine on the hallway coffee table, headed to the kitchen for a cerveza, his mood filling the house quickly, like dinner cooking. Maricela could smell his musk from the day, his frustrated labor, the hours of being diminished by haunting silence of glances and cold tones of voice. Roasted red chilés. They had always hung at the entryway to the kitchen, a red draping that reminded Maricela now of just how much fire can be released from a thing once it is cooked. *Santa Teresa*, she whispered to herself. She stood and swept her feet through the thin layer of surf to rinse them of sand. As she turned back toward camp, the whoosh of a large bird's wings mixed with the breeze. Maricela did not notice.

Cielo slept on the cabin roof again. Feeling the night air against his skin was a revival. Freedom settled in his spirit as the boundary between his body and the sky dissolved. Stars stared back at him like the reflected light in the eyes of animals inside a cave. He crossed his hands beneath his head and wiggled his toes, feeling the day's tension evaporate. Smiling, he listened to the sleep talk of trees. Ocean's lyrics. And the sayings of peace.

He noticed a darkness within the darkness, in his peripheral vision. Sitting up, he was face to face with a shadow form sitting cross-legged. The shadow had arms, and hands, which it rested on its knees. Cielo pushed down the fear that wanted to come up in him. All things deserve my kindness, he said to himself. "Hola, amigo," he said. "Have you come to visit with me?"

The shadow did not speak.

"Can I offer you something?" Cielo had nothing to offer but his sleeping bag and his company, but nonetheless, he was sincere. The shadow extended its right arm and pointed into the trees. Cielo looked. What looked like a family of five people was standing at the tree line. Cielo blinked his eyes several times, trying to wash away the illusion. The family was still there. They were small people, their faces ruddy and warm. They wore little clothing. And held hands. *Indios*, from the old days, Cielo thought.

The shadow morphed, shrinking from Cielo's size down to the size of a child. It lifted its hand to its mouth. An instrument emerged from its shadow body. A flute. It pursed its lips and began to play. A sound came out that entered Cielo's heart. Tears fell out of the descendant of Aztecs before he could even grasp what he was feeling. The family by the trees was dancing slowly, turning in a circle, hands still joined. Cielo watched through his own water as the three children moved to the center of the dance circle. The two parents closed in after, collapsing the circle. All five sat gradually on the ground, still swaying side to side as the shadow played its flute. A star leapt from a far constellation all the way across the ocean and shot in a white arc into the center of the family's tight cloistering. Cielo saw the starlight disappear into the hearts of the children as their parents hugged them tightly, still swaying. A particular note came from the shadow's flute. A single punctuation so pure that Cielo shivered. At that note, the family, now glowing with starlight, became a single tree before Cielo's eyes.

As Cielo gushed emotion and trembled a kind of happiness that changes the shape of memories, the shadow put down its flute and became the night. Cielo lay back down and allowed his tears to continue to their liking. He saw the bare spot in the distant sky where the star had jumped and descended. An owl hooted in the tree that had just been a family. The sound of it brought Cielo to sleep.

Ashia slept that night as close to Balanta as their bodies allowed. She wanted her warmth to flow into him without pause. Her arms remained around his slender waist, and his chest. When he moaned and shifted, she moved with him. Starlight slid through the crease in the cabin roof and landed on her face. She caught the balm of light on her lips and kissed it into Balanta's skin. Ashia thought of Antonia's earlier words: *The island won't bite. Unless you need it to.* Ashia sang an old Ga tribal song to Balanta, its ancestral richness and plaintive melody pouring through her own body, stirring emotions. She was caught off guard, surprised that she still remembered the song. Still vibrating from the song she had become, she drifted to sleep with her face resting on Balanta's laboring chest.

By morning, Ashia's body felt heavy as a boulder. Her eyes burned. Balanta was on his side, turned away from her. She moved up and over his girth to inspect his face. He opened his eyes at the brush of her soft breath against his cheek. He sat up as Ashia cradled his face in her hand, asking with her eyes. Balanta answered with his lips on Ashia's forehead and a strong hand patting her thigh, gratefully. Intuitively, he placed his hand on the skin of her tender womb. The warmth soothed her cramping. "Sorry you are feeling your pains," he said. His eyes were still sleepy, his lids draping.

"Hold me, Balanta."

"You want me to get you some water?" he croaked.

"No. Just hold me."

"What is it?"

"It keeps happening each time I breathe. Love comes in."

Balanta stared at Ashia. The needful boy in him felt his mother's touch. His father's pride. And the first wondrous drops inside his being of a new and tender rain.

DAY SIX

Morning was still young and dark. Doves. Cooing like miniature trains. Eloni was swept into a vivid dream. He was naked and walking over a hot bed of coals, arranged in a long line that stretched out beyond the limits of his vision. Of course, his feet were burning, blistering, and he was dying to jump off the coals. Except, on both sides of the coal bed were snarling, vicious wolf-like animals, their eyes fire red, deep, powerful growls bellowing from their chests. They wanted to destroy him.

His feet were burning. He could not jump off. His greater pain though, was that these animals were baring their teeth at him. They were afraid of him. As far as they were concerned, he was the monster. This broke his heart. He wanted to tell them to relax. Reassure them that he was kind, safe, not violent. But they weren't in a listening mood.

Eloni looked down at his burning feet, now flaming up to his knees. He was being devoured in fire that he did not understand. And he was being assaulted by a deadly pack of... not wolves. Adults. Adults who wore labels and badges, and they were all afraid of him. That's why they were baring their teeth.

The vicious pack was calling him names. "Convict!"

"Felon!"

"Thug!"

"Criminal!"

"Scum!"

They were stoning him. Eloni wanted to die. Better than to live with the whole world being so afraid of you that they wanted your death. Eventually the despised oblige the world and die in one private way or another.

"I made a mistake! I was hurting and alone and confused!" Eloni screamed the words, pushed them out on gushes of desperation and anguish. "Why can't you see that? Why *won't* you? I'm not a criminal. I'm a child and I want to stop hurting like this!" His last words were drowned out by the rumbling of the onrushing pack as they descended upon him. Determined to kill the beast.

Eloni put on a sweatshirt, which quickly soaked up his cold sweat. He went outside and started pacing. He kicked a log from the circle around the fire, sending it rolling, nearly breaking his foot in the process.

Eloni shook Maricela by the shoulder, stirring her from sleep. "Don't be so rough," said Maricela, frowning as she turned over. "Wake me tenderly. Pretend you're making bread or something."

"Sorry. Can we talk for a minute?"

Maricela pulled a thick shawl over her shoulders as she rubbed her eyes. "Rough dream, huh?" she asked.

"Like a rodeo," he answered. "Do you ever wonder what the wood and weight of the cross felt like on Jesus' skin? I mean, the splinters digging in, the force bearing down on his back?"

"Nah, Loni, can't say that I have."

"Just wondering. Sometimes I think it must have felt something like what people's ideas of me feel like against my skin."

"You want to go sit down by the water?" Maricela asked. "We can bring some blankets."

"Sure."

They sat there for a long time, then gravitated slowly downward until they lay completely supine. Eloni's head rested on Maricela's belly. She stroked his hair, comforting him silently. He cried dry tears and asked the ocean's roar to move through his soul and cleanse him. The closer Maricela grew to Eloni, the more it felt like slipping into the warm, soft lagoon water when she was near him. It was time. She could feel it.

"Well, if you ever plan to kiss me, you better get on with it," Maricela jabbed. "These lips have an expiration date. I don't want to become dust waiting for you to figure out what your hormones are saying."

Eloni blushed something fierce.

"Are you sure you want to do this?" Maricela asked.

"What, kiss you?"

"That and whatever it brings between us."

"Yeah. I think so. You smell so good. I don't want to talk anymore."

They didn't. Maricela took over, pulling Eloni's face close. Not all the way. The man needs to do some of this, she thought. Eloni kissed her. It was good. More than that.

She liked the way Eloni kissed her: his lips lingered on hers, savoring their time brushed up against a dream. For once, he wasn't rushing. Peace played a perfect note in her heart. They held each other. Maricela sang old songs that sounded like spiritual surrender. A chill moved into her bones. She pulled Eloni closer and let him be a warm, strong breeze all over her body. A gull flew by as a silhouette in the darkness. A bitter salt wove itself over a loom of ocean mist, became a quilt that claimed them both.

Mende, Balanta, and Pikea went spearfishing in the bay to stock up for breakfast. The warm water soothed their skin in the morning coolness. They headed for the coral colonies. Parrot fish crapped this stuff out. That's what Ivory had told Mende, Mende recalled as he brushed his hand over the coarse, tumorous coral. Eloni corrected Ivory that it was actually the white limestone beach sand that had been passed out by the parrot fish after they ate coral. Ivory was convinced that it was the coral itself that was parrot fish waste. How else does the coral end up shaped like dung on top of dung? he had asked.

Mende adjusted his mask and poked around in the colonies, seeing what he could stir up. He liked the silence down here underwater. Muffling of the whole world.

Shellfish scrambled from holes and cracks as Mende's spear tip violated their haunts. Mende felt a jab on the bottom of his right foot. Turning, he saw Pikea behind him, her spear at his foot. She was gesturing over toward Balanta. They swam over. Balanta pointed their attention down to the sandy bay floor, where a large octopus was wrestling with itself, it seemed. They treaded water overhead for a while, watching. Then the ball of tentacles released itself, streamlined its shape, and blurred away. As the sand cloud cleared, they saw what the animal had been occupied with. An intact coconut floated up past them to the surface. Still wondering whether an octopus could manage to crack open a coconut, they returned their focus to catching breakfast.

"You told Balanta *what*?" Maricela exclaimed, her eyes wide.

"It's no big deal," Ashia replied. "He doesn't pardon dishonesty. My stuff was glowing. He couldn't miss it. I just spoke what he already knew." Maricela wanted to take advantage of this moment alone in their cabin. She had the jar on her lap. Her knees rose and fell nervously. The scent from Shonto's morning offering of sweetgrass drifted through the cabin.

"So... show me the scroll," Ashia said. "Let's see what has you so spooked."

Maricela slowly opened the jar, her eyes wide. She was smiling with embarrassment. "Don't laugh. I'm probably making too big a deal. You tell me." She took out the parchment scroll and handed it delicately to Ashia. "Go ahead, open it and look."

Ashia unrolled the scroll, half expecting something freaky to jump out at her. Her gaze fell to the words:

One day a tribe will come. As it is written inside the great mouth of this earth. And they shall die of fire. And begin as light. Their shadows to be released like crows to the sky, as the mountain of water crushes their false seeds. Forever.

Ashia's face grew thoughtful. "Okay..." she whispered in along exhale. "I can see how this would frighten you. And you think those stick figures in the cave have to do with this message? And with us?" Maricela's expression answered.

Ashia took a deep breath and reread the words. *A tribe will come... they shall die of fire... mountain of water...* She straightened her back, set down the scroll on her lap, and tied up her locs with a cloth wrapped around her forehead. "Cela, I... this could mean anything. I don't think we should assume."

"Yeah, but I can't shake the feeling."

"Okay. Let's tell the others. See what they say. Don't know what we could do about it regardless, but maybe it will help you to feel safer."

"I just don't want to ruin the trip," Maricela said.

"Calmaté, amiga," Ashia said, placing her hand on Maricela's shoulder. "We've already come through some wild stuff here. I have a feeling, whatever this is, we'll be alright." *They shall die of fire...* Ashia thought about the words. She felt guilt. For Ivory had come to her mind.

Fresh fish crackled over the fire, its skin curling up and browning to the heat. Eloni basted away with orange peel zest in a honey, pomegranate juice, and jalapeno sauce. His wrist and hand moved with the light fluidity of a symphony conductor. Maricela admired Eloni's passion, grateful that he had something in his life to counterbalance his pain. She knew that Eloni, like all of them, would in the end have to make a choice between passion and pain. Her hope was that he would drown so much in the passion that no room would remain for anything else.

Birdsong flushed the morning sky with a joyful spirit. Sun gathered its momentum and climbed. The early chill departed quickly. Brightness flourished in the trees.

Ivory and Pikea piled their plates with perch bacon, fried potatoes with onion, garlic, and peppers, fruit salad, and cornbread. "You two have the craziest metabolism," Promise said, laughing. "I'd hate to take you on in an eating contest."

"Throw Shonto in there, too," Cielo said. He kept their cups filled with steaming coffee with coconut milk, and ginger-hibiscus tea. They had grown in tune with how much they needed to hydrate themselves in the morning to avoid succumbing to the island's long days of heat.

After breakfast, Cielo washed his face ceremonially in the cool brook water, then took a nude swim in the bay. He thought it gracious that the others always let him have that alone time. They, however, thanked God he didn't ask them to join.

Maricela and Ashia gathered everyone and told them about the jar Maricela had found, and the scroll with the message. They passed the scroll around the fire ring to let everyone read it. Ivory got a look and jumped up, pulling at his afro, which seemed to have expanded by a foot in diameter since they had arrived. He ran around like Chicken Little, forecasting legendary new varieties of doom.

Shonto ran to get a handful of sage and sweetgrass braids, and came back to smudge the entire clearing in purifying smoke.

Lake and Binda looked at each other big eyed and giggled at the drama, albeit nervously.

Promise suggested that Ivory be banned from fire duties, to which Ivory pitched a fit and filed loud verbal grievance against his perceived persecution. Privately, he, too, wondered if the scroll was a mystical foreboding of a fatal regression into fire play, just as he had always feared.

They argued the meaning of the scroll inscription for half an hour, then Binda asked anxiously if anyone had tried to open the security box lately, to see if they could phone Antonia. Ivory said he had tried at least 50 times since yesterday. Ashia reminded them that if Antonia thought they were in any real danger, she would send the boat for them, and that she probably had people keeping an eye on them from an obscure distance with binoculars. Eloni recommended they drill in fire survival, but he was interrupted by the sky itself.

A pained sound lifted in the distance. Thoracic. Suffering. Even from that distance, it shook the air. Everyone jumped except Balanta, whose eyes grew laser-focused. His hand gripped his spear.

"Is that that freaking wolf?" Promise asked.

"That's not a fox. And it's not a goat," said Shonto, his voice flat and concluded. "What we saw... it was supernatural."

"I don't care nothing about all this debating," said Ivory. "All I know is, I'm sleeping in the middle of the cabin tonight, and all ya'll are gonna sleep around me and shield me with your bodies."

"Okay, Braveheart," Maricela chided.

The long, booming howl was plaintive, soaked in lament. Its quality made Binda's heart bleat. Maybe the animal is in pain, she wondered. Her nature tugged at her to go help the animal. Her common sense reminded her of the danger.

Ivory was haunted by the howling. Even more by the mystery of what creature was making that pained sound. His natural habit was to run in the opposite direction from anything that scared him. But this island flipped everything upside down. He was beginning to be drawn toward risk. It was not an attraction he had known since before he lifted the shotgun in his grandmother's bedroom. Its return to him now made him nostalgic for the days when his grandmother and mother both lived in the world. His face burned with emotion, then became a bog of tears. This only angered him. He was beyond childish needs. He was becoming a man, no matter how others saw him. He wiped his nose and eyes as he embraced a conviction that made no sense: He would search for the howling animal. And he would not give up until he had met his fears. It was time to kill the slave.

Eloni convinced everyone to make a return to the dunes. They took off before morning grew any older. And hotter. On the way, they raced up and down rolling hills covered in bunny tail grass and bright clover. They came to a hill covered in a peculiar groundcover vine. Cielo cautioned that they avoid this area, to which Ivory responded that he would not be deterred in his quest to roll down every hill on the island before they left. In the middle of his exclamation, his foot caught against a large rock. Ivory pitched forward despite furiously swinging his arms backward for balance. He landed face-first in the cluster of vines. Within minutes, his entire face puffed into a grotesque shrine of pain. Eloni was back at the poultice again, just as with Balanta's snakebite, patient and attentive. He applied white clay, willow bark, yarrow, and witch hazel. By the next morning, Ivory's face would calm down close to normal. This did not keep the group from greeting him endlessly with joyful chants of "Poison I-vy!"

They made up games as they hiked. In one game, Promise teetered on one foot atop the tip of a jagged boulder. Surrounding the large rock was a circle drawn in the dirt by Eloni. Inside the circle, between the line and the rock, were dozens and dozens of bleached-white seashells. If Promise fell, she would either manage to jump just beyond the circle, avoiding the shells but violating the circle, or she would land on the shells, smashing them. Either way, if she lost her balance and fell she would fail Eloni's test. Test of what, no one was quite sure at this point.

Promise and Mende got the group back to playing the dozens again, cracking on each other all around the circle.

"Your head's so big, you went to a hot air balloon festival and the crowd cleared out to give you space for takeoff."

"Your head's so big, a deep space satellite picked it up and scientists announced a new planet."

"Your head's so big, you wear triple x hats and they still fit you like a thimble on a pumpkin."

"Your head's so big, your people were disappointed to find out you have average intelligence. They coulda swore you must have had two brains."

They moved into the shade of a narrow canyon. Fat black grapes piled over each other on the leafy vines overtaking the canyon walls. The canyon held its own microclimate, cooler than most of the island, though just as sun-dosed. Promise tossed a grape in her mouth and almost fainted with pleasure. The dark juices painted her mouth and overwhelmed her tongue. The grape skin was thick, almost chewy, slivers of it remaining in the folds of her teeth, a succulent and addictive aftertaste.

Promise saw what looked like large globs of candlewax dripping down the trunk of a towering oak. Closer up, she saw that the candlewax was an initiative of gigantic mushrooms, their caps ballooning in a dazzle of shapes. The mushrooms seemed to have infiltrated the oak's bark, raising generations in the dark and damp of the bark's private parts. The assemblage curdled from the height of Promise's waist down to the ground, where it spilled and gathered in heaps.

Eloni knelt and plucked one of the mushrooms loose from its mooring. "You have to be careful to distinguish the poison ones from the edible ones," he said. With a gleam in his eye he pronounced this variety fit for supper. "I can tell by the coloring," he added, without clarifying what he meant. He nibbled from the tan rubbery cap, which was the size of his palm. "Yes. Clearly a prize winner. This should make good soup."

When they got to the dunes, the brilliant cream gypsum had already shed its morning cool. The lower dunes were covered in succulents flowering in pastel yellows, blues, and pinks. Higher up, the sand was bare and unadulterated. Wind washed the dune contours continuously, covering every footprint soon after it had been left.

Mende observed that clouds were gathering in the distance, and for the first time, the clouds were darker, heavier.

"We need to keep an eye on that," Ivory said. "We don't need no biblical flood to catch us while we're up here on Mt. Sinai. We either need to build an ark right quick, or maybe we should head for camp. Last I checked, no one here is named Noah."

"Okay, Ivory," Promise said. "You're being extra again. Those clouds are so far away, you can barely see them. And even if it did rain for once, is that so bad? How do you think all these plants are growing like crazy around here?"

"I wish it would rain," Lake said.

"Why?" Promise asked.

"I Love the sound it makes at night on rooftops. At least corrugated ones. Sounds like a whole tribe drumming."

"Me, too," said Binda. For her, the sound of rain against corrugated tin was a steel drumbeat. A sound of Old Ones calling for a gathering. It had always called her to sleep.

"If I see any more corrugated tin, I'll choke," Shonto said.

"You guys, stop worrying about the clouds," Eloni said. "They may bring rain, but that's the only way sky can feed the earth. That's what clouds are for, remember? If the sky wants to cry, it is good to let it. A heavy sky only weighs everything down."

"Hey, Loni," Binda asked, "why do you like being on the dunes so much?"

"Don't know. It's a feeling. When I put my foot down and take a step, the sand moves. The earth gives way. I can feel my power." Eloni thought about the self-hatred he struggled so hard to bury each day, and wondered how many generations before him had suffered the same self-allergic reaction. Clouds. Sky. Eventual sunshine. His way of reminding himself of the possibility that one day he could Love himself.

They finally made their way up to the highest ridge of dunes. As they sat on the dune peak, letting the wind cool their faces, the earth beneath them suddenly ruffled, like a horse shaking off flies. Ruffling turned to a rippling, and a sound of muffled thunder came from the land. Lake, being the smallest, was the first to be dislodged into flight. Her body bounced several inches into the air. She landed forward, on her face, then began tumbling down the dune.

Binda tried to stand up when she felt the sand sifting itself. This caused her to wobble and pitch on spaghetti legs before she, too, was sprawled out and tumbling.

An avalanche of humans and sand dropped toward the sea under a sky remarkably absent of birds and bereft of the slightest sound other than screams. They were flung into a depression between two dunes. The earth opened up, caustic and hot, revealing giant ores that seemed to pulse and throb with pressure. Binda's momentum carried her over the edge of the new crevasse. She managed to grip the sand enough to keep from falling in. Eloni and Pikea crawled to her frantically, each grabbing one of her wrists. They pulled her up onto the sand and pulled themselves away from the deep yawn in the dune.

"Earthquake!" they yelled, as if by calling it by its name, it would relent and go away. It did not.

"Keep flat on your stomachs!" Balanta yelled. Sand bounced into their faces and around their bodies as though it were being snapped into the air from a trampoline. Ivory pulled into a fetal position and sucked his thumb. When he saw Promise notice him, he weakly faked a laugh as though his thumb sucking was just a joke to relieve tension. Promise crawled close to Ivory and held his hand.

Binda noticed that the usual birdsong was still completely absent from the sky. Then, slowly, she noticed the air begin to clear of sand clouds, and bodies appear around her. The growling, squeaking of the sand faded. When the earth trembling stopped, they sat for a moment staring at each other. Then, following Ivory's lead, they raced down the dunes and back toward camp, wondering what madness was coming next.

They ended up retreating to the lagoon. Its warm womb of calming water and walls of trees and vegetation made them feel safer.

"Well, at least we can say we were all there for the thunder in the earth," Shonto said. "That's what we're calling it. *Thunder in the earth*. Once we tell the story seven times that makes it a legend. Once it's a legend, it means we survived to tell it." They told the story seven times in seven minutes.

On the way from the lagoon back to camp for lunch, they felt the sun grow instantly eclipsed. The darkness vanished just as suddenly, breathing sunlight down onto the group. Ashia shuddered. Just ahead, they passed under a towering eucalyptus. Something large above rustled the tree's thickly leafed crown, which shook at the force, shedding flocks of leaves. As they stared up at the tree's crown, its branches parted. An umber figure emerged and opened its wings, cloaking the sky again in darkness. Everyone fell to the ground in fear, covering their heads. A great rushing sound roared over them.

"Did any of you see what that was?" Promise asked, looking up at the eucalyptus crown.

"Weird," Ashia said. "I saw it. But I didn't see it. Not clearly. Its form was blurry."

"Me, too," Lake said. "I feel sleepy all of a sudden."

Balanta and Eloni were standing already, up against the tree's trunk, peering into its foliage. "I think I see a nest up there," Balanta said.

"*If* that *was* a bird," Mende said, "It was a mutant."

"I told y'all I saw a pterodactyl!" Ivory shouted.

"Condor," Ashia said. "I'm telling you."

"Who's going to climb this tree and check out what's in the nest?" Mende said. "This thing keeps buzzing us, playing with us all week. We need to know what we're dealing with."

Promise cracked up. "So, your bright idea is to climb up to the nest? Just in time for it to come back and have you for a snack?"

After a quick silence, Eloni said, "I'll do it. I used to climb trees all the time. Just make sure you catch me if I fall."

"Riiight…" Promise said.

"Loni…" Maricela said. The look in her eyes was all she needed to convey her concern. Eloni looked back at her, assuring. She wasn't having it. She folded her arms over her chest in silent protest. Eloni was already stretching for the climb.

"At least pile together some leaves or something," Eloni said, "so if I fall, I can land without breaking every bone." Eloni took off his shoes and rubbed dirt on his hands.

"Don't you want your shoes on?" Promise asked.

"I get a better feel this way," Eloni said. "Trust me."

Like a jumping spider, Eloni was up to the first set of branches in a single burst. The large eucalyptus gave up some of its powdery white bark each time Eloni dug a foot in and sprang upward. Soon, he was at the nest. "You all keeping lookout?" he yelled down. He scanned the sky behind him before pulling himself up high enough to look down into the nest. Gigantic. The size of a king bed. And empty. Not even a scattering of feathers, which spooked him. "Nothing up here!" he yelled.

He climbed back down quickly, scraping the insides of his legs until they were abraded skin and blood.

"Feel better now?" Maricela said, sarcastically. "What were you expecting to find? A printed sign identifying the species?"

"Loni," Shonto said. "I didn't know you were a chimpanzee. That tree has skin like baby powder. How'd you even get a grip?"

"We used to climb trees all day long on Moloka'i," Eloni said, huffing for breath. "Sometimes for the fruit. Mostly just to get up in the sky. Makes for strong feet. And keeps you from suffocating."

"Suffocating?" Shonto asked.

"Yeah," Eloni responded. "Sometimes down on earth, dealing with people, you just can't breathe. Your *Mana*, your power, is good up there."

They argued on the way back to camp about what the flying creature was, not even sure if it was a bird. "I'm telling you," Ashia said. "That was a condor."

"Not a condor," Shonto said flatly. "Thunderbird."

"What's a thunderbird?" Ivory asked, still cowering on the ground.

"It's a good sign. That's what it is. A creature of legend."

"Urban legend?" Maricela asked.

"Funny. No," Shonto said. "Our people's legend. For us, legends aren't fairy tales. They are real. We better be on alert. Someone is about to get swooped up into the sky and taken." Shonto's expression was calm.

"And that's a good thing?" Promise asked.

"Not abducted," Shonto said. "Changed. Big difference."

"We call it *Tuli*, bro," Eloni said. "Our legendary bird."

"Y'all can call it what you want," Ivory said. "I'm calling it, Get our butts back to the cabins and pray."

As they ate lobster tacos with plum sauce, and washed it down with Mende's special lemonade, they looked forward to that night's fire talk. Ashia was eager to dance the day's anxieties out of her system.

"I just hope the talk is lighthearted and not all deep and stuff," Pikea said.

"Pikea's going dark again!" Ivory warned.

Eloni rolled his eyes at Pikea's comment.

"Immune response!" Ivory shouted.

"What are you squeaking about?" Eloni snapped.

Ivory lowered his volume in reaction to Eloni's tone. "Remember what Cielo said? Blood flowing toward a wound?"

"Why are you acting so crispy?" Maricela said, intervening, fearing a repeat of Eloni's earlier violence. "You yourself have ranted about your stuff plenty of times. You have that privilege, but no one else does?"

"I just get agitated," Eloni said.

"You're like eating burnt toast, sometimes," Maricela replied. "You need to tear that crust off."

"I need to get out of here," Eloni huffed.

Maricela frowned. "Okay, walk with me, brother," she said, grabbing Eloni's upper arm. "We need to powwow. Cause you're tripping like you think somebody's gonna pay you for it."

They walked up the beach. The limestone sand was cool even in the heat. Two large sea turtles were sunning just beyond the lick of the tide. They barely turned their heads to acknowledge the two-legged ones. Sand grains on the turtles' faces sparkled. Maricela and Eloni sat beneath a banana tree awning. Maricela dug her bare feet into the coolness of the sand beneath the surface.

"Blow," she said.

"What?"

"You have so much steam built up in you, then go ahead. Blow."

Eloni was silent. Then silent some more. Maricela knew the struggle of bringing up something from the deep, from the place that hurt the worst. It took massive courage. And an exhaustion from long suffering. She remained quiet. A squabble of birds bobbed by on the surf, just off from shore.

"Cela?" Eloni said, his voice high and cracking. "Would you... feel any differently about me if you realized I was a lie?"

Maricela looked tenderly into Eloni's face. She could see the boy in him clearer than ever. She brought her arm up around his shoulders and pulled him close. "Speak it, Loni," she said softly. "Put it on the wind."

She felt his strong body hitch. Jerk. Tighten. Spill. Tears. Eloni cried so hard, his wail chased the large turtles into the sea. Maricela was caught off guard. Then thankful. "There you go..." she whispered. "There you go..."

Eloni emptied himself of his saltwater. When he was nothing but a desert inside, he gathered his grains and spoke them. "I was five. She. Wasn't supposed to even be there. I didn't know. No one stopped her. Worse thing was, my family made me call her *tuafafine*. *Sister*. She was 17. I shouldn't have... smiled at her. Now. Cielo. Those... poses. I can't. See that. She made me bend like that.

The last sentence brought up Eloni's shame in a volcanic explosion, putrid shale from his core, molten and spewing. Its boiling rosary met the cold ocean of Eloni's male identity, cracked, exploded, blackened to crust instantly. Great plumes of steam rose from Eloni's skin. He sizzled. Like all volcanic islands, Eloni's eruption had expanded his territory. Maricela held her arms around his entire shoreline. She was inside his reef now. Her heart stopped grasping. She had gathered enough of him. Only now, in his utter weakness, could she feel his power.

The group fell into a bout of medicine talk. Pikea led the way. "Only people who feel sorry for you say things like, 'I'm so proud of you for coming through what you did.' Don't be proud of me for surviving. Rats can do that. I'd rather have your understanding, know what I mean? That way you won't keep imagining me, cause when people imagine you, in sympathy and condescension, the outcome is never gonna be good."

"Pain is portable," Shonto said. "You can take it with you anywhere. Not that that's a good thing."

"Is dysfunction a virus?" Promise asked. "Can you catch it? Or pass it on to your children?"

"Parents, you Love and admire them too much," Cielo added. "Even the bad ones. So much awe. You can never be yourself all the way, share everything. Because you care too much about pleasing them. Making them proud. You don't want to let them down. Nah, friends are for daring. Parents are for performing."

Ivory jumped in. "You know how you're walking along a sidewalk and you come up on a section or two that are a darker color? You know work's been done. I feel like people can see that in me. That my color, my aura, is different than most people. That work's been done. Except it's not repair work. It's disassembly work."

"When you grow up apart from your parents, do you become less like them, or more?" Pikea asked.

Ashia shared some philosophy. "Some people are so intimate with the world, care so much... that they end up bursting like unpicked cherries in summer heat."

Cielo went into the woods to walk off his lunch. A lush rain of jacaranda petals fell on his face as he moved through their neighborhood, then on to a cul-de-sac of silk trees. He leaned in to study an ant train moving on the bark of one of the trees. Cielo reflected on the civility of ants. A chemically induced social order. *Not much in the way of a moral code,* he surmised. *But brilliant, chemically speaking.* He continued chewing a sprig of willow and moved on, his mind already drifted to the string instrument philosophies of Robert Johnson, Hendrix, and Santana. His belly growled, intoxicated with hunger.

Cielo spotted and followed the three-legged deer as it moved with surprising grace along a stream bank. The deer nibbled often, looking back at the human stalking it. They came to a washed-away embankment crowded with tree roots hustling for survival. The deer hopped the embankment, and looked back at Cielo as if urging him to follow. Cielo followed, climbing the slick wall of mud and roots. Up top, the deer had lain down under the shade of a sweetgum bush. A gurgle of water percolated nearby. Cielo knelt and sipped from the brook. A small crustacean scampered over a stone at the bottom. He watched his reflection grow clear as the water calmed. The ripples on his reflected face diminished. For the first time, he noticed something in his appearance: a man. "How about that," he said softly. Then, his face changed. He saw an old man looking back. His father? Abuelo? Another change. Now, the face of a boy. The reflection moved through a progression: Incan priest. Aztec warrior. Troubled soul on the streets. A serene monk at home even without shelter.

He saw something else in the reflection. A trail of fine dust moved upward into the sky in a pronounced column. Upward. *Could be pollen. Or detritus.* He looked over at the deer, who was licking its legs and chewing sweetgum leaves. The deer's coat shone. It occurred to Cielo that the island seemed to purify itself. Any toxicity appeared to be swallowed, transformed, released. The island was a perfect compost. *A self-healing organism.*

The ladies soaked in the warmth of the lagoon. As of morning, they were now all in their moon times.

Pikea was enjoying Lake and Binda's peaceful energy. Her cramping had been particularly sharp during the dune hike. "This lagoon is *tapu,*" she said. "Sacred. I can feel the mineral water take the pain away from my body."

"Me, too," Lake said.

"I remember," Pikea said, "A long time ago... this *Kaumtua,* an elder, she told me when it's your cycle time, the whole universe is trying to come through. Your ancestors are knocking at the door, wanting another shot.

239

That's your cramps. Then, when they give up and go, they leave an offering, as if to say, see you again in 28 days. That offering is your flow."

"I like that," Binda said. "Makes it seem worth all the trouble."

"Maybe some of it," Lake said. They broke into laughter, and savored their solitude in the healing waters. Old pain came out in the security of the moment. Maricela shared something difficult. Binda offered the perfect words.

Maricela hugged Binda tightly, retrieving something lost and precious. Binda noticed that Maricela's scent was honeysuckle. She wondered if Maricela had been writing more Love stories in her journal. "Binda, you give such amazing hugs," Maricela said. "It makes you feel all oozy."

"Let me get some," Pikea said, embracing Binda, who gave back mutually.

"Pikea, when you hugged me, you smelled like anise seed," Binda shared softly.

"Yeah? That's good, right?"

"Yeah. Maybe you are coming into a healing season. Maybe... something sweet is being planted in you."

Ivory thought he heard a chirping coming from one of the cabins. When he got closer, it sounded more like clattering. Ivory stepped into the cabin, and noticed something on the floor. The jacaranda pods from Promise's waist chain were scattered about. "What the?" Ivory said. Hurt rose in a flash. He kicked one of the pods, sending it flying, and ran out of the cabin.

Out by the fire, Eloni was talking about how they might want to stay closer together, considering how much weird stuff had been happening on the island.

"Stop slurping my juice!" Ivory demanded.

"What are you prattling on about now?" Eloni asked.

"Every time I come up with a great idea, you make like it was your idea. Stop slurping my juice!"

Ivory's voice screeched like a piano left outside in a rainforest, making it hard for Eloni to take him too seriously. "Let me get this straight," Eloni asked. "You saying I'm stepping on your toes, little brother? I'm sorry. I don't mean to. Just ratifying, I guess. I'll leave your ideas alone, promise." Eloni muttered under his breath as he walked on: *Stop slurping my juice. Wow...*

"What's Ivory pitching a fit about?" Maricela asked as she came over from the garden. "He's stewing bigtime."

"I have no idea," Eloni said. "And I'm staying calm. Don't worry."

Ivory grabbed Mende's djembe drum and pounded until his palms grew past raw to blistered. Until blood broke through, streaking the drumhead in dark red bolts of lightning.

"What's your ailment, Ivory?" asked Promise. "You've been beating the devil out of that drum."

"My drum all right, man?" asked Mende. "Sounded violent."

Promise saw pain in Ivory's eyes. "Come on," she said. "Let's go over here for a minute. They went over by Cielo's hammock and sat on the sand. Promise waited for Ivory to spill.

Ivory chewed the inside of his lips. His fingernails were deeply embedded into his palms. "Why'd you do that to the waist necklace I made you?" he asked.

"Do what?" Promise asked. "I don't know what you're talking about."

"If you didn't want it, you didn't have to break it apart like that. I put a lot of care into making it."

"Ivory, stop doing your Shakespeare tragedy thing on me and co-mmu-ni-cate." Promise was heated.

"I just went in your cabin and found the waist chain broken apart all over the floor."

"You did? Man... Ivory, I liked that waist chain. I've only been wearing it *every* time we dance. Don't act like you don't notice. So why would I break it apart? Did it ever occur to you that it could have happened by accident? I could have stepped on it half-asleep this morning. Or one of the others could have."

Ivory remained quiet. "What's your real grievance?" Promise asked. "Dig for it. I know it's somewhere in there."

"Sorry, P." Ivory said, sighing. "I don't know what my place is around here. In the social order. It's making me antsy."

"Don't have a low blood sugar fit about it," Promise cautioned. "Figure it out. Stop squirting adrenaline."

"That's your compassionate response?"

"Ivory, I don't have time for wallowers. Know what I mean? I used to do that to myself, like Winnie the Pooh's friend Eeyore. Always choosing to stay in the mud, pitying myself. I look back on it now, and man, I must have wore people out. I drain myself right quick now anytime I fall back into that. The only social circle that matters is the circle of your truth. Hang out there and it's all good. Even when it's bad."

Promise saw Ivory's confusion, so she pressed her point. "I always feel my past embedded on my forehead, okay? A scarlet letter A for *Abnormal*. No matter how hard I scrub my face at night or in the morning, I can't get that scarlet letter off. So, early on, I learned to lie by trying to be seen as normal. Lied about my parents. Lied about my money situation. Lied about my relationships. Just trying to get inside the circle, you know? That circle where the normal ones hang out. Prime territory. VIP space. Eventually, I started to figure out that lying doesn't get you closer to the inside of the circle. It just gets you isolated in your own circle with others who are also lying because of their own pain. Then, even they can't stand being around your lying. Your circle ends up being a circle of one."

"Okay." Ivory looked hurt, but tuned in. "Then, can you explain how you learned to get stronger? More secure?"

"I got stronger by getting stronger. You with me? I practiced strength. That's the only way to change, brother. Practice. Nothing sexy about it. But it works. Here to testify."

Ivory's breathing slowed. He wiped his eyes, scratched his chin, and picked up Mende's drum. This time, he touched the drumhead gently, apologizing.

"Hey, Ivory," Promise added. "Don't be so insecure. It's suffocating. Just one example. You look at me like you're a cannibal, Ivory," Promise said. "Knock it off."

"I'm sorry. I don't mean to make you uncomfortable."

"Stop stalking people. Desperation smells bad. Stalkers don't make friends. If you would just be you, all that you truly need would come to you. That's how it's working for me. But first, you gotta get to the root. Find out what put that insecurity in there. Then go get it out of you." They hugged. Promise stood and pulled down on her blouse. "Peace, brother. Peace," she said as she began to walk away.

"Hey, Promise?" Ivory said as Promise turned back around. "I write my own songs."

"Yeah? Let me hear one," said Promise.

"I haven't written any yet."

"Then what are you talking about, 'you write your own songs?'"

"I haven't released a song yet that I didn't write. So, I can legitimately say that I write my own songs."

"Boyyy… how much time do you even spend on this planet?"

Lake moved through the oaks, pines, and aspens easily, enjoying her pace. She wanted to be alone with the spirit of the woods. Flower blossoms pooled with water in her wake. A tenderness was rising in Lake. She was going to miss this place. As she had grieved so many places. Leaving and arriving. The two movements had become a long, tedious blurring for her, silos of confusion, not knowing what to feel, for how long, or what to do with the sorrow and joy. One thing was clear: she missed her culture. More than specific people, she ached for the spirit her people occupied. Ritualized. Turned from wild plants into woven baskets of meaning and sacredness. The places she was assigned to since then seemed by law to be soulless. Without any tribal memory. This had always been the hardest part for Lake. Being expected to bond with soulless places, and the hollow people who existed there. Hollow not because they were born hollow, but because they had long ago bonded with hollowness. This fact always made Lake think of the Great Killing. Not of buffalo. Of her people. The endless trails of tears. The programmatic placements in which people had to choose: *Do I accept this concentrated abandonment they call a reservation? Do I bond with hollowness? With a culture of no true memories*? Lake could feel moisture beneath her feet. So she stopped this thinking. Her whole life she had feared what would happen to the world if she let her feelings go all the way. Ivory, back on the dunes, had mentioned a biblical flood. What Lake felt inside seemed like a more unimaginable flood.

A shadow passed over, stealing warmth for a moment before returning it. She heard a swooping, and the shadow dropped to earth. A large prey bird was on the ground, about 20 steps ahead of her on the path. Wow, that's one big bird, she thought, her heart fluttering.

She tiptoed forward, not wanting to alarm the bird, but curious as to its strange flapping and tumbling. As she came closer, she saw three, four wings. She realized two birds were balled up together. A light bulb went on. *Lake, that's not a bird in distress. It's two birds. Mating.*

Reality slowed into its magical trot as she filled with adrenaline. *Two hawks are mating right in front of me. Does that even happen? Don't they feel exposed with me right here*? As the large birds fulfilled their primal drive in a flurry of wings and dust, it occurred to Lake: *As long as a thing feels safe, even its most intimate nature will be revealed.*

"Let's go back to the tree that rains." Pikea said to Shonto. She was speaking quietly. "I want to feel that on my face again."

Shonto put down his spear and followed. They lay under the tree for a long while, wondering how no one else had found this magical tree yet. Pikea and Shonto could not know that the island was full of them, and that those magical trees would touch their lives fatefully.

"I'm kind of disappointed I'm not feeling some kind of big change at this point," Pikea said.

"Did you think we were all going to be magically healed all of a sudden here?" Shonto replied.

"That's what I was hoping for. It's so exhausting carrying this stuff around. I wanted us to leave here... and be new back in the world."

"I don't think that healing is supposed to happen instantly," Shonto said. "Pain is like mist in a valley. With the rising sun, it burns off eventually. But I get the feeling that with pain, *eventually* is over a lifetime."

Pikea looked up into the canopy, letting the mist cool her face. "I don't know..." she said. "Once you fold a piece of paper, it's weaker at that point, easier to fold again. Is it like that with trauma? Once you're damaged, is it easier to get damaged again?"

"I choose to think of it differently," Shonto said. "Like with a broken bone. Once it heals, it's often stronger at that location than it was before."

"So, it's better to break than to fold?"

"I wouldn't say that. More like, whatever we survive becomes minerals to build our power, if we use it right."

"Our families seem to break like brittle old beer bottles left over in the ashes after the fire," Pikea said.

"Maybe any family would break if it were left in the same fire too long. Anyway," Shonto said, "as long as you're learning something about yourself as you go, that's what matters. Don't sell that short. It's kind of a big deal to figure out who you are."

Shonto turned on his side toward Pikea. "*Hongi* with me," he said, barely containing laughter. "Let's exchange some sweet *ha*."

"Man..." Pikea warned, balling her fist, "you better roll back over or we'll exchange something, all right. And it won't be sweet *ha*."

Afternoon matured. Mende and Ivory went on another mini-quest, this time armed with two spears each. In reality, they didn't stray far from the center of the great meadow, where they could see anything coming at them from a good distance, on the ground or from the sky. Most of the others had come back to camp and were relaxing or napping.

"Mende fell in the cactus patch!" Ivory yelled as he ran into camp. "Boy is in some kind of pain," he gasped, catching his breath. "How do I say this? His backside is a pincushion." Balanta and Eloni got up to go get Mende. When they reached him, he was limping toward camp, his face contorted.

"Why did Ivory have to tell the world?" Mende complained as he saw his brother and Eloni. "This is embarrassing." They lifted Mende, one on each side, and headed back to camp. Inside the cabin, Eloni tended to Mende's backside, which was punctured deeply, the skin seeping blood. Ashia and Binda offered to help, to which Mende raised the roof in protest. "Don't you dare come in here!" he pleaded. Mende's mood plunged. He knew his booty would be the target of jokes the rest of the time on the island, and that his legend would likely travel beyond the island. Not quite the reputation he had in mind.

Maricela lit a small Tahitian vanilla-scented candle for her patron saint, Teresa of Ávila. Placing it in the dry sand just up from the tidal plain, she kneeled and opened up her journal. In it, she had listed the names of those who had left her life like unfeeling tendrils of smoke snaking up into sky. Pursing her lips and clearing her throat, she spoke to her saint. "Santa Teresa, I can feel you watching over me. Thank you for staying with me here on this island. For giving me strength. Keeping me in a peaceful place.

"I need to ask a favor of you, Santa mia. I pray you will show me the right way to say goodbye to these people. You know I don't do separation well. Please, Santa mia, I pray you will help me to not be hurtful. Not be distant. I want to leave here with people feeling warm about me. I want to be that ripple in the water that people wish would return. Please, Santa mia. Won't you bless me with the strength to do this... Gracefully? Yes, Santa mia. That's what I pray. I pray for Grace. Amen."

The Amen didn't do it for her. A scotch broom bush poured its fragrance around her. Maricela remembered a scent like this. Nostalgia was forcing its way into her. Boarding school emotions. Absent-birthday party emotions. *Manos stuff.*

Maricela ducked through bangs of vines, and stepped into a small open space carpeted in a deep, rich-colored moss. It smelled sweetly acrid. The enclosure was nearly sheltered from the sky by a ring of willows, their branches weeping and swaying. Any space like this felt like a sanctuary to Maricela. *Cathedral*. She knelt on the moss and crossed herself. *Don't know where I am going. Please, Santa Teresa, lead me there*. Archives of emotion suddenly fell from their ordered places inside of Maricela. She could not stop them.

She placed her hands on the moss, her forehead on her hands. "Oh, Madre, take me to the sanctuary... Let me smell the baking bread. Let me taste clay." Her eyes quickly drowned. Tears found grass blades, then the ground. Her breath heaved and hitched. Maricela opened. Words came out. Crying. Singing mournfully. Wailing. *"Ayayayay Aay... men. Aay... men. Aay... men.* Deliver us, oh Solicitous Silence, deliver us this day from the storm descended upon us. Lift us up into your clouds of Grace. Oh Lord, you have been our Shepherd. We are lost on the hillside, and the storm has already taken us. Find us. Shelter us. Be our haven. We are so thirsty. Please... rain. So empty. Please, fill us. Sweep us out to sea. Let us drown in the deep water. Let us sink to the floor. Bury us there. Bring us up as something new. Bring us to the surface. Let us taste the salt air with new tongues. We do not wish for these eyes any longer. Let us see You for the first time. Let us see ourselves the way You see us every time. Take our skins. Leave them on the rocks to dry up and blow away. Oh, Precious Love among us, weave us. Make us nightingales. Pour song down our throats. Place us in the choir of songbirds. Shower us in solitude. We want your breath as our atmosphere. Levitate us from this suffering. Burn our belongings. Make us homeless. Make us roam this... foreboding land, until our feet bleed. Sweep us onto the cross. Please, God. Take us to Paradise. We don't want this earth. We want the world of Light. Seal our wounds. Make us new. Oh, God. You know our hearts. Make us new. Make us. New."

Maricela's voice drowned in tears. She was the sound of water falling over roses. Her hair had become black moss in the tear-fall, wet and dripping. She stayed, kneeling on the ground, until shadows stretched into totem poles shaped with effigies of the charismatic Unknown.

Ivory headed out while everyone else was at the lagoon or in the meadow. He knew they would try to stop him. He also knew he might be endangering his life. But his old spirit of extreme self-preservation had gone quiet. A new spirit had become his roaring inner voice: recklessness.

He followed the direction of the earlier howling through the woods until the land began to rise into gentle hills covered more sparsely in maples and willows. His breath began to deepen as he felt the earth tilt into a steeper slope. Climbing over boulders, Ivory stayed in his self-hypnosis: *"I walk through the valley..."* He knew that if he lost his mental configuration he might also lose his composure. "No rabbiting tonight. Who put that rap on rabbits, anyways? I'm sure they aren't more cowardly than other animals. Can't shake a reputation once it falls on you." Ivory's mind ran with the rabbits for a while, until he realized he was climbing Jade Mountain.

Ivory's legs and lungs burned as he hopped up on a large boulder, finally cresting a lower peak within the mountain's range. From here, the lagoon looked more like a puddle, and the valley beyond stretched out into the dust haze.

He heard panting down on the other side of a nearby jumble of sizeable rocks. *"Walk through the valley..."* Sweat drenched his shirt, breeze cooling his skin. Jumping down, he crouched, slowly approaching the panting.

"I better pick up a stick or something."

He found a thick dry branch, not too long but sturdy.

"Is this going to be one of those *last word* moments?" he wondered aloud. The animal was lying on its side, shaded from the baking sun by the rock cropping. It was heaving, rib cage rising and falling laboriously.

"Is that a wolf? I can't believe how big that thing is. *Walk through the valley...*"

Adrenaline flooded his muscles, his sweat grew cold. "Am I about to die?" His impulse was to poke the beast with his stick, but that would have put his hand in range of being chowed down. He bent lower to the ground, looked closer. The animal's eyes were teary, its tongue hanging slightly from its mouth.

"Is this thing about to die?"

Everything in him said, *run*. Except for his heart. It said, *care*. Ivory chose to care. He didn't have the first idea as to what that meant, but he was already walking a chosen road.

Hawks spiraled overhead. Surely waiting.

"Water. I should give it some water." He found a wide, flat volcanic rock and spent several minutes grinding a shallow bowl into it with a smaller, harder rock. He poured out half of the water from his gourd into the bowl.

The animal lifted its head slightly, looking at Ivory with a stark vulnerability. Ivory noticed its tail. Patches of fur missing.

"Now, how do I get this close enough to him without getting bit?" It took about 15 of the scariest minutes of his life, but Ivory slid the rock and water inch by inch toward this unbelievable creature. Leaning backward toward safety, one hand nudging the rock, one hand gripping the stick so tightly sweat poured through his fingers. Finally, he reached a point where fear wasn't going to let him push the rock any closer. *"Yea though I walk through the valley of the shadow of death, I shall fear no evil..."* He took a step back, pulled some fish jerky out of his pack and tossed it down by the rock bowl. Then his senses returned.

"Outta here." Ivory ran down the mountain at record speed, falling twice along the way. He heard flute music, seemingly coming from precisely the location of the animal. Ivory wondered about tricksters. And just how far they were capable of going.

Promise awakes from her nap as a tiger, with a primal hunger that makes her second guess if she ate at all yesterday. Cranberry sauce on her arm, sticky like a candy apple. She licks it. It is not cranberry sauce. It is blood. Confused, and still drowsy, she tries to look back into her sleep for a clue. Vaguely, in a veiled image, she recalls flailing while asleep. But why? As her mind clears, she remembers what day it is. The feelings return, fortified and furious. An abject depression at the thought of leaving the island and returning to the emotional habit of her life. A habit so ritualized and rote, it has burrowed into her like a rabid mole, digging wide-eyed and snarling, digging for her heart, dislodging clods of her earth as it descends, past her polished veneer of joy, down further, past her stubborn smile, her abrogated peace, her peace so revoked and retracted it has become a dried umbilicus too deep inside to reach. Promise feels something that is *not allowed* surface up through the mole tunnel, sniffing its way for the open prairie that is her secret. Shuraa Solomon comes back. *Mom, pleeease... go away. Pleeease... come back. Never leave. Don't do this to me.* It is done to her. Promise opens her mouth. A silent terrorized heartbeat comes out. Then a scream that stains the memory of everyone there that day. A scream that bleeds and does not end. It is a Thursday. And Promise so much more than cries.

Binda remembers. She remembers her mother and grandmothers. She remembers Alkina (moon), Ekala (lake), and Nerida (flower), all standing witness around her, their maternal faces looking down at her as though they are trees. They *are* trees, and she is on her back looking up into their leafing vitality. She is barren and will never grow such leaves. That is what she is telling herself. But they won't let her persist in such self-destructive thinking. They boil her brain in an enormous vat of something tribal. Something that steams and hisses and pops and coils. They boil her brain and all the nerves evolved there in the petri dish that is her mind. All those nerves disintegrate. No more pathways for false thoughts foraged into being by sickened squirrels. Only a nothingness that hums. And then... only when the innards of her skull are cremated to emptiness, do Alkina, Ekala, and Nerida reach down with their enduring branches and lift up Binda into their bosomed boughs. Only then, from that great height, does Binda begin to sense her skull spark and fill with primordial light, with pristine conceptions, unrefracted, unpolluted, as though filtered through glaciers galaxies thick. Only then does Binda look down to the vat in which her brain was boiled. She sees the boiling element, still simmering in the vat. She sees Love.

"You feel that you and Balanta will keep going after this?" Mende asked Ashia. They were catching up over by the brook while Balanta rested his still swollen ankle and weakened body.

"Putting me on the spot with the man's brother?" Ashia chided. "I don't know, Mende. I have my desires. I've learned not to put my stock in them. Besides, you boys have your moods. Don't know if I can endure Balanta's intensity beyond a week," she joked. To herself, she thought, *I would take a lifetime*. She felt an eclipse pool out over her heart. "I think I'm going dark, as Ivory likes to put it." She smiled, but was concerned.

Mende put as much confection into his voice as he could, urging Ashia to reconsider. "Balanta's not common. I know you see that."

"Yeah. I see a lot."

"You know, I had bones with you earlier," Mende said.

"Bones?"

"Bones to pick. Then I had to reckon. I was just insecure about you taking Balanta away from me. It's always been just him and me."

"I can't believe there haven't been others. Females, I mean."

"You'd be surprised. Not that they haven't tried him. He's just usually not to be tried. My brother is..."

"Complex?"

"Back in the village they used to say he carried light. I think they meant that he was born to be a leader."

"That kind of weight can contort a person," Ashia said.

"Balanta stayed the same shape. He just hardened. He doesn't know this, but I've seen some of what runs through him. It's whole worlds of spirit."

"What do you mean?"

"He says I write letters to ghosts. I know he's told you. I'm not sure what's coming out of my mouth when that happens in my sleep, but I know what I'm experiencing."

"What's that?" Ashia's body language had relaxed.

"The masses. All the souls that have come to have counsel with Balanta. They come from all over and they are desperate to pour out their pain at his feet. They depend on him to make their lives better. I'm there, seeing it all. It takes place in the desert. Sometimes in the woods. Always masses of souls. And Balanta, every time, he stands there, listening to every single soul. Receiving their generations of pain. Their flood of fear. And he eats it. Balanta thinks I'm communicating with ghosts, of our family maybe. He's afraid that I'm missing them too much. That's not what it is. I'm begging the masses to let my brother rest. I know he can only take so much. One day, it might be too much. Even for one who carries light."

Balanta sucked a nutmeg seed, which soothed his throat as a natural lozenge. He drank bowls-full of spring water, hydrating and flushing his system devotedly. By late afternoon, he was feeling more like his usual self. He found Eloni, down by the ocean, skipping stones. Feathers from a seabird were scattered along the sand. *Something had a bad night*, Balanta thought. Grebes and egrets stood in formation, facing the bowing sun.

"Hey man," Balanta said. "You went to the wall for me."

"You did the same up on the cliff," Eloni said. "That would have been a long fall."

Balanta picked up some stones and started skipping them. He and Eloni spent the moment letting the ocean entertain them with its liquid gravity and its infinite appetite for swallowing things whole and final.

Something dorsal lifted from the water and cut the waves not 20 feet from them. Eloni crouched into his *haka*, his Maori war dance. His feet spread wide, more than shoulder width, his thighs crouched parallel with the ground, spine postured straight up like a spear on its way to pierce the heart of sky. Balanta was impressed with the way Eloni's spirit changed. Eloni genuinely was inhabited by the *haka*. He didn't exude ego or competitiveness. Just pure, raw, warrior light.

A pelican skirted over the water, impossibly close for not touching it. "Dude's just showing off," Eloni said, breaking his stance and trance. "Hey. We're 18 now. I've been thinking more about my journey ahead. Are you going to stay in the system, so you can get those resources? I don't like feeling registered-up like that. I want my freedom. But everyone tells me I'm crazy if I age out."

"I don't know," Balanta said. "I just wish they wouldn't keep trying to erase me and Mende's family," Balanta said. That's not African. You don't take a family's trouble as an opportunity to break them up. What kind of insanity is that? My mom used to say, 'A family isn't just the part of the tree you see above ground. It's most important part is the roots below ground. Only a sick culture can't see that.' She said that if children need to be moved, then move them among the roots, the other relatives. She believed that the only reason you wouldn't do that is if you have some deep down sickness that makes you despise the whole tree. What's worse, a damaged tree, or a culture that by nature kills certain trees?"

When hunger came around, the group built an extra-large fire. "Ivory," Shonto observed, "each night you make the fire bigger. You ever heard of using only what you need?"

"Yessir," Ivory replied. "You ever heard of the principle of keeping the bad things away? By the way, y'all haven't given me my propers yet for my exploits with the wolf-type beast."

"Ivory," Promise taunted, "we're not sure what you saw. Could have been a fox pup. Or dead log for all we know." This ignited Ivory, who spent much of his breath the rest of the day demanding that the group bow down to his bravery. Privately, he was shocked at how content he felt just knowing what he had done, and how little affirmation he actually yearned for.

As the maple and oak burned, the air sweetened and softened with dusk. Eloni baked more fish in the earth's belly, its steam and scent permeating from the sand pit and soaking camp in rich aroma. "You wrap up some of those potatoes in banana leaves, Loni?" Shonto asked.

"Yup. Added ginger shavings, too. There's some corn cobs down there too. Soaked them with almond butter and sugar cane juice. Seasoned them with black and cayenne pepper. Should come out crisp and sweet."

That wasn't all. Eloni served mofongo, a West African dish also popular in Puerto Rico. Plantains, olive oil, garlic, cashews, vegetables, crab, and shrimp, all in a sea bass broth soup.

Pikea, Shonto, Lake, and Binda had gathered heaps of wild berries, plums, apples, mangos, and starfruit. They peeled and sliced it all up for a salad. Cielo used the peelings for a tea, which he boiled in a large mango-wood pot. They ate, savoring. Slow. Focused. Not too many of these meals left. Dusk deepened, pronouncing the truth of this. They drew out dinner for a long stretch, letting their weariness keep them in camp.

After dinner, they brought out the drums. Ashia and Maricela got their journals, wanting to use the last daylight. Everyone changed into their warmer evening clothes.

"Hey, Shonto, are you fire dancing tonight?" Ashia asked.

"Dunno. I think I ate one too many potatoes. Them things were good though. I like what Loni did with the cayenne and garlic cloves."

"How many did you eat?"

'Maybe seven."

"Shonto! That's crazy. I'm surprised your guts haven't seized up."

"I know. And thus, I may take a pass on the fire dancing tonight. Don't want to spew on the crew and ruin the ceremony, sis," he said, smiling.

Ashia stared up at the heights of Jade Mountain. Its presence had loomed in their every moment on the island. She could feel it. Old. Enduring. "We need to all go to the summit," she said, catching their attention.

"The summit?" Ivory asked. "*All* the way up?"

"Of course!" said Maricela. "That's it! It will hurt like I don't know what, but it will be the perfect ending if we can make it. Balanta, you feeling up for it?" Balanta nodded, smiling slightly.

"We should leave early in the morning then," Eloni said. "Going to be rough climbing."

"Great," Ivory muttered. "Hey, Loni and Shonto constructed a sweat," Ivory said.

"A what?" Promise asked.

"A sweat lodge."

Shonto and Eloni had worked in the cool of prior dawns, gathering willow branches and banana leaves. Using the willow bark twine Eloni made, they managed to put together a small dome-shaped structure, with palm frond draping for an entrance. They dug out a depression in the middle of the lodge, two feet down by three feet wide. Shonto found the spiraling horn of a mountain goat to use as the tool for placing and turning the fire rocks. They finished the whole thing in two hours, eager to put it to use.

"This is a sacred thing," Shonto informed. "We're really not supposed to do this on our own. It's for the elders. For the leaders to do."

"Yeah?" Eloni said, more of an evasion than a question.

"I guess if we let the Spirit guide us, and we take it seriously, it won't be so bad." Shonto had his hands in his pockets, and he was shifting side to side with energy. "Yeah, I guess it will be okay. But we need everyone who goes in to do prayers and offerings."

Medicine talk commenced. They targeted stigma and bias and the quandary of acceptance: acceptance into college, jobs, society.

"If your résumé reads foster homes, group homes, shelters, and juvee, people aren't exactly going to see you as a Rhodes Scholar," Pikea lamented.

"So then what do you do?" Lake asked. "What's the hope?"

"I say go revolutionary on them," Cielo said, chewing a bunching of peppermint leaves. "Rally the people. Go Cesar Chavez. Go harder. Never quit. People don't just believe. You have to show them. Then show them again. Then, they *might* believe. Not exactly the stuff of faith, but hey."

"Cielo, you're such an addicted optimist," Ashia said, smiling.

"Amen, Hermana. Amen." Whereupon, Cielo bowed.

"Heck, even a small splinter will leave trauma behind in you," said Promise. "You mean to tell me we're some special class of wounded souls, and everyone else is trauma-free? Not buying it. All of humanity is just pain coexisting with pain."

"It's about holding the circle together," Cielo said, twitching his bare toes against the flames. "We are designed to live as long as it takes to pass a generation's consciousness down to the next three generations, to bring them to personhood. We are not supposed to live longer than that, or more briefly. To be young and dying in spirit means that the circle is broken."

How do you Love someone fiercely and still escape their gravity? That's what Maricela wanted to know. She thought of Manos, and envisioned the atmospheric burn that happened for her at every liftoff as she distanced herself from him, and at every reentry. With every attempt at reconciliation. *Atmospheric burn*. His atmosphere burned her up. Is that supposed to be the case with a father and daughter? How much incineration was required? She wished that Manos had been better at landing blows in the ring and less of a champion at landing blows on women. And children. Like her.

"How do you repair a wound still being torn open?" Pikea asked. "Where is the gauze for that? I still have to go back to my family one day, and they are so dysfunctional, I'm afraid I will go right back to the way I have always been. That's what they want."

"I'm sure if they Love you, that's not what they want for you," Ashia said. "They just can't help pulling you into the only way they know."

"That's a cop-out," Pikea snapped. "I can't stand people who refuse to change. It's like I keep jumping back into a pot of boiling water, hoping not to get scalded. That's crazy thinking, when you're honest about it."

"What else are you going to do?" Lake asked. "That's your family."

"Does that mean I have to go down the drain with them? Shouldn't I fight for my survival?"

"Balance, I guess," Ashia said. "We all need to walk the fine line between our relationships and our sanity."

"Shouldn't our relationships *be* our sanity?" Pikea asked. "And why do we have to walk the fine line from 1,000 feet above earth? How about from five feet up?"

"No, that's where everyone else walks," Ashia said. "We have to do the high-wire act. Even if we never chose to join the circus."

Promise opened up into song. Her soul found a river of old slave spirituals and followed it:

Lord… how come me here?
Lord… how come me here?
Lord… how come me here?
I wished I never was born…

The river flowed around jagged bends and dropped down into a swirling eddy current:

Sometimes I feel like a motherless child,
a long way from home…

The sound of the surf repeating framed the end of Promise's song.

They were all surprised by what Eloni did next. With sap popping in the fire, and baked fish still in the air, Eloni stood up. No spear. No chest out. He pulled out a crumpled piece of paper from his pocket. He shifted from side to side as he opened and flattened the sheet. "I wrote this for my mom while Promise was singing last time. Her song inspired me. So… my *tin'a*, my mom, she died of breast cancer when I was seven."

Maricela, hearing Eloni's voice sound the way it did, teared up. The group grew hushed. Eloni read.

"Dear Tin'a:

I hope you are eating plenty of mango and papaya where you are. And some primo poi. I hope you have found the peace that you never could on earth. And I hope you found a nice man who is good to you.

I don't want you to worry about me. I'm learning that molten lava doesn't always have to become a volcano. I'm figuring out what you meant when you used to tell me: Son, the harder you swim, the harder the water becomes. Ease up, and the water will ease up on you.

I found some people here, Tin'a, who I feel like for the first time in my life I can show myself to and it won't come back on me. Least, I hope it doesn't.

And I'm learning how to breathe, Tin'a. I didn't even realize I wasn't breathing all the way before. No wonder it always felt like my ribs were breaking, even when no one was touching me.

Tin'a, I made it plenty hard on you, probably before I even left your womb. I'm so sorry about that. I hope you can forgive me. I was so confused.

I make this promise to you right here tonight, Tin'a. I promise that I am going to keep grinding until I learn to Love myself, so that I won't keep on hurting myself and hurting the world. I promise you that I'm going to take everything that you put into me, Tin'a, and I'm not going to let it go to waste. I'm going to figure out a way to become decent, so that I can put you out into the world by the way I live. People need some of your spirit in their lives. It's so rough out here.

This ain't no perfect letter. I just want you to know that you're the first person I think of in the morning, when my brain comes back into my body. And I miss you. I miss you so much it hurts worse than anything.

They sat together in the raw ambiance of Eloni's letter. Shonto offered sweetgrass to the fire. To Eloni's words. To the moment. They all covered their faces and bodies in the sweetgrass smoke, as Shonto and Lake had shown them.

Lake was looking up, her spirit ascended in the darkening sky. The moon was now only a tracing of light. A crack in the veil. "The giant is more in sleep land now than awake," Lake said. "He's just entering his dreams."

Lake pulled her braids out from beneath her blanket and laid them against her chest. Shonto saw the fire in her eyes. For Lake, nights like this made her grieve her brother, and the light that never shone on him in his life.

"The full moon gets all of the attention," she said, her voice strong. "It's bright and shows off, and everyone admires it. It's in about a billion songs and poems and movies. But then, when you can't see the moon anymore, when it becomes the so-called *new moon*, people act like the moon doesn't exist at that point. It's forgotten about. And no one admires it. Just like us.

"We don't have much shine on us, so people take that to mean something is wrong with us. That we're inferior. Not worth any songs or poems about us. The only attention we do get is negative. People are resentful toward us for not being like the full moon. For not shining.

"But we are shining. They just can't see it. And a lot of the time, we can't even see it in our own selves. You see in yourself what people see in you. We get our identity from the world, become a reflection of their prejudice. Somehow, we need to put the shine back on our moon.

"My people don't call it a new moon. We call it a *Clear Moon*. It's not new. It's the same old moon. And when it's not full, you can't see it with your average vision, but it's always there. It isn't invisible. If your vision is good enough, if your spirit is right, you can see it. It's just clear. You see through it, into the darkness.

"We say the Clear Moon changes the sky around it more than the full moon does, because the Clear Moon exists and thrives on its own light. This inspires the entire universe. The Clear Moon sees *itself*. This is enough for it. It has true peace. Its peace shines a spirit light that inspires the whole night sky."

Promise, touched by Lake's words, wept emotion. "I'm not crying because I'm on my... moon time, okay?" Promise said. "I just never thought of my... of our lives the way Lake just put it. I need a moment here." She was laughing as she cried. The cocktail felt so good.

"We're just happy to see you cry on a Thursday, woman!" Maricela said, crying herself.

Clear Moon. The notion soaked in as they warmed by the fire. Ocean's sermon in the background seemed to be looking for an *Amen*, Promise thought.

"With the moon growing clear," Binda said, "it will be all the way clear tomorrow night, our last night. It will be wearing its own light. Should we have ourselves a ceremony?"

"We need new names!" Ashia announced in a burst of inspiration. "What we've been through here, we can't just go back the same way. We need new names, right?"

After a pause from the group, Promise spoke up. "That's a great idea! Should we choose our own, or have the group choose for us?"

"What do y'all say?" Ashia asked.

"We've gotten to know each other so much better being here and going through everything," Lake said in her soft voice. "Better than some of our own friends and family. I feel that we should name each other based on what we've seen in each other's nature. That's how it has been done traditionally back home."

"No goofing off though," Ashia clarified. "Nothing disrespectful. The names should come from in here, she said, gesturing to her heart with the palm of her hand."

"Our people give a baby a childhood name," Balanta said. "Sometimes, a healer shares a name secretly with the child. They are the only two that know. Then, when the time comes, they expect the child to choose a man or woman name. It is okay to have others name you when you are born and have not yet remembered yourself. But at a certain age, you should know your true self. And when you do, you should give that truth a name. Without a true name, you are like a field mouse. Any hawk can pick you off and make of you what it wants you to be."

Balanta told them about a man back in the village named Territory. Some names you are given, Balanta said. Others, you catch, like a virus, or a fungus. *Territory*. A name coughed up in a self-centered spasm, as are so many names, by a man who had been obsessed with owning land but whose rights to soil had never extended to anything beyond a few flower pots.

Shonto and Lake told some Diné legends. *The Skinwalker*. The Diné *Creation Story*. And the legend of *the Monster Slayer*.

Ivory and Promise took turns telling slave stories set in cotton fields, caves and grottos, secret places in the woods. Stories reaching back to West Africa's Rice Coast and spilling forward into modern tales of souls refusing chains and shackles of any sort. Stories of rebellion. The kind that leave slave master spirits nervous. Stories of beauty and brilliance that make polluted, falsely superior souls retch with the Truth.

Balanta and Mende told stories of the *Balanta* and *Mende* people's fierce spirit of resisting slavery and oppression. They told of *the Chain Breaker*. And, *the Man with a Fire Heart*.

Pikea shared some Maori legends. *Kawariki, the Shark Man*. *How Maui Slowed the Sun*. And, *How Maui Brought Fire to the World*.

Eloni told soulful Samoan legends. *The Turtles of Tigilau*. *The Story of Pili and Sina*. And, *the Tree of Life*.

They were energized now. Drums talked in baritone and bass. The air hummed with anticipation. Of an ending. Many beginnings. And ceremony. Ivory was deeply affected by Eloni's letter to his mother. For the first time in his life, Ivory felt something break open in his chest that felt good. Hope. Skies parting. New life.

"I'm through with this... suffering," Ivory said. "I don't want to be outside of myself anymore. All my life I've felt homeless. Always pitying myself for it, digging the ditch deeper.

"This one dude I heard speak one time at a youth event talked about this Vietnamese Monk, Thich Nhat Hahn, who teaches that it doesn't matter if you do have a home, as long as you're not being true to yourself, you're basically homeless. Had no clue what he meant at the time, but he must have planted a seed. Now I get it. When you tell yourself that you're on the outside looking in, that's how you'll always feel and think. That's how you'll create your life."

"Like a self-fulfilling prophecy?" Mende asked.

"Exactly. I know it's not as easy as just telling myself that I'm home. But maybe it is. Maybe that's where you start. Start lying to yourself until you believe, and then once you believe, you make it so. Eventually, you just peace out. Peace out on all this fear and insecurity that's ruled you.

"I want to be true to *me* going forward," Ivory continued, his pace rapid and feverish, "which means I need to let a whole lot of stuff go. Relationships, first and foremost. And my thoughts. I got a lot of crazy thoughts running free on the range in my brain. They've been there so long, they think they own the place."

"Time for a new sheriff in town!" Promise shouted. She couldn't have been prouder.

Lake listened as Ivory spoke and realized that she had felt homeless all of her life. The pervasive sensation of being on the outside looking in. The shameful private posture she assumed that left her without belief in herself. *Unworthy*. That's what she had felt herself to be. It was her precious possession. She clung to it as a bag lady, and even though it did not serve her, this stained identity, it was her most secure identity. She knew what to do with it. How to approach others with it. And how to use it to run from anything too bright and shiny.

Homeless. Not always in a real way. But maybe in the realest way. I've been telling myself that I'm homeless, that I'm not where I need to be. Not safe. Not there yet. And it's been eroding me like the ocean. I'm a sand dune, constantly shifting on the inside, always uncomfortable. That's why my emotions are so unpredictable. I'm a honeybee that won't land. Even when it's the best flower I could possibly hope for.

She realized that until she learned to be true to herself, she would always be homeless in her head, which is where it counted most. Homeless inside of relationships. Homeless on her own. Homeless regardless of her grades, her job, her clothes, her friends. Just plain homeless.

Lake remembered the two hawks mating. It came to her again her that all living things will perform their most intimate duties as long as they feel safe. At home. And that such fulfillment has little to do with having a wealth of resources. *I can bring my tribe with me*, she whispered. The thought of it felt good in such a way that in that very moment, a ribbon of water leapt from the lagoon, arced over the trees, and jumped into the ocean. Jubilated.

Pikea was wound up by all the testifying. "I'm coming to a point where I'm through with letting life have its way with me," she said. "For real, I'm way too good at feeling sorry for myself. That's not a good life skill. Something's been happening to me since we've been here. I feel like this place... this place is waking the warrior in me. I'm ready to fight for my life. Ten rounds, 20, I don't care. People can keep throwing blows. I'm gonna throw back. Not violently, but just… I'm ready to be determined, to make the effort and keep on fighting, scrapping. I'm gonna make my life come true."

Ashia applauded. "They see you struggling, and they think you don't want it," she said. "That you don't have the heart to make it in life. What they don't understand is that your orientation toward yourself has been thrown off. You aren't seeing yourself accurately. You want the same things everyone else wants, but you don't see your own worth, your own promise. That has nothing to do with heart. Heart shows up after you can look in the mirror and see your true self. Until then, you're just telling yourself lies and living in fiction."

Cielo stroked the head of his bongos, feeling the moment. "I've got a Love story for you," he announced. "You ready?"

"Go 'head, Cielo," Maricela replied. They threw more wood on the fire, wrapped tighter in their blankets, and settled in for the tale. Cielo spun it proper. A famed blacksmith who fell in Love with a peasant girl. Unbeknownst to the blacksmith, she had been betrothed to the king's son, a lazy, slithering prince. What followed was a riveting tale of heartbreak, tragedy, and redemption. Cielo's story was so entrancing, Shonto and Pikea forgot their hunger. Momentarily. Pikea sang a Maori *waiata*. Shonto followed in the Diné way. Then Cielo, and one after the other. Their singing, more passionate than skilled, brought new stars out from their caves, decorating night anew.

After the fire talk, Ashia and Balanta retreated to the lagoon for a swim. Balanta's arm found Ashia's waist beneath the water and pulled her gently to him. Her breath was on his lips now. The bobbing of the water had them dancing to a silent music. The spring's current spilled out phosphorescent sand grains, enshrining them in a rich blue-green glow, a meadow of light within the water.

"Do you think we'll ever be in a place like this again?" Ashia asked.

"If I'm with you, I'm every place I need to be," Balanta said, chastising himself for how cheesy he sounded, even as he spoke the words.

"That's sweet," Ashia said, blushing. The waterfall's mist enveloped them in a surreal cloudiness. In the distance, an island bird called out deep in the foliage. "Can you hold me while I float on my back? I want to see the stars like this."

Balanta placed both hands beneath Ashia, one under her back and the other under her thighs. As Ashia gazed up into the brilliant black and glinting universe, Balanta swept her around slowly in circles, sand grains glowing as they formed trails from Ashia's hands, Balanta's sense of reality melting into a lagoon with no bottom or shore.

After their swim, they stayed beside the lagoon, talking. "Balanta," Ashia asked. "Do you feel a lot of pressure with the way people look up to you?"

"No… Maybe. Why?"

"I see how people are. Not just Mende. Even the way you breathe is an example. Must be hard sometimes. Lonely, too?"

Balanta looked at Ashia. His eyes were sincere, then warm and grateful, but still protective.

"What are you feeling right now?" Ashia asked. "I sense something simmering." Ashia could feel the jagged, serrating presence of Balanta's own coral reefs. Just below the surface. A coiled defensiveness on edge and ready to wreck and shatter anything that got too close to his shore.

"Binda told me that it takes courage to heal," Ashia said, rubbing Balanta's back. "It takes a reason. She can't just heal someone. All she can do is touch them in the right way and place, and if they have a reason, that touch stimulates the healing. But the reason is the fertilizer." Balanta listened. Silently. With the reverence of a man, and the stubborn resistance of a boy.

Balanta's voice was the density of coal as he told Ashia of the countless nights he lay awake through the night, listening to his parents' scream their pain at each other. Only a thin cotton cloth separated the boys' bedroom from the kitchen area where Shanté and Yara assaulted each other with words and volume. Balanta told Ashia about how Mende would crawl into a fetal ball and try to talk over the screaming. How Balanta himself would clench his jaws so tightly that his teeth began to hurt, a pressing pain that continued into his sleep as he grinded molars. He told Ashia of his migraines that bloomed like algae on fire almost weekly and left him spent and trembling for days. He told Ashia of the sparks of pain that traveled his nerve endings like lightning across the sky, the inherited rage, the painfully secret self-doubt that he kept trapped inside. He told Ashia everything. By the time he was finished, great knots of tension had released like coils, spewing a phlegm of toxin from Balanta's core, out through his bones, his muscles, his pores. He kneeled on all fours and vomited vapors of exorcised trauma onto the grass as Ashia rubbed his bowed back and cried with him, wordless and grateful to God.

That night, the group made their offerings to the four directions. They used water, sage, sweetgrass, and corn pollen, and covered themselves in smoke using a long, smoldering piece of pitch. They prayed silently. Shonto drummed them into the sweat lodge, as they walked over cedar boughs. What happened inside was sacred and cannot be told. As they departed the lodge, reemerging back into the open, they took deep breaths of the cool air to clear their lungs. Their spirits had changed. They were something closer in nature to night itself. Shonto instructed that they not immediately wash their faces in water. It was important to let the spirit imparted by the smoke sink further into them. The sweat brought intense dreams that night. And for Ivory and Binda, appetites that would not cease.

Ashia raised up on her elbow, her face covered in candlelight. Balanta rubbed his sleepy eyes. They had been lying on the beach for an hour, intertwined blissfully.

"I wrote something for you," Ashia said, lightly. "Can I read it for you?"

"Sure," Balanta said. He was secretly swollen with emotion. The concept of someone caring deeply enough to pour herself into words, written words...

Ashia began.

My soul has become a song. Dawn worships a new sun now, as my heart notes flutter from the trees to sip pools of dew.

When you sing your joy, I am you. When you bridge rivers of beauty, look down to the water and see. I am you.

I am your ropes of yearning, tied like ribbons round the trunks of eternity. I am the sweet mist on your lips of spring. I am you.

I am the ink of your mystic tattoo. The light that softens your dreams. Your coral reefs, too. I am you.

Even without the starlight, Ashia would have been able to see the waterfall shimmering down Balanta's face. His eyes overtaken, his tongue so incapable of expression. He placed his large hands around her bare shoulders and brought her to him. His hands felt warm against her skin, and soft, like maple leaves in October. The ocean stopped. Sound went away. Until she heard a pounding drum that was her heartbeat.

"I'd like to stay out here tonight with you," Ashia said.

Balanta looked at her, registering her sincerity. "I'll go get a blanket."

They lay there, warm and in wonder, in the pooled aftermath of her poetry, for a moment naked of boundary.

"I'm going to sleep out on the feather grass tonight," Cielo said. "Who wants to join me?"

"I will," Lake said. "Binda?"

"Okay. Sure. Let's bring a lot of blankets though."

"You people done lost your minds," Ivory said. "Don't you know there's a goat killer out there?"

"Bueno, 'cause we're not goats, amigo." Cielo was laughing.

Out in the meadow, the feather grass was a luxurious mattress, ushering them toward a blissful sleep. Lake held on as long as she could, awed by the stars above, and the moon, its aura so strong in Lake's heart, even as it burrowed its light into the soil of night.

Cielo rested his head on his hands as he lay on his back, scanning the heavens. "God doesn't play," Cielo said. "God creates. This island. Every day, over and over. By sea, salt, sun, and survival."

He thought about what Lake had said earlier. *Clear Moon*. "I read that the word lunatic comes from the idea of people being entranced by *la luna*, the moon. It didn't mean crazy, necessarily. More like delirious... delirious in the moonlight. So, if we're lunatics, well, there's worse than that, right?"

Lake was already drifting. Binda's spirit was traveling. Cielo felt the ground pulse. A deep boom came from the earth. The boom repeated several times, rhythmically. "Now, *that's* how you play a drum," Cielo said. He turned over and grinned himself to sleep.

Binda had been waiting all night to write in her journal. Fireflies swarmed the meadow. Along with starlight, this provided Binda all she needed to see by. She cradled her papyrus-bound journal in her lap and smiled dreamily like someone getting her fix on. The procession of words poured out, spring water at last liberated:

I belong to paradise, not to pain. I belong to the blossoms after rain. I sink slowly in the blue and come up new. On the sand of the cove, for me, I sink I rise, I come up new.

As Binda drifted to sleep, she felt the ocean shaping the island, the island depositing its silt into the ocean, shaping it in return. The mutuality was a sleep tonic. Her sleep was good. Binda dreamt of a woman holding the hands of a little girl whose eyes wore fear. The woman, hair of silver cotton, said to the girl, "Until she turns her compassion inward toward herself, she can never be the healer she is meant to be."

Mende ran down to the beach for a moment alone. He lay down and placed the side of his face on the sand. In the starlight, he saw a flood of hatchlings liberate from their eggshells and turn, still wet and placental, toward the sea. The sand became a rolling darkness of turtle shells, heads, and flippers. Small black eyes reflected starlight. Air smelled rich with birth. So much life, racing for shelter, for safety. For home. Mende lost himself in this rhythmic cycle, a circle dire with a need to complete itself. A ritual of preservation and predation. Predictable seabirds arrived and dove to eat from this massive birth. Their success pained Mende, who wanted to chase them away. Instead, he lay still, his head on the sand, looking sideways at carnage and escape. Thousands of hatchlings tasted saltwater for the first time, achieved at least a momentary shelter. Mende wondered if turtles felt something like hope. And how long they held onto it. The tide turned dark with the new life that had joined it. Mende remained for a long while, his body and face against the sand. Eventually, the tide turned back into its brighter, frothier self, resuming its nature against the shore. Up by the break between foliage and sand, eggshell fragments littered the ground, glistening and swarmed with miniature sand crabs. They too wanted to feast on the offering that is birth.

In the cold, still hours of night, Ashia turned over restlessly next to Balanta. She heard feet shuffling. A tall silhouette emerged. The figure took her hand and led her toward the center of the campground. A fire grew, towering over Ashia and Balanta. An army of snails came oozing from the thick forest line, heading for them with nonsensical speed. Just as they reached Ashia's feet, she was swept up into the air in a vortex. Looking down, she saw a village of people, all sewing blankets, murmuring *Come back home, children. Come back home.*

Ashia was an eagle, locked into a high draft of wind. Her human heart cried to be united with the village people below. She heard her voice wailing, "Wait for me! I'm up here! Can't you see me?" Not one soul looked up from the blanket-sewing tasks, except for a little girl with eyes like watery globes who walked on crutches and was missing a leg. The girl stared at *Ashia the eagle* and pointed, but no one was interested in paying a little girl any mind.

Ashia felt herself falling. Faster than could be possible. She fell all the way through the earth, through molten chambers and families of boulders squatting in the center of the earth. She landed in a field proudly featuring its thick waves of lavender and buttercups. She was on her back, with her legs propped up at the knees and spread. Her belly obscured her vision as she looked down and saw only its glistening rise. Balanta was holding her hand, wiping her pouring forehead with a cloth as a mountain forced itself out of her womb and into the world.

Before she could see what she had birthed and hold it close, a tall waif of a man in a black bowler hat and circular spectacles appeared from nowhere and snatched her offspring. Ashia leapt from her supine convalescence and roared a primal alarm. She chased after the now-fleeing ghoul, and fell flat on her face into an ocean. As she drowned, Ashia felt more alive than ever. She was falling into the depths as ancestors floated up past her by the hundreds, each smiling at her and chanting, *Welcome back, child. Welcome back to us.*

Those ancestors surfaced and became living waves of the ocean, all surging over Ashia as she continued drifting down. All surging and tumbling for a shore where somehow Ashia, even now deep in the maw of the sea, could recognize the shape and movement of a little girl running back and forth along the coastline, holding the billowing string attached to what appeared to be a kite so far above her. It was not a kite. It was Ashia's own heart, spread flat and broad and blood-red in the sky, a giant blushing butterfly. *But this cannot be.* It could not be. Ashia awoke in a panicked movement, soaked and heaving, wondering aloud at what the Lord was doing to her.

Balanta pressed his thumbs into the sweet spot at the back of Ashia's shoulders, down into the soft tissue just outside of her shoulder blades. A tremor ran through her nerves, melting her muscles. She purred. He massaged her entire body as she passed through realms of sleep and ecstasy. They lay on their sides, Balanta behind Ashia, his arms around her, their hands entwined. As Balanta slid back into a peaceful sleep, Ashia felt his breath pour over her neck and shoulder, a warm breeze moving over hillsides into the valley of her contented heart.

DAY SEVEN

They headed out an hour before sun bloom. Starlight lent enough for early vision. Nocturnal creatures were just beginning to pack it up for sleep. A salamander hustled off the trail just ahead of them. A shadow in the bush shifted and was gone.

"Moose?" asked Ivory, still groggy.

"What is it with you and Moose?" asked Maricela.

"Read about them one time. They seem cool."

They moved into the woods, most of them still drugged with sleep, their silence resounding. The way up was hard, steep inclines and declines on shifting surfaces. Eloni, Balanta, and Pikea kept pace. Pikea moved up the slopes easily, her limbs pliant and strong. Jumping, hopping, reaching, she ascended, waited, bounded on. Promise's legs felt like gelatin. She fantasized of oxygen. "Sit down, girl," Ashia said. "It's not like you're trying out for the Olympics. Take a knee."

A hawk, its breast auburn and prideful, cut the sky with liberated wings, banking in circles. Mende felt the hawk was showing off. He wondered whether the hawk was keeping tabs on them, hoping they would succumb and it could feast. Compassion seeped in at the thought.

Cherries, apples, and plums were thick in the higher valleys. Promise and Balanta picked the fruit. The others ate from their long-limbed labor. As they gained altitude, they left behind the paradise of shade and entered a kingdom of sunlight. Everything was bright. Stones glistened with quartz and brilliant lichen. Light bounced off gems and flower blossoms. Even dirt shone. Lake liked the skin on this part of the mountain. The lichen and moss softened things for the group's squinting eyes.

Air thinned. Promise wheezed. Binda rubbed her back. Balanta limped. His leg was aching at this altitude. Higher they went, spears and walking sticks tapping rocky soil, creating a rhythmic companion to their climb. The mountain here was frugal with its shade. Everything grew low and flat. Heat ran unencumbered over the terrain, blistering everything into a hardship of being. The rocks at this altitude were dorsal, almost as though they had been blown back against the slope by interminable wind.

They summited. Eloni and Pikea first. The mountain peak was scripted in spires of granite and shocks of dwarf pines, their hair blown drastically sideways. A crisp wind howled over the peak. Mende felt a vertigo he would never admit. Balanta and Eloni drew deep breaths. Promise, Ashia, and Maricela walked the perimeter, looking down the sheer slopes in wonder. Cielo pulled out a pen and wrote lyrics on his palms. Majestic lyrics. *The syrup and cinnamon of sins absolved.*

Junipers and cypress grew at this altitude in small communes, shedding their needles over the area, scenting the air in pungent saps and oils. One particular juniper towered over the rest, a giant bonsai on the plateau. Beneath its cover grew two shrubby piñons, their seeds coffee-hued and ready. Cielo grinned and pocketed three handfuls. A third tree grew next to the piñons. The tree was leprous, its limbs gone. Only stumps remained, melted like candle wax down its trunk.

Even the hulking juniper looked small sharing the same plateau with a family of 5,000-year-old bristlecone pines. Five of them grew here, each colossal and blotting the landscape like oil spills in the air. Snow gum trees completed the arboreal village, anchoring down in the rocky soil. Vines thick as a farmer's forearms clung to the snow gum trunks, as though merged into the bark, varicose and thriving. The roots of all the trees dared to transcend their subterranean territories. They snaked over one another above ground, appearing to both jostle for space and wrestle like children.

It was cold at the peak. Mende pulled his jacket tighter against him. Cielo was sweating, seemingly oblivious to the drop in temperature. "Cielo, you have more insulation than us, with all that body fur," Mende said.

"We all have our gifts, qué no?" Cielo responded, smiling. "If you want to huddle up for warmth, come on over."

"No thanks. I'm good."

Pikea walked over to an edge of the peak, moving straight into the wind's howl. She leaned over the precipice and looked down, curious to see just how high up they were. Spotting the earth below, she felt a slight dizziness rush through.

"You might want to step back from that edge," warned Shonto.

"You don't want to end up a pastry on the canyon floor for the animals to enjoy," Cielo added.

"As only you can put it," said Promise.

"Should we make an offering up here?" Cielo asked, looking at Shonto, who was already pulling sage and cedar from his pouch.

"The winds up here will carry out prayers a long way," Shonto said. They stood at the precipice of the peak's cliff side. Wind buffeted them backward. Shonto leaned in. They spoke prayers and wishes, their voices captured by the gusts and swallowed. The sage and cedar they tossed blew back in their faces. Into their mouths. They laughed and shouted nonsense into the wind. The view took their senses and made them delirious. The foliage and canyons below stretched on and on in their peripheral vision. Ocean's teal pasture extended indefinitely. Existence was irretrievable here. They could feel its raw freedom. Intoxicating.

Cielo drew in the crisp air and nearly bleated, his sigh was so elevated. "That... was not attractive, son," said Promise.

"Breathe with me, Promise," Cielo said, unembarrassed and immersed in pleasure. "This is the pure stuff. They bottle this and sell it back in the circus tent that is civilization. Get it for free while you can."

Ashia took in the air and groaned. She felt like her molecules were purifying with each breath. "We need a rite of passage to seal this bond of our time together," she said.

"Okay," Pikea said, "but can we not make it so formal? Why does everything have to be turned into rules?"

"Not rules. That's not what we're going to do. We need a ritual. Just an understanding between us of what we've been through. An act to seal things in our memory."

"Whales and dolphins get all the Love," said Ivory. "What about porpoises?"

"What are you even talking about?" asked Eloni.

"You gotta be the right species, or you're not even in the game."

"Are you feeling nervous up here, Ivory?" Promise asked. "You seem to talk gibberish when you're anxious."

Ivory didn't hear the comment. Instead, he turned to Mende and asked, "You think a raven could take a crow?"

"What?"

"You know, a fight. I'm playing that out in my mind. Not sure who would come out on top. I do that a lot. Take two different things and put 'em at each other in my mind."

"Ivory, why are you so random?" Mende asked.

Ivory lifted his eyebrows. "Why aren't you so free? Why don't you let your mind run every now and then?"

"Maybe I'm afraid of where it would go," Mende answered.

"Or maybe you're afraid it would never come back," Ivory said. "Anyway... in a footrace between a turtle and a salamander, who wins?"

"In the water or on land?" Mende asked. "Regular speed, or when frightened?"

Ivory ignored the questions. He was already on to the next mystery. He squinted, inquisitive. "If the plural of goose is geese, shouldn't the plural of moose be meese?"

Promise slapped him lightly upside the head. "Ivory, how much sugar have you had today?"

"Miran, mi gente... check this out, my people," Cielo shouted into the wind. "I am declaring myself a self-healing organism. From now on, I make no excuse for any suffering I incur. I give myself permission and power to heal what ails me. I guess you could say I have become a medicinal Mozart. Ironic, I know, since the lad died young. Nonetheless, I pronounce myself a restorative genius."

"Good for you, Buddha," Eloni said. "Don't know half of what you said, but if you're talking about being happy, more power to you."

Happiness had always been theoretical to Lake. A thing to observe in others. To muse over. Not to feel. Now though, standing in this sacred wind, she believed she might be pregnant with it. With happiness. She was terrified. Would she be a good caretaker of this new life form growing in her? And would it ever leave her? Once found, is it kept? Or is it like snow that falls on the high mesas and then is gone? She didn't know if she could give herself completely to something that could so easily be lost.

"Cielo, what are you thinking about?" asked Maricela. "You look funny."

"Pancakes," he replied.

"What?"

"I'm craving pancakes bigtime. Whole grain. With bananas and blueberries in the batter."

"I don't know about bananas. You can have that. I'll take the blueberries though."

"Waffles!" Ivory blurted out.

"Now we're talking," Promise said. "Fat, buttery waffles."

"With anise and cinnamon," said Cielo.

Shonto's belly took the conversation as a cruel taunting and began to curl and gurgle in familiar protest. He looked at the distant clouds and thought about what his basketball coach had told him: "A dry riverbed, if it wants to change its face, first it has to drown. It has to call on the rain and let itself be run over by the floodwaters. Then, after it dies in the new water, that water can leave, and the riverbed can have a new face."

A thoracic throttling of cicadas in the trees made Shonto feel like he was inside of a circle of people shaking their rain sticks. The energy of it aroused his tribal pride. Reflexively, he flexed the wrist of his shooting hand, felt his heart valves dilate. His drummer inside was awake and hungry for a sacred dance.

"Let's head back down, yeah?" Shonto asked. Today is a swift river. It goes too fast."

Promise didn't want to say anything, but she was hoping not to pass out before they got back to lower altitude. Shonto's urging to leave was bliss to her lungs. They took their last deep breaths of the scintillating peak air and headed downhill.

After half an hour of descent, the gravelly ground revealed a faint trail. The trail ran back toward a precipice, which they approached to check out the view. The canyon floor loomed hundreds of feet below. Pikea spotted the vine first. It was the thickness of Eloni's arm and it ran from its rooting on the plateau, over the precipice and down. It extended like a zip line over the canyon, angling downward until it reached into the trees deep in the forest. "How is it possible that it grew like that?" Cielo asked. "To get from up here on the plateau and across the canyon down there like an acrobat's high wire, that is impossible."

"Apparently not," Promise observed.

Though the vine sparked the same idea in most of them, it was Pikea who spoke it first. "That looks like a prime candidate for getting back to camp a whole lot quicker."

"Ride it down?" asked Eloni, his eyes widening.

"You people done blown a fuse, a gasket, and a fuel pump all at once," said Ivory, backing away from the edge. "Somebody get me a helicopter. I'm outta here." They spent the next 20 minutes arguing over the risk of death versus getting back to camp much later and hungrier, and with much more effort. Most of that time was spent keeping Ivory from fainting.

It was inevitable that Eloni got on the vine first. They used cuttings of another green vine for handles. They each looped one several times around one wrist, then threw the handle over the master vine and looped the handle tightly around the other wrist. Eloni jumped out over the canyon with no hesitation, yelling his freedom as he dropped with gravity, the master root holding his weight easily. "This is flying! Haaaiiiyyyaaa!" His body picked up speed as he reached the midpoint. Beneath him he saw a green blurring. Air flattened his face and filled his lungs forcefully. Eloni bicycle-kicked his feet as he hit the canopy and disappeared. They heard him shouting for the next one to come, and something about it being over too quickly.

It was also inevitable that Balanta had to endure the humiliation of being the one to slide down the vine with Ivory cradled against him. Ivory's face was buried in Balanta's chest. His thin legs were wrapped around Balanta's thighs in a death grip. They both held their handles and jumped. Promise and the rest covered their ears as Ivory screamed, "I walk through the valleeey!" all the way down.

After surviving the vine zip line, they were still up in the hills and a ways from camp. They paused for a rest. Cielo broke out the plantain chips and snapper jerky. Promise noticed Ivory's unusual quietness and calm. She came over and put her arm around his shoulders. "I'm going to miss you, boy," Promise said wistfully.

"I'm going to miss you, girl," Ivory said. "But don't get all so and so on me. We promised to keep close, right?"

"Yeah, I know. Just make sure you don't let life get in the way. You know how grown folks do," she smiled.

"Oh, so now we're grown!" The old feeling was inside Ivory again. A nervous shifting in his spirit. A need to change something. To prove his existence. A bush he spotted was taunting him, so barren and desiccated. Bare of leaves. Empty. Like a surrendered soul asking Ivory to put it out of its misery. *I told myself I would never do this again. I can't be burning down this island. These people are trusting me.* But the itch had already matured. It spread through Ivory's skin, viral and rampant. The bush was so ripe for this. Sun was high and inflamed. The hillside sweltered. Groundcover plants were limp, seeming to want to join the sacrifice. And that's the thing about it, Ivory reasoned. If I set this bush free, isn't that a good thing? No more suffering. Just rebirth. Ivory's thumb reflexively rubbed backward over the mid-joint of his index finger, as though igniting a cigarette lighter. His wrists dewed with sweat. He felt his heartbeat gaining. He could already smell the distinctive sharp tinge of burning wood. He could hear the crackling, see the orange ghosts of flame swirling for the sky. Time had left Ivory. His senses grew acute, knives sharpening against the stone, prepping to make and bear witness to change.

"Man, my feet hurt," said Maricela, baiting Eloni. "We must have put in 10 miles today." They were swinging in Cielo's hammock.

"Take off your feet and give me your shoes," Eloni said, his voice slurred.

"Um, are you sure you're okay there, buddy?" Maricela replied. Eloni was not okay. His eyes were gauzy. His normally sturdy legs quivered noticeably. His balance was clearly off. "Are you sure those mushrooms you just ate from yesterday weren't poisonous?" Eloni was about to answer, but before his swollen lips could part further, the Samoan mountain had fallen and was flat out on the cabin floor.

Eloni came to with a sudden nonsensical blather. He sat up, sweat soaked and steaming. "I guess those weren't the mushrooms I thought they were," he said.

"You think?" Maricela was wiping down his forehead with a wet cloth. "You boys are something else. What's next? One of you going to get poison ivy or accidentally smoke some peyote?" She handed him a gourd filled with cold spring water from the stream out back. He guzzled it sloppily, streams of it pouring down his chest. It was like throwing water on a campfire. He felt the burning of his organs immediately subside.

"That was the best water I ever had," Eloni said. "You think you can help me with dinner tonight? I'm not exactly feeling so great."

"Sure, maestro. It will be my pleasure."

"You think I'm cute, don't you?" Eloni said, winking at her.

"Loni, please," Maricela said. "You got a head like those statues on Easter Island. Just as big and hard. Fat ol' lips and nose. Crusty skin like you been left in the rain for a few centuries."

"Watch it, Cela. I'll put some ghost pepper in your food. I found some in the garden."

"They're about to find *you* in the garden. Nothing but a mound of dirt with a raggedy wood cross that says, *He Tried Maricela.*

"Man. You're drastic."

"Don't flex on a Mex."

It was while the group ate lunch that their fears came true. Summiting the peak left them beat and dehydrated. Midday sun painted camp in ribbons of heat. Only their hunger moved them out to the fire circle. Had they been napping in their cabins, they would have had no chance.

"Fiiire!" Ashia screamed, blood in her throat. "Fire!" A towering black cumulous cloud was avalanching toward them, rolling over itself, its base glowing crimson with spikes of sparking light. The bright sky was obliterated into darkness before they could grasp reality. They dashed chaotically the way panicked goats jump into barbed fences. Maricela's leg caught against the jutting shard of a tree stump as she tried to run around it, ripping open her flesh. Blood streamed down her leg and pooled in the sand, sacramental and warm.

Cielo tripped over his own leg as he pivoted, pitching backward. His head thumped on the sand as he landed, his vision filling with swarming worms of light.

Maricela's stomach turned. Sweat broke out over her entire body at once, dampening her shirt against her skin. *Is this it? Is this how we die?*

As flames raced forward with an impossible speed, and smoke rose like a geyser, Binda prayed for rain.

"Lake! Please!" Promise shouted.

"I can't! It doesn't work like that!" But Lake tried. She clenched her eyes closed tightly, pursing her lips in concentration. She sought out memories. Of when water came. Because of her. The memories poured through. She tried to taste the water. Tried to smell it. It still seemed so far away. Her lifelong mantra swept through her, taunting: *I can't control it. It just happens.* She bit her lip and cast the mantra away. Her eyes still clenched closed, she found her brother, out by the fence, his head bobbing. Lake knelt by her brother and wrapped him in her arms. *I Love you*, she said. *I miss you, and I need you. I'm so sorry I let them take you.* His head stopped bobbing. He turned to his sister. His eyes were ancient. His mouth opened slowly like an old attic door. A prophet's voice came out: "Lake. Make rain."

In the woods between camp and Jade Mountain, the trees that rain heard the plea of Lake's brother, and the prayer of Lake's water spirit. A cohort of monkeypod trees huddled, whispering and urgent. Their crowns shuddered. A fine mist eloped from their leaves, grew into larger drops, and swept toward the camp as a horizontal torrent. Rain was a pounding bridal shower. Torrents of water flushed through the cottonwoods and eucalyptus, recruiting moisture from every leaf, branch, and trunk. Gathering wind on the way.

The first drop landed on Maricela's cheek. A small lake sparking hope in her heart. Then, a ponderous downpour. The fire kept coming, lustful, scathing. Smoke had reached the camp and was prowling and serpentine, probing for spaces to fill. The air heated, almost scalding faces. Eucalyptus trees exploded, their oils blasting into conflagrations above the canopy.

Just as the fire seemed as though it would inevitably reach them, a howl bloomed in the sky as loud and terrible as in a dream. It grew instantly, achieving a deafening level, racing over the water from the western edge of the island, heading toward camp.

"Everyone hit the ground!" Balanta yelled at his loudest, straining his throat. They huddled and lay with their hands over their ears as the wind, still mounting a hurricane-like force, slammed over land, sand blasting their backsides as it passed over. Binda, Ivory, and Maricela were nearly lifted off the ground. Cielo lost his hold and was rolled over several times, a helpless stick in a storm.

The roar seemed to pause directly over their bodies, taunting them. Terrorizing. Binda screamed. Her voice was lost in the sheer volume, unheard and swallowed.

Time stopped moving. And then, after forever, it twitched. The howl diminished slightly. Binda prayed even more fervently, petitioning Hope. Mende lifted his head slightly, opening his eyes just enough to see something that could not be. The wall of wind had reached the oncoming fire, whose raging red sheets suddenly skidded to a stop, their onslaught aborted. The flames seemed to stand up straight, as though they were looking up at the gust.

Then, the fire leaned backward. Toward the ocean. The gust appeared to Mende to pick up the acres of light and push them downhill, toward the water. He saw Pikea standing. Her arms and hands stretched wide. She was shouting at the fire fiercely.

Now, the rest of the group began to slowly lift their heads, rise from the ground, and take stock of the damage around them. The camp was disastrous. Not one of them cared. They forced their gazes toward the wildfire, not knowing if it was already atop of them.

What they saw was what Mende was already in shock over, straining to process. The great howling wind and the horizontal deluge of rain both had hands, humanlike hands, and they were corralling the fire, pushing it ever closer to the water. Lake's eyes were closed, her breath deep and calm.

The fire was a rampageous soul. It was fighting back, as though it was determined to reach the camp and incinerate those who had dared to awaken it. The wind and rain were stronger. As the group watched, dead-still like petrified wood, the fire was pushed into the sea.

Just as after the cave-in, their faces were dusted like ghosts. Ash covered their world. The air reeked with things burnt and blistered. They stumbled around in shock until heartbeats pounding in their heads diminished enough they could hear themselves think. Thinking dragged panic back inside through the wall of their numbness. Balanta worked hard to calm the others. He had them fan out across the area to check for smoldering spots in the underbrush. They kicked dirt and sand over everything that wasn't dirt and sand. An hour later, soaked in sweat and exhausted, they still were throwing handfuls of dirt on every blade of grass, branch, tree trunk, bush, and flower. Either due to shock or resignation, or a strange kind of peace, no one thought to once again try to open the security box and access the phone or the flares. It no longer occurred to them that they could leave this place before their time.

Ivory kept to himself, far from the others. Crying. Flooded with shame. "I didn't do this," he repeated to himself. "I didn't do this. They all think I did this. My life is over. I'm so sick of this pain."

Promise approached, coughing badly and wheezing. She touched his shoulder tentatively. "Ivory. Talk to me."

Ivory's face was covered in tears, distorted in pain. He looked at Promise with a suffering defiance. "I didn't do this. I know you all think I did this."

"Ivory, look. We're alive. That's what matters. You can understand why people would wonder, right? With your history?"

"I can't escape my history!" Ivory screamed. The others looked over.

"Ivory, the way I see it is simple. If you didn't do this, tell me. I trust your word."

"Yeah, right. No one here is going to believe me."

"Okay, Ivory. We already talked about the self-pity thing. That's not gonna cut it, and I'm not having it from you. We all deserve to know the truth, including you, so we can figure out what we need to do. If the island doesn't burn down, I'd personally like to finish this last day off right."

Promise sat with Ivory. She gave him 10 minutes to sulk. Then she demanded an answer to her question. Did he or did he not set the world on fire? She held him as she asked. He fell into her, bawling as he answered. When they walked together back to camp, 20 eyes stared at them, wondering.

The rest of the afternoon was spent taking therapy in the lagoon. Its minerals soaked into their skin, into their nerve endings. They grew calmer as the sun began to dip.

Sitting on a flat rock just beneath the water's surface, Binda cradled Promise in her lap. Promise's coughing and wheezing worsened even after the smoke had cleared from camp. Too many particles had gotten into her scarred lungs, triggering them to tighten. The group carried her to the lagoon, where Binda took her into her lap in the water. As Promise's legs bobbed in the warm element, Binda massaged Promise's chest with yarrow pulp. Binda sang to her. Promise's breathing cleared. Her body released its tension into the water. Binda grew quiet. Her eyes looked deeply into Promise as Promise, looking up at Binda, shared her heart.

"I wish I could keep you with me," Promise said. You're like my ointment. It's going to be hard when we leave here. I don't want life to sweep us all away from each other."

"When you need me," Binda shared softly, "just sing me to you."

"What do you mean?"

"It is our way. We believe that each of us carries our own song, one that's different from everyone else's."

"Like fingerprints?"

"Yes. Our Old Ones tell us that people get into trouble when they forget their song. Or when no one ever taught it to them in the first place. So, first, you need to make sure that you know your song."

"How do I do that?"

"By paying attention to yourself, in every situation. By the way your spirit reacts, it is telling you what your song is. Giving hints. It's not as hard as it seems. You start to learn how to put the puzzle together the more pieces you have in place."

"Okay. Then what?"

"Once you know your song, you have to practice it, or you will lose it. Just like anything else. And once it's strong in you, you can call on it anytime you need, to calm you, or inspire you, or show you the way."

"How do I sing you to me?"

"Just by being you. When you need to, think of me in the world. Really, not *think* so much as *feel*. Feel me out in the world. Then, just send out your song and I will hear it. I will know when to come to you in spirit, and when to come for real, when I can of course," Binda laughed.

"But, how will you know it is me?"

"Our time here on this island has been teaching time. You have been teaching me your song, and I have been paying attention. I see you. I will recognize what you send out."

"Cool. Does it really work?"

"Better than modern technology, sister," Binda said, laughing again. Promise laughed too, with plenty of relief tossed into it. "And it works both ways," Binda said.

"Do you really feel that I know how to recognize your song?" Promise asked.

"Girl, when you bleed together; talk story together; sleep, eat, drink, and dance together, you better know each other's song or something is wrong with you. It's in there. The recognition, I mean. It's just a matter of becoming aware of your ability to recognize."

"Thanks, Binda. That helps me feel better about leaving tomorrow. Not so nervous. I'm not used to relying on people. Including myself."

"I know," assured Binda, placing her hand on Promise's shoulder. "But some scar tissue is good to break."

Promise felt the lagoon's tonic soak her bones. Old adhesions unraveled. *Surreal*. That's what it felt like as she realized she was no longer afraid of her summer wounds. The ones that hatched anew when the temperature rose. Portals to a place and time when hurt was made. She could be with those wounds now. Even hold them gently, and still be in the world of light. Those wounds had lost their virility. She knew this. Her lungs loosened. She could breathe entirely. From her belly. She felt her bones remineralize with the oxygen of peace.

Lake came upon the cave in the hour of whispering winds. It was late afternoon. Tide was high. She had been walking for a good hour. Out beyond the estuary, over a modest hillside crowned in maples, and, back down into a thicket of bushes: morning glory, jasmine, and hibiscus. She rubbed her palms with the wet fiber of the jasmine blossoms, burying her nose in the luscious perfume. She chewed a hibiscus petal, its sharp flavor rich with minerals of the forest. She was still close to shore, and when she felt the ground grow soft beneath her feet, and puddles rose, she grew attentive. She was so used to water blooming around her, she did not know if this was her doing, or if it was just the ocean rising. A shadow passed overhead, fluttering. She walked out into an opening, a stretch of sand leading farther down to the sea. Warm wet sand embraced her bare feet. Carrying her sandals, she stepped across the sand, moving down a slight decline toward the water. Smooth stones grew out of the sand. Then larger polished rocks grew from the stones. She put her sandals back on, and skipped from rock to rock, sea water now surging beneath her feet. Lake's heart began to lift, like a hot air balloon. She felt anxious, in a good way. *Something's coming.* High tide brought in drifting branches and a rich recycled mist from the open water. She followed the shoreline until it became a rise of cliff. Compelled forward, she dared stepping out into the deeper water, determined to navigate around the cliff and continue. Lake moved, focused and committed, water now up to her waist. She felt no anxiety at losing contact with the shore. Every cell in her body vibrated. An energy pulled her, forcefully. She felt like this when she danced. Sometimes it was sun calling for her. Other times, it was earth. Or water. Water Spirit had its hands around her shoulders, from behind. It pushed her firmly forward. She rounded the cliff, moving again into shallower water. She froze. On the other side of cliff, a broad cave opened up before her, smelling of calcium and lime. The cells in Lake's body broke open and gushed. She felt fluid, released. She moved dreamlike into the cave. Its high roof swept over her, a roughly surfaced awning. Her heart paused, then started again. She knew now where she was. *It's the turtle cave.* The water was warm. Air was warm. As her eyes adjusted to the darkness, Lake's people emerged in their multitude. Turtles everywhere. Unprecedented joy filled Lake. She fell into the water, inches deep, at the cave floor. With daylight pulsing from the sea into the cave and across the immaculate hillsides of turtle shells, Lake placed her hands on the living, sentient beings completely surrounding her. Great mountains of emotion erupted from the bowels of her trauma. Lake drowned her troubles in the silent friendship of her spirit animals. She floated on her back. They climbed over her. She cried and cried, touching so many shells in disbelief. Surf swamped her legs as she sat, dislodged from the world of human people, initiated into her truer tribe with every brush and nuzzle from their old and tribunal souls. Lake asked them to judge her. They told her she was already forgiven. She asked them: *Stay with me.* In that moment, the cave's sanctuary wrapped her in a blanket of peace. Lake's shell, no longer useful, cracked and fell into the water. Taken by the tide. Lake stayed, naked and new, in the cave until her tribe of turtles assured her they would never leave her, and that they would be her protection in her season of nakedness, which they hoped would last for the rest of her sacred life. Lake left the cave, peaceful and proud. She left behind memories that had lost their utility. New ones awakened in her. Ones that painted the way to a turtle cave where she divinely belonged.

Balanta still felt weak. His leg ached badly. "You need to eat some Poi," Eloni suggested. "Get your energy back up."

After Balanta had his poi, Ashia walked with him into his cabin. Balanta rested on his cot with his ankle raised.

"Balanta?" Ashia said, her eyes locked into his. "I want to know the curvature of your soul. Are you cool with that?"

Balanta smiled, his eyes tearing.

Ashia held her gaze. "I need you to speak, African."

Balanta took her hand. Placed it on the warm skin of his chest. His weary voice was a midnight river. "Here is the drum that holds my spirit. My motive. My desire. What you feel beating is my word to you."

Ashia slipped Balanta a note. She kissed his forehead. Then she smiled and left, leaving him to rest. Balanta opened the folded paper. Ashia's scent lifted from it. Amber and brown sugar. He smiled as he read the words:

I drink your potent spirit from the seed husks of words you speak. Speak fresh spring water. Speak gentleness and affection. Speak warm touch. Offer me a bridge to your enduring heart. The one that remains after each rain washing. The deposited silt of your song. Story me close to you. Evaporate your emotion from your warm lips onto my dry plains of feeling. Let yourself condense into clear water on my heart meadow. I will soak you in, and we will bring forth so many wildflowers, each one bright and new for the world.

Make my nights tidal.
Wash over me,
steady as a metronome.
Migrate closer.
Let us choose the same land.
Learn this soft bright language
growing in the willow groves.
Burn away my underbrush.
Ointment my burning.
Discover the flower
I have chosen to
raise for you.
Touch its
every
petal.

A warm river flooded Balanta's arterial plains. He folded the note back up and pressed it between his palms. He rolled over on his side and let sleep take him for a while.

"Ready, go!" Eloni had spontaneously declared a footrace on the beach. Shonto, Mende, Promise, and Ivory obliged. They traced the shoreline, heads flung back, feeling their bodies with the intimacy of limitation. Promise's long legs carried her to the front, alongside Mende, with Eloni and Shonto right behind. Their bare feet dislodged sand in heavy sprays. Shonto tasted blood quickly. Memories of boyhood came back, marbled as salt and cream. They raced the ocean, its tide now moving sideways and up shore with them. Salt air saturated their lungs. Even beyond their endurance, they kept running. If they had air, they would have been laughing to tears. Tears flowed anyway, flung behind in their draft. Ocean announced their movement in its slushy alto. Seabirds above followed their pace, intuiting a meal, or at least reacting to some aberration in the natural rhythm on earth. Eloni and the others had lost their breath, their voices, even the sensation of groundedness. They were exerted into a wild dimension. And it was good.

Some of them gathered in the meadow for a last union with its splendor. A strong breeze ruffled the grass, which rippled for 100 yards. Two damselflies, locked and coital, surged upward against gravity, dipping and bobbing like earrings in the air. A kaleidoscope of butterflies lifted from the tall grass and tie-dyed the sky.

Balanta approached Cielo, who was lying on the grass with his eyes wide, searching the sky. Tears streamed down his face and fell to the grass. "You okay, man?" Balanta asked.

"I was crying," Cielo said, as if it wasn't obvious. "Just washing myself in pure feeling. I like to go there, you know? It's cleansing for me. Baptism. Or, short term enlightenment."

Cielo cleared his throat. His face was wistful, ruminative. "After someone who's supposed to protect you punches you in the liver, just because he doesn't like the way you're dressed for school, it's a negotiation after that, for the rest of your life. A negotiation between yourself and your own heart. Where, in your heart, do you place an abusive parent? There aren't any convenient places, so you rig up a makeshift room. Thing is, the room isn't supposed to exist, so it's jacked up. Roof leaks. Walls bend, creak. Floor sags when you step on it. Cold air comes through the window frames. I wish I could kick him out, altogether. But then guilt takes over, and I have nightmares. I prefer the complications of having a cactus in your heart. Even a cactus has its sweet center, amigo. I drink from that."

Balanta said nothing. He sat beside Cielo, his eyes at the level of the tall grass, their tips sparking in sunlight. The wavering blades were an amber sea.

Small creatures with translucent wings alighted from there, making the grass appear to be popping up insects. Balanta fell into rhythm with the meadow as Cielo went back to crying. Cielo's face, covered in tears and sunlight, was the color of cognac. Balanta's perspiring skin was a dark rum under the same gracious sun.

Ocean's mood was cobalt. Ivory swam out to a depth of about 10 feet and dived down close to the bottom. Treading to stabilize his depth, he watched fleets of silver minnows and other smaller fish. He stayed down as long as his lungs allowed. Sea anemones, sea cucumbers, and crayfish skirted by, kicking up clouds of detritus. Ivory glimpsed the large form of a sea turtle in the distance, before it turned away. Shrimp poked about. Sea horses keeled back and forth, peeking from behind kelp. Urchins bristled blackly. Small octopi and squid noodled bashfully over rocks and quickly back into shelter. The water refracted the appearance of everything down here, and Ivory felt as though he was ensconced in a house of mirrors. With his head growing faint, he broke for the surface. He gasped for a while, recovered his air, and dived back down. This was his moment in the public library that was the ocean, and he was going to read every last book.

Promise found small white seashells by the hundreds at the bottom of tide pools. Their surface was polished into a shine. She collected a handful before heading back to camp.

"Ashia, I found something for you," Promise said, as she held out the seashells she had gathered. "I thought we could put a couple in your locs, a couple in my 'fro, and some in the other girls' hair, if they want."

Ashia's eyes filled quickly. "That was so sweet of you. Maybe Ivory can figure out how to drill a small hole in them?" They ran off to find Ivory, who was more than happy to be wanted.

Ivory used a needle from the first aid kit to tap holes in the seashells. The shells were no more than an inch long and wide, so he made sure the holes weren't big enough to split the shells, while still big enough to fit the soft milkweed fiber through. He worked patiently, his face inches from the shells like a jeweler placing a diamond. Sweat dropped from his forehead as his fingers worked with needle and stone.

When the crickets started, the group knew it was near to dusk and time to eat.

"Eloni, what's your grand finale going to be?" Promise asked. "I don't know how you're going to top what you've been cooking all week."

"It's all Aloha, sister," Eloni replied. "I've got something for you." His expression was elfish as he rubbed his palms together, anticipating. They dove into preparations, savoring the ritual that dinner had become, knowing this was their last. Sadness mixed with seasoning as their food grew magical.

The meal wasn't fair. Ivory began to cry as he realized how spoiled they had all been here, and the food they were about to return to. But they had *this* meal. And it had them. Salmon fillets stuffed with mushrooms, shrimp, mango. The salmon skin was cooked crisp, the tender meat melted on the tongue. Boiled snow crabs, their flesh falling out of the shell with no resistance. Lobster drenched in almond butter. Swordfish ribs rubbed with brown sugar and serrano peppers, and braised in plum sauce. Halibut poppers dipped in pumpkin pudding and crusted with browned coconut shavings. A salad heaped with vegetables and fruits and drizzled with raspberry honeysuckle dressing. A large gourd brimming with spicy, old school gumbo. Ginseng peppermint tea. Cielo and Eloni concocted an alcohol-free sangria, with strawberries, plums, lychee, lemon rinds, black cherries, and jicama slices. The storm of scents steamed into the air throughout camp and traveled the island. Every living thing twitched at the savory scent.

For dessert, Mende made his way around the circle with a high stack of zucchini cakes, steaming and fragrant.

"You made this, Mende?" Promise asked, taking a piece.

"Yup. Loni isn't the only brother with skills."

"Mmm…" Binda hummed with pleasure. "More, please!"

"I'm proud of you, Mende!" Ashia delighted.

"Me, too, brother," Balanta said.

Mende downed three slices of cake himself, though it was Ashia's pride, and his brother's, that really filled him up.

Following dinner, the ladies disappeared into one of their cabins.

"What are they doing in there?" Cielo asked.

"Who knows," answered Eloni. "I'm sure they'll be mysterious about it."

They were in the cabin for a long time. Long enough that Shonto and Ivory grew hungry again, and did a yeoman's work cleaning up the leftovers. Then, female voices resumed in a rush of syllables. Maricela, Ashia, and the rest came trailing out of the cabin with bright, satisfied faces. Each had two white seashells tied into her hair. They had affixed them for one another, each shell in a unique location inspired by the one whose hands did the securing. Promise's hair was framed in a mudcloth headband. Her smile was genuine and free. She walked even taller than usual. She was regal. Reclaimed.

"How do you like our shells, boys?" Maricela asked, her teeth disclosed freely.

"Why two shells each?" Cielo asked.

"One for the woman. One for the womanhood," Ashia replied. The six initiates took their seats around the fire, next to each other, their postures supreme. Their demeanors were secure and relaxed, like the way sun moves doubtless along its arc.

Ivory was inspired by the show of cowrie. He dipped into his cabin. When he reemerged, he strolled out glistening in oil, naked except for puffy white shorts that resembled diapers. "Ladies," he cooed with a wide grin, "Do *not* worship me. I know it's hard, but remember, *Thou shalt have no false idols before me.* Or something like that. This is the last fire. I have come clean and supreme."

As the women fell out on the ground screeching, cracking up, and covering their eyes frantically, Promise shouted, "Ivory, you are a scientifically proven mess!"

Sun gave out its last call for daylight, streaming through the boughs with a soft luminescence that spilled long shadows over camp. They intuitively knew to move silently down to the shore for their libation ceremony. The ocean tossed its foamy phlegm up onto the sand, a light merengue that popped and dissolved against their bare feet.

They each carried crystal clear geodes gathered from the dune quake. Silently, they held their geodes up to the sunlight, filling the crystal orbs with solar prayers, private petitions, and remnants of memories. Silently, they crouched to the water and let go of their sun-swollen treasures, entrusting them to an ocean that promised no gentleness.

Ashia used a calabash to bring spring water from the brook. Facing the others, she explained how the water was the spirit of their ancestors. And that by pouring it into the earth, the water was a channel between them and their ancestors. Water was their people's true Love for them, not Love distorted by human pain, but the Divine heart their people were born and died with. By pouring the water, Ashia explained, we are bathing the ones who came before. We are calling them to be with us. We are creating a space for us all to gather and make amends. We pour for our sake. To shower us in their goodness, and return us to their arms. Now... Name the ones you Love.

Ashia poured out a brief stream onto the ground. "Grandmother Nila..." she called out, reverently, then poured out another small amount of water. "Elia..." she said, honoring her departed best friend, who was born with a faulty heart.

Maricela picked up the roll call. "Nomar..." Ashia poured for Nomar.

"Jonas..." Balanta spoke forth. Ashia poured for Jonas. The names came spilling...

"Mom..."

"Uncle Adrian..."

"Coach Boston..."

"Auntie Alma..."

"Sundera..."

"Running River..."

"Rahim..."

They went on like this for a while, pouring libations and paying respects to ancestors, family, and friends they wished could be here to enjoy this island with them, to witness their *becoming*. Their grief was measured in water, and in the long line of names that grew like a vine as they spoke them. Everyone cried except Lake. Her water came from the trees, who wept such Grace that a fine mist rose from the ground, consuming the clearing in an ethereal haze. On the far horizon, behind a misting of clouds, the sun dipped into the ocean, a ripe tomato into an avocado oblivion.

Their last fire smelled the sweetest. Old cypress and maples gave their lives for the burning. An ointment of smoke billowed delicately up and out. Shonto had just returned from walking through the woods, smudging the island with smoke from thick braids of sage and sweetgrass. He had given deep thanks. For all the island had given them. All it had been. He wished for the group to leave the island's spirit clean from any pollution their presence might have brought. He covered many trees and bushes in smoke. He washed boulders in smoke. He walked with a face of smoke. A heart of smoke. Lake felt his purity from back at camp. African lilies not far from her wept like fountains.

"Clear Moon, now," Lake said, looking up at the scratchless night sky. "The giant is all the way inside his dreams. He's caring for us. Good time for change."

"New days. New ways," said Pikea, winking at Lake.

"You know," Ivory said, "I think I figured out the meaning of the scroll message. I think the words *and they shall die of fire* didn't mean that we would literally die, but that we would shed our old skins. Die in spirit. You know? And the words about the mountain of water crushing our false seeds forever? I think the wildfire and the crazy sideways rain... all of that was like Jade Mountain putting a punctuation mark on our time here. We've had a lot of negative ideas about ourselves crushed. False seeds. Crushed. Yes?"

"Yes, Ivory," Maricela said. "I was so used to doom and gloom that when I first read those words, I assumed something bad was going to happen to us. I freaked myself out for no reason. The scroll was for us. It was trying to tell us to relax, take a breath, open up to this amazing place and let ourselves be changed."

"I told you," Shonto said, "Thunderbird doesn't come to kill your body, but to remake your spirit. No need to fear change the way we do. Thunderbird brings us blessings."

"Tuli, brother," Eloni said, his eyes bright and warm. "Tuli brings us blessings."

They all stared up at the portraiture of night, pondering the Clear Moon, the way it considered itself, exuded itself, even now in the absence of sunlight on its skin. Lake reminded them that now, this night, was the time for them to wear their power fully, to not depend on affirmation from the world. This night, they would each feel the full blushing of the Clear Moon, and they would need to use it in their heart. To become their own medicine. To thrive on their own light.

"Maricela," Ashia said, "tell us that story about the salamander that you told me. That one was wild." They wrapped up in their blankets and passed around peppermint leaves to chew. Maricela sat on the sand between Eloni's legs. He was on a large log, his fingers in her hair, massaging her scalp. Eyes closed, she smiled blissfully, tension running from her body. Her soul ran backward through its seasons and shook itself free of troubles like a golden retriever in the surf drying its coat blissfully. She told them of Axoltl, the legendary giant salamander who lived in two lakes in Mexico City, considered a sacred keeper children's sweetest of dreams, and who found salvation in a little girl who taught the great salamander that what appears lost is really only a greater gift waiting to be found.

"Yes! Ivory shouted. "Now *that's* a story! Big-ups, Maricela." After the applause settled, Ivory claimed with great conviction to have seen a giant salamander at the estuary. He dropped onto the sand and started crawling around, mimicking the creature. This earned him a kick in the pants from Promise. The group talked about Axoltl's loss and grief, and their own. They wondered how life would be when they returned home.

"Maybe time passes differently here, and when we get back, all the people we know will be old," Maricela wondered.

"Or we'll be the old ones," said Cielo.

"I can't believe morning will be here in just a few hours and we'll be leaving," Mende said, his arm around Balanta's shoulder. "The boat will come, and that will be it. You know what? I don't even feel that I need photos of our time here. My heart holds the memories in a clear way. Clearer than ever before."

"Brother, that just tells me you have been fully present here," Balanta said. "Clear memories grow from the ground of being present. Time *has* slowed for us here. We have fallen into this place, into each other." The group admitted one by one to feeling the ache of missing each other already. This caused Binda to lean her head on Lake's shoulder and cry.

"Here," Lake said, tearing a sheet of paper out of her journal. "Put your hand down on this." Binda put her right hand on the paper. Lake traced around Binda's fingers and palm. "There," Lake said. "Now, I'll keep this with me. Wherever I am in the world, and wherever you are, if I am missing you and want to feel your presence, I'll just place my hand down on your handprint. It's an old Native way for staying connected."

"Can I get yours now?" Binda asked.

"Of course. Spirit resides in objects. My spirit will pool up in my handprint, and you can always feel me there." Binda traced Lake's hand. Binda felt anxiety leave her as she moved with the pencil along each of Lake's fingers, like rowing in a canoe beside the comforting closeness of shore before turning out to sea. They all took turns tracing each other's handprints, gathering their own form of memory.

Balanta looked at Ashia's face cast in the firelight. She looked like a woman. Not a girl becoming a woman. An achieved womanhood. Beyond age. Flames reflected in her eyes became dancers. Women dancing. Their hips moving under fierce red wraps, arms grasping for the earth, lifting for the sky. They moved as one, to an old drumbeat within, and they knew their dance deeply. They were dancing before time. Without time. Embroidered in their innate beauty. Their backs wet with exertion, their faces solemn, proud, joyful. They danced laughter and grief. Hope and wisdom. Their bare feet wrote a story into the earth. With each step they recalled their collective journey. Their Ghanaian pronouncement. Their skin was night, their hips the wind. Balanta's eyes welled and released their stored up lakes.

The owl returned to a cabin roof. The owl's head ticked side to side in metronome cadence. Its dark eyes reflected starlight. Its face reminded Balanta of an old man from back in the village, who always looked stern and assessing.

Just as Shonto wondered aloud about the three-legged deer, it too appeared at an opening in the trees. It sniffed the acridity from the wildfire, looking up quizzically at the humans.

"I wonder what my animal spirit is," Ivory asked.

"We can choose which animals to inhabit, you know," said Binda, looking at the owl. "But we can't just have our way. If our spirit is not aligned with the animal's spirit, we can't enter. The animals sense us. Might not want our junk. I don't blame them. Harmony is the doorway."

They riffed on the future.

"You all got housing for the summer?" Ashia asked.

"Nope."

"Not sure."

"Depends."

"I think I burnt my bridges."

"First I got to get a job."

"No, first you need to have an address, so someone will hire you."

"No, first you need to have a job so someone will rent to you."

"My dream is to live in an orchard," said Ashia, smiling. "I mean, a home in an orchard, you know? I daydream all the time about being able to walk through those endless rows of fruit trees. I'm walking down one of those rows, and the trees just keep going and going. My arms are stretched wide and I'm brushing the leaves with my fingers. The fragrance of the blossoms overwhelms me. I'm so happy. Then I turn and walk down another row. I just keep moving inside a sea of trees. It's my own private paradise and I'm lost in it. I want that to be my front yard. My backyard. My whole life. And a gurgling brook would be nice. With ducks that come and go. And maybe a heron or two." Ashia daydreamed a scene: She was in a rocking chair that creaked, on a broad porch that groaned. Her yard was bright. A bowl of mangos in her lap. She sliced a mango. Splashed it in sunlight. Slid its sweetness into her mouth, which bloomed. She held the pleasure and the moment for a long note that sang praise. This was her life. Plentiful. Purified.

"I want to travel while I still have energy," said Shonto. I don't want to wait until I'm 30 or something, just sitting on a couch all day because I'm completely wiped out from walking to the fridge."

"Sounds promising, Shonto," Pikea said, smiling.

"I want to be a nutmeg farmer," Binda announced.

"I thought you wanted to be a nurse or a social worker or something," Promise said.

"Sure. I can do all of that. If I have a nutmeg orchard, I can bring people out there to relax and renew."

"Why nutmeg?" Ashia asked.

"I Love the way its spirit behaves. It's good medicine. Hard to explain."

"I'm thinking about getting into criminal justice. Maybe juvenile justice," said Pikea.

"You going to be a PO?" asked Ivory, his voice squeaking.

"Maybe. Who better to add some decency and sensitivity to the mix?" Pikea smirked.

"Pikea," Mende said, "you got some of that Tubman spirit in you. Harriet Tubman. Or, Sojourner Truth. The kind of woman whose spirit is stronger than man's desire to subdue her."

"I hear that," Maricela said. "A woman's spirit needs to be stronger than a man's muscle."

"When someone goes to whipping you," Pikea said, "don't just get better at taking a whipping. Take the whip from them and don't ever give it back. Cause clearly they can't be trusted with a whip."

"What about you, Cielo?" Ivory asked. "What do you see yourself doing for a career?"

"Groundwater conservationist. Or banjo repairman."

"Banjos?" Promise repeated. "I don't know that there'll be too much work for you."

"Maybe not. But what work I do get... supreme bliss."

"Sometimes I feel like the last spokesperson for my family. For my people," Binda said. "After me, we go extinct. When I'm really tired, I can hear my grandmother speaking to me in a soft voice. She says, 'My precious earth. You must never lose your light. You don't carry a torch. You *are* the torch. As long as you keep your light, we can never go extinct. For light is a virus perfected by God. It will only spread. Remember that. Now, go and play. Not so much worrying.'"

With Binda's encouragement, Lake stood to recite a poem.

You eaters of night, swallowers of moon,
forged in dream fire,
loosed upon the world of ghost walkers
to flood canyons in soul water,
glacial pain plowing mountain passes,
shelter raised after storm,
righteous seed freed from bondage,
breakaway sprouts, sun seekers,
prayers of dust, orchard air,
fruit of pain, joy trumpet,
holler on the clouds,
synonym for silence,
shatter these seashells
that are your souls.
Be the grain
of a whole new land.

When Lake finished, there was silence. Then roaring applause and snaps drowned out the silence.

Pikea whispered to Lake, "That was amazing. Can you help me? I want to write a letter to my father, but I'm stuck."

Lake hugged Pikea around the shoulders and laughed. "Pretend you're writing a poem, only, have it make sense."

Ivory started casting out riddles.

Can a sun get a sunburn?

Can cold catch a chill?

Does weariness ever grow tired?

Have you ever seen a smile grin?

Does peace ever get a chance to relax?

"Ivory," Promise said. "Sometimes, you just need to go to sleep."

"I'm not going to sleep tonight," Ivory proclaimed, his voice sounding like a small child. "I'm staying up the whole night."

Later, Ivory would be the first one to fall asleep. While still at the fire.

Ashia and Maricela took Pikea's hands and walked her into her cabin. "Here, put this on," Maricela said, handing Pikea a long white cotton dress.

"Yours?" Pikea asked.

"Sí. I think it will fit you just fine. I only brought it because I always wanted to wear something like this on a beach. Romantic junk, I guess. I'm glad I brought it. Now, stay here until we're ready." Maricela and Ashia headed back outside.

"Ready for what?" Pikea asked. "I don't like surprises!"

"Then get ready to not like this!" Maricela shouted.

Pikea waited in her cabin. Its air smelled charred from the wildfire. She heard voices and activity outside as her curiosity grew. Their island time replayed in her mind. The pontoon ride over. Discovering the lagoon. The dunes and cave. The pollen and dust of emotional flaring and fears. *Fire*. When Maricela and Ashia came, Pikea was deep-thinking about the next morning and the boat ride off the island. "It's about time," she said. "I don't know what you're up to, but let's get it over with."

Maricela and Ashia smiled at Pikea. "Close your eyes and keep them closed until we say," Maricela ordered. They led her out of the cabin, then Cielo took her hand and walked with her toward the fire. Pikea struggled to trust Cielo's guidance, fearing she would trip on something any moment. She heard no voices. Just the ocean lapping. And birds. "Okay," Maricela said. "Go ahead, open your eyes."

Pikea anxiously lifted her eyelids. Darkness had deepened. She focused her vision, which was drawn to bright lights bobbing in the air. Not in the air. In the trees. The group had strung Chinese lantern fruit, with its bright orange and red papery husk, through the tree branches all around camp. The skin of the lantern fruit husk was translucent, a fine embroidery of snowflake patterns. Ivory and the others had removed the small tomato-like fruit from within the overgrown husks and replaced each fruit with small kelp bladders filled with lagoon water and its radiating microorganisms and phosphorescent algae. This caused the bladders to glow with an astonishing brightness inside the papery husks. Trees were lit brightly in the cusp of night. Pikea's eyes grew wider as she looked to the bay. Its waters were filled with an armada of floating, glowing kelp bladders. Everywhere she looked, Pikea saw lanterns flaring. In the sky of stars and fireflies. On the water. In the trees. Scattered across the sand throughout camp. She could not believe her vision.

"How did you?" Pikea stuttered, her voice high and cracking. "Why?"

Maricela's whole face grinned. "Hermana, we wanted to give you your very own quinceañera!"

Emotions welled in Pikea. "But how did you?—"

"Ivory came up with the idea to gather the lagoon water. We hoped that the little critters would still glow inside the kelp and not be offended."

Ivory beamed. "We worked on this since yesterday, Pikea!" he enthused. We kept the husks and bladders hidden back behind the garden and just made sure you didn't wander back there."

"This must have been hard work," Pikea said softly, tears pouring.

"Everyone pitched in," Lake said. She was dressed in a traditional Diné ankle length skirt and velveteen blouse, with a turquoise and silver necklace shining on her chest.

Ivory placed a tiara of willow branches and lehua blossoms on Pikea's head. Females and males paired up as *damas* and *chambelanes*, surrounding Pikea in a circle. Shonto stepped forward as Pikea's *chambelanes de honor*. He bowed to Pikea as everyone cracked up. They all wore leis that Eloni and Ivory made using hibiscus blossoms and nutmeg shells. Shonto draped one around Pikea's neck.

Pikea and Shonto performed *hongi*, touching at the forehead as their sacred *ha* passed between them, purposeful and true. Pikea turned to Promise. They performed hongi, shared their breaths of life. One by one, they all did the same with each other, until their *ha* had been passed in a complete circle.

Lake embraced Binda, anticipating tomorrow. Their tears became one water. "I am so grateful that you exist," Lake whispered.

"I will pray for your ancestors," Binda replied.

"My Love goes with you," Lake said, quietly.

"My Love goes with you," Binda said in return.

Cielo brought out the plantain chips and avocado dip, and his roots beer. They toasted Pikea.

"Salud!"

"Mozel tov!"

"Nostradamus!" Ivory shouted.

The ladies put on their jacaranda pod waist chains and anklets. The drumming started as the fire solicited the sky. Mende was the first to ask Pikea for the honor of a dance. Then the others, waltzing, twirling, dipping. Bare feet gave to the earth in dance. The women felt their moon time power surge from their wombs and flush their skin. Lanterns glowed and swung in island breeze. Trees stood adorned and winking as a daughter of the Maori was showered in her very own quinceañera.

Pikea was taken by her emotion. A dam inside broke. What gushed through was her own permission to grieve. She was swamped in a sweet desire to wrap herself in all her relations. Her Tipuna tone (grandfather) and Tipuna wahine (grandmother). Her Matua tane (father) and Whaene (mother). Her Tuakana (elder sisters), Taina (younger sisters), and Tungane (brother). She wanted them all. It was for her a shocking desire. Foreign. Painfully welcomed.

When they sat down for a break in the dancing, Promise called on Pikea for a speech. Pikea gathered her thoughts. When she spoke, it was in a voice they had not heard before. It resonated with ancient vibration. Soul pooled at the surface of her eyes. Her breathing grew rapid.

"Complete that breath, Pikea," Ashia said. "Let your breath out all the way. That's it. Deep breathing. Let your trauma and tension go. That's what calms me more than anything else."

Pikea's facial twitch disappeared with each deep breath. "My grandfather told me, keep your ways," she said. "Or you will become weak and fall apart. Then, other people will be happy to build systems to carry you forward in their ways. Shape you in their ways. And you may never return to your true self. You will make your ancestors cry for eternity."

The group stood and applauded. Said their *Ashés* and *Amens*.

"When people impose their culture on you," Pikea continued, "it does to you what an ocean riptide does to anyone who dares it. Takes you out to sea and drowns you. Your ancestral culture is an anchor that keeps you close, in the shallow waters. It is a compass that orients you to your mainland. Don't lose your heritage. Once you lose sight of your own shore, you are doomed."

The fire circle roared with "Go on, girl!" and, "Preach!" and, "I can feel your power!" Drum voices grew louder, faster.

Pikea was flowing now. "When your people lose their continent, then they lose their culture, and then *you* lose your people, that's a lot of loss. Hard to know what you once were. Harder still to become it again."

Now they were bouncing. Wearing faces of fire. Spines erect. Pogoing like Maasai warriors, their spears thudding on the sand. Drumbeats, pounding. Deep throat chanting. Trees shaking their lanterns. Pikea jumped up on a boulder, spear in her hand. Clearing her throat, she looked deep into the fire, then faced the group. "My name is Pikea. I come from the deep sea. I am a tame whale. My father is Moana. I am his daughter."

The roar from the group startled the three-legged deer, which had bedded down in the grass by the cabins to behold this human drama. It wagged its tail and twitched its nose before nestling its head back down atop its forelegs. Many tears fell as the ladies warrior-stepped around the fire, laughing and calling out in their deepest voices, "I. Am. His. Daughter."

"I think this moment calls for a late night swim, y'all," Ashia said.

"Okay, but let's be careful out there," Ivory warned. "There's night snakes."

"What is a night snake?" Promise asked, sweetly annoyed.

"They drop out of the trees. Right on your head," Ivory replied. "They're nocturnal. On the prowl for foolish prey such as yourselves."

"Okay, Ivory," Pikea said. Nonetheless, they all looked up at the trees as they raced out of camp. They ran down to the ocean, giggling and shouting. On their way there, Shonto and Eloni wrestled in the sand. They got into a food fight, tossing needle-skinned lychee fruit at each other like Chines throwing stars. Balanta and Mende threw spears at an imaginary target. Ashia threw hers the closest. Lake, Binda, and Maricela imitated bullfrogs for no reason at all, squatting and hopping around, croaking from their chests.

Maricela made sure Cielo kept his drawers on. They all noticed Ivory peel his shirt off. The tree of scars on his back leaned toward the tide. Their 12 tanned bodies dove into the warm surf and swam through the luminescence of lanterns. Ocean warm and fallopian encumbered them. They moved as a pod out toward the barrier reef, feeling their muscles, feeling tide's cumulative power. Lanterns bobbed and brushed against them, casting living light upon their bodies. They let the dense saltwater wash them of fires and earthquakes and cave-ins. Bravely they kept on, all the way until the coral rose to meet sea's surface, and they could squat on the sharp cobbling so far out into the ocean.

Mende continued beyond the reef, his arms powering into the taller waves, his body pulling away from the others. Ivory followed for a few strokes, then turned around.

Pikea and Ashia yelled out to Mende to come back.

"Let him go," Balanta said softly. *Let him go.*

Mende came to a place far out into the ocean. Deep into the black sky. He treaded water there, staring out at star territory, listening to whale song and heaving sea. Looking back toward the incandescent bay and its neon armada of lanterns, its glowing trees and sparking fire, he barely made out the silhouettes of bodies in the water, also treading water and facing his direction. Peace filled his chest. His bones. His being. He dipped his head into the brine and stroked back to the many lights of shore.

Ashia enjoyed the lightness of her body in the ocean as she watched, relieved that Mende was heading back. Buoyant in the warm bay, she felt whatever it was that was coming with the next morning and their departure. She felt change fluttering, prenatal. She thought to herself, *Someday I am going to sit by a lake and write this story.*

They returned to the fire. Maricela and Ashia presented Pikea an almond coconut cake with 12 candles made of dried willow sprigs. Ashia led the group in a traditional Ga womanhood song. Pikea blew out the candles, with a prayer for each one. They ate cake, and drank more roots beer. Then, a shadow appeared, with a sack on its back. In moccasins. Adorned in eagle feathers. The shadow laughed, so the group laughed with it. Its laugh was deeper than a cave, and contagious. Soon, the shadow had them all rolling on the ground as it told the most magical stories, and recounted the infinite tricks it had played on so many souls crossing the desert of their lives.

The shadow grew quiet. Pulled out its flute. In between the notes, the shadow spoke these words in a voice that sounded like it was *Shanti ko Samjhana*. Like it was *Remembering Peace*:

Name the ones you Love. Name them beautifully, so that their souls may shine and resound with the substance of your heart. Name them like a flurry of snowflakes. A river's white frothing. Soft feather grass in a waving meadow. Incense of a temple. Sanctity of ancestors. We cannot carry too many names given in Love. Far better to possess 1,000 Loving names, than to be named without recognition of your true soul, in which case you are truly nameless. Name the ones you Love. Including the one that is you.

The young ones were taken. As the shadow sat with them and played flute music from the souls of many deserts, they began. Across the field of flames, they gave each other names. With each name spoken, they joined hands and raised fire sticks to the Clear Moon, which radiated down on their ritual its nocturnal authority.

"I call you Rabia," Ashia said to Maricela. "It means *Springtime*."

"I call you Raisa," Maricela said in return. "It means *Rose*, and *Beloved*."

Shonto gave Pikea *Haseya*, for *She Rises*. Pikea gave Shonto *Rawiri*, *Adored One*.

Cielo bestowed *Alula* upon Promise. *Winged One*. Promise shared *Ayo* with Cielo. *Happiness*.

Lake giggled and kissed Binda on the cheek with *Ajei, My Heart*. Binda blushed and kissed Lake back with *Apanie*. *Water*.

Eloni spoke *Matai* over Ivory. *Chief*. Ivory glowed at the blessing. Nearly singeing Eloni with his fire stick, Ivory announced that he had made up a new but yet sacred name for Eloni: *Yowzah*. When Ivory explained that it meant *Feast in Your Fingers*, Promise punched Ivory in the shoulder. Eloni laughed and claimed the name proudly.

Balanta, his arm draped over his brother, blessed Mende with *Kirabo*. *Gift*. Mende, his face a fountain, looked up at Balanta and spoke the name *Kayode*. *He Brought Joy*.

They kept going. Names flowing out with joy and brio. Names for each other. Names for themselves. Fire Dancer. Dragonfly Seer. Bashful Mountain. Morning Yelper. Wolf Feeder. Waterfall Diver. Earth Shaker. Falls Plenty. Few Words. Mouth Like River. Bone Eater. Poet Tree.

They sealed the naming ceremony by holding hands and raising them to the Clear Moon seven times, each time shouting *Ashé* (*Let it be*)! louder and louder, their *Mana* growing, until the entire island and all its living things could hear their exaltation.

By this time, the shadow had departed. Then it appeared again, just inside the tree line. Balanta invited the shadow over. It moved like mist, rolling over the ground. "We'll be going soon," Balanta said, his voice tired and even deeper than usual. "I guess you'll have your silence back."

The shadow swelled, as if inhaling. It spoke in an ancient voice. "Silence is a music that makes some souls nervous, others at peace. The ones who are running from themselves grow anxious in quietude. The ones who are comfortable residing in their true self greet silence with gratitude and peace."

Balanta regarded the comment. "You speak in a strange way," he said to the shadow. "People say that about me."

The shadow's torso curled and leaned toward Balanta. "Sometimes, speaking in your own instinctive, innate language is by itself revolutionary," the shadow said. "It changes the dominant language, burrows into it. Before you know it, your word changes the dominant mentality. Words can kill ideas. And birth them."

Balanta thought about the group's entire experience, from the moment they were first contacted by Antonia. Like Ashia, he wondered if Antonia actually existed and if this was a dream.

As if reading Balanta's thoughts, Kokopelli drew close to Balanta's ear. Kokopelli's lips became a flute. The flute whispered a secret in song: *There never was a world. All of this is the Great Spirit dreaming.*

Love, like pain, is a wild thing. It roams. And so, it roamed the island that night. It got into the tree branches and wept out through the leaves. It filtered into the sand and bled out into the ocean. It revived the meadow. The fireflies and butterflies and dragonflies multiplied. Feather grass tips grew so close to the stars, they could almost kiss each other. The lagoon deepened, clarified, swelled like a pregnant belly. And Jade Mountain. Jade Mountain was a proud parent, beholding the glory of its family of living things. Night wrapped itself around all of this, cloistering its galaxies in an intimacy of humming and hymns.

The tribe of 12 went on deep into the darkest hours, talking truth as sap popped in a passionate fire and hearts unknotted in reverie. The island's drumbeat chaperoned their stories. Djembe, hand drum, and bongos spoke back to the earth drum, affirming its paternity. Fire glowed glory through the trees. A forceful whooshing sound repeated itself overhead as a large form in the shape of a great bird flew close enough that the fire nearly went out. The flute player came down from the trees, and joined the circle again, creating the purest of music. The young ones grasped the miracle of their survival. Not here on this island. *Here,* in their lives. And they dared conceive of achieving something beyond survival. They glimpsed the boldest of possibilities, and slung their souls, woven in sweetgrass and sage, around that prize. Claiming it as their birthright.

The earth around them still smoldered with aromas of baked seafood and burned trees. Incense of emotional bonding blended by the fire with the gaining anticipation of tomorrow's unknown dawn. The young ones gave themselves permission. To hurt. To grieve. To laugh and Love like free souls do. They cried like trees that rain, and it was sweet water. It was song.

And they danced. Oh, how they danced.

And felt their power.

Jaiya John is a descendant of many tribes. He was born and raised in New Mexico, and has lived in various locations, including the former kingdom of Nepal. He uses the written and spoken word to walk a Medicine Road. He is the founder of Soul Water Rising, a global mission devoted to the healing and empowerment of dehumanized populations.

Jacqueline V. Richmond and Kent W. Mortensen graciously and skillfully served as editors for *Clear Moon Tribe*.

Jaiya John titles available where books are sold.

To learn more about this and other books by Jaiya John, to order discounted bulk quantities, or to learn about Soul Water Rising's global work, please visit us at:

soulwater.org

jaiyajohn.com

facebook.com/jaiyajohn

youtube.com/jaiyajohn

@jaiyajohn (instagram & twitter)

To subscribe to our literary journal / newsletter, SOUL BLOSSOM, please visit soulwater.org. *Soul Blossom* offers ongoing news of our global human mission; new book release notices; speaking engagement insights; and invited literary contributions. *Soul Blossom* is also a gathering space for the writing and artwork of young people from around the world.

www.ingramcontent.com/pod-product-compliance
Lightning Source LLC
Chambersburg PA
CBHW021952050726
47495CB00023B/2687